D1147317

WESTERN ISLES LIBR

Mary Selby is a doctor, married to another doctor, with six children. She lives in a quiet Suffolk village where she plays the organ in the local church and once hosted the village fête. Her previous novels, *A Wing and A Prayer*, *That Awkward Age* and *Gargoyles and Port*, are also published by Black Swan.

Also by Mary Selby

A WING AND A PRAYER
THAT AWKWARD AGE
GARGOYLES AND PORT

and published by Black Swan

ALL THAT GLISTERS

Mary Selby

WESTERN ISLES
LIBRARIES
£ 30026798
WITHDRAWN

BLACK SWAN

ALL THAT GLISTERS
A BLACK SWAN BOOK : 0 552 99764 1

First publication in Great Britain

PRINTING HISTORY
Black Swan edition published 1999

Copyright © Mary Selby 1999

The right of Mary Selby to be identified as the author of this
work has been asserted in accordance with sections 77 and 78 of the
Copyright Designs and Patents Act 1988.

All the characters in this book are fictitious,
and any resemblance to actual persons, living or dead,
is purely coincidental.

Condition of Sale
This book is sold subject to the condition that it shall not,
by way of trade or otherwise, be lent, re-sold, hired out or
otherwise circulated in any form of binding or cover other than that
in which it is published and without a similar condition including
this condition being imposed on the subsequent purchaser.

Set in 10pt Melior by
County Typesetters, Margate, Kent

Black Swan Books are published by Transworld Publishers Ltd,
61–63 Uxbridge Road, London W5 5SA,
in Australia by Transworld Publishers (Australia) Pty Ltd,
15–25 Helles Avenue, Moorebank, NSW 2170
and in New Zealand by Transworld Publishers (NZ) Ltd,
3 William Pickering Drive, Albany, Auckland.

Reproduced, printed and bound in Great Britain by
Cox & Wyman Ltd, Reading, Berks.

To unconquered mountains and forgotten ambitions, and to Barnardiston Hall Prep School, whose staff and pupils would all ascend Everest tomorrow if Colonel Boulter put his mind to it.

'All that glisters is not gold,
Often have you heard that told;
Many a man his life hath sold
But my outside to behold.
Gilded tombs do worms infold.
Had you been as wise as bold,
Young in limbs, in judgement old,
Your answer had not been inscroll'd.
Fare you well, your suit is cold.'

Shakespeare, *Merchant of Venice*,
Act ii scene vii

Chapter One

There were hoof marks in the soft ground when Penelope Forbes settled down by the mud spring with her pad and pen. Just over the brow of the hill the church bell was sounding a funeral knell. There was absolutely no wind at all – and also no animals, despite the tracks. Not cattle, she thought absently. Deer, maybe? No matter. This was perfect poetry weather.

It was actually peculiarly awful weather for the end of June. Above the small tower of St Alupent's church in Parvum Magna, the sky was the tired, instant mashed potato grey-white of one who has been pursued relentlessly by the Blood Transfusion Service over a number of months. It was not even mottled by any of those curiously shaped clouds that someone, somewhere, always takes as proof absolute that Elvis was abducted by aliens and is even now singing 'Love me tender, love me true' on an exquisitely distant planet whilst it cheerfully orbits a lonely and uncharted star. The kind of rain which falls lightly but *relentlessly*, as penetrating as the smell of chip shops, landed featherishly on the old pumice-grey headstones which marked the final resting places of so many Greatbottoms before this one, and inveigled itself wetly through cashmere, through silk, onto the silent figure of Carol Pendragon as she stood beside the hole in the ground into which her erstwhile uncle had just been solemnly put. In the distance the soulful cry of a peacock added just the right touch – mournful but odd – to this awkwardly sombre occasion.

Carol was unsurprised by the weather, just as she had been unsurprised both by the manner of her uncle's death (involving as it did a large quantity of Napoleon brandy and a woman of negotiable virtue dressed as Cruella de Ville) and by the peculiarity of his funeral (no address, no readings, just a rousing chorus of 'Waltzing Matilda', a jolly tune

9

which had proved capable of surprising poignancy in the circumstances). You expected the weather to be miserable in Parvum Magna – all her memories of Suffolk were miserable, after all. She was, though, surprised by the brass plate and mahogany box for which Uncle Percy had apparently paid in advance. Who would have thought that a man so mean and twisted that his greatest pleasure had come from watching his tea bag drying in the breeze prior to reuse would be prepared to pay for anything so blatantly unnecessary? She was even more surprised by the turnout for his funeral.

A fair proportion of the population of the village – many of them strangers to her after her eighteen years away – seemed to be present. Yet Percival Greatbottom had been a miserable, miserly old sod (*that's right, SOD!* She glared defiantly at the steeple, which imperviously failed to be struck by lightning despite her ungodly thoughts), eking out his (almost) solitary existence on a diet of pot noodles and alcohol. He had also been a man with the innate charm of an outbreak of dry rot, so it was, she felt, extraordinary that the funeral directors themselves had bothered to turn up, let alone all this lot.

Look at them all, sombre in black, like bedraggled crows. Even that rich old bat Mrs Featherstone who used to shout at us for walking on her wall (*'You'll wear it out, and who's going to pay for the repairs?'*) and whose stupid son Cosmo got expelled from his posh school for smoking pot. Priscilla Featherstone had never liked Uncle Percival – had called him a godless old reprobate to his face on more than one occasion. Still, she can't have been right terribly often in life, having such a low opinion of everyone other than the immortal Cosmo. Her face was still set in the mask of disapproval Carol remembered so well. It had presumably stuck that way years ago – probably at just around the time Cosmo was conceived. One of life's shocks, no doubt. And there, extraordinarily fat, next to the Dragon Featherstone stood her own old friend Dippy. Serendipity Forbes – well, that's what she was before she married Clive Rowan. Carol tried not to feel even the slightest hint of smug satisfaction at the fatness, and failed by a factor of a billion. Still blond

– still the same long flowing hairstyle as at sixteen – you'd think she'd have had the decency to have it cut into a smart bob, by her age. She looked like a would-be pop star. Fat Spice. Neil wouldn't fancy her. Neil hated fat and didn't go for blond. Absolutely not. Carol averted her eyes from her once-friend. Jezebel. Not that I care now, of course. She sensed Serendipity looking over at her, and resolutely gazed at the ground where an inordinately huge heap of wreaths and flowers were stacked in anticipation of their final resting place on a mound of wet earth. What a shame, she thought absently, then, if he says 'Earth to earth, ashes to ashes and dust to dust' I swear I'll laugh out loud.

Robert Peabody, now vicar of Parvum Magna as well as neighbouring Bumpstaple – there had been something of a reorganization of parishes (meaning that the Church had no money and so one vicar now had to do the job of three) – smiled at her gently.

'Do you want to drop some earth on the coffin?'

I'd like to drop a gigantic boulder on the old bugger, thought Carol, and shook her head, then was annoyed when some of the other mourners started dropping it. Whose uncle was it anyway? Not that he had ever been much of an uncle, even when she and her mother had lived with him.

She smoothed her Armani jacket – hardly the thing for flinging mud pies at coffins, really – and frowned. Would she mourn her father's brother? She had spent her childhood under his roof; she ought to feel a little regret at his demise. But she didn't. She was not one to harbour grudges, no, she was a Nineties·woman, she did not carry the unwanted baggage of her life around with her, a burden to drag her down (wasn't that how her therapist had put it?). But she had hated and loathed the old goat – why should she pretend otherwise now that he was embarking on his final journey, the one about six feet in a downwards direction. He was, apart from all of his other failings, the last representative of the family who had bequeathed her that most hated name, a name evocative of hysterical matrons in giant frilly bloomers (bloomers, never just knickers) shrieking with laughter at the antics of overpainted Mr Punches with strings of recalcitrant sausages on Brighton beach. Greatbottom. Carol sniffed and thought, not for the first time, that she had married Neil as much for his name as for his personality. Pendragon – it had had such a relieving and classical ring to it, especially for a girl who had spent much of her earlier life trying to avoid ever meeting men whose surname was Concert, Service or Singer.

It was over – at least partly. They seemed to be heading back towards the farm by common consensus, as if, she thought, some sixth sense told them that the dreadful Baggins woman had made twenty billion sandwiches out of tinned pink salmon and low-calorie mayonnaise.

She was in the farmhouse kitchen trying to avoid Mr Fosdyke, the slight but pompous solicitor with the Brylcreemed hair (well, hairs, to be technically accurate, as there were about five of them plastered across his head – making him living proof there really are men who have never seen *The Harry Enfield Show*) when the voice she had once known so well said, 'Hello, Carol. It's been a long time.'

Serendipity had taken her coat off. *Bloody hell*, thought Carol with a jolt, *she's not fat, she's pregnant.* Still, it didn't suit her – made her look like a spacehopper. 'Hello,' she said aloud, not wanting to say Serendipity, a name she had always rather coveted back in the Seventies when girls wore flared jeans with fringing sewn on and wanted to be named anything other than Carol – but not liking to say Dippy, the teenage nickname which conjured up memories of a friendship long gone. 'Yes, it has.' She's aged, too. Well, probably no more than I have, but her face is fatter. I bet she's got cellulite.

'I like your hair.'

Carol touched the dark, layered cut, dry already. She knew it would be as elegant as ever – it was designed to dry like that. 'Thank you,' she said, coolly, then, grudgingly: 'You look just the same.' It was true, actually, apart from the pregnancy. But then perhaps pregnancy does that, stays the ravages of time – all those mysterious hormones, presumably. *Mysterious to me, anyhow.*

'You still haven't forgiven me, though, have you?'

Carol frowned, surprised at the directness of the

12

approach. In Highgate you expected people to make small talk for at least three minutes before they went for the jugular. She met Serendipity's clear blue gaze with a good attempt at curious amusement. Her once-friend saw straight through it, she could tell. Perhaps that's what happens when you go home – as you belt up the M11 in your blood-and-sweat-acquired top-of-the-range Mercedes sports car with eight-speaker CD, such a thing as these yokels can only dream of, those few miles strip away the veneer of civilization and leave you as vulnerable as you ever were. 'What do you mean?'

Serendipity sighed, her blue eyes probing Carol's in that way they always had, like the searchlights you used to see from the Albanian coast when you holidayed in Corfu. 'You know. For marrying Clive.'

'Don't be ridiculous,' said Carol awkwardly. 'Why should I care that you married Clive? We lost touch well before your wedding.'

'It was when I told you I was going to marry Clive,' said Serendipity stubbornly, 'that we lost touch. You never wrote to me after that.' Her eyes never wavered. She always did that, thought Carol; made her seem so bloody honest.

'We moved away,' she said aloud. 'Life went on. Surely you don't think I've spent the last eighteen years in mourning for a boy I once fancied, ever so slightly, when I was a spotty adolescent?' *Has it really been that long? Where have eighteen years gone?*

'No, of course not. I know you're married.'

'Oh?'

'I saw it in *The Times*,' said Serendipity, and Carol remembered what a thing her friend – her ex-friend – had always had about marriages being in *The Times*. And deaths. She wondered suddenly if it had been Serendipity who put Uncle Percy in there.

'You always did read the social page,' she said, reluctant to take the conversation to any sort of reminiscent or personal level. Really, the sooner she got out of this place, the better. She needed to get back to London, call in somewhere on the way for some good Thai take-away, snuggle up in front of the fire with red-hot monkfish tails and a steamed snow pea salad. Alone, of course (Neil was in Geneva or somewhere) – but it would still be better than here.

Serendipity smiled, and her face lit up the way it always had. 'I didn't think you were pining for Clive,' she said. 'I mean you haven't forgiven *me*. For going out with him when you left.'

Carol shrugged, then gave up the pretence, suddenly tired of the day, of the place. 'Well, you were my best friend.'

'I know.' Serendipity bit her lip. 'I'm sorry.'

'Sorry you married him or sorry you let me down?'

'Sorry you thought I let you down. And you never were, either.'

'I never was what?'

'Spotty. That was me.'

'Oh,' said Carol, suddenly and vividly remembering the two of them pooling their paper-round money to try out the coloured Clearasil, and going to school with bright orange faces.

In the silence between them the titanic figure of Mrs Baggins, the woman who was to catering what Genghis Khan was to neighbourly visits by Mongolians (a very poor advert), sailed in to proffer salmon sandwiches and gherkins ('Go on, dear, it's low-calorie mayonnaise'), wobbled eavesdroppingly for a moment (rendering them, Serendipity realized, lurking gherkins) on hips reminiscent (Carol thought) of the massed volume of walruses that gather on beaches in the southern Barents Sea, then heaved to and sailed away again. The silence was, though, somewhat warmer than before. They were both trying not to laugh.

'So you're happy then, with Clive?'

'Yes. You wouldn't fancy him now, though.'

'Why?' Carol was fascinated that, however much she wanted to remain icy, they seemed to be slipping inexorably into their ancient roles, as if they had not been estranged for eighteen years. She was tempted to ask if this was Serendipity's first child, but did not dare, for then Serendipity would ask how many she had, might pull her face at the lack: families with children and families without them always feel sorry for one another.

14

'He's got such a belly. You always said that was grounds for divorce.'

Carol thought of Neil's visible *rectus abdominis*, honed daily at the office gym. You could scrub your washing on it. She smiled suddenly. 'I did, didn't I?'

Serendipity wondered at the reason for the smile – it was too smug to be simple amusement. 'Of course, I'm not the sylph of the century, am I?' she said with cheerful resignation, and she saw Carol's features tighten slightly beneath the even layer of vitamin-E-enriched camouflage.

'Congratulations. When is it due?'

'She, she's a she. I'm good at she's – about a month to go. And thank you.'

'That's all right.' Carol sought swiftly for something different to discuss. 'How's your mother?' *Oh God*, she thought, *please don't let her be dead*.

'A complete spaceman,' Serendipity grinned; 'so still no change there, then.' She put a hand on her arm. 'It really is good to see you, Carol. It's been . . .'

'Ladies? Time for the will.' The dreadful Mr Fosdyke and his hairs. 'Do come through to the drawing room.'

'Why . . .?' Carol was puzzled, but he was gone.

'Didn't you know?' Serendipity was watching her in surprise. 'It was in his last instructions, apparently. He got Fosdyke to invite the whole village to his funeral, and to the will reading afterwards. Something of lasting importance to the community, he said.'

'The community? I'm surprised he even knew what one was. Anyway he only really had the farm. Surely they don't really think he's left them anything?'

'Some of them probably do,' said Serendipity. 'It's human nature to hope. That's why the lottery makes so much profit. And some of them are just nosy. It is a Saturday, after all. There's nothing else to do except watch B movies on satellite or join the queue for things you don't need in the garden centre.'

Carol shuddered. 'I hope to God he hasn't left you all something filthy. I wouldn't put it past him to have bequeathed a consignment of those disgusting blow-up dolls you see in the small ads.'

Serendipity smiled. 'No-one would care. You'd soon see them being used as scarecrows all over Parvum Magna and Bumpstaple.'

'Oh no, not Bumpstaple,' said Carol; 'imagine,' and Serendipity smiled. Bumpstaple was far too posh for that sort of thing.

'Ahem . . .' Mr Fosdyke was clearly indicating that they were late. With a sudden urge to giggle Carol allowed herself to be ushered into the drawing room, overwhelmingly aware of two dozen pairs of curious eyes and five well-oiled hairs.

Only two hundred yards away an old, carved wooden sign nailed to a thorn tree proclaimed the philosophy of the mud spring, or, perhaps of someone else who had once contemplated its murky depths. ENVY NONE, AND ALL SHALL ENVY THEE read the board, virtuously. Serendipity's mother, Penelope Forbes, still sat beside it. She had never intended to go to the funeral. Funerals weren't really her thing. Trees were her thing, and writing poetry, and communicating with her spirit guide, a long-dead Native American with the delightful name of Handsome Dog, and walking on the ley lines wearing layered white chiffon when there was a full moon on the night of the summer solstice. Organized religion was about as important to her as penile sports cars and jewellery that wasn't your birthstone. Penelope made a point of opting out of most of the things other people hanker after – she was probably, in fact, one of the only women in England never to have binged on Mars Bars (although even she made an exception for Cadburys' creme eggs). What Percival Greatbottom might have bequeathed her in his will, and how much it might be worth, was of no interest to her at all. She was, therefore, sitting beside Parvum Magna's peculiar spring working on her book about women, for women, in praise of women . . . while the rest of the village variously mourned or celebrated the passing of Percival Greatbottom. (Actually, most of them celebrated, although Cruella de Ville, who had voluntarily forgone her usual fee on the night when he perished in action, did shed a tear. As she was not wearing the wig or the coat – nor the leather basque, as it happened – no-one else at the funeral had the slightest idea who the woman in the blue Burberry was, and so no-one was particularly intrigued by the tear.)

Beside Penelope the mud spring bubbled intermittently beneath the snow, finding pockets of unspecified gas from somewhere several metres and hundreds of centuries beneath the surface. The spring looked innocuous enough – rather like a small, brown bog, a kind of pool of murky quicksand no larger than a wheelbarrow – but it was, in a sense, Parvum Magna's very own Laidly Worm, as it had swallowed all sorts of things, over the years, and occasionally threw up bits of old junk in return – old bottles, bits of broken china, the odd fossil. Indeed, fifteen years previously it had notoriously swallowed not only half a ton of builders' hard core poured in as an attempt to satisfy its appetite for ever, but also, allegedly, a black and white cow called Tulip. Such clear man-eating potential meant that the children of the village were warned of its dangers almost before they could walk, and it was firmly fenced. Seemingly undistinguished from other bogs the world o'er, it was actually a kind of half-submerged dragon, barely visible on the surface, but with a chronic case of flatulence and a penchant, apparently, for other people's livestock.

Of course no-one had actually seen it swallow the cow, but certainly Tulip had been in the same field as the mud spring on the night in question, and by the time Percival Greatbottom filled out his insurance claim the next morning the cow had indisputably gone – so that had been as clear as, well, mud, really. Various geologists had studied and pronounced upon the spring after Tulip's unfortunate disappearance, and it is a truth universally acknowledged that if anyone should know all about a pointless pool of mud of unknown depth and malevolence, then it would be a geologist. After all, what point would there have been to all that studying if, at the end of it, they can't explain how a pool of mud can swallow a perfectly healthy, if a little unproductive, dairy cow, regurgitating in exchange only a Saxon arrowhead and a salt cellar engraved with the immortal words A PRESENT FROM MARGATE?

The geologists from Cambridge University had eventually pronounced the spring unexciting. (Cynics had remarked that this was not so surprising, as it was only twenty miles from Cambridge, and studying it did not involve even a night away in a pub, let alone expenses-paid trips to Iceland, Trinidad or Mexico.) They had, therefore, talked about incompetent sediments and trapped gases, mudlumps and greywackes, diastrophism and density inversion layers until they had completely confused the gentlemen of the press, who had been hoping to explain the finer points of sedimentary volcanism to their readers. *The Times* had resorted to reproducing a diagram of a geyser from an old edition of the *Children's Encyclopaedia* their editor had found in his in-laws' attic, and the tabloids had dropped the story entirely in favour of 'How to tell if your mother-in-law is from Mars' (pointed ears, apparently). Public interest in the spring had been brief and damp-squibbish, and attention had swiftly moved on to other, more world-turning events, such as the colour of the suits worn by the Prime Minister's wife and the usual squabbles on the floor of the House of Commons.

Today the mud spring was having an interesting day. Days to the mud spring were like blinks of an eye to the rest of us: when your life is measured not in years but in geological ages then an hour here or there doesn't seem worth getting excited about. Today, though, was one of those days by which the mud spring's existence was marked out, on a par with the day when the meteorite landed and not only wiped out the dinosaurs but also put paid to any decent sunshine for about a million years, and the day someone fed it half a ton of nice assorted rocks. Today the mud spring had something to regurgitate, something that tickled its lower Pleistocenes into what the geologists (had they not all been in Trinidad) might have termed a reflex orogenic belch. Something shiny.

Penelope did not notice it when it came. There was no reason why she should – one piece of pre-Saxon gold doesn't particularly stand out when it is coated in mud.

'We should all,' she was writing alarmingly, 'cast off the shackles of civilization, should go into the woods, embrace our sisters the trees, and menstruate together.' Penelope's work was, she believed, inspired by the spirit of a long-dead

Native American princess whom Handsome Dog had rather fancied, in his time. She had not yet been published, which was not surprising. She did go on a lot of writers' courses. She preferred the ones where everyone gets together and reads examples of their work. It was perhaps fortunate for the publishing world that they would never know how many promising young talents had been so affected by Penelope's readings that they had given up creative writing altogether and gone into something sensible (and far more lucrative) in the City.

A little later and a short distance away, Serendipity let herself into the house the back way, falling over the small hairy dog, Dog, who was less a dog than a piece of furniture, really, and walking into a wall of sound comparable to that made by the audiences of *Gladiators*. Clive shouted a greeting over the din, which comprised a combination of Felix's ghetto-blaster, Belinda's mini-hi-fi and Lily's rendition of 'a hundred little ducks went swimming one day'.

'Hi. D'you want any scrambled egg and soldiers?'

Serendipity eyed the kitchen floor with distaste. The entire weekly output of their six hens appeared to have been scrambled then flung onto it and trampled there in some bacchanalian ritual. Just for once, she thought, lobster thermidor and a glass of Chablis would have been nice. No – don't be disloyal – at least he's fed Lily. 'No thanks. Where's Miranda?'

'Mummy duck said "quack quack quack quack" but only sixty-six little ducks came back,' sang Lily, who had staying power of a variety more commonly found in fossils.

'Out with Luke,' said Clive. 'Lily, ten ducks next time. Ten little ducks. Ten.'

'Sixty-six little ducks went swimming one day,' crowed Lily, beaming at her father without identifiable mischief. She was happy to correct him, that was all.

'Oh,' said Serendipity. Miranda's relationship with Luke, nice boy though he was, was becoming a bit too intense for Serendipity's liking. She hoped her daughter would make a career outside Parvum Magna before she decided to commit herself to fifty years of washing the same man's socks in the village of her birth. As she herself had done.

'Ma!' Lily had just noticed her and hurtled her greeting like a human cannonball, but stickier. That would be it for conversation until bedtime.

'Ouch.' Serendipity sat down, awkward in her pregnancy. Clive ignored the comment. 'Backache,' she said, to no-one in particular, but Clive was not doling out sympathy. When you were married to a doctor and having your fifth child you came to realize that normal pregnancy was no big deal. GPs become rather blasé about the mysteries of womanhood (all that time they spend looking at other people's cervixes, no doubt). Oh, but how lovely it would be to be fussed over. She wondered if Carol had any children. Fancy that – I never asked her. She couldn't have five, that was for sure – she had looked far too well groomed. Terrifyingly perfect, in fact. Nail varnish perfect. Shampoo advert perfect. Made me realize I still have the same hairstyle I had at school.

'Mum, can I have my pocket money early?' Felix, with his flop of blond hair and the same smile as his father: 'it's really important.'

'It wouldn't be a sci-fi magazine, would it?'

'It's a book,' said Felix, who had long ago decided to be the first man on Jupiter. Or Mars. He wasn't fussed. Any planet would do. 'It's got this theory about hypercubes – they hide behind molecules and suck up the things that go missing, like the teaspoons and your car keys, then they spit them out in a randomly different place and time. Things slip through to the sixth dimension, and if you could get in there afterwards you could tear the space-time continuum and—'

'Felix,' said Serendipity, 'you've lost me, even me, and I once wanted to be an astronaut.'

Felix looked slightly pitying. 'I know Mum,' he said, 'but it's not like in Wallace and Gromit any more, you know. You have to do physics to be an astronaut.'

'Thank you very much,' she said, 'I did physics at school. And before you suggest it, we didn't still think the earth was flat in those days. Anyway, where's my cup of tea? Belinda, haven't I got you properly trained yet?'

Belinda, nose in Tolkien, looked bookish. 'Sorry, I was just at a good bit.'

Felix looked scornful, 'I don't know how you can read that fairy stuff.'

She sniffed. 'It's better than you and killer parsnips from Venus, or whatever it is.'

'Tomatoes,' said Felix. 'Who rattled your cage anyway? Has your mirror been talking about Snow White again?'

'Oh wow, the class six joke. I suppose I'll have to wait a whole year now for your next one.'

'I'll make my own tea then,' said Serendipity, 'shall I?'

Later, when Lily was in bed and some of the other bedrooms vibrated to the rhythm of something unpleasantly repetitive and toneless which their occupiers seemed to think had musical merit, Serendipity put her feet on Clive and wriggled to ease her stiff back. 'Golly, I'm tired.'

Clive smiled indulgently. She was, even after all these years, the only woman he had ever known who talked like the famous five. 'So,' he said, 'you haven't told me anything yet. Why did he want you all at the funeral? Was I right?'

'Well, not completely.' Serendipity watched his face with another, detached part of her mind. He was still very good looking. What would he think of Carol? *What if he fancies her?* She frowned at herself. 'It wasn't just for some nasty practical joke. He's left the mud spring to the village in perpetuity, together with anything that comes out of it.'

'Not to mention the liability for anything that falls into it,' said Clive. 'That's a poisoned chalice of a bequest, don't you think? It's not as though we'd have any use for a dozen Saxon arrowheads and a fossilized worm, but if it swallows any more cows – well, we pay the bill. It could mean unlimited liability – like Lloyd's.'

Serendipity was doubtful. 'It's hardly going to swallow an oil rig, it's not on that kind of scale.'

'Well, I think it sounds exciting.' Miranda was standing in the doorway, tall, slender, rather alarmingly beautiful, to a parent. (Is it inherently more dangerous to have blonde daughters? Serendipity had wondered about this for years, and feared that she had a fair few more years of wondering ahead yet.) 'Perhaps we could throw Alice Bollivant in there. I'm sure Hector wouldn't sue – she nags him to bits.'

Serendipity smiled. 'You're far too young to know all about nagging, Miranda.'

'I know all about oral sex,' said Miranda cheekily.

'Not from me,' said Serendipity cheerfully. She was well aware that the collective teenage knowledge of sexual facts these days was far greater than her own was even now, and thus there was no point in her even attempting to pass on her own hang-ups. 'And I think you'd be surprised by old Hector.'

'What do you mean?'

'Oh, he's a man with a glint in his eye,' said Serendipity airily.

'He hasn't made a pass at you!' Miranda was deliciously scandalized, glad that she was old enough to have conversations like this with her parents.

'Of course not!' She's nuts if she thinks I'd tell her if he had, thought Serendipity, but he hasn't. I'm not the sort of woman who gets passes made at her. Aloud she said, 'I just mean he's wild about his wife. It shows in his eyes, and the way his moustache twitches when he looks at her. If she fell in the mud spring he'd leap in after her, ripping his clothes off as he went.'

'I don't know why they didn't chuck old Percy Greatbottom in there,' said Clive grimly. 'It would have saved on the funeral.'

'Not very nice if he pops back up in a few thousand years,' said Miranda, 'although I bet he'd have found a drink somewhere down there by then, so he'd probably be pickled instead of rotten.'

'You two are awful sometimes,' said Serendipity, thinking, how wise they are at seventeen these days. How come I knew nothing? 'How was Luke?'

'Oh, you know, wildly sexy. Wouldn't wear a condom. Can I have a chocolate biscuit?'

'Miranda!'

'Oh, come on, Mum. I'm seventeen, not seven. If I was going to ignore your advice, I would, but I'm not, so don't worry about me. So where are the biscuits?'

'Top shelf,' said Clive, which Serendipity took to mean he'd been eating them. So much for his diet – mind you, he'd been dieting for four years and for every week of it she'd found the remains of a giant tub of peanuts in the back of the Morris Minor.

'I'm surprised you left any,' she said drily.

'I thought I'd take them with me,' said Miranda, with studied casualness. 'We thought we might go and have a look at the road protest.' It was far too studied when you bore in mind the deliberately ripped jeans, the CND earring and the T-shirt bearing the words ROADS RAPE that adorned her slender person.

'You do surprise me,' said Serendipity.

Miranda affected a surprised air. 'Why?' she asked.

'Call it intuition,' said Serendipity, secretly admiring her daughter for being interested. Miranda had always been a doer. Not like Belinda, who was seriously dreamy. 'Don't go down those tunnels, will you?'

'Don't worry about me, I'll be fine,' said Miranda, for whom the idea of getting down a tunnel was the whole attraction. 'I'll be with Luke.'

Serendipity sighed after they had gone. 'It must be rather splendid to be one of their generation. They seem more adult than we were. Not so driven by sex. More aware.'

'I don't know,' said Clive. 'Our teenage years were dominated by banning the bomb, but I seem to remember we still found time for the sex.'

'I never did anything radical, though.' Serendipity was still wistful.

'You went to Greenham Common for a day.'

'I know, but it wasn't the same. I didn't camp there – it was too unwashed for me. I was brought up to roll on the Mum.'

'I wouldn't waste time envying Miranda's generation,' said Clive; 'they've got AIDS to worry about, and Tony Blair.'

'I like Tony Blair,' said Serendipity, surprised.

'Exactly,' said Clive, 'what they should worry about. A prime minister your parents like is really bad news when you're their age. Did she take all the biscuits?'

'I hope so,' said Serendipity. 'You're beginning to look like a Teletubby.'

Clive looked sheepish. 'I only had one. Anyway, I have to eat constantly to keep myself this shape.'

Serendipity shrugged. 'You're only cheating yourself. I don't care.' He took hold of her foot, began to massage it. She sniffed. 'You can't get round me that way. You're getting fatter.'

'So are you. We'll get fit together.'

'Clive I'm seven months pregnant, with fewer working muscles than an amoeba. Get fit yourself.'

'I've seen some damned attractive amoebas in my time. You love me really. Anyway, was that it?'

'What?'

'The funeral. Was that it? He left the mud spring for the eternal benefit of anyone who ever thought he was an unpleasant mean old git?'

'Clive! He's dead. You shouldn't—'

'Speak ill of him? He was well aware I thought he was a mean old git when he was alive – I can't see that it does any harm to repeat it now.'

'He was just a lonely old man.'

'Not that lonely, from what I heard.'

'We all,' said Serendipity pointedly, 'have our vices.'

'Oh, for heaven's sake. Are we back onto that?'

'Well, I still don't understand how a girlie magazine can sit forgotten in your desk drawer for fifteen years. You must have known it was there.'

'I didn't. Can we just drop this? Anyone would think I'd been unfaithful.'

'Well, I felt betrayed. Especially when I look like the bow of the *Lusitania*.'

'Oh Ren, don't be ridiculous. You know I'm not the sort to be unfaithful. All men like girlie magazines.'

'No they don't – and what sort is that, then? The sort that are unfaithful?'

'I'm going to run a bath,' said Clive, darkly.

'I'll come.'

'Well, I'm going to the loo first.'

'Amoebae,' she shouted after him.

'What?'

'It's not amoebas, it's amoebae.'

'Pedant.'

Serendipity grinned as he left the room, but the humour did not dispel the underlying and uncomfortable feeling of vague dissatisfaction with life. The feeling had been there all day, niggling and unfamiliar. Now that she recognized it she didn't much like it, nor herself for harbouring it. It was seeing Carol, that was it. It was unsettling. The person she might have been herself. They had done the same O levels, after all. She stared at her stomach. It wriggled, like the man's did in *Alien* just before the creature burst out. 'Hi, Phoebe,' she said to it. The baby did not reply, and she picked up the baby magazine which lay on the table.

'Three women describe their labours,' trilled the front page, sisterishly. 'Follow our diarist in the last few weeks of her pregnancy.' God, thought Serendipity, my mother could write this sort of stuff. Perhaps she should. It might earn her a bit more than she got from mediuming, or whatever she called it, not to mention all those terrible rhymes about wombs.

The magazine's diarist was attractive and smiling. She had clearly never been more than a B cup – her breasts didn't even reach her navel. She had a real haircut, not an obvious self-trim with the nail scissors. Serendipity glowered and felt for her stretch mark. There was only one, and she'd had it since Lily, just down one side, but she still checked it every night to make sure that, like a ladder in a stocking, it wasn't creeping up towards her armpits.

'Oh, Lily,' she said, to a spider on the ceiling. Outside the owl hooted, the one that had been calling in the garden for two years now. It sounded like a tawny but she had never seen it. Lily loved owls . . .

She heard the bathroom door unlock, Clive's signal that she could come up now. She toyed with the idea of staying down here, ignoring him, reading about the three real women instead – but when she turned to page twenty-six and saw their appalling smugness (particularly the one who had given birth in a bath of pine-scented water to the music of Vivaldi – played on the original instruments, of course), Clive seemed a whole lot more appealing.

*   *   *

'So who got the farm?' asked Clive when she sat on the bathroom chair, watching him wallow.

'Carol,' said Serendipity, waiting for him to ask what she was like now.

'Was she there?'

'Yes.'

'Well? Just "yes"? Didn't you speak to her?'

'A little bit.' Serendipity sighed. 'She wasn't very forthcoming.'

'I wonder what she'll do with it?'

'Sell it, I should think,' said Serendipity with a hint of bitterness. 'She won't stay. I didn't get the impression that she'd missed Parvum Magna.'

He patted her knee. 'It still hurts, doesn't it?'

She sniffed. 'She's not like us, now. She's very glamorous, very London.'

'I don't know if the people who live under Waterloo Bridge would recognize themselves in that.'

'Oh, you know what I mean. Anyway, she was very cool. I don't think she ever forgave me for marrying you.'

'Surely not.' She sensed his interest. 'It's been so long.'

'We used to be really good friends,' said Serendipity, as if he hadn't spoken. 'I never had another best friend like that. When she left I'd already passed the critical age when you make them.'

'Well, I'm sure she doesn't still fancy me after all these years,' said Clive, with just a trace of ego.

'I'm sure she doesn't, too,' said Serendipity crossly, 'so you needn't sound so smug. It wasn't about you. It was about me and her. We were friends. She dated you – then she left, and I dated you. I broke the best friends' code.'

'Well, she never came back,' said Clive. 'What was I supposed to do? Become a monk and spend the next fifteen years producing an illuminated copy of the Book of Job? Anyhow, I always preferred you. It was you I fancied all along.'

'You're just saying that,' she said, wanting to hear it repeated – but Clive was not a man to repeat himself. He simply didn't see the need to waste time speaking when he could be reading the magic book his partner, John Potter, had lent him. Caroline Potter, John's wife, had warned Serendipity not to let her husband across the threshold with a packet of trick cards or a bunch of feather flowers, but she hadn't listened, and now he was obsessed with producing sponge balls from behind people's ears. Still, Lily liked it.

'Perhaps we ought to have asked her over for supper,' he said now. 'She must be lonely, over there at the farm.'

Serendipity shrugged. 'I couldn't have. There was something . . . I mean, we did speak, and it wasn't nearly as awkward as I expected, but there was something there, hanging in the air between us. Something else, like a glass wall. I couldn't ask her. Anyway, it's getting late. She's probably asleep.'

Over at Greatbottom Farm, Carol Pendragon heard the hooting too as she was not asleep, she was clambering uncomfortably through a mental attic of tangled and dusty memories, trying to find a quiet corner in which to go to sleep. It wasn't Uncle Percy keeping her awake. It wasn't even Serendipity, nor the long-ago faithless Clive. It was her old bedroom. It was pink.

Reluctantly Carol sat on the bed which Mrs Baggins had made up for her, in the room which Mrs Baggins had dusted and polished, and forced herself to confront the fact that it was pink and frilly because she herself – at least, the sixteen-year-old herself – had wanted it that way. She, whose minimalist Highgate home was a dazzling white enlivened only by the occasional daring touch of ecru and the brilliant splash of the original Hockney on the living-space wall, she had come from that person, that person who had chosen pink frilly. Perhaps, she thought, I am not actually the white and ecru person at all. Perhaps the white and ecru person is just a veneer, and the real Carol Pendragon is pink and frilly after all, because she is still Carol Greatbottom underneath.

She stared at the floral print wallpaper and remembered how she had insisted – *insisted* – that when she grew up all of her children would have absolute say in the colour of their bedroom walls, all six of them. She had known, then, for certain, that they would all choose pink. The girls

27

anyway. Serendipity had five children, very nearly, and she'd probably have another one. How could she do that, when that was my plan? She's had my life. *She* always wanted to be a secret agent and the first woman to the top of Everest. Why wasn't she ten thousand miles away with a ton of goggles and crampons, six false passports, an exploding pen and a couple of bad-tempered Sherpas who'd done the climb three times already and just wanted to get home and watch the satellite shopping channel in downtown Kathmandu? That was where *she* was supposed to be.

Carol smoothed the pink quilt cover, faded but familiar. All of my dreams are here, she thought uncomfortably, waiting to ambush me. It was definitely time to phone Neil.

'Hi,' he said, as casually as though Carol had been nowhere, done nothing of any importance. Which, of course, she hadn't.

'Hello.' It wasn't as though she expected him to sound like a lovesick teenager. That had never been their style. 'How's Geneva?'

He launched into some tale about clients and head-hunting, and Carol let his voice drift between her ears like the scent of Bisto.

'I thought I might stay here for a while,' she said suddenly, surprising herself.

'What? But why? You've got a business to run.'

'My business runs itself,' said Carol, more sharply than the shrug-off tone she had intended, 'and you're in Geneva till the weekend.'

'No business runs itself,' said Neil. 'How long are you planning to stay?'

'I don't know. I've got to sort Uncle Percy's things out, make sure the farm is OK.'

'You can't run a farm.' Neil found the sudden mental image of Carol with muddy green wellies on her feet and something's udders in her hands quite unnerving.

'I don't have to. The manager and the men do all that – they'll work the farm till I sell it.'

'Thank God for that. Just get some house clearance people in, then. There can't be anything worth keeping.'

Carol was suddenly annoyed that he should assume that

28

the contents of the house in which she had spent her forma-
tive years should mean so little. Not, of course, that they did
mean anything. Why should they?

'Oh, you never know,' she told Neil, putting her urge to
stay into terms he would understand. 'There are a few old
chairs and clocks. I might get someone in to look.'

'Ah, antiques.' Neil thought of undiscovered Vermeers on
the *Antiques Roadshow* and decided maybe she was right.
'Well, remember the Mountford-Turners are coming to supper on Saturday.'

Carol thought of them with distaste. Edwin Mountford-
Turner had cold clammy fingers and was always licking his
lips meaningfully, like a Barbara Cartland villain. 'Don't
worry, I haven't forgotten.'

'OK. Well, I must go, darling. Entertaining, you know.
Sleep well. Love you.'

'Grmph,' said Carol. For some reason she just didn't feel
like saying 'love you' back. He didn't sound as though he
was missing her enough. Why not 'I love you'? Missing out
that all-important first word almost reduced the statement to
the impersonal. *Now you're being ridiculous, Carol . . .*

After his voice had disappeared into the international
ether she lay on the bed in the dark, fighting off memories
with thoughts of the asparagus starter she planned for
Saturday, and of the floral arrangements she had ordered
from Harrods. She could hear the call of peacocks in the distance, and it felt almost welcoming. It was true, her business
didn't need her, not any more. Certainly to begin with she
had done it all herself, but now that they were the best
employment agency in the City of London, Fiona, her office
manager, had better contacts than she did herself. She still
loved it, of course she did, she was still a city business-
woman through and through, living and breathing
interviews and CVs and lunches at the right places – but a
short time for reflection here seemed suddenly appealing.
Only a little bit appealing, she reassured herself, lest any
alarm bells begin to ring, but certainly more appealing than
old rubber-lips Edwin. Maybe she really *could* stay a little
longer, put Fiona in charge of the office for a while, and cancel the London dinner party . . .

Chapter Two

St Alupent, Patron Saint of Dragon Slayers and of Parvum Magna's solid, rather endearingly ordinary church, also had a Cambridge college named after him. It was said that learned scholars from this seat of wisdom and sagacity had named the village 'Small Large' as a kind of academic joke, the kind that only others of equal wisdom and sagacity find remotely funny.

It was a village people loved to live in, because its heart still beat vigorously in its newsagent's, primary school, and post office and general store, which had always run out of cream cakes by half-past eleven because Jean Clayton, who ran it, could not resist them for any longer than that. Estate agents hated it because however muddy they got their Church's brogues trying to get a picturesque shot of a thatched dream cottage, the inevitable Fifties bungalow next door showed in every picture. In these days of freeze-dried villages, rendered thus by the New Countrified who complain when cockerels crow, cow manure smells, tractors hold up traffic and farmers are too bloody minded to sell them half of a generations-owned field to make a nice Japanese water garden, Parvum Magna remained a real, salt-and-pepper mix of houses, including some rather superior council dwellings that were absolutely never up for grabs. Its inhabitants were, in almost equal numbers, people who were wealthy but thought they weren't, people who weren't wealthy but wanted to be, and people who were far more interested in how wealthy everyone else was to decide whether or not they were wealthy themselves. If oxen or maidservants had been present in any significant number, then the tenth commandment would have been broken there quite literally, as there was always a lot of coveting going on.

Carol Pendragon had lived in the village for the first sixteen years of her life, at Greatbottom Farm with her mother and her Uncle Percy. Now, though, Uncle Percy was six feet under (and that was not an inch lower than he deserved to be) and her mother was living in Italy with her third husband and all the Manolo Blahnik shoes she could ever possibly require, and more than anyone could ever possibly need, the Imelda Marcos of Tuscany. So now there was just Carol, back here in Parochialville, back here where everything had gone wrong for her, where she had had acne, whatever Serendipity said . . . and she was actually contemplating staying for a while. Why am I doing this? she asked herself, as she arranged for Mr Baggins and his merry men to carry on working the farm, and telephoned the surgery for an appointment with Dr Potter, the junior partner (and the only one who didn't know her).

She didn't like the fact that she knew why, but there it was. She did know why. The feeling had hit her just as soon as the square tower of St Alupent's church became visible over the rolling fields outside Broomhill. The feeling of familiarity (and contempt) which told her that wherever she went, whatever she did, Parvum Magna was, unfortunately, home. She had left her footprints here for ever. Home isn't an affinity, she thought, it isn't a choice, it's certainly not a sense of being like everyone else who lives there – or even, thank God, like *anyone* else who lives there; it's a nebulous concept, a feeling that comes over you, one that you can't control, as powerful and unavoidable as the urge to visit the loo when camping halfway up Everest with a frozen zip and no Andrex. Home is indelibly printed on some part of your cortex, along with being right-handed and being sure that pink is your favourite colour for ever, and it can't be shaken off.

It's a funny thing, she thought resignedly. You can go away for years – decades, even – to far more fashionable, interesting or ultraviolet-rich climes, but when the going gets tough we are all rabbits at heart. We all want to go back and hide in our burrows.

Rabbits. Now that was an unfortunate analogy.

The fact that Carol Greatbottom (nobody called her Carol Pendragon – some names are just not escapable even by

31

marriage) seemed to have taken up residence at Greatbottom Farm, even temporarily, caused enough speculation to power a rumour factory. Life in Parvum Magna was normally so uneventful that the annual rose-growing competition was conducted with the pleasant easygoingness of Genghis Khan's Asian campaign. Serendipity, calling into the post office to collect her child benefit, was conscious of a hint of unexpected irritation at this parochialism, even though normally she loved the village for just such smallness.

'She was a friend of yours, wasn't she, Mrs Rowan?' said Jean Clayton, a postmistress so postmistressy that she made the one on *Postman Pat* look appallingly miscast. She patted her white, postmistressy hair. 'Isn't she glamorous? It's like a breath of fresh air seeing her here, isn't it? And she looks so young.' She herself had turned white at the age of thirty-five, the day her son Trevor got his first tattoo.

As opposed to me, thought Serendipity, who looks about as young as the mud spring, and about as glamorous as a day at the greyhound races in Skegness with twenty lager drinkers and an incontinent dog. 'Forty first-class stamps, please,' she said, a little more sharply than she intended, 'and yes, we knew each other at school, before she moved away.'

Mrs Clayton twinkled her eyes in the way that the Post Office staff training manual has never quite managed to accurately specify (you've either got it or you haven't). 'She doesn't come back very often. Fall out, did you?'

You know bloody well we did, thought Serendipity. She had lived in deepest Suffolk far too long to be deceived by a rural twinkle. Gossip is the nectar of life in villages; it doesn't just spread, like a forest fire, it pulsates in great arterial fountains out from the post offices where it so often begins, infiltrating every cranny of the parish, every ear of wheat, every leaf, every stone – and with every pulsation it mutates further into an awful parody of what was originally extracted by that friendly twinkle, like a game of multidirectional Chinese whispers conducted in Esperanto at the AGM of the Society of Partially Hearing

Esperanto Students who Failed Their Esperanto Exam.

'Mrs Rowan?'

'What? Oh, sorry. No, she and I lost touch,' said Serendipity, thinking, when that piece of information next comes back to me, Carol and I will have been at war for the last eighteen years and our respective solicitors will have resorted to shredding one another's wardrobes during the night.

'Fell out, did you?' Cutting through the chaff to the nitty-gritty like an Inquisitor wielding a very unpleasant hot thing with a point.

'Not really,' she said vaguely; 'you know how it is at sixteen.' She doubted that Mrs Clayton did. Mrs Clayton could never have been sixteen. There are people, plenty of people, who simply cannot ever have been teenagers.

It must have been quite a falling out, speculated Mrs Clayton to her next customer, Alice Bollivant, and by the end of the day conjecture was rife.

Carol, for now unaware that she was being discussed with such relish, had decided to go to Sainsbury's for supplies. When your office is a stone's throw from the King's Road, she had told Mrs Baggins, you come to expect to shop where polenta and fresh Parmesan are sold. (Mrs Baggins had been mystified by the polenta – as she told Mr Baggins later over a nice piece of tripe, why would Londoners want to eat chicken feed? Mr Baggins said that nothing that capitalists did would ever surprise him, but since Mrs Pendragon had asked him to stay on till the farm was sold, then he didn't care if she ate pickled rats, she was OK by him.)

Brian Baggins had worked on the farm for fifteen years. He was a tall, dark and surly man with a moustache like a bottle brush and a face like a passport photo, a man whose far-left-wing principles did not allow him to like very many people at all and whose facial hair allowed him to kiss even fewer. He was probably the human equivalent of a walrus – totally uncuddleable – and his wife Brenda had almost as much facial hair as he did. Working the land suited Brian: it was noble and proletarian. True, he was now working for Carol Pendragon, and she was clearly even more of a capitalist oppressor than her uncle – but she had raised his wages, and a man has to work, so if anyone thought it compromised his principles then who did they think they were to judge another man, anyway? He knew he ran the farm well, and that was all that mattered. Just as long as he got what was rightfully his, Brian, for all his socialism, was content.

The temperature was a little higher than the previous day, and TV weather girls were getting terribly excited trying to cram an explanation of occluded fronts into a twenty-second slot after the lunchtime news yet still display enough personality to land a job presenting *Gladiators*, but the sky was still that drab colour which so completely fails to flatter the complexion and which is so unsuitable for June, and there was a light but persistent drizzle. Driving along the Broomhill road towards Bumpstaple, a pretty but rather smug village about four miles from Broomhill itself, Carol was startled by what appeared to be a giant sheep which leapt over the deep-worn lane, from one side to the other, at the very periphery of her vision, the bit God programmed to see spiders, and by the time she had slammed on her brakes and explained to the man behind that she wasn't just another stupid bloody woman who had stopped in the middle of the road to do her eyelashes, it had gone. She continued on towards Sainsbury's, puzzled. Do sheep jump over hedgerows? It was quite a big hedgerow. Perhaps it was part of a secret government experiment on mutant sheep. Maybe they were training them to crawl undetected behind enemy lines and seduce the footsoldiers . . . Carol shook her head. That was the way she and Serendipity used to talk, years ago. Suffolk was making her regress. Should she really have cancelled the Mountford-Turners in favour of spending more time in a county populated by giant mutant sheep? Mind you, there were plenty of grounds for thinking Edwin Mountford-Turner was a giant mutant sheep too. One with thick lips. The thought of avoiding him, and the prospect of availing herself of both polenta and Parmesan in the supermarket, cheered her immensely, and she forgot all about it.

*   *   *

As Carol immersed herself in the art of making sure her shopping trolley said all the right things about her (no nappies, no own-brand products and no low-calorie meals; lots of lapsang souchong tea, a side of smoked salmon, and all the air-freighted asparagus there was on the shelf) Alice Bollivant was hurrying through the light drizzle to call in on Serendipity, supposedly to remind her that it was her turn to distribute the parish magazine, but actually to remind her whose children were the better educated, even if Hector wasn't a doctor, and to get an invite to dinner and a chance to interrogate Carol Pendragon.

Alice Bollivant had lived in Parvum Magna for thirty years, and she ran most things that needed running, and several that did not. She had a sense of self-importance rare in those who are not prime ministers, pop stars or teenagers. Her husband, Hector, was chairman of the Parish Council (a post he hated, but she had given him no choice in the matter) and she herself ran the WI, the Young Wives, the church (well, the vicar thought he ran it, but then he was hardly ever there, just the odd hour on a Sunday), the cricket team teas, the PTA at nearby Rope Hall prep school, and the Village Hall Appeal, not to mention being the leading soprano in the Broomhill Amateur Operatic Society. She was forty-two, with two children (privately educated at Rope Hall Prep and now Butterton School, of course) and she was the kind of woman who would rather die than take part in the Daz doorstep challenge. She oozed friendship, affection and confidences, but Serendipity was always left with the odd feeling that Alice did not really like her – worse, that just beneath the surface of the conversation Alice had another voice that was saying, 'This village would really be a much nicer place for me if you'd just clear off and go to live in Bumpstaple.' Now Alice drank Serendipity's tea with the pained expression of one more accustomed to china.

'Sorry, Alice, I've only got unbreakable mugs. I haven't done the washing up yet.'

'Really,' said Alice, 'I can't imagine why you don't get Clive to buy you a dishwasher.'

'I don't want one,' said Serendipity, affronted, 'and if I did I'd buy it myself. I wouldn't need Clive's permission.'

'But everyone has one,' said Alice, mystified that anyone should *want* to wash their own dishes.

Serendipity grinned. 'It's like all those small objects of desire, Alice. They start off as optional extras, then there comes a point when everyone thinks they're essential. But just because other people want things it doesn't mean I have to want them. In the great cosmic scheme of things possessing a dishwasher seems relatively pointless. Anyway, I like washing dishes. It's a therapeutic breathing space in life's vast lagoon of chaos.'

'No, but . . .' Alice hated it when Serendipity pretended to be clever. It was not as if she'd been to college. Everyone knew she'd been pregnant when she sat her O levels.

'Look, Alice,' said Serendipity, firmly, 'do you want – I mean really *really* want – to breed peacocks?'

'Of course not,' said Alice, not seeing the point. 'Yours eat your delphiniums and do things on your patio.' The twitch of her nostrils made it quite clear what kind of things these were.

'Well, I wanted to,' said Serendipity, 'which is why I do. And that's my point.'

Alice was offended. 'I don't think it's fair to suggest that just because I have a dishwasher that makes me a sheep.'

Serendipity suppressed a smile. 'Of course not – I'm not suggesting that. I'm just saying I've no reason to want a dishwasher. I've got everything I want.'

Alice saw an opening, and seized on it like a rhinoceros spotting a rhinoceros-sized hole in the fence at Whipsnade Zoo. 'Speaking of getting what you want, your friend Carol seems to have done well for herself.'

Serendipity shrugged. 'She leads a different sort of life now. You can tell by the fingernails.' Carol had proper ones, oval shaped and filed and polished, rather than trimmed to the quick with baby scissors and scrubbed with the kitchen brush while in glorious contemplation of a soaking lasagne dish that wouldn't come clean despite the dazzling claims of the Fairy advert.

'That was an Armani suit,' said Alice, who always ignored Serendipity's more obscure statements. Serendipity assumed she must have read the label – only people who wear Armani suits can spot them on others without reading the label. Isn't that, like the Freemason's handshake, the point of wearing one? Your true peers recognize you, and nobody else counts. Mind you, if that were so, then why had Carol worn it to Uncle Percy's funeral? He certainly wouldn't have appreciated it any more when dead than he would have done when he was alive.

'I don't think Armani does maternity wear,' she said aloud.

Alice shrugged. 'Personally I prefer Jaeger,' she said. 'I think designer clothes are rather vulgar, when you think of the third world.'

Serendipity knew exactly what Alice thought – and it was, as always, 'I want.' She was tempted to ask if Alice thought about the third world when she was buying out-of-season strawberries for her dinner parties, but thought better of it. Envy is painful enough, without making its bearer the object of mockery, so she restricted herself to saying, 'I thought she looked very smart.'

'You two were bosom buddies when I first came here,' said Alice. 'Inseparable in and out of school, I seem to remember. And didn't Carol once date Clive?'

'Yes, before I did,' said Serendipity, as casually as she dared. Even after all these years her rift with Carol was not for public airing – teenage wounds often run the deepest – 'but that was a long time ago. Carol always had grand ambitions, beyond this place.'

Alice raised an eyebrow. 'I seem to remember you both did. Your mother once told me that you planned to become the Prime Minister, and wasn't there something about Mount Everest?'

Serendipity smiled, hiding the wishful dream of high and snow-capped places that had been with her all her life. 'Oh, you know what teenagers say, but that was before I felt the cellulite coming upon me in the night. I'm too old, and any-how, I can't even climb the stairs at the moment. I wouldn't be much good on Everest, not unless they've installed a stair-lift.'

'How the mighty are fallen,' said Alice, rather cattily Serendipity thought. 'But I should like to meet Carol properly again. Why don't you have one of your marvellous dinner parties? You're so lucky having a husband who cooks.'

'I . . . er, yes, I am.' Serendipity was caught unawares, as she always was by anyone who went straight for the throat.

'Oh, that will be marvellous. We must all fix a date.' Alice was happy now she had, as the marines say, achieved the prime objective. 'I think Thursday of this week would be a good day, don't you? There's nothing on your calendar, look.'

Damn, thought Serendipity, why haven't I written something on there for every day? I ought to keep a false calendar in the kitchen, one that has me living my life in a wild social whirl which doesn't leave enough of a gap even to open a can of soup for anyone else. 'Actually I'm working on the main road dressed in leather and fishnets on Thursdays – I didn't want to put it on the calendar, in case the vicar came round,' she began cheerily.

Alice looked blank. 'Really, Serendipity, sometimes your sense of humour is really rather odd – what on earth has fishing got to do with anything . . . ? Thursday,' she wrote on Serendipity's calendar whilst Serendipity glowered ineffectively at Dog, who always hid under the kitchen table when Alice came round, probably smelling her little Papillon dog, Fleur. Fleur looked like a rat and Dog had once failed miserably in a mating attempt on account of size, Fleur being not even as long in total as the part of his anatomy he had tried to show her, leading him to conclude that there are times when a dog cannot be a dog. He had retreated, humiliated, and had never been able to look Alice in the eye since. '. . . and how is Miranda? Still seeing Luke Stewart?'

'Yes. He's a nice boy,' said Serendipity, more defensively than she had intended. Still, hopefully Carol wouldn't come for dinner – she'd have gone back to London.

Alice sighed, getting to her feet. 'I can see you worry, dear. Of course, this was why I felt Olivia and Geraldine would be much better off boarding in a girls' school,' she said. 'None of this teenage sex. Oh, I'm sorry, I didn't mean . . .'

It was nice to see her flustered, thought Serendipity meanly. Serves her right, after inviting herself to dinner. She had obviously intended a dig at those who sent their children to state schools, before it turned into the accidental insult. She was tempted to ask how sure Alice was that Olivia and Geraldine weren't rampant lesbians enjoying wildly unfettered sexual activity, not to mention endless marijuana, in the privacy of their expensive boarding accommodation – but didn't. After all, poor Alice had a hard enough time bearing the fact that Serendipity's children were nice, drug-free and responsible, even though she and Clive hadn't bankrupted themselves to pay for a public school where they could rub shoulders with the titled and rich. The Bollivants had only spent all those thousands on Butterton School because Zoe Ormondroyd, daughter of the Ormondroyds of Great Barking Hall, had gone there, and then Zoe had immediately dropped out to go to Broomhill Comprehensive. Alice and Hector couldn't possibly pull their own girls out, though, not after all the pointed comments they had made about the place. So now Serendipity said, 'That's OK, Alice. I was a teenage mother. That's no secret.' But after Alice had gone she found herself discontented, remembering her old ambitions. Is that why I worry so much about Miranda and Luke? she thought. Clive always says it is, but until now I'd never agreed . . .

A short distance away, the mud spring lay alone beneath the dishwater skies – as it usually did, for if you imagined its whole life compressed into twenty-four hours, humanity's entire existence was the equivalent of a five-minute wild aberration by a disconsolate junior god with nothing better to do than make trouble for the senior gods to clear up. Slowly, and with the kind of patience that only insentient objects and cricket commentators are capable of showing, the bowels of the spring brought another bubble up to the surface, a few more coins with it, and with them a little more of its indigestion cleared. The gentle drizzle cleaned the mud off one of the coins, and it gleamed very slightly in the last of the daylight. It was a golden gleam.

Penelope Forbes, who did not write feminist poetry on cold days (Handsome Dog had got rather chilly last time and had sulked for a week, disrupting three seances and a private reading for the Broomhill chief of police, who had wanted to contact his mother-in-law and tell her, at last, what he had really thought of his Christmas present), was not there to see it – she was busy with her other hobby; her passion, as she saw it. Despite the failure of her poetry to bring her the sisterly recognition she so clearly deserved, she had a sizeable income from the trust fund her father had left her, and today she had driven to Lowestoft in order to buy all the lobsters she could find. Penelope loved lobsters – and the sheer numbers of them that she purchased had enabled her to acquire a whole network of contacts who would sell to her direct. Now she was on the A14 with Handsome Dog at her shoulder and a consignment of crustaceans in the back of her green Morris Minor traveller, humming along with the whale song on her cassette recorder (she was, perhaps, the only woman alive who could hum along to whale song). She was happy. The lobsters, as far as one could tell, were cheerful too. They seemed to like the whale song (although, oddly, she had discovered that they also liked Michael Jackson. She had accidentally tuned in to Radio 1 earlier whilst trying to find *The Archers*, and the lobsters had become quite excited at the sound of 'Thriller').

Handsome Dog was not so cheerful. Bad luck was in the air, he told her, his old enemy Jealous Wolf was abroad. Penelope should watch her path, he said, for there is little more destructive than jealousy.

Penelope was not worried – Handsome Dog could be a miserable old pessimist at times, and had been in a funny mood since she had watched *Pocahontas* with Lily, though she did wonder if Carol Pendragon's return might have something to do with it. Still, perhaps she should keep an eye on Serendipity . . .

'Is there anything on TV tonight?'

'Nothing,' said Serendipity, looking up from sewing the name tapes into Lily's gym kit. 'Lily Hebe Sage Rowan,' they said, which meant an awful lot more sewing than if she had just put 'L. Rowan', particularly when multiplied by the six dozen which she had ordered from Cash's. Serendipity believed in full names, though. What was the point of having all those lovely names if they only got mentioned at your christening and your funeral, neither of which you were likely to remember much about?

'There can't be nothing on,' said Clive, annoyed that she seemed to have thrown the TV listings away, and trying to access Teletext with the remote (Lily had been sick on the listings earlier, but Serendipity didn't bother him with such ordinary details of life), 'unless of course there's been a coup since I left work, and all the TV transmitters have been taken over by a shadowy revolutionary group with an insane desire to abolish *Panorama*. Where are the batteries out of this thing?'

'In Lily's night-light,' said Serendipity, 'and no, you're right, there is, technically, something on.'

'What, then?'

'Well, there'll be the seven o'clock news, the nine o'clock news, the ten o'clock news and the eleven o'clock discussion of the news, there'll be *EastEnders*, *Coronation Street* or *Brookside* – or maybe all three – then there'll be a quiz show involving either Paul Daniels, Ronnie Corbett or that woman with the teeth, an ex-Python actor travelling to somewhere peculiar like Bhutan or Clacton, something introduced by Noel Edmonds with a live audience who laugh constantly, something involving animals and, probably, Rolf Harris, something medical, a drama about the police, an opera we've never heard of sung in the original Norwegian, something about a group of Americans in a bachelor pad all being very amusing, and a fly on the wall documentary about juvenile crime on a Brixton council estate –' she did not look up from the name tape – 'same as every night.'

Clive switched it on anyway, and flicked through the channels. Annoyingly, she seemed to be right. He switched away from a jolly presenter who seemed to be talking about llamas (no doubt Rolf Harris was about to befriend one and pull a thorn out of its hoof), and back to Channel soap. 'Do you want to watch a magic video?' he asked, with what he hoped was a cheekily endearing grin.

Serendipity looked up at last, and eyed him with mild

exasperation. 'I have about as much desire to watch some bloke in a white DJ showing me how to produce a rabbit from someone else's knickers as I have to go on a three-week potato-cultivating course with Dr Jekyll, Fu Manchu and the entire Von Trapp family,' she said, with careful precision, 'and I don't know why you think your lascivious expression will win me over, either.'

'Oh,' said Clive, 'should I take that as a "No", then?'

She giggled, suddenly relaxed. 'I'm sorry, I'm taking myself too seriously again, aren't I? OK, I give in – put the beastly video on. I'll even have Paul Daniels's Christmas special if you'll make me a cup of tea first. I've had a dose of the Alice Bollivants today.'

'Poor you. You shouldn't let her get to you, she's only jealous.'

'I don't see why she should be jealous of us. Look at her. Tennis court, private school, in charge of everything.'

'She's just the sort of woman who's always jealous of everybody. The other man's grass and all that.'

Serendipity sighed, 'I feel a bit like that myself sometimes. Look at me – no career, nearly five children, a dog who wants to be a pouffe, the thickest peacocks in all Suffolk . . .'

'I thought you were happy.' Clive was surprised. 'We always wanted a lot of children. I remember you were really flattered when Caroline Potter said you were a real earth mother.'

'I know. I was – I do. I am. I just wasn't ready for *her* to come back and remind me,' Serendipity muttered.

'Remind you of what? Better days?' He sounded hurt.

'No, of course not. Of the two paths, the other path.' Then, as he looked puzzled, she became exasperated. 'Don't you see? When we were both sixteen we had choices. We talked about it. We thought we could be anything, absolutely anything we chose to be. We talked about being astronauts. I wanted to climb Mount Everest. We discussed whether to have ten children, or just have six and be Prime Minister. We really thought we could choose.'

'So you made choices – or are you saying that the choices chose you?'

'Don't they always, in a way? They come along and ambush you when you least expect it, and before you know it, you've decided.'

'I would have thought Chris Bonington gave Everest slightly more thought than that,' said Clive wryly.

Serendipity sighed, suddenly deflated, feeling the baby kick. 'Don't you ever wonder, Clive, what you might have been if you hadn't become a GP, if you hadn't married me?'

'No,' he said honestly. 'I've always wanted to be a GP, and I've always wanted to marry you.'

'No you haven't, you dated Carol.'

'Only to get at you. Do you regret it all, then?' He was looking hurt.

'No, of course not.' She leaned against him, tired of feeling confused, not wanting to upset him. 'I just meant – I never realized I'd made all of my choices, that I was on the final road there was for me, until I was so far down it past the last junction that there was no going back.'

'You mean you wish you'd been an astronaut?' He was trying to prod her into humour with the ridiculous, but she was still serious.

'No, not necessarily, I just wish I'd actually decided not to be before I wasn't. I never planned it properly. Carol did.'

'Ah, Carol again.'

'What do you mean, Carol again? I've hardly mentioned her.'

'She hangs, unsaid, all around, in the very air that we breathe,' said Clive theatrically. 'You're jealous of what she has, what she's become.'

'I'm not. I don't even know what she has. She might have herpes for all I know.'

'Exactly. You can't want just some of what she's got and expect to keep what you've got too. What *did* she want back then, anyway?'

Serendipity muttered something, then added '. . . and I'm such a frump compared to her.'

'Don't be silly. Come on, answer the question. What did she want, when you decided to be an astronaut?'

Serendipity sighed. 'To marry you and have six kids,' she

said, 'actually. Although before you get any ideas, she likes her men thin.'

Clive sniffed. 'We all play with the hand we're given. I was dealt the fat git cards.'

'No you weren't, you chose to be a couch potato. I mean, is this really, honestly entertaining?'

Clive glanced at the TV screen, on which a bevy of apparently seriously depressed soap opera stars were glowering at one another over several pints of best (no change there, then). There was a thump from upstairs.

'Lily,' said Serendipity on a sigh. Lily fell out of bed with monotonous regularity, but steadfastly refused to sleep in a bed with a guard, screaming hysterically if anyone tried to force her. They didn't know why – that was the trouble with autism. You never knew why.

'D'you want me to go?' Clive felt suddenly guilty. Poor Ren was so breathless when she climbed the stairs.

But Serendipity had already gone.

Lily Rowan didn't see the world the same way everyone else did, and she didn't see people the same way everyone else did, either. The difference was impossible to explain, since Lily had no more idea of how everyone else saw the world than they did of how she saw it, and in any case she was only five and her speech left a bit to be desired.

Lily was autistic. Only mildly autistic, as Serendipity felt obliged to assure anyone who asked her, just in case they expected Lily to recite telephone directories or play Rachmaninov. To Lily the ability which we all have (apart from those who sit on parish councils) to see the other person's point of view seemed to be entirely lacking. Thus it was Lily's habit to treat other people like insentient objects. Although some of those in the House of Lords during a twelve-hour debate on ECUs and Eurosausages probably are insentient objects, for most people the sensation of being sat upon by a wet but chunky five-year-old child when sunbathing on the beach is a little unwelcome. Lily was a handful on the beach. She was a handful when shopping, too, when by a river or a road, and when in restaurants, especially in Southwold where she had once been sick all over a tearoom carpet because the drinking straw in her milk was blue.

Lily was, it was turning out, a very bright child, and she looked like a blonde angel – but she was also entirely extreme. Everything Lily felt she felt keenly, so she was always either terribly happy or terribly sad – even about the littlest thing, such as which of six apparently identical dishes she was given her breakfast cereal in, or whether she had the right name tape sewn into her knickers. Therefore, even though Lily went, thus far at least, to the same school that Miranda, Felix and Belinda had been to before her, any clothes that had been handed down had to be re-named for Lily. She might be only just five but, as Mrs Cherry, her broad Yorkshire extra-classroom helper (courtesy of the special needs department at the education authority) had put it with some astonishment, by heck the lass could read.

When Serendipity reached Lily she was curled into a ball on the bedroom floor, howling like an abandoned wolf cub. Serendipity scooped her up, despite her pregnant back, and woke her, wondering what the dream had been. Lily clung to her like a lost soul, whimpering softly. Serendipity sat on Lily's bed and hugged back, knowing that was all that was required, but that it was essential. How stupid I am, she thought, to think that I want what Carol has, for the only way I could have it would involve not having all of this. Yet I can't help wondering what it would be like to stand on the top of the world . . .

Lily calmed down, snuffled a little, and dozed off, so Serendipity settled her back into her bed with three dolls named Mavis and a plastic Thomas the Tank Engine, all of which were essential for Lily's peaceful sleep, and went back downstairs to find Clive immersed in Paul Daniels's apparent attempt to divide his wife into her component parts. A cup of lukewarm tea sat beside him. Serendipity picked it up and snuggled close.

'She's rattled you, hasn't she?' asked Clive without looking at her.

She smiled. 'Mmm, I suppose so,' she said. 'I just feel unsettled since I've seen her.'

'That's only natural,' he said, understandingly.

Serendipity thought about that. 'You're probably right,' she said. 'I just can't help thinking that Carol has done all the things I said I'd do when we were at school.'

'Oh. Been up Everest then, has she?'

'No, stupid. You know what I mean. In principle. She left here, went out into the world.'

'If it was so great out there,' he said, 'then why's she back?'

'She's not – at least, only temporarily.'

'I wouldn't bet on that,' said Clive.

'What do you mean? Have you been talking to her?'

'She's registered as a new patient,' he said, 'though not with me.'

'Thank God for that,' said Serendipity, thinking, I may be a tolerant woman, but I don't want my husband doing breast checks on the woman who preceded me, even if it was eighteen years ago. Actually, let's be fair. I'm not actually a tolerant woman – but even if I was, I wouldn't.

'It's always odd,' Clive said, surprisingly wisely, 'when you see someone from your past. It's like holding up a mirror to yourself and seeing what you could have been. It reminds you of what you're not, the things you never did.'

She sighed. 'I sometimes feel I'm defined by my fertility,' she said. 'That's all people see when they look at me. I'd have made a useless astronaut, though. Can't bear dried food.'

'I always thought,' said Clive with horrible medical gravity, 'that the worst thing about being on a space station would be if somebody farted.'

'Ugh. How do you mean?'

'Well, they don't take up a giant can of fresh air, do they? They recirculate it. For months. Imagine the scene: "By Stalin's knickers, Ivan Ivanovich, vot iss that terrible stench?" "Ah, zat is ze fart of Vladimir Ilyich from four months ago."'

'Sometimes,' she said darkly, 'I wonder how I ever managed to marry a doctor.'

'You didn't,' said Clive smugly. 'I wasn't a doctor when you married me.'

'You should have come with a warning notice,' she said. 'Remind me to sue.'

46

Even in June it is dark by nine, so people with tennis courts can only get the full use of them if they have floodlights. Yet nine is such a splendid time to play – time for cocktails first, then a light supper afterwards, and perfect for those who want to redistribute their thighs – preferably upwards about twelve inches, and then forwards about five.

Hector and Alice Bollivant had a splendid tennis court although, to her endless chagrin, it only had one floodlight. Hector had been far too mean to buy two at that price – so playing on the court late in the evening ('but you never want to *play* after eight, dear,' he had said) was impossibly unfair: one person had to serve into the light, to someone who couldn't see where they were serving from. Hector said that evened the odds, but Alice thought he was being ridiculous. How could you invite other parents from Butterton School for tennis weekends with only one floodlight? They would return to the Home Counties in their Rolls-Royces saying, 'My God, Laetitia, what a weekend. Wonderful food, but did you see their *floodlight*?' If only the man who'd laid the out-door electrics would take Barclaycard she'd pay for it herself (it escaped her conscience that Barclaycard was not a method of her paying, but a means of postponing Hector's paying).

Therefore, as it was half-past nine, the Bollivants were inside their child-free house (Olivia and Geraldine being involved in a marijuana smoking experiment in faraway Butterton) watching a recorded performance of *The Flying Dutchman*. Outside all was quiet, save for the occasional, wistful yawl of an indigestive peacock and the endless hoot-ing of those bloody owls.

Alice did not honestly like Wagner, which is generally all about dying heroically and splendidly and taking everyone else with you, and Hector would far rather have watched the snooker, the documentary or even the test card, had it been available and not obscured by, in his opinion, several chan-nels of drivel. Unfortunately for him, Alice had run into the dreadful Mrs Baggins in the video hire place, and had wished to impress her, particularly as Mrs Baggins was, astonishingly, in the process of hiring something obscure and French which she had apparently ordered in advance. Alice would have thought she was strictly a Bruce Willis woman.

Just along the road Miranda Rowan was being dropped off outside Peacocks' Barn by Luke, and was involved in the kind of prolonged snog common only to teenagers and those starring in art house films (everyone else moves on to full sex after the first five minutes).

Everywhere else was quiet as Penelope Forbes headed back out on a secret night-time mission. Humming softly to herself, a tune which would have excited several minke whales had they been in the river (it was lucky that they weren't, the River Stour being slightly too shallow for cetaceans much beyond Ipswich) she pulled up on the bridge and got out of her car. This was the part she enjoyed most.

Chapter Three

The following day was the beginning of high summer, as defined not by calendars, weathermen or popes, but by Belinda Rowan's observation that morning of the first red rose, unfolding magically to greet the watery sun. Roses were not, as it happened, the only things to make a surprise appearance that day.

It was Saturday, and Clive was on call. The phone had not stopped ringing all morning with a succession of people who were ill, people who thought they were ill, and people who knew they weren't ill but wanted a free prescription for nit lotion. (There was a huge black market in nit-lotion-obtained-by-deception in Broomhill, currently under investigation by a pair of police officers with very itchy heads called Roger and Charlie, who had been sent to join the Broomhill Nit Squad as punishment for over-vigorous pursuit of a personal vendetta against Morris Minors.) For a GP, the knack was to tell these three groups apart – but Clive suffered, in his wife's opinion, from an excessive urge to please, so he had gone to do a particularly long and nit-troubled morning surgery. At least the surgery telephones were no longer patched through to the house, so Serendipity was free from telephone duty to take Lily on a language-enhancing, flower-observing walk. This was really just like any other walk: Serendipity always felt that the things that the speech therapy service suggested she did for Lily were just the things she would have done anyway, jazzed up a bit with speech-therapy-speak and thus imbued with extra value. Things like walking, talking, cutting gingerbread into people, baking them in the oven, wondering why they always came out looking like gingerbread gorillas with underactive thyroids . . .

'Did you hear?' Alice Bollivant hurried up behind her as she drew level with the drive to Greatbottom Farm. She was looking conspiratorial, a look Serendipity hated as it usually meant she was about to hear something about someone that she would really rather not have known, like the time there was that ridiculous rumour about the vicar and the mobile library.

'Did I hear what?' Lily was becoming extraordinarily excited over a lone earwig. It probably didn't stand a chance, Serendipity thought – but please God don't let her decide to eat it in front of Alice. That would rank on a par with the day they were all invited over to lunch with Clive's senior partner, and Lily had got their hamster out of its cage and dropped it in the fruit salad, or the time she ate the post office goldfish and left incontrovertible evidence of her misdemeanour by dropping its tail back in the tank.

'The Great House has been sold. For cash, too. I heard it from Edwin, our estate agent friend in Broomhill.'

Edwin, mused Serendipity, had the sort of mouth that could have saved BBC Radio a great deal of money, so effective was it at broadcasting information without recourse to technical equipment. 'Oh, really?' she said aloud. 'Well, that's good. Mrs Featherstone was desperate to move.'

The Great House was Parvum Magna's answer to a stately home, a large grand house set in a walled garden and inhabited by, till now, Priscilla Featherstone, a woman with all the charm of a bird dropping. Mrs Featherstone had decided to move to Glastonbury to be with her son, who she liked to say had a high position in the town. (In fact he was one of those New Age crystal worshippers who like to wear white robes and congregate on the Tor at the equinox, and he didn't have a high position at all, although he was often in the position of being high.)

'Yes, but *cash*.' Alice clearly wanted to make something of it: her blue eyes were glittering hopefully. 'What sort of people would pay cash for a house? It was half a million. D'you suppose they brought the money in a suitcase?'

Serendipity entered into the spirit of it. Alice was easier to wind up than Lily's Thomas the Tank Engine (and had more or less the same propensity to go round in circles tooting furiously afterwards). 'Drug dealers? Mind you, I did read in *The Times* that a lot of high-class prostitutes were moving to Suffolk and opening, you know, *brothels*, in posh country houses. They advertise – you know – *it* – as music lessons. Flute.'

'Oh God, how dreadful. Oh, Serendipity, you don't think we should make discreet enquiries, do you?' Dear Olivia plays the flute, Alice was thinking in horror, what if this should lead to some terrible misunderstanding in later life? Perhaps I should insist she converts to the oboe at once.

Serendipity grinned. Alice had not been discreet since the day she was born. 'I was joking, Alice. Honestly, you are so gullible. Anyway it's probably some boring banking type with a wife who works in PR, buying it with his annual bonus.' She realized with a jolt that she had just described Carol and Neil, quite accidentally, and with a certain scorn, but fortunately this was lost on Alice. Why, she wondered, is it so acceptable to sneer at the higher-earning middle class? Surely being born middle class doesn't come with an obligation to buy economy baked beans and make your greatest aspiration a bedroom furnished entirely at Marks and Spencer? After all, she thought, everyone knows the wealthy middle class are now the new upper class, and their greatest dream is a trip to meet Tony Blair – whilst the old upper classes are mostly inbred and barmy.

'I do hope you're right,' Alice said. She could think of no more delightful neighbours than a PR-and-banking couple. Better than doctors (so inclined to talk about unacceptable parts of the body at dinner parties). And she could think of nothing worse than a brothel – except, of course, a horde of the working classes. The working classes, Alice was fond of saying during political discussions, are a wonderful lot, but isn't it odd how they like pork pies and have such awful taste in carpets?

Behind Alice, Serendipity could see that Lily was clearly contemplating eating a worm. She couldn't bear to let that happen. 'Lily! Put it down!'

Stupid of her, really. Shouting at Lily always had the opposite effect to what you intended. She should really have shouted 'Lily, eat it!', because Lily grinned triumphantly and put it in her mouth. Serendipity counted a mental ten. Alice, who had turned to watch, averted her eyes dramatically. She was rather an expert in dramatic gestures, now that she was an opera star – and in any case it was all she was allowed where Lily was concerned. She knew better than to say anything to Serendipity about her management of Lily. She and her friends often discussed it, though. It wasn't that she approved of smacking children. Olivia and Geraldine were never smacked – they never needed it, of course. She had told Hector it was in their genes. (He always agreed, then walloped them surreptitiously when she was at Sainsbury's.) But how did Serendipity know that Lily was autistic rather than just stupid and naughty? Weren't autistic children supposed to play Rachmaninov and recite telephone directories?

Serendipity knew exactly what Alice thought about Lily. It shone out of her eyebrows, which were now raised in that way that some people raise them instead of saying 'Oh really?' It was one of the (many) reasons why she could never have seen Alice as a real friend. 'I must get on,' she said, wanting the encounter over. 'I'm sure we'll find out soon enough who's moving in.'

Alice nodded. Watching children eat annelids was not her idea of fun. It was annoying, really, that Serendipity had managed an array of such beautifully blond children, like something out of a catalogue, whilst Olivia and Geraldine were distinctly mousy. 'I'm off to call on Carol Pendragon, to renew our acquaintance.' It was said with some pride, as if Carol's eighteen-year absence had turned her into a trophy to be displayed against the Osborne and Little wallpaper, along with the Butterton School annual photographs and the picture of Hector as president of the golf club presenting a trophy to the Lord Mayor. We are the sort of people, shrieked Alice's trophies, who rub shoulders with councillors and do not possess a copy of the Argos catalogue. (Hector did, actually, but he kept it hidden in the garden shed. Alice's emerald ring had come from there, although it was in an Aspreys box. So what if it was manufactured emerald? She would never know.)

'Oh, give her my regards,' said Serendipity – but as Alice sailed off self-importantly towards the farm, an old imp of mischief, buried long but obviously only shallowly, made

Serendipity pop into the phone box by the pub and ring an advance warning to Carol.

'Hi. It's Serendipity.'

'Oh. I . . .'

'Alice is on her way up your drive.'

'I shall conceal myself immediately,' said Carol, catching the mood, 'behind the sofa.'

Serendipity laughed. 'See you,' she said, then hung up. Now what had made her do that? An echo of old loyalty – or are we still best friends underneath? Perhaps, she thought hopefully, best friendships are like quarry tiles in the kitchens of old houses. They get concreted over, or covered in sticky gunk and carpet tiles, but they're still intact under it all, still better than all the alternatives, still too valuable to replace, even if you could find anything like them again, and still yours in exchange for a lot of effort with a chisel and a scrubbing brush to get rid of the mess you've dumped on top.

When Serendipity got home, Miranda was upstairs, entertaining Luke in her room. This was something over which Serendipity and Clive had agonized long, but they had come to the conclusion that the room was Miranda's own space, and not to allow her to entertain Luke in it would have been an unfair restriction of personal liberty. In any case, if they were having sex perhaps it was better that they did it in the house. Look what had happened to her and Clive, Serendipity had pointed out when he raised objections at such parental liberalism; look what had happened when they had done it in the darkness of the back of a car. They had certainly learned very quickly that condoms are not easy to find when dropped into a pile of unlit crisp packets and teenaged car-owner debris, and that there are things in such insalubrious litter sharp enough to make holes in them. Only small holes, probably, but then sperm are very small things, and very determined.

Serendipity had decided to bake a cake. Cakes took considerably longer to bake than they did to eat at Peacocks Barn – in fact, most of her cakes were lucky if they even got a chance to cool enough to be iced.

Lily appeared in the kitchen, terribly excited.

'What is it, darling?' asked Serendipity, stroking the top of her head.

'Pants!' shouted Lily, desperate with bliss. 'Lovely Lily pink pants look!'

Indeed they were pink. 'Yes,' said Serendipity in a feigned excess of delight, 'lovely pants, Lily.' It had taken some effort to persuade Lily to actually wear underwear – and even now she would only wear it if it was pink. But Lily had taught Serendipity to be immensely grateful for progress, however qualified it might be. A bird in the hand may be worth two in the bush, she now felt, but a bird in the bush is better than none at all.

Lily beamed and retreated, happy, to the sitting room where she was watching *Pocahontas*.

There was a knock at the kitchen door. Hoping desperately it wouldn't be Alice again – not while there was flour all over the kitchen and Lily was running around dressed in nothing but pink smalls – Serendipity opened it to find Carol Pendragon on the doorstep, glamorous in the sort of jeans Serendipity had never owned, the sort that fitted properly and were proud of their label, an indigo jumper such as Belinda would have died for, perfectly applied lipstick, perfectly perfect highlights, even nail varnish, a different colour from last time. When Serendipity applied nail varnish the one coat had to last all summer. 'Oh,' she said, feeling rather like Mrs Bun the baker, only dumpier and with worse hair, 'hello.'

Carol looked hesitant. 'I've come,' she said, 'out by the back way and through the fields. To mend fences.'

Serendipity wondered if Alice Bollivant was hiding by the front gate with a video camera and a long-distance microphone, so as to report the reconciliation to the rest of the village. Sod her if she was. She beamed. 'Come in,' she said, 'and have a coffee.'

It was lunchtime when twelve-year-old Belinda Rowan, a child whose addiction to books was matched only by her addiction to a group of teenage pop idols each of whom sported fewer body hairs than earrings (and each wore only one earring), wandered up to the mud spring with a book and a cheese sandwich for a little bit of peace. Here she could daydream. Here she could imagine the arrival of a handsome prince on a white charger. Here she could just be Belinda.

Belinda was a dreamy child, and Belinda was also acutely lonely. It was hard to say which of these was causal, and which consequential, but it had all certainly been exacerbated in the last year by the fact that all of her schoolfriends had raced, shrieking and blooming like a herd of uncontrolled rhododendrons, into puberty, with the kind of effervescent sexuality that renders available boys completely mad with terror and entirely clears chemists' shelves of acne potions within minutes. Belinda, spotless, bra-less and smaller than the rest by several inches, was suffering acutely the pangs of feeling she had absolutely nothing in common with her peers, not to mention the pains of being teased about it by a dozen boys who thought twelve-inch blond plaits were perfect for yanking, and a dozen girls who had little to say to someone with, in their eyes, less street cred than, well, a road. All of this meant that peace was very important to Belinda.

Belinda shared a bedroom with Lily, so that it was never that haven of calm and tranquillity that she would have liked it to be. It wasn't that she didn't love Lily – how could you not when she loved everyone back so extremely? – but sometimes she wondered, secretly, guiltily, what it felt like to be an only child with a TV in your bedroom and a complete set of Tolkien novels that no-one had scribbled in. (Lily had cut Smaug the dragon off the front cover of *The Hobbit* and insisted on sleeping with him under her pillow every night. When Belinda complained her mother had pointed out that Lily was to be commended highly for the skill with which she had employed the scissors. The rest of the front cover was entirely intact, and it hadn't spoiled the text now, had it?)

Of course Felix had followed her. You'd think a boy of fourteen might grow up a bit, instead of having the self-restraint of a herd of starving fourth-formers in front of a McDonald's, but he didn't. He always had to know what everyone else was doing. Perhaps it was because he was the only boy – maybe he had a persistent feeling of not quite being in on the secrets.

She leaned against the fence surrounding the mud spring and glared at him. 'I thought you had a French test on Monday?'

Felix shrugged. 'I have. I know it all. I saw you sneaking off and I thought I'd see what you were up to.'

'I'm reading,' said Belinda. 'Haven't you got any friends of your own? And why are you wearing my jacket?'

'They're all learning stupid French vocab. And property is theft. That's what Mr Baggins says. What're you reading?'

'*Lord of the Rings.*'

'Not again.'

'It's brilliant,' said Belinda defensively. She did not want to admit to Felix that she so longed for it to be true that she had named every landmark in the village after places in the book. She believed, in her heart of hearts, that if she spent long enough waiting in the right place, and believing, then the Elven kings would return to Middle Earth. So, the woods were called Lothlorien, the river the Brandywine, the road-building scheme down in Broomhill was Mordor, and this, her haven, was Rivendell, Tolkien's last retreat of the Elves.

'What's that?' Felix wasn't listening anyway.

Belinda shrugged. No taste. He didn't read Tolkien, he read Biggles and science fiction, and endless stupid books about black holes. 'What's what?'

'Listen.' Felix had that intent look of someone whose ears are trying to focus. There was a sort of slurping, sucking, creaking, *grunching* noise. It seemed to be coming from the mud. It *was* coming from the mud.

'Oh my God,' hissed Belinda, clutching Felix's arm, 'what on earth is it? It's never made any sort of noise before. We'd better move back in case it erupts.'

'It's not going to erupt.' Felix was scornful. 'It's not a bloody volcano, you know.'

'Well, it's doing something,' said Belinda, stepping back. 'It sounds like your whole class drinking milk shake in chorus.'

'I always thought there were Druid sacrifices in there,'

said her brother, meanly, 'blondes, probably. It was always blondes.' He eyed Belinda's blond plaits. 'Perhaps they're coming back up, dripping and pale. Or maybe it's Tulip the cow, all ghastly and white. Mooooo!'

Belinda was unimpressed. 'Oh, shut up, Felix, I've heard better ghost stories from Lily. Don't be stupid. It's bubbling – look!'

The mud spring strained horribly, gurgled unengagingly, then emitted a gigantic belch, the sort of noise a thousand nomadic Mongolian tribesmen might make if asked to show their appreciation of the annual dinner for very greedy Mongolian men in the usual way. It was the most effort it had gone to since all that appetizing rubble had been sucked in. For several seconds it grumbled and glooped and glollopped. When it had finished it subsided into silence, but this time there was no mistaking what lay on its surface.

'Those are coins over there,' said Belinda, after a brief astonished silence, 'and pieces of metal – those over there look like gold.'

'They can't be gold –' Felix peered at them – 'there are dozens of them – and what's that other thing? It looks like an old rusty crown. Shall I fish it out?'

'Oh no, Felix, don't. You might fall in.'

'No, I won't. I'm not going onto the mud – I'll use a stick.'

'Shouldn't we wait for someone else? Fetch someone?'

'There's no-one about,' said Felix, 'and it might all disappear down again like Tulip – if that *is* where she went.'

'What do you mean?'

Felix grinned. 'Brian Baggins told me he thought Tulip was alive and well and living in Great Barking, and that Farmer Greatbottom was just after the insurance because she wasn't a good milker.'

'That's terrible.' Belinda was shocked. 'How did he know?'

'Said he recognized her.'

'Gosh.' It did not strike either of them, as rural children, as odd that Brian might recognize a cow. Such things are commonplace in the country, where many people relate much better to livestock than to people. Indeed some have commented rather nastily in the past that some of them probably *are* more closely related to livestock than to people.

'Come on.' Felix was climbing over the fence. Belinda followed cautiously, not wanting to take her eyes off the assorted heap of objects on the surface of the mud. They might, after all, be mere precedents for some other, magical event – a hand bearing Excalibur, for instance. What if the seven sleepers and Arthur their king were actually dozing under Parvum Magna? Now that would be a story for the *Broomhill Gazette*. Belinda hoped to be a reporter like Lois Lane when she grew up, assuming she hadn't already married a prince by then.

Cautiously, using a broken branch, they swept the odd objects off the surface of the mud to where they could reach them, retrieved them, and climbed back over the fence, each secretly fearing that, with a big enough repeat gloop, the mud might heave up and suck them down to avenge the theft. Once on solid ground they investigated, rubbing one of the coins clean on Felix's school tie – as it couldn't have been much grubbier it seemed reasonable to use it.

'It does look like gold,' said Belinda cautiously. 'You don't suppose it is, do you?'

'No,' said Felix, certain that it must be. 'What's on it, then? You're the one who's good at Latin.'

'It's not Latin,' said Belinda, peering. 'They're not normal letters. There's a head on it, but I can't tell what it says. I think we should go and tell Mum.'

'What if some more comes up?'

'Well, we can't wait here for ever, and there's quite a lot here already. Come on. We'll be quick.'

'Shall I wait here?'

'No chance. I'm not coming back with Mum to find just your legs sticking out.'

'Oh Belinda, so you really do care.'

She sniffed. 'Certainly not, I'm just looking after my jacket.'

Serendipity's kitchen was not entirely relaxed, despite both of their efforts to make it seem so. It felt as though she and Carol were, metaphorically, circling one another cautiously, each trying to make the first move but not quite risking all. Things were not improved by Lily's attempts to interest them in various pictures she had drawn, most of which seemed to be of bosoms.

'It's because I've – er – grown so much,' said Serendipity, embarrassed. 'She draws what she notices.' She dragged Lily, protesting, off to the sitting room to be bribed with a Wallace and Gromit video.

'Tell me about the children,' Carol said, trying to sound interested, when other people's children had never interested her in the slightest. She didn't even know how old Serendipity's were. It was enough to know that there were four already.

'Oh, you know,' said Serendipity vaguely. 'The usual moans, really. I always had this vision of myself in a huge farmhouse kitchen, serving up—'

'Well, you've got the kitchen.'

'Yes, but I saw myself in it serving up these splendid family meals. All nourishing and sensible. Kedgeree, shepherd's pie, huge plates of vegetable lasagne.'

'Ugh,' said Carol.

'What?'

'Nothing. So what's wrong?'

'If I tell Miranda it's shepherd's pie for dinner she makes that dog food noise you just did, the one you always made at school semolina. If I say, "There's nothing for dinner, open a can", she's over the moon. Her idea of bliss is hot dog sausages and beans.'

'Don't you remember being like that?'

'No – well, maybe a little – but then everything my mother cooked was absolutely disgusting.'

Carol didn't say the obvious thing, but it hung between them anyway, unsaid, and Serendipity blamed her for it. 'My food is not disgusting,' she said emphatically. 'You'll see. Alice Bollivant wants to have dinner with you so you have to come here and try it. She insists we make it Thursday – she even wrote it on my calendar. I hope that's OK with you – you will still be here, won't you?'

'Yes, I thought I'd stay for a week or two and sort things out,' said Carol, who hadn't really decided to till that moment. It was just, she realized now, that she needed very very badly to step off the treadmill for a while and have a break from her life. It was a marvellous life, of course, successful and energized – but a rest would be nice. Just a little one. And this was home.

'Well, Thursday, then,' said Serendipity, 'although I warn you, Clive doesn't cook on weekdays. Everything I make turns out looking like the end product of first year home economics.'

'Clive was always more interested in home economics than you were,' said Carol. 'I remember the fuss when you wanted to do metalwork instead. Girls didn't do that then.'

Serendipity sniffed. 'Clive still cooks.' She didn't like Carol claiming to remember some Clive of the past, of whom ownership was possibly in doubt.

'Maybe,' said Carol, 'you should be flattered that Miranda hates your food, if her favourite thing is hot dog sausages.' She imagined Miranda to be about sixteen, with the long pigtail that Serendipity had always had.

'I suppose so. I just always expected her to be like I was – trying to avoid calories and live on cottage cheese and coleslaw.'

'Coleslaw went out with the Osmonds,' said Carol, 'and we all live our lives believing that everyone else is just like us.' As she said the words she suddenly realized how little they applied to her. *No-one is like me*, she thought, *because of my secret.*

'You don't,' said Serendipity. 'You know you're different to us.'

Carol blinked inwardly. 'What do you mean?' Had Serendipity guessed so quickly at the hollow empty feeling she had in her womb?

'You never did,' said Serendipity, sailing a different channel from the one Carol so feared exposing. 'You never thought you were the same. You were always different. You looked beyond this place. You were the one who wanted to leave at sixteen with your mother. You could have stayed.'

God, thought Carol, *how deceived you all were. Of course I couldn't have stayed.* She shivered, squashing any hint of a memory. 'I seem to remember we both wanted to be James Bond girls.'

Serendipity smiled: 'Silly, hey?' The smile didn't reach her eyes. It didn't even quite reach the corners of her nostrils where the muscle with the longest name, the *levator labii superioris alaequae nasi*, sits awaiting its calling as hoister of smiles and as the subject of Trivial Pursuit questions. The not-smiley-enough-smile said she hadn't quite got over her personal Everest.

Carol didn't notice. 'Parvum Magna got me in the end, though, didn't it?' There was a trace of bitterness in her voice – not lemon bitter, just kumquat, an altogether more sophisticated type of bitterness, subtle and delicate.

'How do you mean? You've still got your career. You've only got Greatbottom Farm for as long as you want it – it's not a millstone.'

'I suppose so.' Just for a second Carol longed, really *longed* to tell her what she had actually meant. To tell her old friend that she had finally discovered that all that work, all that backbiting, up-clawing, defensive-aggressive ladder climbing in the City had all been for nothing because, at thirty-four, all she really wanted was a farmhouse kitchen and five children who thought shepherd's pie was dog food. Old friend. That had a nice ring to it. I never had a friend that close again, she thought, and when you've had a best friend, and you've shared everything, all your secrets, how do you go forward alone? She even might have spoken, such was the remembered urge to confide, to share, but the door burst open to admit two highly excited children.

'Mum, Mum, guess what? Just look what we've found! Oh – hello.'

Felix and Belinda stopped, uncertain, on the kitchen threshold. What beautiful children, thought Carol, shaken, all blond – they look like something out of *Chitty Chitty Bang Bang* – and they're hers and Clive's. I wonder if she's got any others that look like this. The girl is stunning – that hair – and the boy is the spitting image of Clive at that age, and I adored him so much. That was why I couldn't bear to stay . . .

'Felix, Belinda, this is Carol, who was my best friend at

school. Carol, this is Felix, who's fourteen, and Belinda, who's twelve.'

'Ooh,' said Belinda, '*that* Carol. From when you were at school. Gosh.'

Carol felt like a fossil. 'Do you have a best friend?' she asked with forced cheer.

Belinda sniffed. 'Not really, I'm one of a three, and the other two both have periods. It's awful when everyone has something you haven't got.'

How right you are, thought Carol, wincing slightly. 'Isn't it just,' she said aloud, 'but you'll get there in the end.'

Serendipity sighed inwardly at Belinda's isolation, finding herself unable to help. The biggest mistake a mother can make, she thought, seems to be to imagine your children are like you were, and that you therefore have the ability to find the right thing to say.

'Is there a bucket,' asked Felix with ringing clarity, 'that I can just put my head in while you women all menstruate together?'

'Felix!' said Serendipity.

He raised an eyebrow. 'I was only quoting Grandmother, and she's a poet.'

'That's open to argument,' said Serendipity wryly.

'Penelope? Do you remember that poem she wrote about Cosmo Featherstone?' Carol giggled. Suddenly, she thought, I'm relaxed.

'Gosh, yes, Priscilla has never said a civil word to Mother from that day to this.'

'You still say "Gosh".'

'I evolved it,' said Serendipity, 'as an acceptable way of swearing in front of the children.'

'She still says "Shit" when she burns the dinner, though,' said Felix smugly. 'Don't you?'

Serendipity raised resigned brows. 'You have to have something kept in reserve for dire adversity.'

'The trouble is,' said Carol, 'if you get an awful lot of dire adversity, the word you had in reserve loses its impact and you choose another, and another, till your language is absolutely appalling.'

I wonder how much adversity Carol has had to face?

thought Serendipity, feeling suddenly guilty at her own smooth and easy passage through life. OK, there were problems, but nothing at all on the scale of war, domestic violence and major illness.

'What do you say then?' asked Felix, grinning appealingly at Carol. She felt her heart lurch slightly. How I would love a son like you, she thought. Aloud, she said, 'Bother. I say "bother".'

'Felix.' Belinda nudged him, becoming impatient: 'Haven't we got something to show Mum?'

Mum. How ghastly. My children are never going to call me Mum, thought Carol, then bit her lip. Who am I to criticize? Serendipity's an old hand at having children. I haven't had any.

'Haven't we just.' Felix was obviously burning with enthusiasm for something. He looks just like that boy who was on TV, thought Carol, the one in *Just William*. 'Guess what we found.'

'I don't know,' said Serendipity.

'Three guesses.'

'Felix, you are so annoying. OK, you've found three dozen Afghan tribesmen, half a pound of sprouts and a dead armadillo.'

He grinned. 'Don't be daft – even I know better than to bring sprouts into this house – but just look what we've got here. The mud spring just chucked it out.'

'We found this old feed sack in the corner of Farmer Greatbottom's field,' said Belinda, glancing apologetically at Carol. 'Well, of course it isn't his field now, since he's dead . . .'

'Don't worry,' said Carol, 'it takes a lot longer to die in language than in life.' Then, as they tipped the contents of the sack out onto the kitchen table: 'What on earth is all that?'

Serendipity was wiser. 'OK, is this some practical joke? Own up, Felix, you made all this in metalwork, didn't you?'

Felix grinned at Carol. 'She's never got over not being allowed to do metalwork. See how jealous she is of her own son.' He rolled his eyes tragically. Belinda sighed loudly and flicked her plaits backwards, a gesture she liked to use to express exasperation.

Carol smiled, remembering Serendipity doing the exact same thing when Cosmo Featherstone lay in wait for them on their way home so he could leer. She fingered the crown curiously. 'Did this really come out of the mud spring? Honestly?'

'Honestly,' said Felix and Belinda, 'about ten minutes ago. We should go back to see if there's any more.'

'They are honest,' said Serendipity to Carol, 'although often deluded and occasionally quite mad. It comes from my mother, you know, although of course it skipped a generation.' A thought occurred to her. 'Felix, you haven't been onto the mud? You wouldn't be that daft?' She was suddenly alarmed, remembering Tulip. After all, she thought, if our children are even as foolish and daredevil as we were in our time then we have a great deal to worry about. Carol and I used to run right across the mud spring, for a dare. If you were quick enough it couldn't get a grip on your leg, but once Carol got stuck in it up to her calves and I had to pull her right out of her wellies. Those wellies are probably nearly at the centre of the earth by now, communing with dinosaurs.

'No, of course not, d'you think we're crazy? We fished it off with a branch. Can we go back and see what else there is?'

'I think you should wait till your father gets home. He's due back any minute – the call service take over this afternoon.'

'I'll go with them,' said Carol hastily, 'if you like. Then you can wait for Clive.' She felt, suddenly, that she needed to be a bit more, well, *girded up*, to meet Clive. She hadn't thought so before, of course, it was just since seeing his son.

'Are you sure?' Serendipity's glance took in the designer jeans, the pristine shoes, the nail varnish.

Carol laughed, suddenly. A light laugh, a laugh that she had forgotten she kept inside her for moments of relaxed amusement. 'Don't worry about me. A bit of mud never hurt anyone.'

'Apart from that cow,' said Serendipity.

'Especially not that cow,' said Carol. 'I happen to know that cow was fraudulently disposed of. The mud spring was wrongly convicted – it was a stitch-up.'

'Told you,' said Felix.

By the time Clive got home Serendipity had polished a few of the coins – there seemed to be literally hundreds of them, not to mention the other bits and pieces – and was becoming increasingly excited. Lily was even more excited, as she had managed to abscond with four of them and, having ascertained that they were not chocolate, had stuffed them into a sock and poked it down the side of the bed, to join with the four assorted Barbies and yet another doll named Mavis who lived down there already.

Serendipity was unaware of Lily's squirrelling; she was too involved with the very large pile of coins that remained. 'I think it's genuine,' she told Clive excitedly. 'Carol and the children have gone to see if there's any more.'

'Carol? So she's been round here?'

'Yes. Mending fences, she said.'

'It's about time,' said Clive, 'although I'd have thought they needed completely rebuilding. If they had been stock fences your cattle would have run amok years ago.'

'She was the one,' said Serendipity, 'who didn't keep in touch. It wasn't my choice to fall out.'

'It takes two,' said Clive, 'like the War of the Penises.'

'The what?'

'The War of the Penises. Two tribes in Sarawak started trading insults about the size of one anothers willies and ended up at war.'

'Honestly, Clive, what's the connection between Carol and me and a handful of Sarawakians with delusions of penile hugeness?'

'Well,' said Clive, 'it proves it's not only what they throw at you that makes a row, it's what you throw back, too.'

Serendipity pursed her lips. 'If you don't stop being so bloody wise I might throw all this stuff at you. What d'you think of it, anyway? You went to university.'

'Believe it or not,' said Clive, 'medical students don't spend their entire university years gathering random bits of information that might help them win *University Challenge.*'

'No, that'd be why your college always loses. I just thought a bit of knowledge and culture might have rubbed off on you during all those years when we lived on a hundred and one recipes with a baked bean and a minced mad cow. I thought that was why you chose St Alupent's – so you'd mix with people who did things like history and literature.'

Clive grinned. 'Ah well, St Alupent's has other, finer qualities that Jeremy Paxman failed to appreciate,' he said, 'but in any case, I know even less about buried treasure than I do about medicine. I do know a man who can probably help, though. Giles Perry. He was an undergraduate at St Alupent's when I was – played rugby in the first fifteen – read ancient languages, but he was always into archaeology and ancient history.'

'That's no recommendation,' said Serendipity. 'All the rugby club were interested in was beer and debauchery.'

Clive grinned. 'Most of them only ever managed the first. Apart from me with you, of course. Giles never had any luck with women – he was always far too nice. Anyway, I read in the last college journal that he's back there now as Director of Studies in Anglo-Saxon, Norse and Celtic.'

'Oh. All really useful stuff, then,' said Serendipity drily.

'It is for St Alupent's,' said Clive. 'Most of the fellows are only interested in philosophy. You can't have a decent conversation with someone who hasn't decided whether or not you exist outside his own imagination.'

There was a commotion at the door as Belinda and Felix poured in, jabbering incoherently, and carrying three grubby Marks and Spencer carrier bags. Felix looked like a winning contender from *The Krypton Factor*, covered in mud from waist to feet and looking awfully pleased with himself.

'My God!' Serendipity exclaimed, and he smirked.

'Very flattering, but actually I'm Felix, your son.'

'Oh, shut up, Felix. You've been in the spring, haven't you?'

Felix shrugged. 'A bit – but look what we've got.'

'I don't care if you've got the crown jewels, together with Excalibur, the Lady of the Lake, and the combined cast of *Me and my Girl*,' stormed Serendipity, 'you've been in the spring. You could have been sucked away. Felix, how could you?'

Belinda leapt to his defence. 'It wasn't his fault, Mum. Carol got stuck in the mud. We had to go in after her – at least, Felix did, and I held onto him.'

'Carol? Oh God, she isn't still in there, is she?'

'Looking for the cow? Don't be daft, Ren, I think *even they* would have told us by now,' said Clive. 'So where is she, kids?'

'She went home all muddy,' said Belinda; 'said she'd see you later. We brought the other things back here. There's quite a lot more, but the spring's gone quiet now.'

'Quiet? What was it doing before?' Serendipity had a mental vision of the mud spring launching into a drunken chorus of 'The Hippopotamus Song.'

'It was rumbling,' said Belinda; 'you should have heard it.'

Felix sniffed, disappointed that his heroic role had been so lightly passed over. You'd think they'd have been more interested. He obviously should have let Carol sink a lot deeper before he pulled her out – more chance of getting a gold Blue Peter badge that way. After all, he'd soon be too old for one.

Belinda tipped the contents of the carrier bags onto the kitchen table, and the four of them were reduced to silence. There was now a heap, a real heap, of ancient metal. Mostly it consisted of coins, but there was something that could have been a linked belt, a couple of big bangly things and, of course, the crown. Here and there, through the mud, there was a glimmer of gold. Serendipity picked up the crown. Simply shaped, it was set with smooth but unidentifiable stones. It reminded her suddenly of the one Miranda had had to wear when she was the Sleeping Beauty in Broomhill Ballet School's Christmas production some ten years ago – but that had been plastic. Somehow, this one had a whole different feel to it. It was bloody heavy for starters.

'I suppose,' said Clive in a slightly strained voice, 'we could set up a scrap metal business.'

Serendipity stroked the crown. 'The way I see it,' she said, 'either it's an elaborate hoax, or this is worth a lot of money. Just think – it could belong to King Arthur, or Queen Boadicea.'

'Boadicea,' said Belinda, 'was publicly whipped by the Romans.'

'God,' Felix was impressed, 'is that what you're doing in history this year? We did the boring Tudors when we were in Year Four.'

'The new National Curriculum,' said Belinda, giggling, 'has to include the kinky bits.'

'You're making it up,' accused Felix. 'Mum, tell her.'

'For heaven's sake,' said Serendipity, 'this might be a thousand-year-old crown, and all you can do is fight about the National Curriculum. You should definitely go into politics – you'd be well suited.'

'Well, fake or not, either way,' said Clive, 'it isn't ours. It was on Greatbottom Farm land.'

'That's where you're wrong,' said Serendipity. 'He left the spring to the village. It belongs to us all. It belongs to all of Parvum Magna.'

Belinda raised her eyebrows. 'This place can't even agree on where to put the parish litter bin,' she said, 'so this is bound to set the cat amongst the pigeons.' As it turned out, she wasn't wrong.

Giles Perry was one of the newer fellows of St Alupent's College, Cambridge, an ancient seat of learning which had achieved fame in recent times when it was nearly flattened by a rival college. It also boasted an exceptional museum, recently endowed by an ex-engineering student who had made a fortune out of inventing a pink foam. The museum specialized in early Roman and Celtic artefacts, and Giles Perry was responsible for looking after it. He was most interested to hear from Clive. 'Of course I'll come and look. Mind you, it had better be good if I'm to miss Formal Dinner for you.'

'Formal Dinner? At St Alupent's? The last time I was there they had that chef who looked more crustacean than human – surely that's no great loss?'

'It is recently. Hubert's been replaced by a giant

microwave. The food's rubbish but the wine is great. The philosophy fellows have decided that philosophically we can't be certain that the college cellars are full of great wines unless we drink them. No port, though – they set it in concrete to stop us drinking it.'

'Well, we've only got supermarket lager here, but hopefully we can cook something palatable.'

'I'll look forward to it. You know, I believe you're quite close to the Red Field there, where the Iceni are said to have fought the Romans.'

'Really? In Parvum Magna? Are you serious?'

'Deadly. The Roman Ninth Legion marched south via Cambridge to meet Boadicea, and she sent her forces along the Stour Valley. They met somewhere on the Cambridge–Suffolk border, a great and bloody battle, you know, nasty spiky chariots and so forth.'

'Poor Boadicea.'

'Poor bloody Romans, mate. She won. Never take on a woman. Especially not a redhead. History's not your subject, is it?'

'No, but I'd like to see you take out a set of adenoids,' said Clive, 'and surviving in a house full of blondes is pretty heavy going. In ten years' time I will probably be completely submerged in mascara. Come at eight.'

Chapter Four

Carol felt ridiculous. It was ridiculous, of course, to feel like this about seeing Clive again. After all, if what Serendipity said about the paunch was true then she would find him about as appealing as tripe with onions – yet she still felt edgy and uncomposed. It was because Felix was so like the Clive she remembered. For a moment, when she saw him, the years had fallen away, and it had been as though she and Clive were conducting their first date by the spring, uncoloured by subsequent events.

Those owls were hooting already. She glared at her reflection in the mirror. It was all very well in London, at the office, but faced with Serendipity's fresh face and unhighlighted hair this morning, she had felt suddenly false and over-finished. Staring back at her less familiar self, this one with only a touch of powder ('darling, a shiny nose is never acceptable, however natural you want to look': that was her mother, Zsa Zsa Gabor's undiscovered twin), she wondered if it wouldn't have been better for her to have gone back to London straight away, putting the farm in the hands of an agent. Of course it would have been better. Neil thought she was quite bonkers. Bonkers. Now that was another of Serendipity's words. OK, so Parvum Magna had, for the flash of an inkling, felt like home, but she had moved so far on from all this Bumpkinism – village halls and cricket teas and arguing over how much to charge for admission to the annual fête. In London the only people with ridiculous names were members of long-deposed European royal families, not people whose mother belonged to the flower generation and thought it appropriate to attend school open days wearing caftans but not shoes.

In the end, though, when Clive met her at the door as she raised her hand to knock, the tension fled from her like air from a punctured spacehopper being sat on by a very fat man, slowly, silently and comfortably – but with infinite relief. There had been nothing to fear, no ghost of a teenage crush to sneak out of the past and rock the luxury cabin cruiser of her new existence. Clive might have passed on his charm to his son, but in doing so he had, she felt, retained very little of it for himself. OK he hadn't lost much hair, but had the man perhaps donated his abdominal muscles to a good cause? Serendipity hadn't been exaggerating. Imagine him on the beach at Juan-les-Pins. And of course he wouldn't tan, either, not with that colouring. She remembered how proud she always felt when she and Neil were in the South of France and she saw other women noticing his honed and browned body that complemented her own so very well. She ignored the little voice in the corner of her psyche that thought perhaps she was protesting a little too hard.

'Hello, Clive. It's been a long time.' God, how corny, she thought. I sound like a long-lost extra from *Brief Encounter*.

'Carol! Lovely to see you, do come on in. We're expecting you to have supper with us – Serendipity's in the kitchen arguing with the pasta maker. I gather you've been mud-wrestling with Felix.' And Carol found herself absorbed into a warm noisy house that she had never expected to enjoy, enjoying it.

In the kitchen Serendipity had given up on the pasta maker, which she had never used before, which she planned never to use again, which insisted on producing pasta in giant, dumpling-like globs bearing no resemblance whatsoever to the ravioli she had seen done so effortlessly on morning TV. Clearly she had been watching take number one hundred, after the chef had made ninety-nine gloopy globs just like hers. If her ravioli had been people it would have been the Teletubbies. The TV chef probably had an army of trainee TV chefs under the counter, being paid sweatshop wages to beat and whip, and beaten and whipped intermittently themselves when their soufflés failed to rise to the required degree. He hadn't mentioned those, though, had he? Probably the producer did the beating whilst the adverts were on. She would send them the globs she had made by special delivery to prove she had sussed their secret, and use the Sainsbury's stuff in the fridge for dinner. After all, this was Carol. There was no need to put on an act.

'Ren! Carol's here. Come and have a drink.'

Ren, thought Carol. That's an improvement on Dippy, anyway, although if I'd been called Serendipity I'd have changed it to something sensible like – well, Carol. Penelope Forbes liked to tell people that she had chosen her daughter's name because her conception had been a serendipitous delight, a chance touching of the karmas of two souls, glancing off one another as they drifted unguided (and condomless) through the huge and passionate orbits of their lives. Serendipity had always said this was the most embarrassing thing she had ever heard (apart from the speeches at the tofu and wine party Penelope held for all her weird friends to celebrate her daughter's first period). Carol thought Penelope Forbes was two lemons short of Pancake Day, and needed an injection of something very powerful and almost certainly unlicensed to sort her out.

She was conscious now of her huge and heady sense of relief, that one of the lions of her past had turned out to be a mere kitten just as it leapt. How ridiculous to have worried that Clive might stir any sort of longing in her at all – and how disloyal to Neil! She was so lucky to have Neil – they were so lucky to have one another. They said that to each other so often, she had almost, just almost, begun to fear they didn't believe it any more – till she came back here.

'Well?' Belinda rushed into the room from her enforced bath. ('You're not coming into the sitting room smelling like that, either of you,' her mother had said. 'That spring smells as though Tulip is still down there and living on rotten cabbages.') She was virtually still dripping. 'Have you shown her?'

'Shown me what?' Carol was intrigued.

'Ah,' said Serendipity, 'we were waiting for a moment of due splendour. She means have we shown you this – the Parvum Magna Treasure!'

From behind the sofa she dragged a pair of large trays on which were arranged the offerings of the mud spring, gently rinsed and dried under the tap. (Serendipity hadn't been so sure about that, but Clive had dramatically drunk the water to prove it was safe. Since he drank it all the time this proved that the worst it could do to the treasure was render it incapable of remembering the punch line of a joke, so she had gone along with it.) There was a surprisingly large number of pieces – hundreds of coins, it appeared, and an array of buckles – and then, that crown. That crown.

Carol stared, and swallowed cautiously. There was something impassive about the collection. Something solid, something old, a sort of air of knowing.

'I had no idea there was so much,' she said, in a whisper that was slightly awed.

'I know,' Serendipity said as they all stared solemnly at the collection. 'There's a scent of history, don't you think?'

'There's a scent of something, that's for sure,' said Clive, who was not a man easily impressed by atmosphere.

'Don't spoil it, Dad.' Belinda was rapt. 'This could be really historical. D'you think it's really gold?'

'It could be brass,' said Felix knowledgeably, 'couldn't it, Dad?'

'I don't know. Wouldn't it rust?'

'Well, it seems incredible,' said Carol, 'that it's been down there all this time. However long that is. How on earth did it come up?'

'The same way as the other bits which have come up over the years,' said Clive. 'Perhaps it's like quicksand but in reverse.'

Felix looked arch. 'It's all to do with the size of mud particles,' he said. 'They roll on one another, and things drop down, and things come up, and bits bubble through and mix it all up, and the bits that are down there with it come up too.'

'Oh, well that explains it completely then,' said Clive cheerily, putting a hand on his shoulder. 'My son the geologist.' Felix glared, having come of age as far as the detection of sarcasm is concerned.

Carol picked up the crown. It was heavy, very heavy. Certainly it had an aura of authenticity, even unenhanced by the presence of an *Antiques Roadshow* presenter coyly asking how much they had it insured for in tones suggesting it was at least enough to be worth a gasp if not complete loss of consciousness (so satisfying to the envious viewers at home). She stroked the metal, surprisingly smooth, and the round, pebblish stones. Could someone, once have worn it?

'You don't really suppose it's anything valuable, do you?' she asked, after a pregnant pause.

Clive shrugged. 'I suppose it could all be an elaborate hoax – although how, and by whom? Still, we know a man who might be able to tell us more . . . he's a fellow at St Alupent's, my old college in Cambridge. I've asked him to come over – should be here any minute.'

'If it is real,' said Carol, 'under the terms of Uncle Percy's will it belongs to the whole village.'

'I don't know . . .' Clive was dubious. 'Ren thinks it belongs to the village, but it strikes me that buried treasure belongs to the person who finds it – doesn't it?'

'Well, I'm not sure. We could find out.'

'Imagine that,' said Serendipity with wry humour: 'it either belongs to a village that can't even agree on whether or not to plant daffodils on the green, or it belongs to you, Belinda and Felix and no-one in the village ever speaks to us again. Can't we just chuck it back in, before the trouble starts?'

'Don't be such a pessimist – it's a nice dilemma,' said Clive. 'Better than the terrible decision of whether we should pay a professional to trim the churchyard blackthorn hedge, or simply wait for it to miraculously self-limit, that took up so much of the PCC's time last year.'

'I don't know what anyone expects,' said Serendipity, 'when they have Alice Bollivant and Priscilla Featherstone on the same committee.'

'It sounds like board meetings I've been at,' said Carol, reflecting that maybe London wasn't so different from the country after all. It was just a matter of scale. Here you got a cup of tea and a front pew for your boardroom time; there you got a Christmas bonus big enough to destabilize the economy of a third world country, and the chance to be seriously libelled in the financial press every time you opened your mouth.

'I can see another problem,' said Belinda cheerfully,

putting the crown on her head and peering into the mirror. 'I think this is me, you know.'

'Belinda,' said Clive to Carol, 'is a born pessimist, when she isn't getting ideas above her station.'

'You'd better decide that when you've heard what the problem is,' said Serendipity. 'Belinda?'

'How on earth will we decide,' said Belinda, with understated grimness, 'who exactly is "the village"? I mean, is it the people who live here right now, today, or the ones who actually own the houses, like the Ormondroyds and the Council – and what about Mrs Featherstone who's just moved out, and people who used to live here years ago, and their children, and the people who've just moved in?'

'Pessimist,' said Serendipity, not wanting to confront a spectre of such Brontosaurian hugeness. 'I don't think we're going to be talking about much money. Once you divide a few thousand pounds between a few hundred people there isn't going to be a lot to fight over.'

Belinda shrugged. 'I bet you anything Alice Bollivant wants the crown,' she said, with the accurate insight of which twelve-year-old girls are often so capable.

'I don't think so,' said Serendipity. 'Anyway, I think we're probably running away with ourselves. It *can't* be worth much, people are always finding old coins and things. We could just buy some new bulbs for the green with it. It will be a storm in a teacup, you'll see.' But she had reckoned, of course, without fate's sense of humour and the incredible inflationary effect of a couple of thousand years of history.

'Tell me about London,' she said to Carol while they drank gin and tonic (Carol had managed not to look superior when they had no Campari) and waited for Giles. 'You've hardly told us anything about London, or about your Neil.'

Carol shrugged. She was thinking: I saw that pasta maker in the kitchen. I can't make decent pasta – I thought only TV chefs could. Is there nothing she hasn't got right in her life? OK, Lily's maybe not turning out quite as she would have planned, but she is lovely, in her way, even if she does eat goldfish. 'There's not much to tell. I live in Highgate Village,' she said aloud, 'by the Heath, and my office – I run an employment agency – is in the City, yet I seem to spend ages in London just getting about. Neil and I have a house. No garden, I'm afraid, just a terrace. We entertain a little. Neil is an excellent cook.'

Serendipity poured more wine. 'Do you have nice neighbours?' she asked.

Carol smiled. 'No-one would ever ask that in London. Nothing changes here, does it?'

'People change,' said Serendipity, more sharply than she had intended. 'You make us sound rather bumpkinish. We do have mobile phones and Thai food, you know.'

'Such things,' said Clive gravely, 'are the markers of civilization. Do lighten up, you two.'

'I'm sorry,' Carol regretted her tone. 'I just meant that where we live no-one expects to know their neighbour. You can go out to work, come back in the evening and you've got different neighbours, and it doesn't even matter because you didn't know the first lot.'

'That's sad,' said Serendipity, 'but surely you do meet them – you know, taking out the rubbish, over the garden fence.'

'Not really,' said Carol. 'The garden fence is a twelve-foot wall and my housekeeper takes out the rubbish. People don't trust friendly strangers – they're all too rich.'

Serendipity wondered if Carol was rich. Sounded it. It must be nice not to worry about money. 'People here are terribly envious of the good life in the city,' she said, a little wistfully.

Carol smiled without humour. 'It has its advantages,' she said dismissively, thinking, it must be nice to speak to your neighbours without them assuming you're either networking, head-hunting or casing the joint. Not that I'd ever want to live here again, of course. That's too high a price for being able to talk about the weather with Mrs Bloggs over the dustbins, or borrow the odd Brillo pad, or whatever people use when they do their own housework. 'So what are we going to do about this treasure?'

Serendipity got the impression she didn't really want to

talk about her home. She probably doesn't want to gloat, she thought, so I won't ask any more.

Carol sighed inwardly. All the things she had always thought she hated about living in the country seemed less awful this evening: neighbours, familiarity, deadheading the roses. London's rules seemed terribly irrelevant, and explaining them like trying to explain the role of the Royal Family to an alien. What's more, she thought, my so-called once-best-friend isn't really interested anyway.

Giles Perry, when he arrived, was accompanied by a young man who made Belinda's heart do a double-treble-back-flip with spin, the sort of thing that would get you eleven points on the vault at the Olympic Games. This was his nephew, Hugh Appleton, erstwhile star of *Just William*, and now, at fourteen, head boy of St Alupent's Lower School House.

Hugh, it seemed, was coming to stay with his Aunt Tessa, Giles's sister, in Bumpstaple for the summer, and as term at St Alupent's had ended that day, Giles had offered him a lift. He was a handsome young man, freckled and fair, with one of those shocks of red hair that only sits on top of the head, rather than across the face, when it is glued there, the sort of red hair that had guaranteed him a front row position on the record cover when he had been a soprano in St Alupent's choir (redheaded boys always look the most angelic, although appearances, in these instances, are almost always deceptive). He also had a genetically encoded interest in treasure, although his shoulder sported not a parrot but, rather startlingly, an iguana, whom he introduced as Ignatius.

'Oh,' gushed Belinda, 'isn't he beautiful!'

Since Ignatius was rather more ugly than the gargantuan potato cod (which is, sadly, very ugly indeed), it seemed fair to assume that Belinda was smitten. She developed a sudden urge to retreat upstairs to 'freshen up', leaving Hugh gazing after her with some interest. Any girl who liked his iguana was worthy of investigation – after all, so many of the pretty ones ran off screaming. His first girlfriend had been an exception, but had in the end been more interested in his pets than in him, and the relationship had ended in an awkward dispute over the ownership of a breeding cockroach. Serendipity watched her go with fond concern.

Belinda attempted to recover her composure from some far corner of the Javan jungle where it had gone to hang upside down to roost. She was in love! At last, this was street cred, she would have friends again! – always presuming, that is, that Hugh could be persuaded to see her good points. But was this puberty? She didn't have much in the way of breasts yet (she checked quickly) but they could be on their way. What if the breasts appeared so quickly, now, that people noticed them popping out over dinner? She certainly couldn't wear this T-shirt, now could she?

Meanwhile, Carol was examining Giles. He was bespectacled, with arms that gesticulated so much that there seemed at times to be more than two of them, a large and rather French nose, and the kind of hair that looks like watercress – spiky at the sides but straight on top as if someone had been over it with a lawnmower. He was tall and lanky, with the sort of twinkly eyes that only Gérard Depardieu can carry off. He had a firm handshake, at least. She couldn't bear men who didn't – but on a scale of nought to ten that only scored him one point. That made one altogether, then. He was definitely not her type. Why on earth am I scoring him at all? she wondered. Perhaps the country air is making me strange. Perhaps we Londoners actually need smog in order to function.

'Dinner before treasure,' said Serendipity firmly, afraid that her efforts with the pasta maker were in danger of being completely, rather than just more or less, pointless.

Miranda was out with Luke as always, but Felix and Belinda joined them. Belinda had changed into some of Miranda's things, apparently on the assumption that Hugh, faced with a micro-skirt and a pair of green eyelids, would see her as a girl with hormones, one of the pubertal crowd. And as soon as he realized she was girlfriend material, he would be instantly enamoured. Wasn't that how it worked? (Belinda's biology teacher had recently taught her class about pig husbandry, where a bit of hormone goes a long way – one spray of boar taint and your average lady pig is anyone's for a tray of mashed sprouts.) To further encourage this rather hormonal event she had applied Miranda's blusher liberally to her cheeks, and brushed out her long plaits in what she hoped was a feminine, Lady-of-Shalottish fashion.

'You,' said Clive, giving her a dark look when she went into the kitchen to help carry things through (although the only things she planned to carry through were Hugh's) 'look like Looby Loo on speed.'

Belinda was unmoved. 'Who's Looby Loo? Is that another of your names for Gran?' She departed, carrying two bread rolls on a small plate, in a cloud of something that smelt suspiciously like Serendipity's Crabtree and Evelyn, and Clive raised his eyebrows expressively. 'This,' he said, to no-one in particular, 'is one sad generation.'

Hugh was impressed to have his own serving wench. You didn't get that a lot at his school – in fact if you wanted to get a bread roll at all you had to throw yourself across the table onto them before anyone else saw them arrive, then eat them in the style of a python, but quicker and with slightly less innate delicacy.

'Did you really find the treasure?' he asked Belinda, and she glowed gently. Hugh, who had had a great deal of experience with female hormones and felt that he had come to grips with them, over time, missed the glow. Thus are the mighty fallen: a boy who is obsessed by treasure is often ill placed to pick up subtle warning signs – or even, as in this case, signs as subtle as a very unsubtle avalanche.

'Yes,' she said proudly, 'in the mud spring in our village. It's centuries old – there's a cow in it, and maybe even dinosaurs.'

Hugh was intrigued. 'I'd love to see it. Will you show me? I'm staying with my aunt in Bumpstaple for the summer while my mother gives birth.'

'She can't be giving birth all summer,' said Belinda, fascinated by the idea.

'You don't know my mother,' said Hugh cheerfully.

'What about school?' asked Felix jealously.

'Oh, we finish a week before everyone else,' said Hugh.

'Makes up for being chained to our desks all term.'

'Really?' Belinda was round eyed.

Hugh sighed. 'Of course not.' Girls, he thought, they're just so gullible.

'Don't your parents want you at home?' Serendipity could not imagine sending a child away to school, much less not being at the school gate the very second term ended wanting to drag them home and keep them there.

Hugh looked solemn – he had discovered that sympathy was a useful thing. 'It's my mother,' he said, a trifle mournfully. 'She says I've got a bad track record with labouring women – just because I tried to get my aunt to give birth in a field. At least they make up for it by buying me presents.'

'Really?' Felix perked up behind his bread roll (which he had had to fetch himself. When he had children the girls would be trained to wait on the boys: it would be good practice for when they were married.) 'What sort of presents?'

'Ignatius,' said Hugh, with some pride, 'was one.'

Serendipity aimed a chilling look at Felix. 'Don't even think about it,' she said.

Felix said nothing. He had a feeling there was a lot to be learned from Hugh. Belinda needn't think she could hog him with her stupid eyelid stuff.

Dinner was, Serendipity felt, a successful meal. Belinda was hanging onto Hugh's every word (and there were plenty of them), and Felix was, she thought, concealing his jealousy of Hugh's position as a teenage icon very commendably. Carol and Giles Perry seemed to have hit it off quite well – they had, after all, both been to university, she thought rather wistfully – and Lily only came downstairs once to interrupt things. Admittedly, when she was down she stayed down, and ate most of what was on Serendipity's plate – eating being one of Lily's strong points, together with noise, strength and obstinacy. She also gazed with impressed fascination at Ignatius, to the extent that she forgot to insist that everyone sang. (Many of Serendipity and Clive's dinner parties had ended with a rousing adult chorus of 'ninety-two little ducks went swimming one day', before their guests stumbled, exhausted, to their cars.) It was not long, though, before they were ready to unveil the Parvum Magna treasure to their guest.

Giles Perry had not been expecting much. He had come wearing his indulge-the-public hat, an invisible hat that archaeologists put on whenever someone claims to have found the missing link, Excalibur, or part of a saint who already has ten accredited arms, seven legs and more ribs than a millipede. Archaeologists had learned a collective lesson when Piltdown Man had turned out to have been recently constructed out of bits of tall people and bits of gorilla. Archaeologists, since that débâcle, have not been, as a group, easy to excite. Not academically, anyway. Giles was a cynic as far as buried treasure was concerned. There might be a few gold coins this time, perhaps, maybe something Roman if they were very lucky. There had been finds before in this part of Suffolk, after all, and whilst all that stuff about the Red Field was supposedly true, men in anoraks with metal detectors had thoroughly explored this area many times. (He had been there himself, and felt the anorak to be the most innately practical and useful garment in his wardrobe.) But by the time he had finished looking through the find, with an interested Hugh at his shoulder (sporting an uninterested iguana on his) with Lily gazing at the iguana and Belinda at Hugh with similar levels of adoring fascination, he was feeling stunned. 'I feel,' he said, in stunned tones, 'as though someone with a very large stunning device set on maximum stun has been my way and, well, stunned me, for lack of a better word.'

'You think it may be real?'

'I'm sure it's real,' said Giles, 'and I think what you have here may be the most important find of Icenian gold yet discovered. It's absolutely incredible. This . . . this mountain of history, just regurgitated as if it were an old milk bottle top. Incredible. Phenomenal . . .' He touched the metal crown reverently, having temporarily run out of superlatives. Archaeologists are rarely speechless for long, though, and he said, 'I think – I really think – you might even have the crown of Boudicca, Queen of the Iceni. Boadicea, of course, is her popular name.'

There was an impressed kind of silence, since no-one

could think of anything intelligent to say – or indeed, anything at all that didn't sound greedy. It was broken by Hugh.
'Boudicca was stripped and beaten by the Romans,' he said,
with some relish, 'naked. And then she marched along the
A12 to fight the Romans.'

'Still naked?' asked Felix, awe-struck.

'No, I think she put her leather stuff back on for that.'

Felix grinned. 'Sounds like you've got a better
history teacher than we have. They didn't tell Belinda's class
she was naked.'

'That's probably because there were girls there,' said Hugh
earnestly. 'They'd have said it was sexist claptrap. My
mother did. Fancy you finding her crown,' he added to
Belinda, turning so that Ignatius impaled her on his baleful
stare.

'It was nothing,' said Belinda nobly, watching Ignatius
with a wary eye. Perhaps beautiful hadn't been quite the
right word. Right now he reminded her of her biology
teacher. 'I didn't think the A12 had been there for that long.'

'Aunt Carol threw herself after some of the coins and
nearly got sucked down,' said Felix, feeling left out. 'It took
Belinda and me ages to pull her out.'

Hugh eyed Carol with new respect. A woman who would
risk deadly mud for treasure was definitely worth knowing.
'Next time,' he told her wisely, 'you should lie down. That's
the way to get out.'

'I'll remember that,' said Carol, liking him a great deal,
'thank you.'

'If you and the children found it,' said Giles, 'then there is
an argument that it's yours. Finders keepers.'

Carol frowned. 'My uncle left the mud spring and everything that came out of it to the village.'

Giles shook his head. 'It's a tricky one. It does
normally get split between the finder and the landowner –
provided you have his permission to hunt for treasure on his
land. If you don't specifically have that, though, it's not so
simple.'

'But we all own the mud spring now,' said Belinda, 'so
how can we not have permission?'

Giles smiled at her. 'There won't ever have been a case

like this one, but I've seen a fair few other wrangles in my time. In this case the whole village now owns the plot, and without everyone's specific permission to look for treasure, rather than to just sit there and look at the mud, then you probably don't have the right to more than an equal share with everyone else – especially when you didn't really look for it, it just appeared by itself. When there's a dispute about ownership then the Secretary of State decides.'

'Fancy someone's secretary deciding,' said Belinda. 'You'd think it would be more important than that.'

'The Secretary of State,' said Hugh kindly, 'isn't a secretary. He probably can't even type.'

Belinda blushed. 'Why isn't he called something else, then?'

Hugh looked sympathetic. 'If people my age made the rules,' he said, 'he would be.'

This one has the charm of his uncle, thought Carol. Perhaps it's genetic – do nephews have enough of their uncles' genes to be like them? I should like a son like Hugh . . . 'Ah well,' she said, 'no-one agreed we could hunt for treasure. And it was Belinda and Felix who found it, I just helped extract it.'

'You found as much as we did,' said Belinda loyally, 'and we never hunted. We just found it. It was just there, on top of the spring.'

'I'll look into it,' promised Giles; 'ask a few people what they think.'

Clive sighed. 'This sounds to me,' he said mournfully, 'like a can of worms. It might be Carol's, it might be Belinda's . . .'

'And mine,' said Felix.

'. . . Indeed, and Felix's. It might be everyone's. It might be priceless, it might be worthless. It might cause an unholy row.'

'You're such a pessimist,' said Serendipity. 'Don't listen to him, Carol, he's a pessimist.'

But Carol was watching Giles thoughtfully. How could a man with such a nose as that be so charming? Too skinny, though. Too skinny by half. Neil would say he had probably stayed in academia because he couldn't cope in the real world. And the great thing about being married to Neil was that she and he had always thought the same way.

By the time everyone had gone, and Belinda was lost in a Hugh-centred daydream, Serendipity and Clive were just beginning to take it in, although they still could barely believe it. Things like this don't happen in ordinary Suffolk villages. Ordinary Suffolk villages have outbreaks of dry rot and the occasional trouble from bored housewives forming covens and hexing the milkman. Icenian treasure, though, is encountered slightly less frequently than plumbers who are happy to call round the same day, which is not often at all.

'Perhaps we'll wake up tomorrow and discover we've taken part in a mass hallucination,' she said sleepily, 'perhaps there are strange substances circulating in the Suffolk air. Perhaps the Broomhill coven have put a spell on us . . . there might, even as we speak, be a black mass in the churchyard.'

'A black mass of what?' asked Clive, and she giggled.

'Sometimes I feel as though I've married Des O'Connor,' and, as Clive took a deep breath, 'except when you sing, so don't.'

Clive sniffed. 'Belinda seems to have found a friend.'

Serendipity smiled. 'I worry about her. She's such a loner. Hugh seems a nice boy.'

'If you like zoo animals,' said Clive.

'It was only an iguana,' said Serendipity, who did not have the benefit of Handsome Dog at her shoulder, warning her of things to come. 'I could handle the iguana if Belinda would come out of herself a bit.' They were the sort of words that can come back to haunt you.

They made love later in a particularly relaxed way. It was always so much better, thought Serendipity, when she didn't lie there convinced she would get pregnant. She had never trusted birth control, or Clive, not to get her pregnant, not since the first time. At least when she already was pregnant she didn't suffer the images behind her eyelids, of electron-microscoped sperm and eggs doing what they do, just at the critical moment.

Imagine, she thought, feeling like this and *not* being pregnant. She'd be mobile enough to roll over without several practice moves to get the momentum going, and to make more imaginative advances than a minimal hip-wiggle. She snuggled as close to Clive as the unborn Phoebe would allow.

'Ouch,' he said mildly.

'What?'

'You prodded me.'

'It wasn't me, it was Phoebe.'

'We are not calling her Phoebe.'

'She's already called Phoebe.' Clive knew he had more chance of winning Wimbledon than winning on this point, and Serendipity knew that he knew. 'Clive?'

'Hmm?' He was hypnagogic, hovering between sleep and almost-sleep, a good time to get an honest opinion if she could only wake him just enough to speak.

'When you saw Carol, what did you think? You know.'

'Umm.'

'Clive?'

He sighed from a dream. 'Nice legs. Nice bum. Too much lipstick.'

'I've always thought men like lipstick on their mistresses but not on their wives. She's grown unfairly tall.'

'Hmm?'

'Unfairly tall. Women who are unfairly tall can walk with a sort of languorous grace. If short women try it they just look as though they've got gall bladder trouble. Do you think I'd look better taller?'

But he was gone. Too much lipstick. Was that all that was wrong with Carol? Lipstick washes off. I really hope, thought Serendipity insecurely, I really hope she's got cellulite. And a varicose vein.

'Well, it really does seem possible that it's genuine treasure,' said Carol to a cynical Neil on the telephone that night. 'He thinks it's Boadicea's crown. Although she's called Boudicca, apparently.'

'Really?' Neil didn't care what she was called. 'It was found on Greatbottom land, wasn't it?'

'Well, no, not really,' Carol frowned, 'not any more. I thought I told you – Uncle Percy left the mud spring to the village.'

'Oh ha, as if that will stand up in court. I'm quite sure it could be challenged, darling. He was an old drunk – probably wrote his will when he was half-soaked.'

The thought hadn't even occurred to Carol. 'I don't think I'd want to do that,' she said, 'it seems a bit hypocritical, when I hadn't been back here for eighteen years and I said I didn't want a thing from him.'

Neil was horrified. 'But didn't you find most of it? Surely it's yours on two counts? You found it and it's your spring.'

Carol was suddenly tired of this. It wasn't as if they needed a few hundred pounds – not even a few thousand, for that matter – but Neil could never let anything pass. This had, she realized, always bothered her. 'It's not my spring, Neil, and I didn't find it, either. It's not my spring and it's not my village. We wouldn't be wanting to challenge the will if someone's cow had just fallen down it.'

'That's completely different' – Neil was irritated – 'the village would be challenging it then – which is another good reason why you should be now.'

'Neil, I don't want to challenge it. In any case, I'll get a share like everyone else, if there's anything to *be* shared. The village includes me, I'm a part of it.'

There was a silence, then Neil said, 'Carol? you don't sound quite yourself.'

'Why? What do you mean?'

'You sound – well, you've always hated Parvum Magna. You never wanted to go back.'

'I didn't,' said Carol, 'but now I'm here it's – well – not as I expected. It's nicer than I remembered.'

'I think I'd better come down to Suffolk when I'm finished here,' said Neil, thinking, this could mean real money and she's going to fall victim to her hormones and give it away? I think not.

'Really?' Carol rather liked the feeling that he was concerned enough to rush to protect her.

'You don't mind?' Neil was surprised. Usually she hated any suggestion on his part that she might be less effective alone. Carol made Boadicea look clingy and helpless. He had always admired that.

'No,' said Carol, 'I'd love you to come.' She wondered what he would think of the pink bedroom. 'We need to talk.'

'Oh, not that again.'

'Yes, that. But not on the phone.'

He sighed. 'This is all because you've seen that friend of yours and she's turned into the old woman who lived in a shoe – but all right, we'll talk. I'll see you soon. Good night.'

Carol stared into the darkness after he had gone, and wondered if he was right and she was only feeling broody because Serendipity had taken childbearing to excess. True, she – she and Neil, that is – had been trying to conceive for months – ever since she realized that they had absolutely everything else that their acquaintances had, and more, except a baby. But now she knew just how terribly badly she wanted a child, and seeing Serendipity had made her realize it. She wanted to have lots of children, and to be the centre of their lives, and to make her own pasta and not care if she got varicose veins . . .

But it was too late – she had already chosen, without being aware that she had chosen, to be a woman of fewer children. After all, she was thirty-five – there wasn't time to have six now, not unless she managed triplets twice over – and if she did that it seemed certain, from what she had read, that she would develop the kind of breasts you fall over when getting out of bed, and her internal organs would drop out of her bottom.

Outside and a few hundred yards away, Brian Baggins stood in the garden of his blue cottage on Greatbottom Farm (Uncle Percy had not held with the ubiquitous Suffolk pink, which he thought far too socialist a colour, so he had had them painted passion blue instead), having one of the most profound experiences of his life. For years he had been hoping for this moment. Communication. Being at one with nature. For the owl had, unmistakably, replied to Brian. He tried cupping his hands again, and lo and behold, an answering hoot. It was incredible, but he was in no doubt.

He was having a conversation. There was an intelligent owl in Parvum Magna.

Unusually, the news of the mud spring's unexpected bequest did not travel around the village at the speed of gossip (which is, as physicists are aware, roughly the speed of light to the power of a few billion), as Clive felt that it might be best to keep quiet about possible treasure lest possible burglars should be listening. The news that a village meeting was being called did travel very quickly, though, and accompanying it with the words 'you may hear something to your advantage' ensured that everyone planned to attend – with the exception of Penelope Forbes, who remained as interested in treasure as polar bears are in the Worldwide Web. (Mind you, who knows how a polar bear might feel after spending an hour or two with Bill Gates?) And Penelope, although not interested, exactly, did wonder, reflectively, *why* had the treasure appeared? Why now? Was it something to do with Carol? A sign? (Handsome Dog was little help – whenever something like this happened he went all obscure and talked about prairie vegetation.) So news of the meeting even reached the village's newest two inhabitants, on the very day that they moved into the village's grandest house.

The Great House, home for many years to Mrs Featherstone and her dissolute son Cosmo, had been sold, and quickly, to a couple who had always loved it, coveted it, longed to own it, ever since the first day that Hilda Antrobus had started cleaning there twenty years earlier.

Hilda and Sidney Antrobus had lived in Broomhill, in a pristine and sparkling council house, since the day they were married, twenty-nine years ago. In fact Hilda felt a secret scorn for all the middle-class women she cleaned for – a pathetically slovenly lot, not a proper job between them yet they couldn't even keep their own houses clean! It gave her a sense of superiority she was always very careful to conceal from them, but it shone in her eyes sometimes, as she polished their stair-rods and scrubbed out their kitchen cupboards.

Sidney worked at the chicken-processing plant in Great Barking. He had worked there since the day he left school, and no-one in Broomhill could pluck a chicken faster than Sidney Antrobus, or Chicken Sid, as he had been known for much of that time. He had recently been awarded the forty years' service medal, together with the kind of anniversary clock which so absolutely defines the certain small objects of desire for a particular generation, one of those which drives anyone under forty-five completely bonkers within four spins and a chime.

Hilda and Sid had expected their lives to go on, more or less unchanged, from now until the day they retired. Even after that they wouldn't change much. They would keep their big, old, tatty caravan (why change it if it isn't broken?) for trips to Margate and Yarmouth, they would still play darts on Mondays and bingo on Wednesdays and there was that lovely Noel Edmonds at the weekend. There had always been, of course, their secret dream of a big house in the country with wisteria on the wall, where their grand-children could play safely within the garden walls and peacocks would cry mournfully into the morning mists – but that was one of those lottery dreams that everyone has from time to time when *Inspector Morse* is on and they can't follow the plot.

Until two weeks last Saturday. 'It could be you,' Terry Wogan had said to the cameras in his Woganish way, and, for once, astonishingly, it had been them. Seven million pounds. The lottery people had been full of clever advice as to what to do with their money, but Hilda and Sid had not required it. They had managed their own money all of these years; they didn't need men in suits to tell them not to put it in a tin under the bed. In any case, their plans had been made and firmed over endless weeks of lottery yearnings, as they had never really been able to follow the plots of *Inspector Morse*, and now they felt they owed it to God, Fate, or the big glittery hand to do exactly what they had said they would do. That was their side of the bargain.

So they had bought the house of their dreams, the Great House in Parvum Magna, together with two Range Rovers and a proper karaoke machine, a big one like in the bars in

Tokyo. They would keep their old caravan. (On top of that they were keeping a million pounds, then a million was going to charity and the rest to their children. If their children wanted to waste it, well, fine, there wouldn't be any more. It's a tough old world.)

Now they were moving into their new home, while people in council houses the length and breadth of Suffolk battled for the right to be rehoused in their much-admired old one. Mrs Featherstone had already grabbed their cash and departed for Glastonbury before they could change their minds – they having offered the asking price without a survey, so much more than it was worth given the state of the listed lead guttering. Hilda would not miss her, stuck-up old cow. As she wandered around the elegant drawing room, looking with satisfaction at the skirting boards that she herself had so recently been paid to clean, she saw someone coming up the drive, and smiled wryly. How nice. The neighbours were coming to say hello.

Actually it was Alice Bollivant, to whom the word neighbour could not really be applied, at least not in its Christian sense. She had come to check out the new purchasers, make sure they drank tea from decent china cups and didn't read any obscene newspapers or anything that had backed Labour in the last election (which didn't leave much these days).

Hilda answered the door. 'Hello, love. Come on in.'

Alice's heart sank. She could tell from Hilda's accent that this was not Old Money. Still, Bob Hoskins had a cockney accent, and he was a respected actor . . . 'Hello. I'm Alice Bollivant from The Myrtles over the way. I came to tell you there's a village meeting in the church hall on Wednesday at eight – and of course to introduce myself, you know, let you know we're around.' She had been planning to offer supper afterwards ('nothing special, just ourselves and a bottle of plonk', before rushing off to the wine cellar for Hector's best claret, the one he thought she didn't know about) but, in view of the accent, she would hold fire on that.

'That's very nice of you, ducks. I was just brewing up a cuppa – Happy House removals will be here in a minute.'

'You're starting early,' said Alice, thinking, *tea bags*? 'Did you pack up yesterday?'

'No, love. It only took an hour to load our stuff on the truck this morning. Chicken Sid and I have never been much for clutter.'

Alice gulped. *Chicken Sid*? 'You're local, then?'

'We are, Alice, in fact we have met. I did for Mrs Featherstone for twenty years. We lived on Brigstock Road, until today.'

Alice frowned, 'Brigstock? Is that the new development on the edge of Steeple Barking?'

'No, dear, it's on the Brigstock council estate just behind the chip shop.'

'Oh,' said Alice, lost for words. She was the sort of woman who would never go into a council estate unless she was reading the road map upside down, who imagined them to be entirely peopled by the tattooed unemployed, with ten unwashed children apiece playing barefoot in the streets and shouting, 'cor, lumme, look at that' whenever they see anyone in shoes, while their pregnant mother, still in her curlers, makes soup out of cabbage leaves and old socks.

Hilda knew Alice's type exactly, and knew exactly what she was thinking. It didn't worry her in the slightest – she had nothing to prove. On her council estate every house had satellite TV and a Gameboy, and the children replaced their football kit three times a year. She did wonder what Alice's skirting boards were like, though.

Alice hurried home, pursued by the call of Serendipity's peacocks, who were presumably mating, or whatever peacocks do that necessitates all that caterwauling. She was far too flustered to notice something white trotting towards the mud spring in the Greatbottom fields. She had always thought it terribly pretentious of Serendipity to keep peacocks. Only stately homes and palaces keep peacocks. Alice, to whom appearance was everything, could conceive of no other reason why anyone should want something that was such a repository of noise and mess than social climbing. That Serendipity claimed to love the birds and their noise was, obviously, a front to cover up pretentiousness of huge proportions. It was like corgis, really, thought Alice. Corgis have bad breath and pass wind without apologizing. No-one could seriously want a corgi. Presumably the Queen only had corgis to keep her staff in order – it's not easy to get ideas above your station if picking up doggy-doo is part of your job description – and of course everyone else keeps corgis to emulate the Queen.

Alice's mood had not been helped by the information that Hilda and Sid had three sons named Wayne, Ernie and Del-Boy, and that between them they boasted more tattoos than the entire crew of HMS *Invincible*. She had been shown the photos. The arrival of a photographer from the *Sun,* accompanied by a man in a spotted suit called Gary, and a girl with the kind of breasts you could tether small boats to, wanting her to pose with Hilda and Chicken Sid as the 'new, posh neighbour' was the final straw. These people, on top of the lone floodlight on her tennis court . . . it was definitely time to think about moving to Bumpstaple.

She was even more furious when she got home, for the eerie wailing which had so irritated her turned out to be coming from her own garden, where a group of peacocks were clearly giving a prearranged signal to the rest. 'Quick, you lot, the coast's clear,' it must have meant, for now there was a line of four of the blasted birds filing smugly out of her greenhouse, each with a tomato in its mouth.

'Bloody hell!' shouted Alice, running after the birds, who merely strutted slightly faster than she could jog. 'Leave my bloody plants alone you . . . you vultures!' It was not her day.

Belinda appeared at her gate. 'Mrs Bollivant, I think the peacocks are – oh dear, I'm so sorry. Lily chased them, you see, and they flew.'

Alice rolled her eyes. Whenever it was down to Lily decency obliged you to say that was all right, no harm done. They'd cleared her entire radish patch the previous spring. 'That's all right. No harm done,' she said between gritted teeth, thinking, the next time I see those birds eat one of my radishes I'm going straight out to buy a Rottweiler. Come to think of it, maybe there were special peacock-eating hounds – there were wolfhounds, after all, and deerhounds. Why not a peacock hound? Something like a Jack Russell but with huge jaws. That would do. 'Would you like to come and fetch them back?' she asked Belinda in her most mellifluous tones.

Belinda was not deceived. She was a perceptive child, though she didn't particularly need to be in order to get the gist. 'She was really peeved,' she told her mother later. 'I could see her nostrils quivering.'

'Oh dear.' Serendipity shuddered. The thought of being assailed by Alice and her quivering nostrils was a little too powerful an image at the end of a long day: 'although at least it wasn't the radishes. Alice is very proud of her radishes. They ate some last year and she went bananas.'

'You ought to say she went radish,' said Miranda brightly, 'it would be appropriate.'

'Ape shit would be appropriate,' said Felix.

'I do wish you wouldn't use those expressions,' said his mother, frowning, 'and we really must keep the gates shut so the peacocks can't get out.'

'It's the American she objects to,' said Belinda to Penelope, 'not the shit.'

Serendipity glared. 'You'll all be worried if we find ourselves at war with Alice,' she said. 'She doesn't have to put up with our peacock noise, you know, and she doesn't have to employ you, Felix, to mow her lawn in the summer. There are worse ways to earn pocket money.'

Felix rolled his eyes. 'Oh don't send me down t'pits, Mam, lawd's a mercy. I'll do anything, only spare me from t'pit.'

'This boy,' said Penelope in some delight, 'belongs on the stage.'

'Sweeping it,' muttered Miranda, who did not want her acting ambitions to be cramped by a younger brother.

Serendipity giggled. 'You'll all be sorry,' she said, 'when the Radish Wars begin.'

'Well, closing the gates won't stop them,' said Belinda: 'they fly out. I've seen them.'

'We should get one of those electric boxes,' said Felix, 'like Alice's dog has – you know, so they'd get an electric shock when they crossed the boundary.'

Serendipity sighed. 'I'm not sure it would do for peacocks

– d'you think it works right up into the air?' She was assailed by the terrible mental image of Alice Bollivant weeding her borders in a state of triumphant territorialism while directly overhead a series of radish-minded would-be trespassing peacocks squawked dreadfully then crashed like kamikazi pilots, dramatically but fruitlessly, into her black-berry bushes.

'I think it's a very good idea,' said Clive, arriving home from work. 'Hello Penelope, how are you?'

'Fine, Clive dear, my biorhythms are in synchrony this month so my powers are on top form. You really should think about letting me do a healing session at the surgery. I know you have a reflexologist, but Handsome Dog's aura is particularly powerful in July. Actually, we should ask him to help me with a seance on the subject of this treasure. You know, dear,' she nudged Serendipity, 'we could ask Percy Greatbottom what he thinks we should do with it.'

'Hmm,' said Clive, who, whilst he had great faith in the powers of the reflexologist, was not sure that Penelope's menstruation-centred brand of healing would go down very well with his partners. It might turn the patients quite mad. Mind you, that would be an improvement in some cases – he had spent a whole hour today trying to explain to one woman that it wasn't surprising that she and her husband hadn't conceived yet when he was a guest at Her Majesty's pleasure on the Isle of Wight.

'I think we can do without Handsome Dog in this instance,' said Serendipity darkly. 'The last time you asked him something for me he said I should go and talk to a bison.'

'Handsome Dog is very wise,' said Clive cheerfully, and Penelope looked suspicious. 'He was probably telling you to emigrate.'

'I asked him if I was pregnant,' said Serendipity crossly, 'and I was. I don't see where bison come into that. And any-way, you never did like my peacocks.' She watched him hang his jacket on a chair. 'They might die of fright if you shocked them. Birds are funny.'

'I don't dislike them,' said Clive, 'it's just that when you asked me if I'd ever fancied exotic birds I had something rather different in mind. A garden full of peacock poo and the unnerving experience of huge blue turkeys less intelligent than a verruca peering in at me through the bathroom window when I'm using the lavatory weren't quite what I'd pictured.'

'Well I can't see some glamorous Oriental girl being prepared to sit on the roof and watch you practising card tricks on the loo,' said Serendipity drily, and Clive shrugged.

'I don't see why not. With my share of the treasure I'll be able to hire a whole troupe of exotic floozies to attend to my every need. Where's Lily?'

'Disposing of your every need for this week – she's got the chocolate biscuits.'

'Oh no.' Clive was heading for the kitchen.

'It's a good job you're not a politician,' Serendipity called after him: 'a few chocolate Hob-nobs and you'd be anybody's. Prime Minister's question time could be blocked for weeks if someone went to the cash and carry and bought you a gross.'

Clive did not bother to deny it. He was too busy wrestling with Lily for one of the last two biscuits.

'I'll show you some magic,' he was pleading, '*and* read you a story.'

Lily held out. She didn't understand the words but she knew the tone, and like all frequent victors she was an excellent judge of when the pleading one had made his best offer. Daddy had better try harder.

·

Chapter Five

'What d'you suppose this village meeting is about?' Alice asked Hector. Hector grunted. 'Really, Hector,' she added, 'I wish you wouldn't make that noise. It's rather animal.'

Hector kissed her cheek. 'I was making love to you, dear. That grunt signified the approach of the climax of the experience – for me anyway – and talking village business actually during the act doesn't make it any less animal. Anyway, you bought the oysters we had for supper.'

'You don't see gorillas chatting while they're mating,' said Alice, annoyed at being mocked, 'and anyhow, I had the oysters too.'

'True,' said Hector, 'but I had six, and I'm a little disappointed.'

'Why?'

'Only one of them has worked so far.'

Alice giggled. 'You are awful.'

Hector admired the giggle a little wistfully. It was a very sexy giggle – although Alice often argued that Hector would find a pound of tripe sexy if she draped it across her bosom. He completely agreed. He often wished Alice would throw a little more passion into things, too. Underneath, he knew, she was as sexy as her giggle – true nature is, after all, so often revealed in the way we laugh – but Alice kept her passions so deeply hidden. When he said this she pointed out that she was openly passionate about the village, but he said that was hardly the point. Being a gorilla would have its good side, he felt now, even apart from the freedom to grunt in moments of ecstasy. The freedom to scratch one's armpits during tennis matches, for example, and no hoovering. (Hector had kept very quiet when they had been joking at the office about men who were under the thumb of their wives, and the degree to which this was directly proportional to their familiarity with the household hoover.)

Now he added, 'Actually, my dear, it would please me greatly if you could manage just the odd grunt.'

Alice blushed. 'The time for grunting in the field of human sexuality,' she said darkly, 'is when the baby is coming out, not when it's going in.' Much as she enjoyed sex, admitting to that fact would have killed her.

'Well, a slight sigh,' said Hector. 'I'd settle for a slight sigh.'

Alice sighed now, pretending asexuality. 'If it would speed things up, Hector. I am, as you know, a very busy woman. My skills are much in demand.'

Hector smiled into the darkness. He knew Alice and her hang-ups too well to be offended.

Hector Bollivant was a terribly reasonable man of quite unreasonable tallness, with a droopy moustache which he hoped made him resemble Omar Sharif (although people more often remarked on his resemblance to John Cleese). He was not a man to make a fuss, but although he was generally quite happy to live under Alice's rules, he could be quietly stubborn, as in the case of the floodlight. He also desired his wife immensely, passionately, constantly and above all else. Anyone who studied him closely would soon have realized that when he felt particularly passionate, his moustache quivered. Sadly, no-one had ever studied him quite that closely, especially not Alice, for whom sex was one more thing to be taken in her stride, along with bridge nights, golf club dinners and the WI. Hector often felt she didn't really know what sex was all about. Mind you, she sang 'Jerusalem' with passion, and she had no idea what that was about either.

'Anyway,' said Alice now, 'you haven't answered my question.'

'Normally,' said Hector darkly, 'you take my every grunt as meaning "yes". That's how you got that floodlight installed on the tennis court.'

Alice snorted: 'Nonsense, Hector, you wanted it as much as I did.'

'I think that was my line,' muttered Hector.

'What?'

'Nothing, dear.'

'So answer me. In this instance, Hector, "yes" was not sufficient.'

'I missed the question,' said Hector. 'I was approaching the ultimate nirvanal peak of my human condition.'

'Really, Hector,' said Alice, who was always complaining to her friends that she was not married to a romantic man (she had never listened to enough of what Hector had to say to realize that she was wrong): 'I was asking what you thought the village meeting would be about.'

'The usual,' said Hector, who thoroughly hated his role as spouse of the Parish Council chairwoman. He knew exactly how Denis Thatcher must have felt: 'arguing about someone's extension, fighting about the date of the village fête, criticizing all those not present for not being there, muttering about Old Percy Greatbottom's ridiculous legacy, and—'

'That's it!' cried Alice. It was the most animated Hector had seen her in bed since the time he had pretended to be James Bond, just as a joke. ('My name is Bond, James Bond,' he had said into the darkness of a January night, and he had sworn he had heard her whimper, although afterwards she had claimed it was hay fever). 'It'll be something to do with that. I bet someone wants us to pay for something – to fill the thing in, or to fence it off with ten-foot-high electric fencing, or to throw in another cow. Maybe it has swallowed another cow – or one of those stupid peacocks. It wouldn't surprise me – it'll be Serendipity Rowan who's behind it. She's clearly in cahoots with Carol Pendragon.'

'I thought they weren't speaking,' said Hector, wondering whether to go and put on his dinner jacket and his Sean Connery accent. Why not? – he was feeling quite potent. Alice was so splendid when she got all officious.

Alice shook her head. 'They weren't, I'm sure, but eighteen years is nothing between friends.' She sniffed. 'They were always as thick as thieves.' There was an odd touch of bitterness in her voice: 'They excluded everyone else.'

Hector was surprised, 'You sound as though that mattered.'

Alice glared. 'Don't be ridiculous, why should it matter? I was four years older than them. In any case, if Serendipity ever finds out the truth about her so-called friend then that friendship will be about as solid as . . . as something not very solid at all.'

'What do you mean?'

'Oh, nothing.' Alice regretted her words, based on loose suspicion. 'Nothing really, just schoolgirl gossip really.'

'Come on,' said Hector, 'you can't say that much then leave me wondering.'

'What's it worth?' Now she was looking quite girlishly sexy.

'I'll massage your back.' Gossiping definitely got her going, he thought, kneading the smooth skin. Maybe I don't envy that gorilla after all. Imagine having sexual partners who were as hairy as you were. Ghastly. (Hector was, like Esau, an hairy man.) Maybe I should find things to gossip about whenever we get into bed.

'All right.' She wriggled against him. 'After Carol Greatbottom, as she was then, left Parvum Magna there was a bit of talk as to why she'd gone. People said she was pregnant. She had that look about her.'

'What look is that?'

'Oh, you know, Hector. Women know these things.' Alice was coy, and Hector took this to be some vague reference to women's psychic skills, something he was not expected to understand or question, along with sanitary towels, cyclical breast pain and Alice's reasons for not wearing a thong.

'Goodness me, old scandals resurfacing, heh? I don't see why that should upset Serendipity Rowan.'

'Well, she was pregnant herself within minutes of Carol's departure. That's why no-one told her, I suppose.'

'Told her what?'

'Well, that Clive was the father.'

Hector was having trouble with all this, particularly as the massage he was performing took effect. He could not understand the complexity of other people's relationships; having only ever wanted one woman he had never been able to understand soap operas at all. 'I expect,' he said, with admirable self-containment, 'that Serendipity knew that. She must, I would think, have been there when she conceived.' He slid his palms down Alice's back, admiring the curve of her waist.

'Not of *her* baby,' said Alice, 'although of course he was. No, I meant, of Carol's baby. Oooh, Hector! Do that again. I say, I don't suppose you feel like talking about floodlights, do you?'

Hector smiled and resigned himself to being persuaded as, outside, the owl hooted wistfully, although this time, as Brian was fast asleep, no other owl replied.

Darkness skulked hopefully over Parvum Magna, but was elbowed aside by a smiling moon, as Penelope set out again on her nocturnal mission. In the back of her car the lobsters twittered at lobster-only frequencies, as she drove towards the river. Driving past the church, a movement from the graveyard caught her eye. Something white, over in the far corner . . . whatever it was, it was clearly skulking. The steady, throaty throb of a passing Morris Minor had been enough to send it scuttering behind a marble cherub.

Penelope smiled grimly. That would be the Broomhill coven, again. Pathetic lot, absolutely no idea about shamanism and the worship of Mother Earth. They seemed to think there was some sort of merit in prancing around gravestones wearing nothing but an old sheet and a pair of knickers with runes on, but they had absolutely no idea how to talk to trees. Actually, from what she had heard, the coven was a bit of a fiasco as they were one short of the requisite thirteen due to the unexpected departure of their Grand Warlock for Southwold (where he was now running a tea-room and putting hexes on tourists). She really ought to find out who was in charge – they might be interested in talking to Handsome Dog about finding a new direction. Following the cycles of Mother Earth, the cycles of womanhood . . . Later, though. Right now she had other things to accomplish.

In the graveyard the object of her scorn was alone, was not a coven nor any part of one, and was not even slightly interested in the cycles of womanhood. He was, though, endowed with a very real fear of Morris Minors, so she was right about that, at least.

Serendipity, washing up early the next morning, could feel her ankles beginning to swell. 'I don't know what you'll all do,' she told her family, glaring at the untidy mass of plates, cutlery, Rice Krispies and Ready Brek and half-empty glasses on the table – there seemed to be several more cereal dishes than there were family members – 'when I'm dead and gone.'

'Oh, we'll just freeze you,' said Felix cheerily, wandering through to the fridge in search of a chocolate mousse. Serendipity had shopped the previous day, and he took the view that you ate the good things as fast as you could while they were there, because by Thursday there would be nothing to eat but the outside of the lettuce and the wax off the Edam. 'We'll thaw you out at mealtimes.'

'I suppose I should be grateful for that,' said Serendipity. The rest would probably be quite refreshing. 'I'm beginning to look like something Barnes Wallis of the Dambusters would recognize.'

'What, a dam?' Clive grinned over his paper.

'The bouncing bomb. And soon,' she told Clive crossly, 'I shall look like an elephant. If you wanted an elephantine wife, I don't know why you didn't go and . . . marry an elephant.'

'None of them would have me,' said Clive cheerfully. 'I tried both African and Indian, not to mention a couple of rather attractive anteaters before I got to you. None of them could cook, though, and the anteaters were useless in bed.'

Serendipity sniffed. 'It's all very well for you to laugh, you don't have to be pregnant. I could have had the title role in *James and the Giant Peach*, and I don't mean as James. I don't think I can face doing this again, Clive. I feel as if I'm actually becoming a hippo, and if I tempt fate too much I might not turn back into a woman.'

'I take it,' said Clive, folding his newspaper, and wondering how many more animals his wife would identify with before the day was out, 'that you're still trying to convince yourself we're doing the right thing. Look. You can't do this again. I don't want to be married to a hippo. So I'm going to have it done. We've got the appointment, it's all arranged. You've just got last-minute nerves.'

'Are you really sure? Are *we* really sure? Don't you think

101

it ought to be me? I'm the one that doesn't want to be pregnant again. Maybe we ought to wait a while.'

'You'd be pregnant again if we waited a while,' said Clive, 'I just know it. We've discussed it, Ren. Every method of contraception known to man has failed us. People stop me in the street these days and ask me if I'm Catholic.'

'We haven't eaten tadpoles,' said Serendipity. 'That's what they do in China. I read it somewhere.'

'Look, if you want to eat tadpoles, that's fine by me, but don't expect me to even nibble a tail. I don't want to do this if you're not sure, but my appointment's tomorrow. Do you want me to postpone?'

She sighed. 'I suppose not. We've been through this conversation before, haven't we? About a couple of pregnancies ago. It just seems to have come upon us so suddenly.'

'Well, there's always abstinence. Preferable to tadpoles.'

'Thanks very much. Now I feel I've been compared to a tadpole and found wanting. Anyhow, abstinence isn't your strong point.'

'Nor yours,' said Clive, grinning, and she blushed. It always intrigued him that, after all these years and all these children, she still blushed. 'You're a prude at heart, you know,' he told her fondly.

'Just a hippo on the surface,' said Serendipity, wondering suddenly if Carol was a prude. 'You could father lots more children, though, if you wanted to. You could donate sperm.'

'No I couldn't,' said Clive firmly. 'The only person I want to have children with is you. Anyway, you'd hate that.'

'I'd never really thought about it. I don't think I would – not if I knew where they'd gone. But they don't tell you, do they? Maybe you're right. Are you really sure about this . . . ?'

'I am sure,' he said firmly, 'absolutely.'

Lily appeared all in a rush, beaming delightfully and wanting her breakfast. Her face changed on entering the kitchen – it generally took only a moment for her to move from exuberant pleasure at being awake, to apparently hysterical fear. 'Wincey spider, Mummy, Wincey spider,' she howled, with a volume that opera singers would kill for.

'Can't we turn her down?' Belinda, appearing behind with a book in front of her nose, was irritated. 'It's like being under the flight path of Concorde. I've got French vocab to learn. I wish we'd broken up already, like some people.'

'If someone would get rid of the spider,' said Serendipity, as Felix and Miranda, responding to the call of muesli, materialized next to the fridge.

'Why don't you get rid of it?' Belinda knew very well why, but she was just reaching the age when she liked to make a point.

Serendipity glowered. 'Because I'm quite sure that if I go near it it will suddenly treble in size, grow teeth and bite my ear off. Why do you think?'

'If it trebled in size,' pointed out Felix, accurately, 'it might be almost as big as a pea. A very small pea.'

'I'm sorry, I can't help it.' Serendipity persuaded Lily into a chair well away from the spider, and put Rice Krispies into her bowl. 'It's a phobia.'

'Lily pour!' shouted Lily, seizing the jug and pouring the rest of its contents into her bowl. Since it was a very small bowl, and a very large and very full jug, this made something of a mess, washing snap crackle and pop across the table and into Belinda's lap.

'God!' she shrieked, 'now I'll have to change into my other skirt!'

'You mean the one you haven't shortened?' Felix was in goad-mode. 'Thank God for that. I was beginning to think my sister was turning into a tart.'

'Nobody wears skirts long,' said Belinda haughtily, departing in a puff of rice dust. Serendipity and Clive exchanged a glance. 'Another one bites the dust,' said Clive sorrowfully. 'I sense the advancing front of pending adolescence. Definitely a low moving in, bringing gale force winds.'

'Well I think,' said Miranda, who was at the age when you feel your parents really need your advice, as they are so clearly getting it all wrong by themselves, 'you have a moral obligation to conceal your spider phobia from your children. You've probably given it to Lily.'

'But Lily eats earwigs.' Felix was shovelling cereal into

his mouth as though auditioning for 'Little Shop of Horrors' (as the plant).

'Mum doesn't mind earwigs,' said Miranda, standing and picking up her plate.

'I don't actually eat them though, if you don't mind,' said Serendipity, and Belinda, returning, giggled.

Felix regarded her in some horror. 'I'm not walking to the bus stop with you,' he said. 'If that skirt was any shorter it would be a belt.'

'I thought you said you hadn't shortened that one,' said Clive, wondering if he ought to be forbidding anything here, but knowing from personal experience that rows with teenagers are never ended, only begun, and like most wars are also never won. This is particularly true where the lengths of skirts are involved.

Miranda started to dry dishes. 'It's rolled up around the middle, isn't it, Belinda?'

Belinda assumed the only-too-familiar expression of a girl who senses criticism of her clothes, the expression a rabbit might wear if invited to be guest of honour at the annual dinner for the People who like to eat Very Tasty Very Fresh Bunnies – a highly suspicious expression. That was the trouble with an older sister: she forewarned your parents. Mind you, if she were older, she'd be too old for Hugh.

'Isn't Hugh Appleton staying in Bumpstaple over the school hols?' Miranda asked casually.

Belinda blushed and muttered something about not knowing, not caring and not even remembering having met him until this very moment. Serendipity took this to mean that a meeting was arranged.

'She's showing him the mud spring after school,' volunteered Felix airily, 'then we're having tea with Gran.'

Serendipity sensed a plot.

A call to her solicitor, the hairily challenged Mr Fosdyke, had confirmed Carol's fears – as Giles had thought, the final division of any proceeds from the mud spring was her job, and hers alone.

'As your uncle's sole executor, the responsibility for administering his will rests with you. So yes, if something of value came out of the mud spring, I'm afraid it would be your task to divide it up between the beneficiaries, such as you judge them to be. A poisoned chalice indeed, although one has to say it's not terribly likely that it will be worth much – treasure very rarely is . . .'

'It doesn't look like much,' said Felix apologetically, when he and Belinda reached the spring with Hugh and his creature, Ignatius. The mud spring, silent and spent after its recent mammoth effort on the regurgitating front, lay, brown and gunky, in the warm sunlight. The wooden sign which had for so long meant absolutely nothing in the context of the spring's general uninteresting brownness, had now taken on the stature of a premonition. 'It's as if,' Belinda said in awe, 'the spring has been trying to tell us that this was going to happen.'

Felix was scornful. 'I don't think a pool of mud could have carved that sign,' he said, but Belinda was not sure. You never knew, she said, what a few centuries of erosion and a bit of magic could come up with.

Hugh was impressed, though. A boy who has been a TV star is not easily impressed, but Hugh felt the spring had potential. Treasure, he knew, is often found in the least likely of places, and a true scientist must be capable of admiring the ugly, the apparently ordinary and the frankly fetid.

'Here,' he said to Belinda, endowing her in a split moment with the elevated status only a few women had known, 'hold Ignatius. I want a closer look.'

'Be careful,' said Belinda, trying not to swoon in Felix's presence, despite the temptation, 'it swallowed a cow once.' If only, she thought, the other girls could see me now. They had refused to believe her at school this morning when she had told them she was meeting Hugh. What was the use of puberty if no-one could tell? Where were the breasts?

'It didn't really swallow a cow,' said Felix scornfully, 'though it probably could. We're not allowed on it.'

'Wow,' said Hugh again, watching a pebble he had lobbed sink silently away to untold realms of ancientness, 'what else has it brought up, apart from the treasure?'

'Just odd things,' said Felix: 'arrowheads, bones, a pepper pot.'

'They do say,' said Belinda, 'that King Arthur and the Seven Sleepers are down there, waiting to arise and come to England's aid in her hour of need.'

'They'd be a bit mucky,' said Hugh prosaically, prodding the mud with a stick, 'and they'd pong. It wouldn't bother the French, of course.'

'Why not?' Belinda was confused.

Hugh grinned. 'It's just one of my dad's jokes. He used to joke about the Welsh, but Ignatius is an honorary Welshman so now he picks on the French instead because of the cheese.'

'Speaking of cheese,' said Felix, 'I'm starved. Aren't we having tea with Gran?'

They found Penelope down by the river with Lily, gazing thoughtfully into its waters and communing with Handsome Dog, and introduced her to Hugh. 'I like your aura, young man,' she informed him, 'and what is that?'

'Ignatius,' said Hugh, 'an iguana of mine.'

Then Lily, paddling in the ford, looked up and rushed Hugh in a show of wild happiness that not even Handsome Dog had managed in his peace pipe smoking days. Ignatius, it appeared, had been on her mind ever since the dinner party. Ignatius was the love of her life.

'Lily dragon,' she declared, 'give,' and faced with such commanding imperiousness Hugh had little choice but to hand Ignatius over to be admired. He was wary though. 'My last girlfriend,' he said, with studied casualness, 'tried to steal one of my insects. It was a doomed relationship.'

Belinda swallowed. She knew Lily. Lily always got what she wanted in the end – well, she did when she wanted something this intently. Was her own relationship with Hugh to be doomed, then, even before it had begun? There was only one way out . . .

'Gran,' she said, 'wouldn't it be great if Lily had one of those?'

Penelope adored Lily with an adoration that bordered on the possessive. Lily had that effect on people – the combination of her peculiarly angelic beauty, her vividly extreme personality, her strange helplessness in the face of life and her absolute unawareness that the difference between beetles and baked beans actually mattered made people lose their hearts in a particularly protective way. Whenever Penelope read of yet another institution where autistic children had been mistreated, she closed her eyes in pain and vowed to protect Lily with every bone in her body. If there was a new therapy for autism on offer, and there were hundreds, Penelope would read about it. One day, she was certain, Lily would wake up and be completely normal, and if an hour or two swimming with dolphins or playing the tuba might speed the arrival of that day, well, it should be explored. So the sight of Lily in love with an iguana had her resolved. After all, if people got such great results with dolphins, was an iguana not worth a try?

'You're quite right, Belinda,' she declared. 'This child must have one of these. You must work on your mother, dear, she never listens to me.'

The village meeting was that evening, and the rather decrepit village hall was the only place to meet. It stood behind the squatly ancient church, as if slightly ashamed to come out properly into full view, a large and tatty building with a lot of years behind it and possibly not very many more in front. Plans had been in place to improve it for years, but there had never been the money to implement them. Even so the hall, leaks included, was still used for everything from rehearsals of the Broomhill Amateur Operatic Society to the old folks' bingo on Thursdays. Unfortunately the acoustics were rather less flattering to the human voice than those on the M4 flyover at Chiswick, and the Tannoy system hooted more than a gathering of owls at a hooting competition, but its single light bulb and blackout-curtained windows now played host to the meeting that Carol had called.

At eight o'clock, when Carol arrived at the hall herself, it was fuller than it had ever been, even late on Christmas Eve (when the once-a-year faithful feel an overwhelming urge to sing 'Hark! the herald-angels sing' and then go next door for a glass of ginger wine, a drink entirely disgusting at any other time of the year). Everyone from the village had heard those intriguing words, 'you may hear something to your advantage'. No-one wanted to miss out. They had seen Agatha Christie – they knew that if you missed the beginning you never got hold of the plot (although Felix had remarked rather uncharitably that there were some of them who wouldn't get hold of the plot if it was written on a naked belly dancer in indelible purple pen.)

Giles Perry and Hugh were there, and Belinda and Felix with Clive and Serendipity, fraught after several hours of trying to get Lily to calm down, culminating in Belinda and Felix arranging the temporary lodging, in Lily's bedroom, of Ignatius. This had not, Belinda felt, been a point in her favour. Her friends, still disbelieving her Hugh story, had advised her by phone to get a life if she wanted a boyfriend, and to stop going on about lizards, but she had the feeling, she told them, that Hugh was not like other boys. She had the feeling that her best chance actually might involve dressing in a green scaly suit and learning to cling upside down to the ceiling. She was beginning, also, not to care – the little-known Attenborough Syndrome, almost unique to girls meeting Hugh, was kicking in.

'Hello Mrs Pendragon. How are you?'

'Oh, hello Hugh.' *I don't really know how to talk to children,* thought Carol suddenly, *I've never had to.* 'Please do call me Carol.'

'That's a relief,' said Hugh cheerily. 'You don't look like a Pendragon.'

'Oh? How should a Pendragon look?' Carol was offended, unused to such directness.

'Dragonish,' said Hugh, 'obviously.'

Carol, unsure how to take this, glanced around at others. Amongst the crowd she recognized the Bollivants, the Claytons from the post office, the Bagginses (she thought of the low-calorie mayonnaise sandwiches and shuddered. Mrs Baggins had clearly learned her catering at motorway service stations in the heady salad cream days of the Sixties) – and wasn't that Lady Sybil Ormondroyd from Great Barking? She looked sprightly for a hundred and three, or whatever she must be by now. They were all mingling, muttering and mumbling, apart from Alice Bollivant, who clearly felt herself far too much above such a gathering to mill or mutter. Lady Sybil Ormondroyd was laughing uproariously and engaging in an impromptu rendition of 'Down at the Old Bull and Bush' with a woman who wore her curlers under a headscarf, while they both served tea from an urn.

Serendipity kissed Carol hello. 'Come and have a cup of tea.'

'No thanks.' The only place where Carol was prepared to drink tea out of an urn was Henley Regatta.

'Don't you think it's amazing,' said Serendipity, 'how tea miraculously self-organizes at village gatherings. It's as if the village urn supernaturally senses a gathering of more than two of us, and switches itself on.'

'It sounds rather godly,' said Clive, materializing at her shoulder, 'sensing, that is, rather than tea making. Perhaps this is what they mean when they say He moves in a mysterious way.'

Carol nudged her. 'I always wonder what they're saving themselves for, the women in curlers. Imagine going out like that, with them still in.'

Serendipity giggled. 'For later. They're probably sirens in the bedroom,' she whispered back.

Carol shuddered. 'I don't think I'll pursue that thought, thank you.' Serendipity glanced at her in surprise – she had sounded quite, well, prudish. She wondered suddenly what the Almighty Neil was like to be married to.

Carol was watching Alice, who she thought looked rather uncomfortable as a woman in a bright cerise suit accosted her. 'You'd think she'd feel secure on her own territory,' she whispered.

Serendipity shook her head. 'It's surprising how few village gatherings include people from the council houses as well as people from our end of the village. It's another example of the great divide. Actually, though, I don't know who that woman in the pink is. Perhaps she's the one who's just moved into the Great House.'

'Our end? God, you sound just as bad. Soon you'll be saying "hice" instead of "house" like Cosmo Featherstone always did.'

'Sorry – I didn't mean to. You know what I mean. It's inverted snobbery. They think we think they envy us, so they snub us because otherwise they think we might snub them. And once you've done it once, you have to keep doing it, even when you've lived here for fifty years.'

Carol grimaced. 'Unfortunately, I remember it well. It's ghastly.' This sort of social division was something you forgot in London, she thought. There people lived in postcodes, not 'ends'. It's not that class snobbery doesn't exist in the city, it's just that people don't have the same opportunity to express it, as the Great Unwashed don't live in Chelsea, and people from Highgate wouldn't be seen embalmed in West Kensington.

'You're right, of course,' said Serendipity, watching her face. 'We still stick to our cliques in this village. I suppose it might drag itself into the twentieth century just as the rest of England chases Greenwich waving and shrieking into the twenty-first. The trouble is, people are only really comfortable with people they feel are just like themselves.'

What does that make me, Carol wondered, the childless one, hanging around with Serendipity? She bit her lip. Giles Perry met her eyes, and smiled, and she felt herself flush, as if he could see what she was thinking. 'What about Lady Sybil Ormondroyd?' She pulled herself back into the conversation. 'She's hardly your average council estate type.'

'Oh, Lady Sybil's a special case. Clive always says that she's the only one of us with true class because she fits in anywhere. Since she moved out of Great Barking Hall she's become quite a major figure in local bingo circles, and she organized the last Darby and Joan outing to Hunstanton.'

Carol winced. 'Hunstanton?'

'D'you remember when we all went, that year' – Serendipity didn't notice Carol's strained look – 'you and I and . . . oh my goodness, isn't that Cosmo Featherstone? Gosh, he's changed. I haven't seen him for years. I wonder how he found out we were meeting.'

Carol shrugged, looking at him through narrowed eyes. 'Psychic messages, probably. He looks older than he is, doesn't he?'

Serendipity nodded. 'Wouldn't you think that all his years of chanting and concentrating on his crystal might have made him into a serene and inwardly focused being?'

'He doesn't look much like the cosmic high priest of the Arthurian Society,' said Carol. 'You'd think he'd look a bit more – well – weird.'

'Well, OK, but he doesn't look normal,' said Serendipity. 'That moustache would look a bit much even on a walrus, and I've never liked men in dresses. Mind you, he always had the sexual magnetism of sago pudding, even in trousers, so that hasn't changed.'

'Your type then, eh?' said Clive cheerily, appearing at her shoulder.

Serendipity raised her eyebrows. 'Not if we were the last two sago puddings on earth,' she said. 'Are we going to call this meeting to order before the tea runs out?'

'No danger of that,' said Carol, 'it's the first law of villages – the tea never runs out.'

'What's the second law?'

'Oh, all the others are about cricket.'

'That figures,' said Serendipity.

'Hello, Carol,' said Cosmo Featherstone. 'Fancy seeing you back here.'

He looked the same, only hairier, thought Carol, and he still had a fat face. She didn't think much of the Druid look. She gave him a cool look. 'I came back for a funeral,' she said icily, 'and to see friends. That's all.'

Cosmo beamed beatifically. 'Just think, it's Percy's time to regenerate. How wonderful.'

'Regenerate?'

'You know. My dear girl, you must believe in re-incarnation. Why, I myself have strong reason to believe I was once Guinevere . . .'

Carol eyed him distastefully. 'How interesting,' she said, in tones of gargantuan uninterest, 'and I suppose this is Arthur.'

The woman on Cosmo's arm, who was only very slightly less hairy than Cosmo, facially, at least, smiled. 'How amazing you should have realized that. You must have sensed my aura,' she said in deeply Californian tones, 'but then any

111

former lover of Cosmo's is bound to have absorbed some of his psychic gifts.'

Carol nearly choked on her tea, but was saved from having to reply by Giles, of all people, appearing chivalrously at her shoulder saying, 'Carol, come and have a word with Clive. Ah, Cosmo, it's a good thing Carol's husband isn't here – he's a T'ai Chi master with fists like hams and a pathological hatred of ex-boyfriends.'

He whisked Carol away before Cosmo could muster a glower, leaving him beaming after them flower-powerishly.

'Thanks,' said Carol, recovering fast, 'I never could stand him, but I was fine, really.'

Giles squeezed her shoulder reassuringly. 'That's OK. You just looked as if you needed rescuing.'

Carol smiled. 'You don't look like St George.'

'Ah, but I'm from St Alupent's College – he was the patron saint of dragon slayers, you know.'

'Cosmo was no dragon. Just a bit of a bastard.'

Giles raised a brow. It gave him, Carol thought in surprise, a rather James Bondish look. 'Really? Mind you, men who hate women . . . after all, I see that he's so far out of the closet he's left the room.'

'Oh he's not,' said Carol, 'he's Guinevere.'

'It's a shame he's not Penelope's age,' said Clive, appearing at her other shoulder, 'they could have been soul mates. Might have saved us all a lot of trouble. Let's find Ren.'

Trouble? What did that mean? Did he know her secret? There was no way Clive could have known, thought Carol furiously searching her mind as she followed him across the room. Clive was only seventeen himself, back then, when it all went so wrong. At that age he'd surely never have guessed that she was pregnant when she left . . . but if he *had* known, then Serendipity would know . . .

As the meeting was called to silence Carol battled with the worry that her secret had never been a secret at all, that Serendipity knew very well that she was pregnant when she left Parvum Magna, and knew who the father of her baby had been too. No-one knew. No-one. That had been her mantra for eighteen years – and now, suddenly, it seemed

112

that her secret had been simmering away all along, ready to pop out at her when she came back, like the treasure in the mud spring.

Giles Perry did the explaining. It took a while for many of those gathered to work out who he was. The knowledge that he was a fellow at St Alupent's College did not help, as most of the fellows there were generally thought to be peculiar old men who talked in riddles and lived on port. Soon, though, by propitious use of the words 'treasure' and 'valuable' he had them all mesmerized. Carol watched him as he spoke, reluctantly attracted to the sparkle of infectious enthusiasm which ran through everything he said.

'I think,' he told them with measured excitement, 'that it's actually possible that this crown belonged to Boadicea, or Boudicca as she was really called. The coins are almost certainly gold, and mostly date from around AD 60. A few are Roman, the rest Icenian, so it's quite suggestive of a hoard from around the time the two sides met. The items of jewellery fit in with what we know of the Iceni at that time, although some of them are of a decorative quality we don't usually see in finds of this age. Even if I'm wrong about the date . . . well, I think it's fair to say that you have a major find here. Perhaps the most important single find on British soil for very many years.'

Clive had brought along a few of the coins, and the crown. Predictably, as soon as the collective intelligence realized that there were no catches (although a couple of people did go home uncertain, still, as to whether or not they had just been to a very clever timeshare presentation, one so clever that time shares had not actually been mentioned at all) pandemonium broke out, and everyone had an opinion which had to be aired at the same time as everyone else's opinion.

'Who found it?'
'I don't care who found it . . .'
'Percy Greatbottom left it to the village . . .'
'I don't know why you think that includes you . . .'
'Well, the Council own your house . . .'
'At least I don't overfill my dustbins . . .'
'What if it's cursed?'

'Shut up, Cosmo Featherstone, you always were two sausages short of a picnic . . .'

'I am a vegan . . .'

'It's like when the rice boils over,' said Clive to Giles. 'You just have to let them settle.'

Eventually everyone became quieter, as those who have drunk more than two cups of urn tea are mostly incapable of sustaining anything more than a plaintive mutter for longer than a minute. The Parish Council, a group of the sort of people who are very good at taking over things and talking very loudly however full of tea, had taken over things, and were talking very loudly. It was Alice, of course, backed up by Jean Clayton, although Sid Antrobus, the village's newest resident, appeared to be right in the fray too.

'I will be the spokeswoman,' said Alice officiously, standing on a cushion for psychological superiority. 'Please direct your questions through me.' She then proceeded to ignore everyone else's questions and ask her own, but this didn't really matter since what they all wanted to know, essentially, was what it was worth, when it would be sold, and if they could have cash, and that was what Alice wanted to know too.

The answer, as Professor Perry was able to tell them, was that there had first to be an official ruling as to whether or not the find was legally treasure. 'The find has to be reported to the coroner,' he said, 'within fourteen days.'

'Why the coroner?' Hector liked a chance to look masterful. 'No-one's dead. Shouldn't we go to a lawyer?'

'Well, the procedure is pretty well laid out,' said Giles. 'People find treasure all the time – although this does seem exceptional, I must say. The coroner will tell you which museum to take it to, and then it gets looked at properly.'

'What, you mean we just have to hand it over?' That was Cosmo. No doubt about his staking a claim, then.

'No, no, it goes there for safe keeping. You just have to go through the legal process. It's all to do with deciding if it's treasure or not.'

'But obviously it's treasure' – Mrs Baggins was becoming impatient with the technicalities – 'it's a crown. If that's not treasure then I don't know what is. When I was a girl we found an unexploded bomb and that didn't go to the coroner. Mind you, it wasn't gold . . .'

'Ooh, I remember that, Brenda. Whatever happened to that nice young man who . . . ?'

Giles was patient. Carol was surprised at how patient he was. It was a nice quality, really. Mind you, men who weren't gifted on the physical side needed a few other qualities to make up for it. She almost wondered what Giles would look like naked, but just managed not to by concentrating on an image of Neil, not patient at all, but with a body to die for.

'I can go through the details with anyone who's interested,' said Giles gently, now, 'but essentially the coroner decides if it's officially treasure. I don't think there's any doubt here, because of the number of coins and the fact that they appear to be gold. Anything gold is treasure trove, generally. Once it's declared treasure any interested museum will pay you for it.'

'Pay whom, exactly?' That was Jean Clayton from the post office. 'Pay the village, or the person who found it?'

'The treasure belongs to you all, as far as we can tell,' he said, 'although usually the finders would get half. In this case it is on what is effectively common ground, and it was found on the surface rather than dug up, so I suspect it should be shared as in the terms of Farmer Greatbottom's will. We can get a formal ruling if no-one can agree. As you can imagine, there haven't been any cases exactly like this before, but if you can't agree then the Secretary of State gets to decide.'

There was more muttering as people realized that Carol and the Rowans might stand to gain more than everyone else. There were sidelong looks at Serendipity, who, they felt, had a bigger house than she needed as it was, and a few nasty comments about Carol's absence, and the lack of love which she had shown her late uncle, compared to the immense esteem in which each of them, they suddenly realized, had held him. There was a general feeling that the government or its representative, the Secretary of State, could not possibly be trusted to do anything other than mess up, if asked to sort things out.

'Who decides what it's worth?' Cosmo, cutting to the nitty-gritty again.

'It has to be independently valued,' said Giles, 'there's a special committee. I can tell you, though, that if this is what I think it is then I'm sure St Alupent's museum will want it, and we'll be more than generous.'

There was a silence while holidays in Barbados, new Mercedes sports cars and all expenses paid trips to the Annual World Convention of Reincarnated Figures from Arthurian Legend rattled around the various hopeful psyches of his audience. No-one wanted to be the first to break it by saying something greedy.

'So who,' ventured Alice, choosing her words with care, 'will administer it?'

'Ah,' said Giles, ever quick, 'you mean, who should share it out?' He glanced at Carol, who made 'no' signals frantically with her eyes, though more in hope than in expectation. Please don't land me in it, said her eyes, just because I'm Uncle Percy's executor. But non-verbal messages never hit home with Neil: he always asked her afterwards if she felt sick, that was all. She obviously had unexpressive eyes.

Giles winked at her, very, very subtly. 'I think that's down to the coroner at the inquest,' he lied brightly. 'I'll have to check.'

Carol smiled, and for a moment she felt really . . . understood. Silly, but thank God he hadn't told them it was her decision. She was executor of the will, she had to share it out – but she didn't have to start arguing about it quite yet. They'd have been queuing up at her front door with tales of woe and debt before dawn tomorrow.

'I bet you're all wondering how much you'll get,' said Hugh cheerfully, catching the mood exactly. Carol suppressed a smile. If I ever need protecting, she thought, he'd be the one.

Alice glared at him. State school, no doubt. 'Certainly not,' she said loftily. 'I'm sure Professor Perry doesn't know yet.' Giles nodded agreement: he did not want, he said, to speculate, and there was then a general, palpable deflation of interest. Alice tried to remain intelligently fascinated (difficult, when neither word could be applied to her particularly). 'Professor Perry, do tell us more about the possible history of the treasure. Do you suppose it really was Boadicea's?' She was determined to try on the crown before the evening was out.

I can see right through this one, thought Giles, *I bet she wants to try on the crown.* Aloud he said, 'I really couldn't say for certain, but it's possible.' Not much chance, of course, but let her have her fun.

'D'you think I could try it on?'

Carol watched Giles handling Alice. You had to admire him, she thought, he had people skills. He also had nice eyes. Shame he was such a runner bean otherwise. Eyes like that could have made him quite a dish.

It took a while for everyone in the village to try on the crown. Some, as Alice remarked rather snootily to Serendipity, suited a crown rather better than others, and even Serendipity was forced to admit that the Baggins curlers didn't give it quite the right air. Cosmo Featherstone seemed not to want to take it off at all. Carol felt an odd twinge when she felt the thing in her hands, and she shivered.

'Someone walk over your grave?' asked Giles Perry sympathetically, and she shook her head.

'No, it's not that. I just had an odd feeling.'

Giles eyed her cautiously. He was not experienced with women, other than those on Dr Who, of which he was a great fan. When *they* had odd feelings it generally meant that something primeval, alien or highly unpleasant was about to appear and zap them with some sort of green beam. Whilst this seemed unlikely in the current context, you could never be too sure where women were involved.

Carol frowned thoughtfully. An odd feeling it had been, a sudden feeling of being hooked up, caught back up in the life of the village as if she had never been gone. Nothing ever happens here, she thought; for two thousand years the only memorable thing in this village's history was a redheaded woman with spikes on her wheels chopping up Romans as if she was planning to open up a branch of Dewhurst's specially for lions with a taste for person Bolognese. Then I come back and, well, look what happens. And it's sucked me right back in, as if I'd never left. She glanced over at Clive. What a nice man he was. No, he didn't know about her baby, he couldn't have done. He was just a sensitive man, a kind man. Serendipity had truly had the best of things . . . except for Neil, of course. But somehow Neil didn't spring easily to mind here: she couldn't imagine him in Parvum Magna.

'There is one suggestion I'd like to make,' Giles was up on a chair, addressing the tea-filled audience. Carol found herself next to Hugh.

The crowd fell silent. ('Here comes the timeshare bit,' muttered old Archibald Clayton to his wife).

'I suggest that, for now, St Alupent's College would be a good place to keep the find. It's basically uninsurable – at least till it's been formally valued – and it's likely that the coroner will direct you to us in the next day or two anyway. We currently have an interesting exhibition of Roman and Celtic artefacts, and this would, if you'll excuse the pun, crown it.'

Clive shifted guiltily at the thought of the rest of the hoard, sitting in two farmers' sacks at the bottom of the junk cupboard. Still, what would a burglar be doing in their broom cupboard anyway? Looking for a haul of old anoraks, odd gloves and wellies that have quite probably been weed in?

Amongst the crowd, meanwhile, there were some general, tight-fisted mutterings of 'I don't know' and 'shouldn't they pay?' But, as Alice pointed out, the College had been very generous in its endowments to the church ('and with tonight's expert advice,' added Hugh in the kind of whisper that opera singers probably use if they stub their toes when they're resting their voices – what it lacked in volume it made up for in penetration) and it seemed very little to ask. Outside, it began to rain. Very shortly afterwards, the same could be said of inside. The crowd became restive, and a little damp.

'I've got a bloody question,' shouted Brian Baggins above the din, and Alice peered at him down her nostrils.

'Yes?'

'Well, if we're all so rich now, couldn't we do something about this bloody village hall?'

Silence gradually fell as they all contemplated the puddle beside Brian, product of the sudden shower outside and a leak in the roof directly over Brian's head.

'He's right,' said Brenda. 'We've wanted to do this place up for years. The plans have been gathering dust ever since the restoration fund was embezzled by that thighs woman.'

Alice glowered, incensed at Brenda and Brian for introducing such a common tone into the discussion. Mind you, what could you expect from communists? 'You mean the woman who ran the body toning club?' she said primly.

'That's right.' Brian was unrepentant: 'old Jessie Thunder Thighs. Ran off to Marbella, she did, with our roof fund, in 1988.'

Alice sniffed, remembering the thigh exercises well. 'Lie on your sides, dears,' Jessie used to boom, 'up, down, up, down, now let's grip with those thighs. Alice, dear, you're not gripping. Imagine you've got Hector between them . . .' Humiliating, it had been, but it had given her thighs like that Linda Leatherstrumpet on the adult channel. Not that she watched the adult channel, of course – she had just happened upon it by chance when staying in a hotel room with a decoder. Now she said, 'Well, I hardly think this old place is worth repairing now. It's throwing good money after bad.'

Hugh nudged Carol. 'I bet Uncle Giles hates her,' he whispered.

Carol was intrigued. 'Why do you say that?'

'He hates strident women,' said Hugh, 'I heard Aunt Tessa say so. She says it's time he met someone decent instead of someone who'll grind him under her stilettos.'

Carol winced. 'Don't look at me,' she said, 'I'm married.'

'It's a shame,' said Hugh regretfully; 'you'd have been perfect for him.'

Carol felt herself blush. She glanced surreptitiously at Giles, found him watching her, and glanced away again.

Hilda Antrobus, meanwhile, was indignant: 'Waste not, want not, that's what I've always said. Chicken Sid and I never throw anything away – why, our old caravan has been taking us to Clacton since 1973 . . .'

Alice put her nose in the air. 'One can take thrift,' she said, to no-one in particular, 'too far.' *One can end up with just half one's tennis court lit*, she thought.

'Well, I think Brian's idea is splendid,' said Carol. 'It strikes me that doing something to the village hall while we wait to hear from the coroner would be a splendid idea, something to benefit the whole village. I'm sure that's what my uncle intended.' *I'm sure it isn't*, she thought.

Alice regrouped hastily. 'Indeed. Let us have a show of hands, everyone. All those in favour of restoring the village hall with some of the money.' *It's gold,* she thought, *there's bound to be enough left over for my floodlight.*

Hands were raised slowly, first a few, then, eventually, all bar that of Cosmo Featherstone, who shrugged and sulked.

'I'll tell you what,' said Carol suddenly, seeing a glimmer of hope, 'I could get some quotes from builders in the morning. We could even make a start – if the money from the treasure doesn't come to much, then Uncle Percy's estate shall pay the rest.' Brian beamed and promised her the plans the next day. She was a good woman, this Carol Pendragon, even if she was a member of the traitorous capitalist class.

After that the meeting dwindled rather argumentatively to a close. Giles Perry collected up the treasure, deftly removing the crown from Alice's head, to which it seemed to be glued, and returned to Peacocks' Barn for the rest. 'I'll write you a receipt,' he said, penning the words, 'one crown, Icenian, two dozen gold cloak fasteners, one large hoard Icenian gold coins . . .' on a page torn out of his diary, and handing it to Clive, and that was that for now.

Carol walked out to his car with him. 'Do you really have no idea what it's worth?' she asked.

He looked down at her, watching the way the breeze caught her dark hair against her cheek. 'Well . . .'

'I just want to know,' said Carol, 'what I have to deal with. Forewarned is forearmed.'

But when Giles told her his best guess she didn't feel forearmed at all. She felt as if both of her arms had dropped off.

*   *   *

By the next day the wrangling was taking off like school-children when the bell goes. Serendipity heard it first, when she went into the post office to buy stamps. Anything to take her mind off what was happening today . . .

The day of Clive's operation had dawned with, she felt, an overlying doomish sort of feel. She had sat in the kitchen drinking coffee during the brief moment of peace before Lily erupted into wakefulness with her usual enthusiasm, and wondered how she had ever got to this point in her life. She didn't feel so far distanced, in time and place, from her sixteen-year-old self, she didn't feel any different, and yet she was irrevocably, not the Everest-aiming fit young thing of then, but a hausfrau whose husband needed his wings clipped before they produced enough mutual children to run an entire Victorian mine.

Clive punctuated breakfast with noises of nervous cheerfulness, eating a huge bowl of something gunky.

'I don't know how you can eat,' said Serendipity, 'when something so momentous is just about to happen.'

Clive frowned. 'I think it's essential to eat,' he said seriously, 'whenever anything even slightly momentous is about to happen.'

Serendipity shrugged. 'I suppose that's the difference between fat people and thin people.'

'Well, in this case it's the difference between local and general anaesthetic. Cheer up, it'll be over in minutes, I'll be home in an hour or two.'

'Are you sure you don't want me to take you? I could hold your hand. You held mine, in labour.'

Clive shuddered. 'It's hardly the same. You'd probably pass out, and in any case, I don't think I want Lily as an audience.'

'Well don't moan afterwards that I wouldn't come. I could at least drive you to Newmarket.'

'It's only two tiny little nicks,' said Clive, trying, she knew, to convince himself. 'I'm perfectly capable of driving myself home.'

'You might swell up,' said Serendipity, rather gruesomely, he thought.

He grinned nervously. 'That's something to look forward to, then.'

'Oh, don't be filthy. You are sure about this?'

'We're both sure,' said Clive, 'you know we are. And now I've got to go, otherwise there would be no point in my having got up so bloody early.'

And then he was gone, waving the sort of jolly wave so reminiscent of the illustrations in early Enid Blyton books. It ought to be more dramatic than this, she thought, something so final. More dramatic than a drive to Newmarket and a quick jolly snip. It's all too easy.

She tried morning TV to take her mind off it, hoping for one of the usual programmes starring a fat jolly chef with a skillet, but everything seemed to be about hospitals. Later, running water mournfully into the kitchen sink and trying to get the last bit out of the Fairy Liquid without cutting the top off, so that Lily could have it for a water pistol, she tried not to think about surgical steel instruments, and instead mourned the onset of dishwashers which had ended the ritual of washing up afterwards that had added so much to her mother's dinner parties. That was one thing you could say for Penelope, she reflected, she always brought interesting people to the house. If some of them had possibly owed at least a part of their quirkiness to the stimulating effect of substances other than nicotine in their cigarettes, who was to say that made them unacceptable? It had been the Sixties, after all. Well, the Seventies, to be strictly accurate, but since many of Penelope's friends were firmly stuck in the Sixties even now, it seemed reasonable to imagine that they thought they were in the Sixties back then.

Lily appeared in the kitchen with a doll called Mavis who had clearly recently suffered total immersion in the remains of the cherries in kirsch from Saturday. Clive couldn't really have liked them, whatever he claimed, for them to have lasted this long in the fridge. Lily, though, was sucking Mavis's hand with obvious enjoyment and, for once, had nothing to say. She had been watching Ignatius in his tank for the last hour, and it had left her oddly calm.

'Oh God.' Suddenly Serendipity had had enough of trying to keep her mind off Clive's nether parts in their current role of heavily manhandled objects. The chaos of the washing up could wait. They would go somewhere genteel, somewhere nice, somewhere where she could have a cup of coffee without getting into a fight over a table, and where she stood a reasonable chance of being able to park in the same county as the shops she liked to visit. She and Lily would go on an outing to Long Melford. They would drift thoughtfully round the wonderful china shop with the kind of crockery that only people without children can use, idly consider the kitchenware and find a gadget to buy. Then they would look at the antiques and fantasize about winning the lottery and about living in a house where no-one drew on the best things with so-called washable pink felt-tip pen that never ever ever comes off. But first she would stop at Parvum Magna post office . . . which was how she heard the bickering gathering steam.

'I might have known that Cosmo would be back here,' Jean Clayton was saying to Muriel Mullins. Muriel ran the Dragon Arms with her husband Dirk, a dour man who usually wore a trilby and smoked untipped Gauloises, apparently in the hope of being mistaken for Humphrey Bogart. 'He was always a greedy boy. He won't get a penny, of course.'

'Personally,' said Muriel, 'I think it should be divided out in accordance with how long one has lived in the village.' Muriel had, needless to say, lived in the village for most of her fifty years.

Jean Clayton looked doubtful. 'I don't know,' she said, trying to sound as though she had no particular axe to grind, despite having lived in Parvum Magna for only twenty years, 'I think everyone should have the same rights, even the children.' Jean's three daughters, two layabout sons and eight grandchildren all lived in the council houses on a diet of fish fingers, sponge fingers and chocolate fingers and twenty-four-hour satellite TV. That share should add up. 'Mind you, I don't see why Carol Greatbottom should get more than anyone else. Nor those Rowan children. Any one of us could have found it. It's not as if they dug it up.'

They looked embarrassed when Serendipity came in with Lily, and tried to pretend they hadn't mentioned Belinda and Felix. 'What do you think, Mrs Rowan? A share of treasure per person, or a share per household? And what about children, and the Featherstones?'

Serendipity was caught unawares. 'I really hadn't thought it through,' she said awkwardly, 'it's something we'll all have to discuss.' *Oh God*, she panicked, *don't let them drag me into it.* 'I expect there will be another meeting when we know more, but I'm sure Carol intends to honour her uncle's will to the letter.'

Jean muttered approvingly, and Muriel patted Lily on the head: 'Hello, sweetie.' Lily frowned darkly and subjected Muriel to a hard stare. Muriel faltered slightly. 'How is she?'

'Fine,' said Serendipity, 'doing really well.'

'Oh good,' said Muriel, obviously meaning well. 'It's such a shame, isn't it?'

Serendipity felt her fury rising. She did her best to stamp it down. 'What do you mean?' she asked icily.

Muriel was nonplussed. 'You know. Her – problem. What is it called? That syndrome.'

'She doesn't have a problem,' snapped Serendipity, suddenly furious; 'everyone else has a problem. Lily is just perfect,' and she seized her daughter's hand and stamped out of the shop. Lily, sensing imminent separation from the Mars Bars she so coveted, managed to seize three of them on the way out.

'Well, really,' said Muriel to Jean, 'that woman is positively strange. Aren't you going to make her pay for those?'

Jean who had had a brother with Down's Syndrome in the days when no-one talked about it, and who still mourned his loss, glared at Muriel. 'Certainly not,' she said coolly. 'It's a privilege to have that child in my shop.'

Carol had decided to avoid the flak, and spend the morning getting a builder started on the village hall renovation. The figure Giles had put on the treasure was more than enough to renovate the hall, even if she were to turn it into Fulham football club (now that would annoy Alice). Why not get things started, then, she thought? It's down to me, and since the London office seemed to be running more smoothly now than when she popped in and out, why should she not make this her pet project for a little while?

At first it was hard work. Several local firms of builders, as soon as they heard the word 'repair', spent a great deal of time telling her how difficult, slow and expensive this would be and how keen they would be to come along with a big bulldozer and one of those big metal balls and demolish it so they could build another hall from the ground up. It would be a little dearer, of course, but better value in the long run, because these old village halls were often built by, you know, cowboys . . .

The throwaway culture. Carol felt irritated with it – unaccountable for a woman who had until recently thought nothing of throwing out a fridge when the hinges got a bit grubby. Perhaps Uncle Percy's parsimony has popped out in my genes, she thought. Still, she persevered, aware that Neil, had he known, would think her quite mad – and at last she found them, Gromit, Flange and Peebles, Builders, Ltd, 'as erect a trio as there ever were in building' (this perhaps, she thought, explained their current lack of work). Feeling she was getting somewhere at last, she arranged to meet them at the village hall.

She found Hugh hanging around there alone. 'Hello,' she said awkwardly. She still wasn't sure how to speak to him. Just think, I was only two years older than this when . . . 'Are you all by yourself?'

'You can never be alone,' said Hugh, 'with an iguana. The others are at school so I'm following my headmaster's instructions.'

'Really? What were they?'

'He said before I unleashed my intellect on the world I should carefully contemplate the mayhem I might cause,' said Hugh, with some pride.

'My God,' said Carol, 'he makes you sound like some sort of alien.'

Hugh was flattered. He liked this woman. 'It's a real shame you're not free for my Uncle Giles,' he told her. 'He thinks you need protecting.'

Carol was startled and a little annoyed. 'Why did he say that?'

Hugh was unabashed. 'He said you were quite appallingly beautiful,' he told her, 'and that you'd opened a can of worms.'

Carol wasn't sure how to respond to that one. 'Er . . .' she said.

'The trouble with treasure,' said Hugh, deciding to enlighten her further, 'is that someone else always wants it. That's the trouble Jim Hawkins had in *Treasure Island*. I had the same trouble with my last girlfriend. She wanted what I had more than she wanted me.'

'It sounds very unhealthy,' said Carol, almost lost for words.

'Oh, it was,' said Hugh; 'it's made me very wary of women. But at least you've got a way out.'

'I have?'

'Uncle Giles thinks so. He said the village gave you complete freedom last night to spend as much as you liked on the village hall, without even realizing what they'd done. I'd gold-plate it, if I were you.'

A voice made them jump. 'Mrs Pendragon?' The man was tall and thin, with a bald-topped and weatherbeaten head, giving him the look of one who spends much of his life up a ladder. 'Bob Gromit, of Gromit, Flange and Peebles, Builders, Ltd, specialists in erection.'

Carol heard Hugh suppressing himself admirably, and kept her face nobly straight. 'Lovely to meet you, Mr Gromit. Well. This is our village hall, do come in and see the plans.' Hugh noticed her use of 'our', but Carol did not.

The plans, retrieved for her by Brian Baggins from the cupboard in the church, were surprisingly complicated and grand, and Mr Gromit was impressed, particularly when she told him she wanted no expense spared.

'We don't often get jobs like this,' he told her frankly.

Carol smiled. 'Then perhaps you should change your advert in the Yellow Pages,' she said, 'get a different motto.'

Mr Gromit looked blank – he was not blessed with extreme intellect, and *double entendre* (indeed, even single *entendre*) was a little beyond him. However when it came to slating your roof, rebuilding your chimney or painting your walls, he was your man. 'So you want this bowling green done as well? And all the kitchen stuff?'

'I should have underfloor heating,' said Hugh, 'if I were you – it's much more expensive.'

Mr Gromit eyed Hugh warily. 'Are you in the trade?'

'Not yet,' said Hugh, with a warning look, 'but you never know what I'll be one day, and I know my stuff.'

'He certainly does,' said Carol. 'Can you handle underfloor heating?'

'Don't you worry,' said Mr Gromit, 'we'll do you proud.'

'I know you will,' said Carol, and meant it.

By the time Lily had melted the Mars Bars on the car upholstery they had reached Long Melford, a pretty and elegant town, which is probably the place where *Antiques Roadshow* presenters go in their best dreams (other than the ones involving members of the opposite sex draped across Jacobean tables or doing the erotic Dance of the Seven Perfectly Preserved Aubusson Rugs). The arrangement of beautiful façades along Long Melford's main street lends itself especially well to echoing and enhancing screams of a certain pitch, a pitch which suited Lily's voice. Serendipity hauled Lily to her feet and attempted to half drag, half carry her away from her favoured position in the middle of the road in the centre of the town. Lily arched her back, kicking and screaming, and twisted her head to try to bite her mother.

'I had planned,' said Serendipity to Lily between gritted teeth, 'to shop. To wander, Lily. To spend a little time away from the middle of the road after driving along it for half an hour.'

'No go,' shouted Lily, like a platoon of US marines in a siege situation, 'no go no go no go!' She wanted her dragon, that was all.

People on the pavement opposite stopped to look. Serendipity could feel them whispering and tutting. Half of them, she knew, would be saying, 'what a hopeless mother – she ought to smack that child', whilst the other half would be saying, 'what a hopeless mother – she's obviously smacked that child'. She could feel herself getting hot and desperate, wanting to be home again. A traffic warden was waiting for her when she reached the edge of the pavement. 'Is this your car?'

'Yes,' said Serendipity, still struggling to avoid being bitten. Lily was not blessed by any of the reticence which makes most children reserve the deepest bites for fish fingers – as far as she was concerned her mother was fair game, and Serendipity knew from experience that it hurt.

'I wouldn't advise you to leave the doors open, madam,' said the warden.

Serendipity began to bundle Lily into the car. Lily attached all four of her extremities, like Spiderman, to the door frame and refused to budge. Serendipity shoved with frustrated futility, then attempted to prise the hands off, one at a time. There was the usual difficulty of them reattaching. It must be like this, she thought, when you're attacked by a giant octopus.

'Can I help?' asked the warden, nervously.

'No, it's OK. I'm afraid she ran off into the road, that's why I left the doors open.'

'Oh, I see,' said the warden, who clearly didn't. She felt she had to ask the unthinkable, given the screaming: 'Er . . . she *is* your child, madam?'

Serendipity sighed. 'Yes, she is. Look, that's her on our disabled badge, with me trying to hold her down in the post office photo booth.'

'Oh yes,' said the warden. 'Er, do you mind if I ask . . . '

'She's autistic,' said Serendipity, 'that's why.'

'Oh. I'm sorry. Poor thing.'

Serendipity could feel the tears behind her eyes, threatening to come out in the usual way. She swallowed hard on what felt like a turnip in her throat. 'She's fine. We're fine,' she said fiercely, hating the sympathy, not wanting it.

'She looks so normal,' said the warden sympathetically. 'That's really sad.'

'She is normal,' said Serendipity, trying to keep her cool, finally detaching Lily's last hand from the door frame. Lily screamed as though pursued by demons, and threw herself onto the floor of the Land Rover. 'She just sees things differently. She's not sad, she just likes roads.'

'Oh. It must be difficult. Perhaps you shouldn't bring her out like this,' said the warden, who was called Jill and liked to solve other people's problems, 'it doesn't seem very safe, in your condition.'

Serendipity lost it. Shutting the door on Lily, who was howling inconsolably on the floor of the car (perhaps leave the seat belts for a minute, then) she shouted: 'What do you mean, not bring her out? What's the alternative, then? Keep her indoors for ever? Build a funfair in our back garden and a simulated Wild West high street on our drive so she thinks she's living like everyone else? Well, like Michael Jackson, anyway. Or glue her to satellite TV twenty-four hours a day so that she turns into a zombie who only speaks American like the rest of the subscribers? It's her life too, you know.' A part of her recognized that she would regret this outburst in a minute, but another part was enjoying the luxury of just letting go for once, of having a good shout at the world and how bloody unfair it was on Lily. 'Children with her difficulties don't get put away any more, you know, they get left to cope. And that's what we're doing, coping. And she's beautiful. She's lovely and I love her and I don't want anyone feeling sorry for her or me!' There were too many tears in each eye, now; even surface tension couldn't hold them in.

The poor warden was obviously distressed. Hysterical mothers had been in the training course, but only if they were hysterical because you hadn't shown any sympathy for their predicament as mothers when you gave them a ticket. She had thought that, compared to the irate clamped diplomat scenario, the one with the hysterical mother had been rather easy – but there had been nothing about mothers who became hysterical when you had shown them sympathy and hadn't given them a ticket. To make things worse there were now several old couples giving her accusing looks from the other side of the road, clearly believing she *had* given a ticket. 'If you'll tell me what the right thing is to say,' she tried somewhat desperately, 'I'll say it.'

Serendipity deflated faster than a balloon someone forgot to tie off, and finished putting her shopping into the car. 'If

I knew what it was,' she said on a sigh, anger gone, 'I'd tell you.'

The warden sighed. 'Well I don't envy you,' she said, 'that's all.'

'Well, maybe you should,' said Serendipity, 'maybe you should.'

She left Long Melford feeling more cheerful than she had in a long time, unburdened by gadgets for peeling garlic or taking the eyes out of potatoes. It wasn't until she passed Broomhill Poultry and thought of all those people inside with rubber gloves on that she remembered Clive.

Clive was indoors, wincing bravely. Lily tore off upstairs to see her dragon without so much as a hello. Unfortunately, he had been returned to Hugh in her absence. Furious, she found a nice pink pen, and began to draw on her bedroom wall, hundreds of iguanas. They looked like bugs, but they were iguanas.

'How was it? Are you swelling up yet?' asked Serendipity downstairs, with the kind of relentless good cheer familiar to all who have seen nurses in *Carry On* films. She was conscious of a feeling of panic that he had done it, of not having really thought he would go through with it, but she elbowed it aside and refused to acknowledge it.

Clive looked noble. 'It was nothing,' he said, looking forward to the fuss, 'really.'

'Oh good,' said Serendipity, who was not a one to fuss. 'Make me a cup of tea, then. I'm puffed out.'

Chapter Six

When Carol got back to Greatbottom Farm after her morning jog there was a very new dark green Range Rover parked by the door. It made her think of Cosmo Featherstone, who learned to drive in one. The Featherstones were the only people she had ever known pretentious enough to have two. Pretentious and slimy. Surely *Cosmo* hadn't come to see her? Even he couldn't be that stupid – but as she reached her door, a beaming Mrs Baggins flung it open to greet her.

'You've a visitor, Mrs H,' she whispered, attempting tones of girlish conspiracy. Unfortunately, tones of girlish conspiracy did not sit well with Mrs Baggins's features and figure, which were a little nearer to the Les Dawson end of the scale than the Baywatch Babe, and she sounded quite unnervingly lewd.

Carol hurried indoors in some alarm, to find Neil sitting in a chair in the kitchen, trying not to drink a cup of Mrs Baggins's tea (Twining's, but stewed within an inch of its life, and laced with enough sugar to keep the entire Chinese army in calories for a year). He looked, she realized with an odd lurch, completely at home, and that was odd because he shouldn't.

'Neil!' She moved towards him, then checked herself as she noted his quick glance towards the ever-gloating Mrs Baggins. 'Neil, it's wonderful to see you.' A sensible kiss. They were sensible kiss sort of people. 'Mrs Baggins, thanks so much for making Neil feel at home. You can finish early – go now, if you like.'

Mrs Baggins was torn between wanting a little more gossip fodder (so far she had 'well, they weren't very lovey-dovey', 'his shoes looked ever so expensive and his coat was from Harrods', and 'such a handsome chap, just wait till you see him') and wanting to go home for a nice cream bun (diets and Mrs Baggins had never crossed paths, something which was immediately apparent on seeing her). The bun, as so often in life, won, and she hurried away.

'Oh Neil, I'm so glad to see you.' Suddenly Carol was rather relieved to see him, although her initial feeling hadn't quite been relief. He was here for her, and he really was a splendidly handsome man. She wasn't trying to make up for that odd conviction that he shouldn't be here, of course, because he should. She had just been feeling strange, that was all. This place was getting to her. 'Is that a hire car?' she asked.

'Certainly not,' said Neil, who felt that to hire a car was to admit to needing something one did not possess, a situation entirely inappropriate for a man of his standing, 'I bought it.'

'You bought a Range Rover? But Neil, you've got a Porsche – and anyway, they cost a fortune! Why?'

'Darling, you sound so middle class. We hardly need to worry about the cost of a car. I didn't want the local yokels thinking we couldn't fit in. You know what these people can be like – inverted snobbery and all that.'

Carol frowned. 'You won't find anyone in this village with a Range Rover. They do surface the roads in Suffolk, you know.' To be a true country snob, she thought, you have to have a deteriorating thatch and a Land Rover County with a fuel pump that doesn't work.

Neil shrugged. He had nothing to prove, said the shrug. Cars and penises, it was a load of complete rubbish invented by inadequate men who hadn't got absolutely everything they wanted. He had everything he wanted. Look at Carol – glamorous, beautiful, slim . . . Of course there was that slight jangling of unease at the corner of his mind, a slight but persistent tinkle, like the sound of those dreadful Filipino shell dangles that his mother used to have in the back yard when he was a boy, stirred by the expected son not having arrived yet . . . could it be that Carol was less than perfect? But Neil did not allow himself to dwell on that. Nothing in Neil's life was ever less than perfect. It was not allowed to be. His mother might not have wanted to leave her house with the back yard in Rotherham, but the place in Kent was much more suitable and he had found her much more appropriate friends. The ones from the old life would only have been filled with envy at the garden and the tumble-drier. It was her own fault if she felt out of place . . .

It was only after they had said hello properly and Neil had noticed the décor of her bedroom − Carol pretended that her mother had chosen the pink, then felt immediately disloyal, which was silly when her mother spent about as much time thinking of her, these days, as she spent bungee jumping in Alaska (none) − that they were able to talk.

He was worried, he said, that Carol was being taken advantage of. Carol shook her head, watching his tanned chest rising and falling with his breathing. Neil was so fit, even serious sex didn't upset his pulse rate. She felt oddly in need of a cuddle, which was ridiculous as she and Neil had never been cuddly people. She ran a hand over his firmly muscled stomach and he smiled then pecked her on the cheek, rolled over and got out of bed. She watched him dressing, wondering if Serendipity got any pleasure out of looking at Clive these days. Hard to imagine how, unless you had a penchant for walruses. No, that was unfair, but how could a man with abdominal blubber be attractive to anyone?

'I don't see how,' she said aloud, 'it's not as though anyone could have known that something valuable would come out of the mud spring. Uncle Percy scraped through life on a wing and a prayer, so I don't think he could ever have imagined that leaving it to the village would be anything more than a last nose-snubbing gesture.'

'But that's precisely my point,' said Neil, adjusting the mirror to view his whole self at once, a highly satisfying arrangement, 'he wouldn't have left it to the village if he'd known it was of any value. You could probably contest his will.'

Carol frowned. 'I don't really want to. I didn't want anything from him.'

Neil peered at her curiously, his self-absorption punctured by the anger in her voice. 'Darling?'

Carol shook herself mentally. 'Sorry. You know we didn't get on at all, though, so it seems hypocritical to chase after his money.'

Neil raised a fine arched brow. 'You should be more pragmatic, darling. This is your inheritance. Ethics don't come into it.'

Carol sensed his displeasure, but knew that, since he didn't have all the facts, it wasn't his fault that he thought her unreasonable. Secrets, that was the trouble. Unexpectedly an old memory flashed across her mind, of herself and Serendipity in teenaged form, sitting by the river, promising never, ever to have secrets from one another for as long as they lived. 'Secrets are like walls,' Serendipity had said, 'they divide people.' Pretty wise for fourteen, but then she'd probably read it in *Tammy* or some other of those equally erudite comics they used to buy every week with their paper round money in order to tear out the pictures of David Essex and the Osmonds and stick them on their bedroom walls. Thank goodness Uncle Percy hadn't left Donny, Jimmy and Co. up on her wall as well as the pink wallpaper. She pressed her lips together grimly. Being exposed as having been one of the crowd as a teenager hardly mattered. Some secrets, though, are not for the telling.

Neil hadn't given up yet. 'I would like at least to see this treasure, before it passes into the common ownership of the Bumpkins of Bumpkinland.'

'Well, I'm sure you will in time,' said Carol, oddly not liking the Bumpkinland part. 'We could go over to St Alupent's College to see it if you like. But in the meantime we're having dinner with Serendipity and Clive tonight.'

Neil's arrival caused something of a stir in the village, his extreme good looks and obviously expensive clothes sending Mrs Clayton into twitters of postmistressy delight, and necessitating Alice's polishing all of her silver frames on the off chance he might call around and feel like inspecting her displayed school uniform shots of Olivia and Geraldine, prominently featuring the Butterton school logo. Serendipity was somewhat alarmed to discover that he had, merely by virtue of arriving in the village, been added to her dinner party list. She hoped he was a person who could hold his own – Alice Bollivant had, after all, engineered the whole thing with the aim of giving Carol at least as good a grilling as the trout. Mind you, she couldn't imagine Carol being married to someone who wasn't high powered and capable. He'd probably eat Alice alive. Would he eat the trout, though?

She had invited her mother at the last minute, to try to balance things out, and that was a pretty terrifying thought in itself, suggesting that a pretty peculiar bunch of people were expected if a menstrually focused vegan medium might add any sort of balance to the whole affair. Ideally Penelope would partially cancel out Alice, rather as aircraft are said to be trialling the use of one unacceptably loud noise to cancel out another.

Now, waiting at the supermarket checkout with a few forgotten extras (well, things that had seemed too expensive the first time round, but affordable on a second shop – though sadly the Switch card is not so easily deceived) she rubbed her back pregnantly and leafed through a food magazine which she had no intention of buying unless the money-off coupons in the front of it added up to more than it cost. I forgot bleach, she thought, and I used all mine trying to clean those pink iguanas off Lily's bedroom wall. But going back to get some is one of those morally unacceptable acts. The queue behind me would probably be happier if I coshed the cashier and stole the takings, than if I left my stuff on the conveyor belt and went to buy bleach.

'When's it due, ducks?'

Serendipity sighed and tried to muster up a glower with which to discourage the woman in front of her in the queue. The woman wore a very cheery smile – far too cheery for a supermarket – and the kind of wildly flowery clothes that speak of either massive extroversion or serious psychosis. She was also astonishingly huge – parts of her were trying to force their way out of her leggings – and very pink. In all she looked like a blancmange.

I am a private person, thought Serendipity, I don't want to discuss my body with complete strangers. She'll be asking me how many I've got, next, then she'll make some insulting personal comment about how I ought to get Clive to have an operation or take up celibacy.

The woman smiled expectantly.

'A few weeks,' muttered Serendipity grudgingly, thinking: I'd better humour her, just in case she's about to flip.

The woman, like most people in supermarket queues, was immune to muttering of any sort. She had, Serendipity noted pettily, eleven items in her basket (they were easy to count as they were all ready-made pastry) and she was in the ten items or less queue, so she must be particularly immune. 'Is this your first?'

Serendipity braced herself inwardly and began to put her mozzarella cheeses onto the conveyor belt. She felt hot. 'No,' she said bravely, 'my fifth.'

'Goodness, you have been busy' – the woman did not disappoint her – 'my daughter has three. She had twins last time.'

'Oh, very good,' said Serendipity, feeling obliged to congratulate the unknown daughter on such triumphant fecundity.

'What have you got already?'

The trouble with direct questioning, Serendipity thought, was that once you started answering the questions you had no choice but to continue. It was the same with doctors. You went in for something for your sore throat, the doctor says are you sure you're fine, you burst into tears and confess about the piles, and two minutes later you have to show him your bottom whether you want to or not. What will I say, she wondered now, if she asks me how my sex life is or whether my bowels are OK?

'Three girls,' she said aloud, 'and a boy.'

'Oooh. Trying for another boy, were you?'

'No,' said Serendipity, properly riled because she had suffered similar advance rilings from similar strangers many times before. 'Absolutely not.'

'You should get your husband to have the chop,' said the woman, smiling conspiratorially. 'I say that to my daughter all the time. Married to the vicar, she is, and they're very fertile, vicars. You tell your husband Mavis Entwhistle said to get done.'

Serendipity raged inwardly, running through a stream of things she wished she dare say, then smiled and nodded. My husband is probably her GP, she thought; if I tell her to go and boil her head he might be summoned before the health authority. 'I'll tell him,' she said mildly.

It was her turn. Her face felt hot and she pressed a packet of mozzarella absently against her forehead. A sign beside the till said, PLEASE DO NOT CONSUME ITEMS UNTIL THEY HAVE BEEN PAID FOR. Serendipity was sure it had been put up specifically for her benefit because of the time Lily ate a whole packet of chocolate biscuits on the way round in the trolley then threw up at the checkout while Serendipity was trying to smooth out the teeth marks on the bar code of the packaging in order to pay for it. She wondered if the use of mozzarella as an antipyrexial was likewise banned.

'Are you OK?' asked the girl at the till. Her badge told the world she was Tallulah (actually she was called Tracy but they were only allowed one Tracy at each store, so the other three had been allocated new names: Tallulah, Tamsin and Tamara). Her makeup told the world that either she had been to a colour consultant or she didn't have a mirror. Surely, Serendipity thought, lipstick that pink could only have been intended for people whose lips need to be seen in the dark – amorous miners, perhaps, or sexually charged sloths.

'Mm, just pregnant. It's very hot in here.' She packed a carrier bag and fished for her Switch card.

'It's not every day you see people with mozzarella on their heads,' said Tallulah, touching up her lips as Serendipity hunted. It was against the rules, but the colour consultant had said she needed strong lips at all times. '. . . although I did always wonder what people did with it. I'm first aid trained, by the way.'

'Oh,' said Serendipity, 'that's good. What would happen if I went into labour now and couldn't pay?'

Tallulah looked hopeful. 'I'd probably get my stage two first aider's certificate,' she said. 'Have your waters gone?'

'No,' said Serendipity, 'and I meant to the mozzarella. What would happen to the mozzarella?'

Tallulah processed her card. 'I don't know,' she said. 'Oh – Rowan – are you Dr Rowan's wife?'

Oh no, thought Serendipity, now the other nightmare conversation. 'Yes,' she said, 'I am.'

'Oooh,' said Mavis, still loading her shopping bag, 'he's

the handsome one with the nice eyes. You are lucky.'

'Why?' asked Serendipity curiously, wondering what it was that she envied.

'Well, people always respect a doctor,' said Mavis, 'even though they talk a load of rubbish half the time. It's a scandal, really. All that HRT.'

Tallulah sniffed. 'Well, I can never get an appointment,' she said crossly. 'I ring up and he can't see me for two days and by that time I'm better.'

'Well, that's good, isn't it?' said Serendipity, who had heard this one before and felt like being obtuse.

Tallulah looked blank. 'Why?'

'Well, it saves you a trip.' She beamed triumphantly.

'Huh,' said Tallulah, 'it's no wonder the health service is going to the dogs.'

'You should try Entwhistle's herb tea,' said Mavis cheerily, 'it's amazing. You wouldn't need the doctor at all then.'

Tallulah looked doubtful. 'It doesn't make you put on weight, does it? I put on tons with ginseng.' She was possibly slightly thinner than a praying mantis.

'Ooh, no dear,' said Mavis, comfortable in her gigantism. 'I drink it all the time, and my Cyril thinks I'm perfect. Must fly, he'll wonder where I've got to.'

If she flies, thought Serendipity, then I'm Guy the Gorilla. Tallulah tried not to roll her eyes.

As Serendipity drove home along the country lane between Bumpstaple and Parvum Magna, she was puzzled to come to a police road block. No police were visible, but there was a large pile of radishes lying in the road next to a sign saying POLICE. She eyed them thoughtfully. They looked very good radishes. She hadn't got any radishes . . .

'I thought grated radish would be wonderful in the salad. Very Japanese,' she told Clive as he boned the trout.

He looked doubtful. 'Sounds a bit trendy.'

'I saw it on a TV chef,' said Serendipity.

'It's better not to try to be trendy,' said Clive, 'if you're basically very untrendy underneath. Normally, we're about as interested in being trendy as we were in comet Hale

Bopp. We eyed it from afar, we said "oh yes" a couple of times, then we went to bed.'

'Well actually,' said Serendipity, 'I stole this radish. It's a hot radish, but I couldn't resist it. It was police property. I think there's a touch of anarchy in me.'

'A touch of your mother, more like,' said Clive, 'but if it would please you you can fence your hot radish to me.'

'Are you two talking in code?' asked Miranda, who had been bathing Lily and who was, therefore, rather wetter than Lily herself.

'You haven't seen any odd gatherings of radishes around the place?' asked Clive.

'What are you two on? Here, Lily's done. Kiss her now, before she finds another beetle.'

'I can't wear any of these dresses,' wailed Serendipity later, getting ready for dinner, 'they're made for women with human silhouettes.'

'They look fine to me,' said Clive. 'Wear the blue one.'

'Fine? How can you say that? And the blue one shows the sort of cleavage you could lose an entire cricket team down.'

'Really, darling, you must get rid of this obsession with Ian Botham.'

She giggled and threw the dress at him. 'Stop being funny when I'm trying to be agonized.'

'I'm sorry. Anyway, I'm supposed to be the agonized one.'

'Oh *I'm* sorry.' She was contrite: 'we shouldn't be doing this, having people round, only the day after . . .'

'I'm fine,' said Clive bravely, 'really. It was nothing.'

'Have you swollen up?'

'D'you want to see?'

'Ugh, no, please. When will you have the all clear?'

'They say after three months, but in America they say after thirty-five ejaculations.'

'That should be next week, then,' said Serendipity, and giggled again.

'So you can stop moaning about your bosom,' said Clive. 'Women pay good money for a bosom like that.'

'Rubbish,' said Serendipity, 'these are like the Virgin Atlantic Challenger. If they were full of helium I'd have circumnavigated the globe twice by now. Perhaps I should offer myself to Richard Branson.'

'In what capacity, precisely?'

'Replacement balloon, of course,' she frowned into the mirror.

Clive tried to look appealingly lascivious. 'Would a massage help?'

Unfortunately, appealingly lascivious, as a look, only exists in the male mind, and Serendipity ignored it. 'No it wouldn't,' she said, 'they feel as though they might explode like the Hindenberg, taking the whole house with them. How on earth can you think I feel sexy? Your operation was nothing compared to pregnancy.'

Clive was annoyed. 'Oh dear, I apologize for not having suffered more. I agree that having my goolies manhandled by a masked man wearing plastic gloves and a blue paper thing on his head didn't even in the smallest of ways compare with five pregnancies, five labours, and the daily responsibility for a dog that thinks he's a hearthrug. But at least I've done it.' He wondered suddenly if Carol and Neil had arguments about sex. He'd bet they didn't. He'd bet they seduced one another every night.

'At least,' said Serendipity darkly, 'it won't have given you varicose veins.'

Lily was in bed before their guests arrived – and, more importantly, Lily was asleep. Felix, Belinda and Miranda had been bribed with a Chinese take-away to stay in the TV room with a recorded episode of *Inspector Morse* and not emerge to disturb the evening, not even for appendicitis unless the appendix actually ruptured.

'Come on,' said Clive cheerily, 'enjoy yourself. This is your social life.'

But Serendipity glowered at the asparagus. 'I'm not looking forward to this,' she said as there was a knock at the door. 'I've got a bad feeling, and it's not indigestion.'

Things began badly when first the asparagus drooped and secondly Serendipity didn't like Neil. It was one of those instant dislikes that image consultants are so fond of telling us all about, but it was, nonetheless, irrevocable.

'Serendipity, this is Neil. Neil, Serendipity.'

Neil was definitely handsome, and he had a certain charm in the direct gaze of a very clear pair of dark brown eyes, the sort of gaze that makes you feel fancied. Liquid dark brown eyes, Serendipity felt, were great on women and even better on spaniels, but on men . . . no thank you. He looked suave and sophisticated and rich, and she sensed that, given the opportunity, he would call her 'my dear', and make it his business to win her over. Well, I won't be won over, she thought defiantly, I am pregnant, and pregnant women are like mountains, they are not easily moved. (Nor easily climbed, Clive would say, but that was another thing altogether.)

'I've heard so much about you,' he said, and he had the kind of voice that could do voice-overs for dark chocolate adverts. 'It's so kind of you to ask me at such short notice.'

'Not at all,' said Serendipity, beaming her false smile, the one she usually kept for Clive's patients and Clive's mother, 'it's lovely to meet you at last. Do come through and meet Clive . . .' He really does make me feel fancied, she thought, and it's quite unnerving. I don't like it at all. Thank goodness Clive doesn't do that. He makes me feel warm and wanted, but he doesn't make it obvious. Neil's making it obvious precisely because he doesn't fancy me.

By the time Hector and Alice had arrived it was too late for the asparagus. It had already drooped. Penelope still hadn't appeared, but they would have to start without her. Serendipity draped parma ham onto it in the kitchen, then drizzled her mother's portion with olive oil instead. This was going to be a long evening. Where was her mother anyway?

Penelope was late because something was following her, and she kept stopping to try to catch it out. She only lived a hundred yards away, and being followed was not unusual for her, as a trail of restless Native Americans tended to be at her shoulder most of the time. The difference was that they didn't rustle. Well, they may once have rustled in the sense of creeping up to other people's wigwams after dark and stealing their bison, out in the Wild West when men were men and women wore corsets and didn't complain, but they didn't rustle in the sense of making small surreptitious noises in the hedgerow. Every time Penelope took a step, there was a rustle. When she stopped, it stopped. If she moved a little faster, it kept up. An owl hooted, and she jumped.

This was ridiculous! I am an adult woman, thought Penelope, I don't believe in ghostly cows. Well, actually, I do, but not in the rustling sense. This was almost certainly someone's stupid horse. She peered into the hedge – but just then the unmistakable throb of a passing Morris Minor broke the peace of the dusk. There was another, bigger, more purposeful rustle, and she heard something trotting off. Definitely a horse – and it had made her late for supper.

Carol was looking very glamorous. Neil was proud that, of all the women present, she was the one that stood out. Serendipity was quite a surprise, though. True, she was as large as he had expected, but he hadn't expected quite such a presence, such a direct personality. He secretly rather liked blondes, too – quite a different hair texture from Carol's. Never having had any contact with a pregnant woman – not since he was gestating in one himself, anyway – he had somehow expected her not to display any signs of rationality or intelligence. She didn't like him, but Neil regarded that as a challenge. Perhaps he should make a pass: it might be quite interesting, having it away with a football. Good practice for if Carol ever managed it. Neil worked on the principle that if you propositioned a hundred women, propositioned them baldly and with hardly any effort at all, the chances were that ten of them would say yes, and one of those would be a siren between the sheets. That was the game he played. He assumed that everyone else played it, too.

Alice Bollivant, on the other hand, was clearly impressed with him, and that was always pleasing. There was something about plump flesh, after all . . . but fat is failure, so admitting to himself that he liked big breasts was akin to admitting to himself that he passed wind. It was unacceptable.

He was right. Alice Bollivant was impressed, but she was not a woman who enjoyed being impressed, except possibly by royalty should the opportunity arise – and that was only OK because it would be such a perfect opportunity to impress others later.

Alice already did not like Carol. It was a gut reaction, she told herself, not wanting to see the real reason. It was absolutely nothing to do with Carol's looks and style, she told herself. (Carol was so tall as to be graceful, with the deportment that only tall women can get away with. Short women, like Alice, attempting the same, look strained in the middle, as though they have a problem with their bile duct.) Carol was wealthy and successful, she had the kind of husband who would clearly not stop at one floodlight, she wore an emerald the size of a large sultana, whereas Alice's was only the size of a split lentil. Mine is a very good one, though, thought Alice, whereas one the size of Carol's is probably flawed. She tried to find a reason for her dislike of Carol, totally failing to recognize it as envy.

'And do you have any children?' She turned a laser-beam look on Carol.

Carol smiled a superior smile she had honed over the years to field just such questions, and pushed back her thick dark, expensively cut, hair. Alice could tell about the cut. 'Oh no. Not yet.' There was a time when she had meant that sincerely – but not any more. That 'yet' word was beginning to seem like a pun, a joke, a ridiculous little group of letters which, as a sound, had absolutely no meaning beyond being the kind of noise goats sometimes make on frosty nights.

'Oh,' said Alice, 'you're a career woman, I suppose.' Her tone said this was on a par with being a transvestite Satan worshipper with a penchant for biting the heads off live chickens.

'Nothing wrong with that,' said Serendipity, feeling an unexpected urge to defend Carol without really knowing why. 'Lots of people start their families late now, Alice, not like you and I.'

Alice's eyebrows rose so fast and so far that they were in danger of hitting escape velocity and making it into orbit. Equating herself, whose first child was conceived *in wedlock* at a self-respecting twenty-two with Serendipity's teenaged and illegitimate fertilization – and of course she hadn't been the only one, had she – she opened her mouth, began, 'Well at least I was over twenty, unlike *some*—' but as she did so Hector kicked her sharply under the table.

Hector didn't want Alice dropping any clangers about pregnancy. He liked Serendipity and Clive. He liked their cosy chaotic house, which still had children in it. His own dining room was as cosy and intimate as Valhalla (and had probably seen even more intrigue, although considerably less sex) and his daughters spent most of their school holidays on the yachts of their friends.

Serendipity saw the kick, wondered what on earth Hector could fear Alice would say. After all, Alice had said most things that there were to be said about teenage pregnancy to her; she was not, never had been, the kind of woman to say nothing when something would do. Often, she had so much to say that no-one else said anything at all. It was particularly unfortunate, then, that most of what she said upset somebody and some of what she said upset everybody. She had a habit of waving her self-righteousness like a banner. You could never imagine Alice splitting a condom, or allowing Hector to make love to her in the back of an old MG in Hunstanton.

Penelope appeared, apologizing (rather insincerely, Clive thought) just as they finished the first course. 'Don't worry, dear, I'll eat mine while you talk.'

'This is my mother,' said Serendipity, 'Penelope. She's a poet.'

'And a medium, dear, don't forget that,' said Penelope cheerfully. 'Hello, you must be Neil. Handsome Dog recognized you.'

Serendipity sighed. 'Handsome Dog is her Indian.'

'Native American, dear,' said Penelope, picking her asparagus up and eating it as though she was practising her oral sex technique, as Neil watched, fascinated. 'One of the noble Sioux. Darling, we must talk about iguanas.'

'Later,' said Serendipity. 'Much, much later.' She turned to Carol: 'I sometimes wish she could appear a little less mad,' she told her, discomfited.

'Oh no dear, a little less mad wouldn't be much help at all,' said Penelope, happily wiping olive oil from her lips with Neil's napkin. 'If you are going to appear even slightly mad it's best to go the whole hog and be completely barmy.'

Neil was looking flummoxed, thought Serendipity, which was nice. What's more no-one, thus far, had collapsed gasping with hitherto unsuspected asparagus allergy, and none of the mice which so plagued the house at the moment had run across the dining room floor or appeared on anyone's plate and exploded (a hazard, she had heard, of the phosphorus bait now favoured by the Pest Man).

'What do you do, Neil?' she asked bravely, sure that after he had finished replying she would be left in an unaltered state of wondering what on earth people did all day in the City, and why they got paid so much. Neil, regaining his equilibrium rapidly and launching into what he felt to be a fascinating résumé of his financial career so far, didn't disappoint her. He fixed her with his undivided attention too – in his experience it didn't matter what you said to women, it was the way you said it that counted.

Carol, recovering from Alice's childlessness rattling, had turned her attention to Clive. Neil was doing his usual flirtatious attention thing with Serendipity, but that was fine, it didn't bother her in the slightest – why should it? She felt absolutely no need to flirt with Clive in response, but then he wasn't the flirting type. He was rather comfortable to talk to, actually.

'So what about this treasure, then?' asked Neil after a while, surprised that no-one else was talking about it.

'It's very exciting,' oozed Alice at once, 'we can hardly believe it – and to think dear old Percival wanted the village to have it.'

'Dear old Percival?' Penelope did not count subtlety as one of her main attributes. 'He was old, Alice, but he certainly wasn't dear.'

'From what I heard,' muttered Hector into his wineglass, 'he was absolutely free.' Alice glared.

Neil was interested, but he hid it well. 'Since I gather he was not well-liked,' he said smoothly, and even Alice had the grace to look embarrassed, 'I'm surprised he left anything to the village.'

Penelope smiled. 'I think he hoped the village might lose a few tractors down the mud spring and have to foot the bill, but that's fate's twisting tricks for you.'

'Really?' Neil filed that away for later. Best not to appear too interested in ownership of the loot at this stage. 'So what is it, exactly? The treasure, I mean?'

'It's Icenian,' said Clive, 'almost two thousand years old. Imagine, all that time . . .'

'Do you have it here?'

'No, it's in Cambridge,' said Clive, 'in the museum at St Alupent's College. The crown is fascinating – to think that it might once have been worn by Boadicea.'

Penelope raised her eyebrows. 'Boudicca,' she corrected him firmly, 'was an example to all womanhood. She was stripped and flagellated by the male ruling class, yet she proved that menstruation is no barrier to warriorhood.'

Serendipity glared at her. 'Mother, you're not with Emily Pankhurst now, you know.'

'Oh I'm so sorry, darling.' Penelope was unperturbed. 'I'm not allowed the "m" word at the table, you know,' she told Neil confidentially, 'it offends my daughter's delicate sensitivities. She belongs to a strange generation.'

'I expect your mother said that about you,' said Serendipity crossly.

Penelope shrugged. 'My mother thought women's power was the sewing machine plug. She had no idea.'

Neil wanted to know more about the crown. 'If it's the real thing it could be worth a fortune,' he said, and Carol felt an odd little shiver.

'It reminds me of that ghost story,' she said, 'the one where everyone who touched the ancient crown got haunted by a man no-one else could see.'

'Oh gosh, yes,' – Serendipity looked at Clive – 'we all watched it, do you remember, one night when there was still an old Roxy cinema in Broomhill. I was terrified of the dark for weeks.' Even as she spoke the words she wished she hadn't – because remembering involved thinking of Clive and Carol being together as a couple. She had been with

146

Cosmo, and had slapped his face when he tried to grope her during the interval. That had been the first double date – and Cosmo had fancied Carol anyway. He had said so later.

Carol remembered that too, remembered kissing Clive in the back row of the cinema. She wondered if he did too, and felt herself blush. He certainly wouldn't admit it now . . .

'I remember us all in the back row, smooching and eating popcorn,' said Clive cheerily. 'I don't think I saw much of the film.'

Neil glared at him, suddenly feeling that one view of them all, not his own of course, might be that Clive had had both of these women, and he now had the one Clive rejected. Not 'had' in that sense, of course, Carol had certainly never slept with Clive . . . He wondered again what Serendipity would be like in bed.

'So who were you smooching with?' he asked her, the thin veneer of humour barely disguising the deliberate mischief.

Carol frowned at him, and Serendipity blushed. 'An old boyfriend,' she said coolly.

'Ah, I beg your pardon,' said Neil, in tones far too smooth to do anything of the sort.

Penelope treated him to a disdainful look then ignored him. 'I hear Cosmo is back in town,' she said, helping herself to tofu.

'I don't know how you can eat that,' said Clive. 'It looks like tripe.'

Alice pulled a face which said that she had never eaten tripe, never been into the sort of home in which tripe might be eaten, wouldn't recognize tripe if it did the jolly tripe dance around her dining room wearing purple sequins and an identity bracelet marked 'tripe'. 'Hector's mother used to talk about tripe,' she said, 'they had it during the war.'

'We all did,' said Penelope, 'we did a lot of things during the war. It was the best of times, the worst of times . . .'

'Oh for heaven's sake, Mother,' said Serendipity, 'you weren't born till VE Day.'

Penelope raised an eyebrow. 'People,' she said, 'used to talk about it a lot. Anyway, I was talking about Cosmo. He was your first boyfriend.'

'Don't remind me,' said Serendipity. 'They were five of the less memorable minutes of my life.'

'Cosmo was at the village meeting,' said Hector, who had hardly felt the need to speak at all till now, finding it all thoroughly entertaining. 'I believe he feels entitled to a share of the treasure.'

'He's a slimeball,' said Carol, before she could stop herself.

Alice homed in on the sharpness in Carol's voice. 'Weren't you friendly with Cosmo?' she asked.

'We were all something of a crowd together,' said Clive cheerfully, before Carol could reply, and now she knew for sure he was protecting her. 'But actually, he's staking a claim for his mother, not for himself.'

'He has a point,' said Serendipity mildly. 'His mother's furniture had barely cleared the village boundary when the treasure turned up. If it is worth a significant amount . . .'

'Those new people,' said Alice, not wanting to name them in case she should be thought of as someone who knew people who wore curlers and had flying ducks on their sitting room wall, 'can hardly be expecting anything.'

'I don't see why not,' said Clive, helping himself to potatoes; 'they live here now, they own a house.'

'They'd barely got here,' said Alice. 'I think any share should be in proportion to how long you've lived here for.'

'What about people who lived here for years and then moved away? We have to draw the line somewhere.' Serendipity looked at Carol. 'It's going to be up to you to decide, isn't it?'

Carol grinned wryly. 'Perhaps I should limit it to friends of my Uncle Percy,' she said, 'but then no-one would get anything.'

There was a brief, guilty silence, interrupted only by the metaphorical sound of Neil's attention seizing upon this like a giant, starving gnat. Then, 'I could get Handsome Dog to ask him what he wanted,' offered Penelope, 'if you like.'

Carol shuddered. 'No thank you. I had enough of him telling me what to do when he was still alive.'

'I don't think opinions from beyond the grave have much legal standing,' said Neil hastily, thinking, we can do without this mad old bat having an influence. Well, I suppose she's not that old. Quite good breasts. But mad, definitely mad. Having said that, a bit of confusion can be a useful tool. He smiled meltingly at Penelope: 'Do you really think you could – you know – communicate with Percival?'

Penelope shrugged. 'Well, he was never a very receptive man. I don't suppose he'd want to talk to Handsome Dog anyway.'

'I wonder what a lawyer would say about it all,' mused Serendipity. Neil smiled at her, slightly knowingly. She avoided his eyes.

'Whatever he'd say, it would end with the words, "here's my bill",' said Clive. 'But I think the electoral roll probably defines who constitutes the village. It's not up to us to bring in people who aren't on the roll. I don't suppose the new people in the Great House are on it yet.'

'Neither is anyone under eighteen,' said Penelope sharply, 'and neither is Carol, but they're still members of the village. Some people would say the people who own properties but don't live here should share in it too.'

'I thought you said property was theft,' said Serendipity mildly. 'I'm surprised to see you defending absent landlords.'

Penelope sniffed. 'I wasn't talking about landlords, actually. The League of Vegetarian Women Poets own a stretch of the riverbank just by the bridge.'

'God,' said Clive, 'this is beginning to sound like the AGM of the Self-Interest Society.'

'It was the same in the post office,' said Serendipity. 'No-one will ever be able to agree what's fair.'

'Well, I don't know,' said Carol, 'but I do know the will said *everyone in the village* should share in it. If I have to decide who that is, then I'll have to call another meeting, once we know how much money there is, to explain.'

Neil listened, frowning rather darkly. In his view Carol was throwing it all away when she could have the lot. But he wasn't going to let that happen, no sir. Not when he'd worked so hard all his life for so little. He'd worked some entire years in the City for bonuses of less than six figures! He wasn't going to see his best chance of a more significant sum divided into scraps by a group of people who thought a rogue trader was a gypsy selling clothes pegs and being bullish was running around a field with your horns showing. This situation clearly needed a bit of subtle management. Carol would thank him for it. She wasn't herself in this place, that was all, there was something pernicious about it.

'Lovely tomatoes,' said Hector, hoping to change the subject, and Alice sent him a baleful look. She would have liked a little more reassurance from Carol that she would be getting her floodlight money before they moved on to tomatoes. Baleful didn't rock Hector, though, and he added, 'Did you grow them, Clive?'

'No, our stupid birds ate ours,' said Clive, 'but these are supposed to be vine ripened.'

'It makes you think of pink Tuscan walls and ancient Mediterranean men with gnarled hands and mouths full of olives standing around drinking Campari and waiting for them to turn absolutely red,' said Serendipity wistfully.

'They came from Kent,' said Clive, 'but they are nice, I agree.'

This is painful, thought Serendipity. We're talking about tomatoes now because most of us don't like one another. Well, I like Clive and Hector, and Carol, and my mother most of the time – but something about Neil irritates me immensely. I hate him thinking I find him attractive.

Alice was cutting up her fish. She ate as neatly as she dressed – she was not a woman you could ever imagine sucking up spaghetti *à la Lady and the Tramp*. People's eating habits say so much about them, thought Serendipity, watching Clive shovel his in while he talked animatedly to Carol. ('You think it's been easy?' he was saying to her. 'I have to eat constantly to keep my stomach like this.')

'We're in the final of the beautiful village competition again,' Alice said, meaning to impress Neil but failing by a factor of a million. 'I had the letter this morning. It means I need to organize you all into the village tidy-up. Perhaps beneficiaries of the treasure should be judged by the effort they put into that.'

'Oh dear,' said Serendipity without thinking, 'one more thing.'

Alice rounded on her at once. 'Aren't you pleased? It's quite an achievement – the fourth year in a row.'

Serendipity sighed. 'I know, but it means we have to cut our hedge.'

'Some people,' said Alice with saintly forbearance and a critical gleam, 'had to collect the condoms from behind the bus shelter last year.'

'Alice, I'm shocked,' said Clive. 'You really shouldn't use them twice.'

Alice blushed furiously and spluttered into her trout, and Serendipity glared at him. Protecting her was all very well, but upsetting Alice wouldn't help anyone.

Carol laughed, relieved to have left the subject of Cosmo behind. Clive really had turned into a lovely man. Actually, she thought, he was always lovely, even back then. It was unfortunate that Hector picked that moment to ask how she was getting on with the renovation of the village hall, because until then she'd started to think the evening was improving.

'Renovations?' asked Neil. 'What's this?'

'Oh, just some plans we're going over, darling,' she said, but she could tell from Neil's face that he didn't like the sound of that.

'I think,' said Alice primly, 'that we should all be consulted before anything is done to our village hall.'

Penelope beamed at her. 'Don't be a lunatic, darling. If we all had to agree, nothing would ever get done, Alice. Look at Parish Council meetings – they usually degenerate into you and Brian fighting over who seconded who in the minutes.'

Neil, putting these renovations into the tackle-Carol-later part of his brain, caught Serendipity watching him and smiled knowingly. She smiled back, not knowing what else to do when he was her best friend's husband, wishing she could shove his smirking face into his supper.

Neil helped her clear the dessert plates, and Serendipity felt herself irritated by that, too. She would have been just as irritated if he hadn't helped – it was, after all, clearly his role to be the one out of the group to chat to the hostess in the kitchen, as he was the one she didn't know. But he was flirting with her, and she didn't like that.

'No dishwasher? I don't blame you at all, dreadful modern gadget,' said Neil, who possessed the ability to adapt chameleonishly into whatever personality was most appropriate. 'I'll just rinse these while you make coffee.'

Serendipity wanted to say 'oh no, Neil, why don't you just bugger off instead', and was surprised at the violence of the feeling. But how on earth could *her Carol* have married this person? He was so slimy a snail wouldn't have had him in its house.

It was still a shock, though, when he made a pass. Indeed it took a moment to realize that it was one. Admittedly, when a man says, 'how about a quickie before we go back in?' while showing complete ignorance of the normal social requirement for personal space, it usually means one is being propositioned, but Serendipity's not expecting it delayed her comprehension as she sought other possible translations of his words.

'Er – I'm sorry,' she said awkwardly, 'but no. Quickies aren't my thing, actually.'

Neil leaned over her and smiled charmingly. 'I could wait till after the coffee,' he offered helpfully, 'if you prefer more time.' I bet he gets away with this all the time, thought Serendipity furiously, because if I say no, subtly, he can pretend he was joking, and if I'm outraged he can make me feel a fool by implying that not only was it a joke but never in a month of Sundays would he touch me with a cattle prod. Outraged, though, was far too all-consuming to be ignored.

Serendipity took a couple of breaths so that her voice wouldn't squeak too much. Sounding like Walt Disney's Snow White didn't add to the intended menace. 'I take it,' she managed eventually, 'that Carol doesn't know you're doing this?'

He shrugged, disarmingly. 'What's that got to do with it?'

Serendipity was as disarmed as Iraq. 'I would have thought it obvious. She's your wife.'

'Of course she is. Look I'm not asking you to marry me. Let me be blunt. I'm as surprised as you are that I'm attracted to you, and I don't know you well enough to tell if you're the kind to agree to a quickie with a stranger that you obviously fancy . . .'

'Actually, Neil,' said Serendipity between gritted teeth, and with all the bluntness of a very very blunt object, 'you have the charisma of a sheep tic and I find you, as a man, perhaps slightly less appealing.' This is a man, she thought, who will very soon find the remains of the orange and basil sauce upturned on his head – but then Carol would know what's gone on, so I can't . . .

Neil looked put out. 'So after dessert is right out, then?'

Serendipity wondered if Clive would believe this. 'Get stuffed, Neil,' she said politely. Neil got the drift.

It was dark by the time they had all gone. Serendipity, scraping the remains of the chocolate mousse into the sink with a reckless disregard for the U-bend, and wishing she could see Neil down there with it, decided she couldn't bear to tell Clive what had happened. He would laugh, he wouldn't believe Neil could have been serious . . .

'Clive?'

'Hmmm?'

'What should we be doing about the treasure? I mean, do you think Belinda and Felix should try to claim a larger share because they found it?'

Clive eyed her thoughtfully. 'You heard Giles – they probably wouldn't win and it would have to go to some sort of hearing. What do you think?'

'I think,' said Serendipity firmly, 'that I've never heard so much grasping and argument in this village before, not even when no-one could decide who should plant the sycamore on the village green, and I can think of nothing more awful than adding our share to it. That's what I think.'

'Do you know,' said Clive cheerily, 'I quite agree. And of course, that's the difference between me and Neil. And that's why he's rich and we're—'

'We're OK,' said Serendipity, really beliving it for about five seconds, after which she rubbed an aching leg, and felt something there. 'Oh Clive, look – a varicose vein!' She sounded as tragic as a teenager with no money.

'Oh, that's been there ages. I wouldn't worry.'

'Maybe you wouldn't,' said Serendipity, 'but you're not a snivelling heap of self-doubt. You're a man.'

'Self-knowledge,' observed Clive sagely, 'is the path to nirvana. And it's tiny.'

'It isn't tiny,' Serendipity glared, 'it's humungous. It may be small compared to the ghastly Medusa-like legs that assail you in surgery every day of your working life, but to me it's immense.'

'Is this more Carol insecurity?'

'No,' lied Serendipity, not liking to admit it was, when it was. 'But I know now how other women feel. I always thought I was different.'

'Different how?' Clive was curious.

'I always felt younger. I thought I was immune to varicose veins and cellulite. Now my mental image of myself has made a giant leap from age twenty-one to age forty in the blink of an eye. There's nothing left to feel smug about any more.'

'That is sad,' said Miranda, coming in and pitying her. 'You thinking you're twenty-one.'

'At least you haven't got cellulite,' said Clive cheerily.

Serendipity glowered. 'It's only,' she said, 'a matter of time. You two finish drying – I need some fresh air.' It still smells of bloody Neil in here, she thought, and anyway, she needed to have a think about whether to tell Clive about Neil's pass – and, more importantly, whether or not to tell Carol.

Could she have imagined it? she wondered, strolling past her dahlias. Would they believe her? Perhaps some things are better left. Yes, some things are definitely better left. Wrapped in her own thoughts she was right up against the hedge when she heard it . . . something chomping menacingly, inches from her head. It sounded like a . . . well, like a large but ghostly cow.

Now, how stupid to think that, she told herself from inside the house a few moments later, it was all that talk about jinxed treasure this evening that had done it, brought Tulip the cow to mind.

* * *

A short distance away there were still people busy in the village. Penelope Forbes, replete with tofu, was out completing another of her midnight missions. Really it was the best time for it – no-one was out fishing then, and the river's sounds were very peaceful. She didn't hear anything: nothing rustling, not even the hoot of an owl – but then, she was playing whale song fairly loudly.

Sidney Antrobus heard the hoot of an owl, though. 'For God's sake, Sidney,' said Hilda from their bed, a water bed with purple satin sheets (well, OK, they had said the money wouldn't change them, but this one thing had been something they had always wanted . . .) 'will you shut that window before I freeze to death.'

'Not much chance of that, dear,' said Sidney, beaming, 'it's about as freezing as Botswana.'

'Oh, really, and how would you know? When have you ever been to Botswana?'

'I watch the world weather reports,' said Sidney, with half an ear on Hilda and the other one and a half on the night air, 'they're very entertaining.'

'For goodness sake.' Hilda noticed the skirting boards suddenly out of the corner of her eye. They were looking a little bit dusty, she thought, and frowned. 'Haven't you got anything better to do?'

'Not,' said Sidney, with a loaded lack of expression, 'since I gave up my job. Stuffing chickens. Did you know, if you hoot, owls sometimes reply.'

Hilda scowled. 'Only,' she said darkly, 'the kind of owls that watch the world weather forecasts. By which I mean very stupid owls.'

Sidney cupped his hands together and tried a little experimental hoot. The first attempt was no great shakes, but the second – well, he gave a good hoot, did Sidney Antrobus. 'We used to do this when I was a boy. We made our own entertainment back then. No TV. No—'

'I know, you grew up in a shoebox on Clacton Pier,' said Hilda, irritated. Sidney was really being very difficult – she knew he was missing his job, but it was hardly appropriate to remain a chicken stuffer with their sort of money. It just wasn't fair to the others. She plodded down the stairs in

155

search of a duster and the Mr Sheen. Dust on her skirting boards. This was the trouble with a big house. It needed time spent on it, and she should know, after all her years of cleaning other people's. But all this money used up her time now. There were so many choices to be made. Shopping took for ever, once you realized you didn't *have* to buy the economy baked beans. And if it weren't for snooty cows employing her all these years, well, how would she and Chicken Sid have afforded to live? Maybe she should have someone – for just an hour or so. To help them out. Just to dust. When you thought of some of the jobs people had expected her to do over the years – cleaning their lavatories, for goodness sake – just having someone to dust wouldn't make her a class traitor . . .

'There!' whispered Sidney in excitement. 'Hilda! It's hooting back.'

Hilda, dusting, was unimpressed, but Sidney felt a glow of something rather splendid. It wasn't just that he had proved he could still hoot like a boy, he thought, as he hooted again and listened for the owl to reply, it was that he could hoot like an owl. 'I feel at one with nature,' he told Hilda, 'with the great, turning wheel of life.'

'You,' said Hilda when he told her, 'have been watching *The Lion King* again.' She put the duster away and resolved to place her ad in the post office next day.

Carol, responding appropriately to Neil in the pink bedroom, could not concentrate properly and found herself pretending. Her mind wasn't on things tonight, but if she told Neil that she was thinking about the past, he would say what past? and if she told him she was thinking about Clive, well, he wouldn't like that at all. But Clive had such kind eyes. Smiley eyes. You really felt that he was interested in you, even though he clearly was not the type of man to flirt.

It would have been such a different relationship with Clive, she thought, I'd have children and no secrets . . . But you can't go back. I'm just feeling nostalgic. Clive is fat. And he's married to my best friend. Giles Perry isn't fat – but he is a bit like Clive. What on earth was that Hugh said about stilettos? Perhaps he had hidden depths.

'Darling?'

'Yes, Neil?'

'You seemed distracted. Are you OK?'

'Just tired,' said Carol, 'it's been a long day.'

'You should have said,' said Neil, not liking to play to an unreceptive audience.

Carol sighed. Now he would sulk unless she took over by being on top in a state of unbridled enthusiasm. Still, every sperm could be the one, and they should have built up a little while he was in Geneva, like water behind the Aswan Dam. It must increase her chances, surely? She pushed Clive out of her mind.

'What did you think of them all?' she asked him afterwards.

'Ghastly,' said Neil. 'Remind me – which one was the Parish Council chairman?'

'Hector – but Alice really, she's the power behind the throne.'

'Dreadful woman,' said Neil, but he was oddly attracted to Alice. She had power, or what passed for power in this backwater, and that made her interesting.

Chapter Seven

'It was chomping, you say,' said Miranda at the breakfast table next morning, 'like a ghostly cow. And what is that like, precisely?'

Serendipity glared. 'Loud,' she said, 'and it puffs and blows at head height.' She turned bacon rashers on the grill pan, crossly.

'Cow says moo,' said Lily cheerfully then, when no-one responded, climbed down from her chair and thrust her face up against her mother's. 'Moo cow!'

'That's right Lily,' said her mother, 'very good, but it went "munch, munch, munch." Rather like Daddy eating bran flakes.'

'Oh my goodness,' said Clive ghoulishly from the middle of a heap of Special K (he seemed to be under the impression it might make him thinner if he ate enough of it), 'it must be the ghastly ghostly gruesome cow of Great Ghostly Cowville . . .'

'There's no need to mock,' said Serendipity crossly, 'you won't mock when you see what it's left of the raspberry canes.'

'They're decapitated,' said Felix, who had been out to inspect.

'Oh my. The headless raspberries . . .' intoned Clive sorrowfully, 'and each in the prime of life. Mind you, would a phantom cow eat raspberries?'

'You can laugh,' said Serendipity darkly, 'but you'll see. Next time one of you will be out there when it chomps.' She loaded several rashers of bacon onto a chunk of bread the size of Merionethshire.

'I'm not laughing,' said Clive. 'You wouldn't laugh if someone had poured you a bowl of Fairy Non-Bio and put milk on it either.'

'Lily just gets confused,' said Miranda. 'It's because there are so many of us and we buy everything in sacks. She probably thought it was muesli.'

'I heard that owl again,' said Belinda, 'it's been calling a lot recently.'

'I think there are two now,' said Serendipity. 'We ought to ask Hugh what he thinks. He knows about that sort of thing, doesn't he?'

Belinda's eyes lit up like Blackpool illuminations. 'Ooh, yes. He could come to stay the night. Couldn't he Felix?'

'He could,' said Felix, plotting. 'He could stay in my room with Ignatius. Would that be OK?'

'I should think so,' said Serendipity mildly, 'as long as I don't have to catch flies for anybody on my tongue.'

Belinda beamed. Felix grinned, and poured more cornflakes.

'Pig,' said Belinda, 'you're just after the toy.'

'I'm not,' said Felix, extracting from his cereal, by odd coincidence, a plastic dinosaur with more than a passing resemblance to Ignatius. 'Here, Lily. I'm hungry.'

'Mavis!' squealed Lily, over the moon with delight.

Serendipity sighed. 'Felix, you're less a boy than a grain silo. I seem to ferry food home by the ton, and it just disappears into you.'

'You should realize,' said Clive, 'that nothing matches the appetite of a fourteen-year-old boy, not even a pregnant woman. I should know, I was one once.'

Serendipity smiled, intending to make something of that, when the telephone rang rudely. That would be Martha, Clive's mother and professional Valkyrie — Serendipity could tell. It sounded shrill, sudden and dramatic, like her.

She picked up the receiver. 'Haven't you had it yet?' asked Martha loudly and predictably, and a rasher of bacon fell out of Serendipity's sandwich in sympathy. Dog, whose mealtime persona was rather more like a giant hoover than anything that ever evolved within Darwinian theory, removed it with ruthless efficiency.

'Hello Martha. No,' said Serendipity, holding the receiver as high as she could so that Lily couldn't reach to snatch it. Undeterred, Lily went off to find a chair. 'We'd have told you if I had.'

159

'Well, just so long as you're OK,' said Martha. What she means, thought Serendipity, is, does Penelope know something I don't.

'I'm fine,' she said aloud. She gazed longingly at the sandwich. If she took a bite she'd be inaudible. Not that it would make any difference to Martha, who invariably unplugged her ears when she switched on her mouth. At her feet, Dog gazed likewise. 'I must dash. The children have an iguana coming to stay.' I must be mad, she thought, putting the receiver down and polishing off the sandwich. I mean, I like animals – but that one is just so prehistoric. Still, it's only for a night.

'Good morning all. How is Lily?' Penelope burst in, splashing jollity to left and right. 'Oh, darling, you haven't been cooking bacon? Ugh, the smell.'

'I confess,' said Serendipity, 'I ate a bacon sandwich. I had a bacon-deprived childhood, so I'm making up for it now.'

Penelope raised one eyebrow. 'How I had you I'll never know. You can't expect to be in tune with your menstrual inner being if you eat sister creatures, you know.'

'For heaven's sake, Mother, I don't have a menstrual being, as you so charmingly put it – I'm pregnant. And please don't use that word in front of Lily.'

Penelope sniffed. 'If you want to bury your womanhood, that's fine.'

'Bury it? I've got nearly five children, Mother, if I've managed that with it buried then for heaven's sake don't dig it up.'

Penelope sat at the table, in staying-for-a-cup-of-tea mode. 'It was very nice tofu last night.'

'Oh, I'm glad you liked it. Clive said it had the culinary appeal of a deep-fried donkey.'

Penelope pulled a face. 'He would know. Still, it was an interesting evening. I thought you said Carol had changed? She seemed just the same to me – although I didn't think much of that crocodile she's married to.'

Serendipity was surprised. 'I thought it was just me that didn't like him. Alice thought he was wonderful.'

'Well, she's a dreadful woman,' said Penelope darkly;

'with all that oozing niceness, you just know she must be horrible underneath.'

'You make her sound a bit like the mud spring,' said Serendipity.

'Not at all,' said Penelope, 'the mud spring is full of secrets, and some of them are nice, although one of them may be a cow. Alice is full of something else, and cow doesn't quite describe it.'

'Bull might,' said Serendipity cheerfully, but Penelope shook her head.

'Envy,' she said, 'that's what drives Alice. She's lost touch with her inner self. Now, if she were in tune with her own biorhythms . . .'

'Mother,' said Serendipity, 'if you say menstruate again to me I warn you, I shall rebel.'

Penelope was unperturbed. 'Going anywhere today?' she asked.

'Yes, I'm taking Lily to the special nursery in Bury.'

'Oh, lovely,' said Penelope. 'I do love Bury, don't you?'

Serendipity smiled. 'Well, I suppose it's very charming, although my heart always sinks a little when I drive in down the Horringer Road and see that sign, you know, "Welcome to the floral town." It makes me think of trombones and Terry Wogan. I hate all those colour-coded flowerbeds.'

'There's hope for you yet,' said Penelope in delight, 'you should join the Floral Anarchists – we spend at least an hour a week sowing the wrong flowers in council flowerbeds.'

Serendipity sighed. 'Now I know why our council tax is so much. Still, I shall think of you proudly the next time I see a weed on a roundabout.'

Over at Greatbottom Farm Carol watched Neil leave for London, with uncomfortable relief.

'You never really told me what you thought of Serendipity and Clive?' she had said over breakfast (well, coffee. According to Neil only failures ate muesli and only the anally retentive ate All Bran. Carol, who had inexplicably fancied both recently, had hidden them away and made the coffee black, the sort successful men drink.)

Neil shrugged. 'Bland,' he had said, 'boring. Thick.'

Unaccountably resentful, Carol said, 'But Clive's a doctor – he was very bright at school. They were both brighter than me, actually.' *I hated that at the time, too.*

Neil shrugged again. 'People become doctors because they haven't got what it takes, darling,' he said. 'That's why none of our friends are doctors.'

Carol had wanted to say 'none of *your* friends, maybe,' but knew this would sound plaintive, childish. 'I'm sorry you're off,' she said.

'Oh, I'll be back,' Neil had assured her and, as her surprise showed in her face, he added, 'I can't leave you all alone here. I'll do a bit of rearranging, that's all. Then we can sort out this treasure business together.'

'I cancelled the Mountford-Turners,' said Carol, thinking, I don't want you to sort out the treasure. It's not your problem.

'Oh, that's fine,' Neil had said. 'His company's in trouble – bad interim report. We don't want to be seen associating with failure.'

Now, thinking 'those who live by the sword, die by the sword', Carol realized that her London self would have understood exactly what he meant. In London their socializing was like chess – complex, carefully thought out, every move calculated. Serendipity wouldn't have cancelled the Mountford-Turners, she thought awkwardly, she'd have offered them advice and support – but then, Serendipity wouldn't have known them in the first place, because she wouldn't have liked a man who behaved like a giant squid who has accidentally ingested a drum of testosterone someone has dropped on the sea bed. I need some decent company, she thought, someone to talk to. Serendipity – or perhaps Giles Perry.

I could talk to him about the treasure, she thought, about having to share it out between a group of people who are already starting to act like squabbling hyenas. There was nothing remotely squiddish about Giles. He was rather like Clive. He was fun. He made her laugh. Neil, she thought suddenly, doesn't make me laugh. He's much better at laughing at people than with them. Now why has that never struck me before?

It was, she thought, washing up the coffee things (Neil had been voluble on Uncle Percy's lack of a dishwasher, but his outrage had not extended to helping her wash up) as if there were two Carols. There was the London Carol that she had been for all these years, poised and wealthy and content. And there was the old Carol, the one she had thought long gone, who had been lurking here in Parvum Magna like something unexpected in the mud spring, waiting to ambush her if she ever came back. But the odd thing was, this old Carol was rather comfortable, like slippers with a hole in that you don't want to throw away in favour of the new ones. She had a best friend. She had roots. She liked to laugh. She was . . . being disloyal to Neil. It was fortunate that the London Carol was the real one, and that this was just a nostalgia attack. Only the London one was Neil's sort. No wonder he had been angry with her . . .

'You offered to do *what*?' he had demanded last night, after the sex, when he had remembered those comments about the village hall renovation. 'You've taken responsibility for it? That means that even if all this treasure turns out to be rightfully yours, you'll have to pay for a bloody tin roof on some stupid Nissen hut.'

Carol had decided not to enlighten him further on the actual scale of the village hall project, nor on the possible value of the treasure itself. For some reason it seemed better that he didn't know. It wasn't that she didn't trust him, of course, but it was her business. She and Neil never talked about business. And he'd only get excited about it and try to take over. 'The treasure isn't rightfully mine, Neil,' she said, for what seemed like the hundredth time. 'It's not my mud spring, and I didn't find any of it either. The children did.'

'You were nearly swallowed by the mud, pulling it out.'

'It doesn't matter,' said Carol, 'it's still not mine. And Giles says it's worth more than enough to pay for a few repairs to the village hall.' I'd better not let him see the plans, she thought.

'Giles?' Neil was immediately suspicious. 'Who is he, and why is his opinion so important all of a sudden?'

Carol sighed. 'Because he's the expert. He's a Cambridge professor.'

'Oh,' said Neil, presuming Giles to be, therefore, both ancient and mad, 'but I still don't understand it – you've no attachment to these people, you've a business in London to put your money into . . . and you're sitting here planning communal lavatories and new lino as if you were Lady Tweedtrousers of Bumpkin Manor.' Eventually, though, when she had remained stubborn and had absolutely refused to agree to 'abandon all this foolishness, darling, come back to London with me and let my solicitor sort everything out', he had left her alone, claiming to be unable to sleep in a room with pink flowers on the wall.

She checked the postbox when he had gone. The usual bills, demands for money from public houses Uncle Percy had frequented, odds sheets from betting shops which had 'missed his excellent custom recently' – and several hand-delivered letters addressed to her.

Rescuing the muesli from its hiding place Carol helped herself to an enormous bowlful, settled down to read them, and became thoroughly miserable faster than you could say 'money' if you were speaking very quickly.

'Dear Mrs Pendragon,' began the first, which was from Terry Clayton, one of Jean Clayton's many dissolute children. He thought, he said, that Carol would have a say in dividing up the money when the time came, so could he possibly have a small advance now – just a few hundred – as he had heard of a dead cert running at York in the two-thirty on Saturday . . .

Then there was one from the Baggins's niece in Bumpstaple. She knew, she said, that she no longer lived in the village, but she came for walks here all the time, and had even lost her virginity in the hedge behind the old village hall, so she was a Parvum Magnate in spirit, and couldn't she have a small share? Sixty per cent of a share would be acceptable, though with a minimum of a thousand pounds because less than that would be, well, a bit of an insult to her virtue, wouldn't it? Carol sighed and opened the third. It was from the Ormondroyds, Lords of the Manor of Great Barking. They would like to point out, said their estate manager, that as major landowners in the area and landlords of several properties, they had a claim to a proportion of any moneys found in Parvum Magna. Greed, Carol reflected, was certainly not restricted to the impoverished classes. And look at Neil, she thought uncomfortably, he was worse than any of these – he wanted all of it for himself.

There were another three: one from a family of ten, demanding a larger share for those with more children, one from a childless couple demanding a larger share for the childless, who took so much less, they said, from society, and one from a man who wasn't from Parvum Magna at all but who wondered if she knew any unattached (though preferably pert-breasted) women who were.

Carol put the letters straight into the kitchen bin, but they still muttered at her from under the lid. She took the bin and put it into the huge wheelie bin outside, where it loomed threateningly, a black plastic repository of grasping dissatisfaction. This, she was sure, was only the beginning. There was an earthquake of discontent gathering momentum. She could sense it already, and she could sense that she was going to be at the epicentre.

Well, she had no intention of being swept away to Oz. Or even back to London, not till she was ready. And there is one thing I can do, she thought, a small thing, perhaps, but it will make me feel better. I can spend as much of it as humanly possible on renovating the hall. The more I can spend, the less there'll be to be shared out afterwards. And since it's for the village, none of them can argue with that. She picked up the phone.

'Mr Gromit? Carol Pendragon here. Those plans I gave you – can we add a tennis court outside? And I wondered about putting a nice big Aga in the kitchen. And solid maple floors. Yes, no expense spared, that's right.' She felt a little better for that. Now perhaps she would go for a walk.

Serendipity, driving back from Bury St Edmunds later that morning, following Lily's appointment with the paediatrician, was struck suddenly by the sheer number of mismatched flowers on the roundabouts. (East Anglia is very good at roundabouts, hence it is a good part of the world for Morris Minors and a bad one for articulated lorries, which sometimes spend entire days wedged amongst the tulip beds somewhere between Thetford and Downham Market.)

They got home to find Clive looking like a man who feels that a really nice lunch will improve his bruises, and made him a sympathy sandwich – tuna with extra mayonnaise. 'Don't ever say I haven't suffered,' he told Serendipity sufferingly.

Serendipity was unimpressed. 'I don't think it quite compares to all the heaving and pushing I've had to do,' she said.

Clive looked wounded. 'At least I held your hand.'

He had gone again, back to work his way through a pod of pregnant ladies, when Carol appeared.

'I've come out,' she said a little obscurely, 'to escape from my bin.'

'Ah,' said Serendipity, 'you're stressed.'

'I certainly am,' said Carol. 'Half the village have already written me letters asking for money.'

'Only half? You do surprise me. Have you heard from Giles, by the way?'

Carol flushed a surprising pink. 'No, should I have done?'

Serendipity eyed the flush curiously. 'He rang earlier and left a message. Just to say that the coroner has agreed that St Alupent's can hold onto the treasure, or the find, as he kept calling it, and that he'll be in touch again soon.'

Carol regretted missing Giles, who seemed to be the only person who didn't want something from her at the moment. 'It seems odd. I left this village in a state of uncomfortable drama, really, and I get the impression that nothing has happened here for eighteen years – and yet now I'm returning for even more uncomfortable drama.'

'We have managed the odd incident in your absence,' said Serendipity, slightly stung. 'Great Barking even grew a penis in its churchyard.'

'A *what*?'

'Just a privet one, but it was quite impressive. In any case, your leaving wasn't so dramatic, was it? I seem to remember you just skulked off.'

'Yes, well, Mother and Uncle Percy rowed fairly

dramatically,' said Carol. 'I just got swept along like flotsam.'

'Poor you,' said Serendipity sympathetically. 'Has Neil gone back to London?'

'Yes, he had work to do. He'll be back in a day or two.' Carol was still uncomfortable with the relief she had felt when Neil left. *Maybe I should go too, leave the old Carol here and pick up the new one again? But I can't, not now that I know the old me is still here. For some reason I need to get to know her again, now that I've found her. And it is nice to see Serendipity too. And Clive.* 'Look, d'you fancy a break from domestic drudgery?'

'Do I? How long are you offering?'

'We could go for a walk,' said Carol, thinking, *I haven't walked this much since I came out of Harvey Nichols last Christmas and couldn't find a taxi till Shaftesbury Avenue* (she would never, of course, be seen dead on a bus).

'Good idea – I'll get Lily togged up,' said Serendipity, 'she loves walking down to the ford. We'll have our daily quality time.'

Carol watched her putting wellingtons on Lily, thinking, *this feels very comfortable. I don't feel this comfortable when I lunch in Harvey Nicks. Are we friends again? Can you be friends with someone when you're this jealous of what they have?*

There. I've thought it now. It's done.

Lily loved the river. She loved it so much that she wanted to be close to it, wanted to be a part of it. Fortunately the river ran over a ford in the middle of the village, so it was fairly shallow. Lily was now in it, sitting fishing for pebbles. The sun shone warm on the top of her head, and behind her a pair of chaffinches flew out of the hedge and chattered breezily about summer. Lily smiled and pointed. 'Birdies.'

'She's got no fear,' said Serendipity to Carol, 'you have to watch her every moment of the day. Sometimes she wears me out till I want to weep, but then I love her so much I weep anyway.'

'How did you find out? About the autism, I mean?' Carol was suddenly curious.

Serendipity waved at Lily, who beamed back. 'She just didn't speak. Even at two, not a word. There were other things, of course. Like the time on the beach when she ran all over the other sunbathers – not just close to them, but actually on them, on their bodies, footprints on their brown gleaming torsos, snatching their belongings as she went. She got all the way to the sea leaving a trail of oiled people doubled up shouting, "what the . . . ?" with other people's sandwiches sticking to their Ambre Solaire.'

Carol smiled. 'I'm sorry. I shouldn't laugh. It's just the mental image.'

'I know,' Serendipity smiled. 'We laughed afterwards – but not at the time. I was too busy apologizing to the most muscled ones and trying to stop Lily from drowning herself.'

'Why did she do it?'

'I've no idea. I think she was just overwhelmed. Too much was happening, too many possibilities, she was trying to find a way of coping.'

There was a silence. Lily, deeply concentrating on the attempted retrieval of something they could not see, suddenly looked straight at the sun and smiled. The light caught her golden hair, giving her the quality of a Botticelli angel, haloed and shining. Carol felt her heart jerk oddly, in a way that hurt. Am I actually ready to have children? she wondered. Everybody does it, you never stop to think that maybe they've all achieved something quite magnificent, not when you're too busy feeling so bitterly jealous.

'It must have been a shock,' she said aloud, realizing suddenly that it had never occurred to her that her own child, when it came, might not be normal. That was something that happened to other people.

'It was,' said Serendipity, oddly echoing her thoughts, 'in a way. You always think things like that are part of other people's stories. We were upset for a day or two, for Lily, not for us. Yet in another way it was like a prophecy fulfilled. I always felt as though something would happen to me. Something hard. Does that sound odd?'

'Not really. I think she's wonderful,' said Carol rather wistfully, as Lily sat deliberately in the water. *Don't complain about the child you have*, she thought, *you don't know how lucky you are.* 'We used to play here all the time,' she said.

Serendipity smiled suddenly. 'Didn't we just. Actually, I still do. I come here for a solitary paddle whenever life feels too fraught.'

Carol watched her curiously, wondering if it was often fraught. 'Did you paddle when you found out about Lily?'

Serendipity shook her head, surprised to realize she hadn't. 'No, it was almost a relief, when the diagnosis finally came. I thought, if something has to happen to us, this isn't so bad. Not when you think of what some people have to face. Look at her now. She's happy. She's lovely.'

'It's a big responsibility,' said Carol. This could have been me, she thought. Serendipity is living part of my life, in an odd sort of way, after all. It was meant to be me, married to Clive, growing the varicose veins. Lily should be mine. I wish she was.

Serendipity shrugged. 'Children are,' she said. 'It doesn't change anything in that sense. Of course I'd go to hell and back to defend Lily – or any of them.'

'And God made man in His own image,' said Carol softly. She could feel a tightness in her throat, linked to the empty feeling lower down. It's a real empty feeling, she thought; not just an absence of fullness but an active, aching emptiness, a cliché of a feeling. Will I ever know what it's like to have a baby? she wondered – and now, for the first time, not just what it would be like to have a baby, but what it would be like to have a little girl, one who drives you to distraction and for whom you'd go to hell and back. Well, there was no chance of one like Lily. She was a rare soul indeed.

'What?' Serendipity was watching her.

Carol blinked. 'She's very sweet. I don't know how you do it, though, how you manage her.'

'You don't think of it that way,' said Serendipity, 'it's not as if there's a choice.'

'Maaaa!'

'Lily! What's the matter – I'm coming, darling!' Serendipity waded into the river. She looks like a hippo, thought Carol uncharitably, blaming Serendipity for the grip of melancholy at her throat, thinking, I wonder if Clive really fancies her when she's like that. He can't do. *I wonder if he still fancies me – even slightly* . . . She pushed the awful, disloyal thought away before it could eat any holes in her recovered friendship. (Thoughts we push away, though, get squashed in the corner of our brains, like springs – the more you squash them the greater the force with which they bounce up to catch you when your back is turned, and the greater the surprise.)

Serendipity was lifting a dripping Lily out of the water. 'Oh my goodness.'

'What? What is it?' Carol wasn't going to wade in. You never knew what there was in rivers these days. It was all very well for little children – they had a natural resistance to dirt (they ate enough of it) but Londoners are almost certainly not resistant to Suffolk river mud. Not Highgate residents, anyway.

'It's a bloody lobster.'

Serendipity waded back, carrying Lily and the lobster. Lily was desperately excited, as always.

'Spider!' she shrieked in a mixture of terror and delight, 'spider Ma!'

'No Lily, it's a lobster. Lob . . . ster.'

Lily looked blank then laughed like a hyena, high and falsely. Carol peered at the creature. 'You wouldn't think it could survive in there.'

'It's a very clean river,' said Serendipity, defending it. 'People fish in this river. There have been crayfish in it for years.'

Carol suppressed a smile. 'If the great unwashed want to stick their toes in this water and dangle their maggots in this water, I feel even less inspired to extol its cleanliness. And if that's a crayfish it has to be the giant mutant variety. But it's not, it's a lobster.'

The lobster wiggled its pincers with ominous lobsterishness.

'It doesn't look English,' said Serendipity.

Carol giggled. 'I suppose it's the striped T-shirt and the string of onions over its shoulder that give it away. It's probably called Sasha and smokes untipped Gauloises in a little attic room just off the Boulevard Saint-Germain.'

'I meant it can't be native to the river, silly. It's huge. It must have escaped from somewhere.'

'Escaped from where, exactly? You're not suggesting it broke out of the Mill House restaurant in Little Barking, climbed several fences, evaded Sir George Ormondroyd's infamous lobsterhounds and then legged it across a couple of fields to dive into the river, are you?'

Serendipity laughed. 'Well, I don't know. No, Lily, you can't pull its legs, it will pinch you. What on earth should we do with it?'

'You could boil it,' said Carol.

'D'you think so? Oh, I couldn't.' The lobster wobbled its front end pitifully. 'It's alive.'

'You've eaten lobster in restaurants, haven't you? Those were alive.'

'Not when I saw them,' said Serendipity, lobbing the lobster purposefully back into the river. 'When I saw them they had mayonnaise on, and a little side salad. Oh, how awful of me . . . perhaps we should tell someone. If you see unusual birds you're supposed to notify the RSPB.'

'Well, unless it flies off I don't think that they'd be interested,' said Carol.

'Spider gone!' howled Lily accusingly, 'spider Lily.'

'I'd better take her home,' said Serendipity. Lily was now face down on the ground, weeping hysterically. 'Lily, darling, spider's gone home. He wanted a swim.'

'Gone,' wept Lily, inconsolable as always, 'spider gone Lily.'

'You can't eat meat,' said Carol, who didn't, 'and refuse to accept it was ever alive.'

'Self-deception is the first necessity for survival,' said Serendipity, 'especially when it comes to lobsters.' She remembered that Carol had always been frightfully holy about vegetarianism as a teenager. Ate meat now, though, didn't she?

'You never ate meat either,' accused Carol, 'you felt really strongly about it, or so you always said.' She was conscious of feeling betrayed. How stupid, she thought, I'm reverting to my teenage values. Simple, but unbending.

Serendipity sighed. 'My children all think that vegetables

were created by God especially to torture them. Felix suffers acute nausea in the face of aubergine, and Miranda's idea of post-traumatic stress is the way you feel after being socially obliged to eat a mushroom. There's only Lily who'll eat salad, and she eats a whole lettuce at a time. She likes them best with slugs on. Faced with that it becomes rather difficult to maintain a completely anti-meat stance, although we do ban beetles from the kedgeree.'

'Your mother's still veggie, isn't she?'

'Is the Pope Catholic? Of course she is,' said Serendipity. 'Rabidly so. That's why there are slugs on our lettuce. She grows it for us, but she can't bear to kill them.'

'Yuk,' said Carol.

As they walked back to Peacocks' Barn, fighting Lily every step of the way, Carol wondered if that were true, about self-deception, and if she, too, deceived herself, and what about. But then, if you've deceived yourself successfully enough then you wouldn't know. 'So that means,' she said aloud, 'that it's possible that everything I ever thought about myself could be wrong.'

'Oh almost certainly,' said Serendipity, cheerfully dodging Lily's attempts to poke her in the eye and make off in pursuit of the hapless lobster. She'd wager all the pocket money she'd ever got (not very much, as it happened) that she knew exactly who put those lobsters in the river.

Alice Bollivant knocked at the door just as they were finishing tea, but Carol, fortuitously visiting the bathroom, hid there for the duration of her visit. It was not a long one – Alice was looking for Carol.

'No,' lied Serendipity, 'I don't know where she is.' What are friends for, she thought, if not to mislead the enemy.

Alice was suspicious. 'Hector thought he saw her come this way.'

'Really? Oh, well, I've just been down at the ford with Lily, so if she was here she'd have missed me.'

Alice was unconvinced. 'Well, if you see her, could you tell her I wanted a word? I think I've some very good ideas to run by her about the distribution of the treasure. I thought if we based it on property values, then that would be a fair reflection of the stake different people have in the village, don't you agree?'

'Er,' said Serendipity, who could think of several people who'd like to put a stake in Alice if she pursued that line of argument, with the charmless and financially challenged Clayton family at the front of the queue, 'I don't know. I think there are a few problems with that . . .'

Alice was haughty. 'Well, I think it's a very good idea.'

'Well, you would,' Serendipity couldn't resist it. 'Your house is worth more than almost anyone else's.'

'That's quite irrelevant,' said Alice, who genuinely believed this. 'I am only interested in fairness. I shall keep my ideas to myself in future.' She arched her eyebrows so haughtily that they disappeared into her perm.

If only, thought Serendipity, you would. But as Alice was leaving she uttered the dreaded words, 'Oh, Serendipity, there was something else . . .'

Alice was often seized by the irresistible obligation to pass on what she knew – such knowledge always seared a hole in her consciousness until she had relieved herself by unburdening it in as many directions as possible. It wasn't gossiping, it was an unpleasant but essential duty to pass on information sensitively, before someone else did it and made a complete hash of it. 'I thought you ought to know,' she told Serendipity primly, 'before someone else told you. Dear Miranda seems to be spending a lot of time kissing that boy of hers. A girl can so easily acquire the sort of reputation . . . well . . .'

Serendipity sighed, thinking, I'd rather someone else had told me. 'Miranda's a teenager, Alice. Teenagers snog.'

Alice shuddered. 'Oh, I do wish you wouldn't use that word.'

'What? teenagers?'

'No, you know very well. It's too like snot.'

Serendipity laughed explosively. 'Oh Alice, how could you? You've ruined a perfectly good word for me. Putting snog and snot together . . . ugh.'

Alice looked pained. 'I don't think you ought to joke, Serendipity, girls can get a bad name, you know.'

'Thank you very much,' said Serendipity darkly, wishing,

not for the first time, that her doormat dog would suddenly metamorphose into a better imitation of a living thing and eat Alice, lock, stock and social conscience.

Alice, though, was horrified at her possible gaffe. 'Oh, I wasn't referring to you – I mean when you and Clive were – well, I mean you're married, now, aren't you . . .'

Serendipity grinned. 'You dig a good hole, Alice, I'll give you that. I'll speak to Miranda and tell her you're concerned.'

Alice looked nervous. 'I'd rather you didn't bring me into it.'

Serendipity sighed. 'Of course not,' she said. 'I will be the epitome of tact.'

Alice, as attuned to sarcasm as modern pop music is to anything at all, smiled graciously and took her leave, satisfied at another deed well done.

'Thank you,' said Carol, who had been listening at the door, 'for sparing me that. If one more person tells me why they ought to get more of the money than the person next door I shall weep.'

Serendipity grinned. 'I know what you mean,' she said, 'but do bear in mind I've got seven mouths to feed and I've lived here all my life . . .'

We must be friends, thought Carol, if I can see the joke.

Later, Serendipity found her mother pottering in her vegetable garden, humming to herself. Clive was by now at home resting with the essentials for suffering men (a plate of chips and a bottle of Chianti).

'Hello darling,' she said, as Serendipity and Lily picked their way between the green beans, 'come and help me cheer up my lettuces.'

Serendipity grinned. 'Olive oil,' she said to the lettuces, 'and balsamic vinegar. Will that do? It always cheers up a lettuce.'

'Really, Serendipity, you know very well what I mean,' said Penelope crossly. 'In any case, my lettuces need cheering up. They have been ravaged.'

'What by? The Suffolk Lettuce Ravager?'

'I don't know what by,' said Penelope, 'but by something that ate all the youngest ones, my virgin lettuces. Look – do you think that's a hoof print?'

Serendipity peered at it. 'Almost certainly the mark of the infamous and terrible virgin lettuce ravager. Perhaps we should tie Alice Bollivant to a tree to appease its dreadful appetites.'

Penelope looked hurt. 'I don't know where your flippancy comes from, darling,' she said in hurt tones.

Serendipity looked bland. 'Well, if it wasn't from you, it must have been from Macclesfield. Lily, please don't eat that caterpillar.'

'Spider,' said Lily hopefully, 'Lily spider dinner.'

'Can't you just give her biscuits like other mothers.' Penelope extracted the caterpillar from Lily's grasp. It reared its head wildly and tried to scarper. 'Poor thing, it's terrified.'

'Perhaps it was schizophrenic,' said Serendipity cheerily: 'you might have tipped it over the brink into madness, but that's not why I'm here. Mother, if I said lobsters to you, would it mean anything?'

Penelope concentrated on her decimated vegetable patch. 'I don't think lobsters can have done this,' she said, 'and the rabbit fence is intact. I can't imagine what else would have eaten so many lettuce in one night.'

'Lobsters in the river,' said Serendipity, 'and maybe it was a highly intelligent mutant rabbit with a little wooden ladder.'

Penelope shook her head. 'It's these hoof prints that bother me. Not cows . . . I think the coven have been in my lettuces.'

'The coven?' Serendipity laughed aloud. 'What on earth would they want with your lettuces?'

'One never knows with covens.'

'You're being ridiculous, Mother, the Broomhill coven are about as seriously occult as *Blue Peter*. Most of their potions are for cellulite and wrinkles.'

Penelope looked hurt. 'Well, you tell me what else makes funny little hoof prints, and eats radishes and lettuce but spits out the rhubarb.' She sighed and stood up. 'Why don't you come inside for a cup of tea? That child seems to be starving.'

Serendipity extracted Lily from the garden and extracted a rather manky lettuce leaf from Lily. Lily screamed in fury, then changed her mind abruptly, leapt at her mother and clung, like a Fijian on a coconut tree.

Serendipity staggered into the house after Penelope, and watched her brewing tea while Lily systematically emptied a small pot of pasta shapes and began to line them up in rows of nine.

'Mother,' said Serendipity firmly, 'you can just stop prevaricating and come clean. There's no-one except you who would put lobsters in the river.'

Penelope affected mystified innocence. 'I can't imagine what makes you think that, dear. Come on, the local news is on TV.'

'Because you're peculiar. You've always been peculiar.' Serendipity switched on the set.

'I don't know how you can say that,' said Penelope, hurt, 'I've been a good mother. What have I ever really got wrong?'

'You went barefoot to school speech days wearing the kind of earrings trapeze artists practise on,' said Serendipity, remembering the whispers.

'You should have been proud that I was different,' said Penelope, 'and in any case, it may be a mother's duty to do her best for her child, but that doesn't involve a promise never to embarrass the child by being herself.'

On the floor Lily made her name out of pasta. 'Mummy, Lily!' The introductory music to *News East* came on.

'That's brilliant, Lily. Good girl. Do Mummy's name now. You did tell me my father was a wildly handsome Irish gypsy who made love to you in a field of poppies.'

'It was a nice story,' said Penelope, a little defensively.

'It fell apart at school,' said Serendipity, 'when someone pointed out I was probably conceived in early February. Not a month known for its poppies – or its circulating Irish gypsies. I felt a fool.'

Penelope was unabashed. 'Your father was an electrician from Macclesfield,' she said. 'He came to rewire me.'

'Obviously,' said Serendipity, who had heard this many times. 'Now tell me about the lobsters.'

Penelope looked sheepish. 'I release them,' she said. 'I feel I should.'

'You do realize they catch them downstream? I read in the paper that you can buy huge lobsters in the market in Sudbury. Where d'you suppose they get them from?'

'At least I give them a fighting chance,' said Penelope. 'But I've been thinking of starting a proper lobster protection society – perhaps your friend Carol could spare a little of this village bounty to start it up. I shall ask her.'

Oh dear, thought Serendipity, poor Carol. Even the lobsters are on to her now.

Miranda came into the kitchen, looking like a teenage boy's wildest fantasy.

'Good heavens, child,' said Penelope in some alarm, 'do you go to school like that?'

'Of course not. I've just got changed,' said Miranda, pulling a pained face. 'I thought you'd be here, Mum. Is it OK if I go to the pub with Luke?'

'In leather trousers? The boy will think he's gone to Heaven,' said Penelope.

'Really, Mother,' said Serendipity, exasperated, 'don't encourage her. Yes, but soft drinks. You know the rules.'

Miranda grinned at Penelope. 'Don't you like them?'

'I fear for your health in them, darling. God only knows how you got into them, but I fear we may need the Fire Brigade to get you out.'

The local news broke with a story about Suffolk farmers growing hemp to be used in making ecologically sound paper.

'Wow,' said Miranda, 'think of the fun you could have if you found it.'

'All active substances,' said the presenter sternly, as if she had heard her, 'have of course been removed from the cannabis plants.' The screen showed nondescript greenery in a field.

'Oh look,' said Penelope suddenly, 'that's one of the Greatbottom fields. There's that funny tree – and the mud spring.'

'You're right,' said Serendipity; 'the secret location is here.'

'Cool,' said Miranda. 'Just wait till I tell Luke.'

'You heard what they said,' said Serendipity: 'no active substances. And I hope you don't smoke pot, Miranda. It's dangerous.'

'Don't be such a prude,' said Penelope. 'I remember you passing out at the Young Farmers' Christmas discotheque after someone gave you a joint, and being brought back on a tractor.'

Serendipity sniffed. 'That's rubbish, Mother, it was because Cosmo Featherstone spiked my drink. You just hoped it was a joint. And I still think those jeans are too tight.'

News East was moving on to a story about road protesters moving into tunnels to block the route of the Broomhill bypass.

Miranda, who secretly longed to be as eccentric as her grandmother, said, 'You haven't lived till you've worn leather jeans, and they have to be tight.'

Penelope sighed theatrically. 'You haven't lived till you have been in the arms of a Bedouin prince beneath the blue light of Sidi-bou-Said.'

'Oh, for heaven's sake, Mother,' said Serendipity, watching Miranda's rapt face, 'the nearest you ever got to a Bedouin prince was when you went to see *Alien* with that man who ran the Moroccan restaurant in Bishop's Stortford.'

'Look, that's the Broomhill bypass on TV. And he was from Tunisia,' said Penelope, unrepentant. 'The Bedouin genes make wonderful lovers.'

'Whereas those jeans,' said Serendipity, seizing the moment with relentlessly groanable humour, 'are likely to kill any prospect you have of being anyone's lover. Speaking of which, could you and Luke smooch slightly less ostentatiously? People are beginning to come and tell me about it.' Miranda did not reply. She was watching the road protest report. The protesters looked rather interesting.

'Alice Bollivant,' said Penelope, 'I bet it was her. The woman is as repressed as a coachload of menopausal nuns on Valium. Take no notice, Miranda, darling.'

Miranda was preoccupied. 'Sorry, Mum, but it was only a kiss.'

'Alice is just jealous,' said Penelope firmly.

'What of?' Miranda wondered what she would look like in combat fatigues.

'Your youth, your passion' – Penelope was back in theatrical mode – 'envy comes naturally to women like Alice. Oh, but what wouldn't I give to have a few of my moments again.'

'One can be rewired,' said Serendipity drily, 'too often.'

'Look!' shouted Lily triumphantly, startling them all.

They looked. The alphabet pasta was lined up. It said, LILY MUMMY SPIDER SPIDER SPIDER BOADICEA.

'Look at that,' said Penelope, 'and she's only five.'

Serendipity smiled sadly. 'When she does these things I never know whether to applaud or weep,' she said.

'Always applaud,' said Penelope. 'You'd be surprised at the difference the bright side makes to your life.'

Felix and Belinda appeared in the kitchen, with Hugh in tow. 'Dragon!' shrieked Lily at once, plastering herself all over Hugh, 'Lily dragon.'

'My Aunt Tessa says thank you for having me to stay, and she hopes you know what you're doing,' Hugh told Serendipity politely, trying to pretend Lily wasn't climbing up him with her eye on Ignatius.

'You're welcome,' said Serendipity, determined not to notice, 'although that creature you keep makes me think of Godzilla. And it's only fair to warn you, I am pregnant and therefore stressed and peculiar.'

'That's OK,' said Hugh, beaming, 'I'm used to that. I could teach you T'ai chi for stress if you like – it gets your mind in tune with your body . . .'

'So I'd get a fat mind, then?'

Hugh sighed, 'My mother does it all the time. She says no-one would ever mug her now. When people see her waving her arms and legs about, they keep well away.'

Serendipity smiled, suddenly happy. Belinda could do worse. 'Well, stay as long as you like. Belinda and Felix break up tomorrow – they need something to keep them occupied.'

'What we probably need is a pet,' said Belinda. 'Actually, you'd be amazed at the difference an iguana can make to your life. Hugh's mother says every home should have one.'

'Really?' said Serendipity, in a tone slightly drier than Yorkshire water's catchment area, 'I'll bear that in mind.'

'Mrs Pendragon!' Brian Baggins hailed Carol as she moved the wheelie bin down to the bottom of the drive, together with the second post, which had been rather like the first lot.

'Oh, hello Brian. Is everything OK?'

'Oh, fine. That agent you arranged has been round, you know, valuing the farm machinery, looking at the standing crop.'

'But I didn't . . .' Neil, thought Carol. He's having the place valued without even telling me. How dare he?

'I – er – wondered if you'd like to read this?' Brian pushed a book into her hand. Carol looked. *Egalitarian principles*, the cover proclaimed, *and the even Distribution of Wealth*.

She smiled grimly. 'Thank you,' she said, trying not to look in any way like a woman who has absolutely no bloody intention of looking at the bloody book (which was what she was) 'that's very kind.'

Brian beamed.

'I'm sorry, darling,' said Neil on the phone, 'I forgot to mention it, that's all. Don't be so suspicious. You said you were selling the farm, I assumed you'd need a property agent to value it. I just happened to run into one at lunch.'

Carol glared at the receiver, thinking there's no such thing as an accidental lunch contact – everyone in the City knows that. 'I'm perfectly capable of dealing with the sale of *my* farm *my*self.'

'I know you are,' said Neil, in the kind of smooth tones which mean just the opposite, 'of course you are.'

Chapter Eight

As school holidays rolled carousingly in the following week, summer reached its height. A million trillion ladybirds were singing in the grass (although when Belinda had written this in her English exam, her teacher had written in the margin, 'Shouldn't this read "googol"?' to Belinda's enduring disgust) and word was spreading through Parvum Magna that the decision on how the proceeds of the village treasure would be divided rested with Carol.

Carol, though, had other things on her mind, because it was day twelve, Neil was up for the weekend, and that nice Dr Potter had suggested she help the conception gods by keeping proper count of the relevant days. So she decided to check that things were doing what they should, which meant a trip to Boots.

Outside, the cacophonous hum of bees and lawnmowers almost, but not quite, drowned out the sound of Broomhill Amateur Operatic Society's final dress rehearsal for their open air production of *La Bohème,* being staged in the bottom field of Greatbottom Farm. It was a truly ambitious project, featuring the plump, Wonderbra-enhanced and appallingly miscast Alice Bollivant in the role of the starving and probably tuberculous Mimi. The rehearsal was not going well. Alice's love interest, Rodolfo, was being played by Dirk Mullins from the Dragon Arms, a man who was to the tenor voice what mating cats are to silent evenings, and she was objecting to the way he kissed her dying persona.

'You wouldn't kiss me like that,' she was shouting, 'I'm dying. You don't . . . don't *snog* someone who's dying.' Snog? she thought, *Snog?* Now I'm saying it! Those Rowan children are affecting me.

'I'm supposed to be full of passionate love and regret,' said Dirk crossly, 'I'm hardly likely to go down on one knee and kiss your hand.'

'You'll certainly be full of regret in a minute,' said Alice, 'and if you could sing a bit more like Caruso and a bit less like the Manchester United football supporters club after a gallon of lager it would help.'

Dirk was wounded. 'You won't find another tenor at this sort of notice,' he said darkly. 'You should be a bit less rude and a lot less warbly.'

'Oh for heaven's sake,' said Marjorie Smythe, the JP's wife from Bumpstaple who was directing them, 'try and act like star-crossed lovers and not like a couple of neighbours having a fight about the height of your hedge. Let's do that bit again, shall we? Alice, do try and *look* tuberculous rather than just bad tempered.'

Alice glowered dangerously but said nothing. She would have liked to explode in temper like the true diva she was, but she was well aware of those waiting in the wings and longing to replace her, and she hoped to take the lead in next year's production of *Madame Butterfly* too. She should look good in a kimono.

A short distance away Serendipity, weeding the garden of Peacocks' Barn, fought down an urge to mow the lawn and drown them out. Amateur opera from a distance, she felt, is even worse than amateur opera close up. From a distance you just get the warbling bits, and when it came to warbles, Alice was your woman.

Miranda appeared, looking awkward and nervous, like a bearer of bad tidings. 'Mum – I have to tell you something you won't like.'

Here it comes, thought Serendipity suddenly, she's going to tell me she's pregnant. It struck her that she had been expecting this moment for seventeen years. She swallowed. 'Yes?'

'I'm going to camp at the road protest.'

Relief enveloped her. Now she realized that Miranda was garbed for protest in ripped camouflage trousers and a jumper that looked like a grizzly bear with Vitamin E deficiency. Serendipity became aware that her mouth had fallen open, and closed it. 'Why?'

'To make a difference,' said Miranda, irritated that it wasn't obvious.

Serendipity forgot she was pregnant and less stable than the melon display at Sainsbury's, sat back on her heels, and fell over. 'D'you really think the Broomhill bypass is the place to start? It's already half built.'

'Half too much,' said Miranda, 'and it's never too late.'

'Just think,' said Serendipity cheerily, 'if you stop it now it will end for ever in that field at the back of the council estate. All those articulated lorries on their way to Harwich and Felixstowe will disappear into the Brigstock estate, only to find there's no way through. They'll be found there years from now, still living off the loads they were carrying, and making their own shoes out of corrugated cardboard packaging. Imagine, dozens of lorry drivers, stripped of the shallow veneer of civilization that parts us from the beasts . . .'

'You're mad,' said Miranda admiringly, 'I hope it's genetic. But the whole world is in a mess – the rainforests, the ozone layer, the whales . . . I have to start on it somewhere.'

'You make it sound as though you're painting the spare room, but I know what you mean,' said Serendipity, managing a squat at last. 'Still, not many whales on the Broomhill bypass.'

Miranda was passionate. 'But I'm focusing on the Broomhill bypass for now. Tomorrow the world.'

Thank you God, thought Serendipity, for not making me a teenager again, even in my worst dreams. Seventeen seems to be the age of recognizing the state of the planet. That's when they grow dreadlocks and pierce their navels, and make their ambitions. 'We all need our personal Everest,' she said wistfully.

Miranda patted her hand. 'You must be the only person I know whose personal Everest *is* Everest.'

It was nice, thought Serendipity, to feel understood.

She drove Miranda into Broomhill later, ignoring the obvious irony of a road protester at a demo arriving in a car, trying not to notice the incredibly filthy state of Miranda's fellow protesters, beside whom the grizzly bear jumper looked like an item of high fashion off the shelves of Harrods' Very Expensive Department, and popped into the

High Street afterwards, but she didn't see Carol slipping into Boots. Alice Bollivant saw her, though, and cornered her next to something unmentionable for treating piles.

'Carol! How lovely to see you,' cried Alice, gripping Carol's shoulders and embarking, to her consternation, on the 'mwah' series of air kisses, so derided by the press. 'We must get together some time. So much to talk about. I have some ideas to put to you about the way we divide out the treasure. You see, as secretary of the Parish Council and of the Church Council too, I am in a perfect position to advise you on who should benefit most, and I have had some excellent ideas . . .'

'Er, yes,' said Carol, trying not to look at the ovulation prediction kits which loomed at the edge of her visual field, edging away from them. She didn't need one anyway – she knew, really knew, that in a couple of days she would be zinging with ovulation. Her menstrual calendar was engraved on her cortex in letters of fire. She glanced into Alice's basket, and saw it was full of those milk shakes bought by woman obsessed with how far out their thighs are, how far down their bosoms are, and how far gone their stomachs are. Then she spotted inspiration outside, on the other side of the plate glass doors. 'Oh look,' she said to Alice, 'isn't that Serendipity's Land Rover?'

'You two always were thick as thieves,' said Alice, jealously.

'She was my best friend,' said Carol, surprised to realize it had generated such envy, even more surprised to find that it still did. So often in life, she thought, those things that everyone else envies are not the things we value ourselves. But best friendship? It's been hard doing without. She abandoned her basket and headed for the exit.

'I'll call in and run through things with you then, shall I?' called Alice after her.

Outside Serendipity tried to turn the car round in a sixty-three-point turn, feeling herself turn the colour of one of Delia Smith's peppers. Dozens of little old ladies with tut-tut expressions criss-crossed the street around her, and Lily started to howl for something unspecified. She was delighted to see Carol appear to direct her. 'It's like playing elephant polo,' she told her after the car had calmed down, 'on a sexually aroused rogue male with very big tusks. Thank you for saving me.'

'Well, you saved me,' said Carol, 'from Alice.'

Alice, watching them from inside Boots, sniffed. Three always was a crowd, she thought. And who wants to be best friends with a couple of ex-pregnant teenagers anyway? Once a trollop, always a trollop, that's what she said.

Clive was not pleased to hear of Miranda's whereabouts.

'I suppose now she'll grow dreadlocks, all of her friends will be called Kermit and Dinosaur Joe,' he said darkly, 'and we won't understand why.'

'Well, I'm proud of her,' said Serendipity: 'she's trying to make a difference.'

'Your mother is behind this. It has that sprinkling of weirdness to it that's almost her fingerprint.'

'It's not Mother,' said Serendipity, 'except maybe by the presence of her genes. And you should admire Miranda – I wish we'd tried to change things.'

'Speak for yourself,' said Clive indignantly, 'I spend my working life trying to change the world by permanently altering the ratio of genuine illness to dubious sick notes. I do make a few people better too, you know.'

'So that just leaves me,' said Serendipity rather miserably, 'one of those women who sits at home and housekeeps, whilst her husband and now her children go out and do great things.'

Clive saw her face. 'Oh Ren, how can you say that? You're letting Carol get to you again. You're a nurturer, a provider, you've fed us and clothed us and answered the telephone and painted a big yellow sun on Lily's ceiling and fish and things on her walls.'

'Fish and things? Is that what will be on our gravestone, echoing hollowly down the centuries? Clive Rowan, respected doctor, Serendipity Rowan, painted fish and things?'

Clive peered into the back of her head via her eyes. 'What do you want it to say? Climbed Everest, fell off, left a grieving family?'

'Had a go,' said Serendipity. 'I want it to say I had a go at life.'

Later still, rooting in the kitchen for a late-evening-pregnant-woman-chocolate snack and trying not to think of where Miranda might be sleeping, she found Felix rooting for an anytime-anybody-chocolate snack.

'Do you think I could climb Everest?' she asked him.

Felix looked dubious. 'You get puffed out on the stairs.'

She was impatient. 'I mean when I'm not pregnant. When I'm forty-five and fit.'

'Course you could,' said Felix loyally.

'It would cost a fortune,' said Serendipity sadly, 'and no-one would take me seriously.'

Felix looked thoughtful.

'Won't be long.' Clive waved casually and left via the back door.

'Where's he going?' asked Felix, who had his own plans for the evening: they included Hugh, but not Belinda.

'He's gone to the Broomhill bypass, I expect,' said Serendipity, 'just to check. Gosh, listen to that car revving off through the village. We ought to have speed bumps.'

Neil's car drove into the night as if he were Jeremy Clarkson test-driving something with far more valves than one engine could possibly need, powered by the row he had just had with Carol over the village hall renovations. She seemed weirdly and obstinately incapable of understanding that money is finite and should never be given away.

At the same time Clive drove more sedately down to the Broomhill bypass road protest site. This was a jolly, rather Heath-Robinson affair of camping equipment, *Guardian* readers and serious tunnels.

Carol, left alone, glared after Neil's departing dust and opened a defiant bottle of Chablis. Spare no expense, she had told Gromit, Flange and Peebles of the village hall reno-vation, and they had taken her at her word. She had never actually told Neil it was just a Nissen hut with a corrugated roof – it was his own fault if he had assumed that. Still, it wasn't surprising he had reacted so badly when he'd been for a look around. The maple worktops in the cooking area, the underfloor heating and full-sized snooker table, the floodlights she was planning on the tennis court they were laying at the back – all these had really upset him.

But it was no business of Neil's in the end. This was her problem, her uncle, her position as executor. It wasn't Neil's money she was spending – never would be, since she had absolutely no intention of challenging the will. And if Neil wanted to say that she wasn't the woman he married, and she'd gone soft, and that he wasn't sure that he could trust her any more, or that he really wanted her to have his son, then that was just jolly well fine. So what if it was day twelve and another missed chance? However badly she wanted to be pregnant, she certainly wasn't going to give in to Neil just for the use of his body. There has to be more to a relationship than sperm.

Clive was relieved to find that there seemed to be almost as many concerned parents as environmentally aware teenagers at the Broomhill bypass. He had a cocoa at a camp-fire with one of his patients and, to Miranda's outward disgust and secret relief, had a look in a tunnel himself before forcing a sleeping bag and a mobile phone into her arms and returning home. On the way back, on impulse, he turned through the gates of Greatbottom Farm.

'Clive? I'm sorry, I wasn't expecting anyone. Come in – I was having an unglamorous night,' said Carol, as unglamorous as Elizabeth Taylor. Clive was suddenly embarrassed. Some impulse of sympathy had made him imagine her, alone without Neil, sitting down to a solitary Marks and Spencer meal-for-one, with a mug of tea and an Inspector MacTavish novel. Instead here she was drinking chilled Chablis and listening to Verdi. It seemed at odds with what she had become, he thought. Not the Chablis, of course, just the Verdi. She didn't seem a passionate woman.

'I – er – was passing and wondered if you might like to come and have supper with us, if you were lonely – that is, I mean, if you fancied some company.' He felt rather awkward.

Why is he here? wondered Carol, trying to calm her still smouldering rage at Neil. Has he come to make a pass at me?

As the thought plopped into her head she realized, simultaneously, that she had been very much hoping that he would, and that her sense of loyalty to Serendipity was now restored enough to make that fact appalling. It was the row with Neil. It had obviously thrown her. 'I'm fine, really,' she said. 'Neil is away so I'm having an early night. He's preparing for a conference in Tokyo next month.'

Clive thought it sounded rather hollow. 'Wow,' he said, 'Tokyo. The furthest work ever takes me is a conference on erectile failure in Watford. You must miss him.'

'Of course.' Carol didn't think about it. She looked at Clive, tall beneath the hall light. He was taller than Neil. Actually, if it weren't for the weight he'd put on, he'd be Neil's build. He had a sweet face, really, nice eyes. She wondered if he had affairs. 'Are you and Serendipity happy?' The question surprised her, but the answer felt important.

Clive was surprised too. 'Of course,' he said.

Carol smiled. 'You're very sure. How can you be so sure she's happy?'

Clive shrugged. 'I ask her.'

Carol was fascinated. 'You ask her? What, all the time? Just, "are you happy?" and she says "yes"?'

Now Clive looked mystified. 'Yes, of course. Don't you and Neil do that?' He didn't wait for an answer. 'I'd better go. Ren will worry – I've been a while.'

Carol frowned. Should Neil and I do that? She wondered. 'Clive?'

'Yes?' He was moving to the door.

'Do you think I'm attractive?'

'Of course I do.' Clive had no trouble with that one: 'You're a very attractive woman. Neil is a lucky man.'

Now that's the response of a man who doesn't have affairs, thought Carol: he immediately brought Neil into the conversation, he didn't even have to think about it. Some demon in her persisted, though, working on a lonely impulse from an unformed thought. 'Have you ever had an affair?' I know I shouldn't be doing this with the conversation, she thought, yet I can't seem to help it. He's just so . . . nice. I wonder how life would have been if . . .

Clive, whose instinct for sensing pursuit was about as

well honed as that of a particularly stupid salmon with a penchant for coloured feathers dangling on threads, sensed the pursuit very slightly, but decided he must be imagining it. 'Goodness, no. I'm not the sort.'

'What if I wanted you to sleep with me? You said you find me attractive,' said Carol, pretending to herself that this was merely arguing a point.

'Not like that,' said Clive. 'I mean, of course you're attractive, but I don't want to sleep with anyone but Ren, so I'm not looking.'

Carol thought, he's a fertile man . . . I need a fertile man, in case it's Neil and not me who fires blanks – and Clive fancied me once. I still remember the first time he kissed me – it was up by the mud spring . . . if only he wanted me enough – just once, and no-one else need ever know. We never did when we were sixteen, so we're owed just one. It would be so easy, and he conceives children at the drop of a hat. Serendipity must say, 'oops, that's another one' almost every time they do it.

But Clive was already going and Carol was already appalled at the impulse that had seized her. It must be my hormones, she thought.

As she was closing the front door something caught her eye – a note, sticking out of the postbox. Not another! She took it indoors.

'Dear Aunt Carol,' it began. *Aunt* Carol? that sounds rather nice. It might be the nearest I ever come, after all . . .

'Mum has always wanted to go climb Mount Everest, and I know you've got the money to give out – so can you fix it for her to go? Love, Felix.'

Oh God, she thought, just when you think you've climbed out of the mud and think you can deal with all the grasping and greed, someone does something noble and you fall right back in again.

Later she put 'Ride of the Valkyries' on really loudly to make herself feel better. Not that she had made a pass at Clive. She had just sounded him out. Asked him if he had ever thought of sleeping with anyone else. Anyone rather like herself. The nasty, other half of her said, well, I had him first. I don't want an affair, I just want a baby. The more the arguments went round in her head the harder she pressed the remote, until the Valkyries were not only riding but howling and battling and galloping all over the house shrieking abuse at one another. She almost didn't hear the phone.

'Hi, it's Giles Perry here.'

'Oh, hello. Hang on a minute.' Carol turned down the volume, putting the Valkyries back inside the CD player, and shook her head to stop her eardrums from vibrating.

'Hi. I just rang to let you know that we have a date for the inquest – the first Tuesday of next month – and the coroner is quite happy for your treasure to stay with me in the meantime. We've also had a good chance to look at it now, so I wondered if you wanted me to come over and speak to everyone?'

Carol wondered what Giles would think of her dilemma. And what would he think of Neil? She knew what Neil would think of Giles. They weren't the same type, not at all. Neil would say Giles was low-powered. He was relaxing, though, the sort of man you could talk to . . . 'How about tomorrow night?' she found herself offering. 'Perhaps you and I could go for a drink first, then you could forewarn me.'

As night fell and the inhabitants of Parvum Magna retired to their bedrooms to engage in rest, sleep, romance, lust or, in Hector's case, wild but unfulfilled sexual fantasies involving Alice, a crown, and a chariot with spikes on its wheels, two people were abroad, two people who had watched the local news and observed just how very local it had been on the subject of hemp. That one of them was Hugh Appleton would have been absolutely no surprise to anyone who knew him. The other was Felix, delighted to have the opportunity to cement a boys-only bond with this most accomplished of schemers. Ignatius had stayed in bed at Hugh's Aunt Tessa's. ('Don't worry,' Hugh had told Felix, 'Ignatius will be fine. If we get arrested my aunt can feed him.')

Felix was terribly impressed with the idea that he might get arrested, but then it's not every day that you plan to smoke your first joint.

There was a bright moon, a hunter's moon, washing quicksilver over the landscape. An owl hooted, then another, then the first again. After a moment the second owl hooted twice, then the first, twice. There was silence, then both hooted together and a third joined in. Hugh stopped.

'What's the matter?' hissed Felix, whose heart was still racing with the success of having crept undetected out of the house, despite the obstinate presence of Dog on the third step up on the bend in the stairs, which had nearly sent him flying across the hall.

'That's not an owl,' said Hugh, 'I know owls. Something's going on.'

'It is an owl,' said Felix, with the confidence of one on his own territory, 'it hoots every night. Sometimes it goes on for ages.'

Hugh shook his head. 'I,' he said with impressive gravity, 'always know when something's going on.'

A little way away, in their respective gardens, Hector Bollivant and Brian Baggins, now joined by Sidney Antrobus, continued to hoot enthusiastically and tunefully, each unaware that the only creature being excited by the noise was one rather less feathery than they imagined. It gave them great pleasure to commune with nature – they had all been doing it for years. They could not have been more excited if they had been scientists broadcasting endless messages on puny radio waves to the infinite immensity of the universe, hoping for some not too revolting alien creature to pick up the broadcast and say to his wife, 'ooh, listen to this, Deirdre, they sound nice', and then one of those radio receivers with which they endlessly monitor the infinite void were to start broadcasting Virgin Long Wave Alpha Centauri, or something equally entertaining.

It took Hugh and Felix only a short time to reach the field where, they believed, the late Farmer Greatbottom had been growing hemp in return for a government subsidy. (It must have made a change for him, Felix said, as most of his subsidies were for doing nothing at all.) Hugh had come equipped with a packet of cigarette papers, a box of matches and a very small quantity of tobacco purloined from Uncle Oliver in London while his back was turned (due to the unfortunate but pre-planned entry of two lizards and a bevy of assorted beetles into his lunch box).

Now Hugh and Felix crouched by torchlight amongst the tall plants with which they hoped to achieve an interesting mental state, and tried to work out what to do with them. Not far away, something else also tried to work out what to do with the greenery, for it was very hungry. It tried an experimental munch.

'Wow,' said Felix, largely because he felt he should, 'man.'

Hugh was not so easily deceived. 'I'm not getting anything,' he said, 'other than a sore throat.'

'You have to really inhale,' said Felix earnestly, 'hold your nose, and pretend you're diving.' They collapsed to the ground, coughing horribly, like a pair of old smokers in a sauna. And when they recovered, there it was, ghostly white, looking at them over the green fronds.

'Bloody hell,' said Felix, 'a giant goat.'

Hugh was equally impressed. 'Just think,' he said, gazing at his makeshift reefer, 'if this is what one breath can do, imagine what would happen if we smoked the whole field.'

'I don't know,' said Felix in sudden distress, 'but I feel awfully . . .' and by the time he had finished being sick in Percy Greatbottom's probably-hemp field there was nothing white to see but the moon.

They staggered home, weary and somewhat chastened by the power of their experience, remarking as they went on how much bigger the world seemed, how much brighter the moon, how much more churchy the church. Behind them in the field the llama ruminated on the greenery he had eaten. He did not ruminate in the bovine sense, which is to churn it indigestively in an extra stomach of huge and tripe like construction, but in the camelid or llama-ish sense, which is to think about it a lot. Then he spat it out, suddenly and effectively, in a huge wad, and loped off in disgust. It was green, it was tall, it was juicy – but at the end of the day it tasted like horse dung.

They were hungover the next morning, bleary and sore-throated in their respective houses – which, Hugh told Felix on the telephone, confirmed it. They could now – now and for the rest of their lives – say nonchalantly, 'Pot? Oh, I tried it, but I can leave it.' Bill Clinton, he said, had nothing on them. Belinda Rowan, interrupting their surreptitious phone call, was annoyed to find that something seemed to be going on without her. Hugh's insistence that sometimes boys had to do what they had to do cut no ice, although when he explained that danger had lurked at every corner and his code of honour was not to endanger women she was somewhat mollified. Still, it didn't quite make up for the feeling of having been left out.

'Anyway,' she told him primly, 'I think you're really stupid. Drugs are dangerous.'

Hugh was airy. 'There are some experiences everyone should have,' he told her, from the viewpoint of one who knows because he has.

Belinda was unimpressed. 'If they said that everyone ought to experience a hole in the head I suppose you'd do that too.'

'Don't be silly,' said Hugh, but Belinda wasn't interested.

'I'll see you later,' she told him loftily, 'when I've finished doing some girl things.' She hoped to taunt him into feeling likewise excluded, not realizing that the last thing in the world that any boy worth his salt would be interested in was girl things. Girls things were pink. Girls things were naff. If girls were offered the chance to play rugby they'd agree if they could wear pink kit and silver trainers and be called the Bumpstaple Barbies. Actually, he admitted to himself with grudging admiration, if girls were offered that they'd be taking on the All Blacks at Twickenham in no time.

Still, Belinda felt that he had scored a point, and took her Tolkien over to the mud spring to see if any more crowns had come up. A silver one would be nice, just for her.

Carol was at the mud spring, gazing into the mysterious slurry with lines of deep thought etched upon her brow. She looked tired.

'Hi,' said Belinda, 'are you out walking a dog?'

'Yes,' said Carol, 'although I've no dog. I'm examining my conscience.'

Belinda was sympathetic. 'My mother is always doing that. She says she's contemplating her personal Everests.'

Carol smiled. 'She always used to do that. Anyhow, what are you up to? I usually see you with that nice young man.'

Belinda blushed. 'He's being a twit today, and he doesn't know he's supposed to ask me out, so I've come to read.'

'Oh dear,' said Carol, who thought Hugh was about as far from being a twit as it was possible to be, 'do you want to tell me about it? I've a good ear for detecting male twits. I think I tend to attract them, actually.' Now why on earth did I say that? she wondered. Did I mean it?

Belinda, explaining about the field of marijuana, thought Carol would make rather a nice mother, and told her so. Carol laughed, rather wistfully, Belinda thought. 'I'd like to be a mother,' she said. 'I'm not sure if I've found the right father yet, though.'

'But you're married.' Belinda was mystified. Divorce does not figure in Tolkien.

Carol nodded. 'I know. But sometimes things look different when you come home. So which field was it, then?'

'This one, they said,' Belinda told her, 'by the mud spring.'

Carol laughed. 'Well, I don't know why they're so hungover,' she said. 'This is a new variety of sugar beet. The hemp is over there, but you'd have to smoke the whole field, really, to even raise a good mood.'

'Oh,' said Belinda gravely. 'From the looks of them they tried.'

'Well, I suppose if they're convinced they smoked pot there's no point disillusioning them,' said Carol, 'then they won't try it again.'

Belinda wasn't so sure. It was nice to have the information, she said, so she could feel a lot smugger when Felix started his inevitable gloat.

They had been gazing into the spring as they talked, each the sort of person not comfortable with looking too directly at the other, so they did not instantly notice the presence that had joined them. And when they did, it felt as though he, if it was a he, had been there for quite some time. Belinda saw him first.

'Oh, wow,' she said, transfixed, 'look!'

Carol looked. 'So that's what it was,' she said: 'a llama.'

The llama gave them a very stupid look – something which, unfortunately for them, is something of a llama speciality. It also looked edgy and ready to flee. But then maybe they always do that too.

'D'you suppose it's tame?' asked Belinda.

'I don't know,' said Carol, 'but how cross can a llama get, really?' She approached him tentatively, surprised at herself, a woman who had never had an affinity with animals, who hadn't even had a cat, who had *paid* a man from the Council to remove a spider from her bathroom. But a window on the past had opened, and through it had jumped Carol Great-bottom, fifteen, who had wanted to be a vet.

The llama was impressed. It nudged Carol's proffered hand, then pushed itself up against Belinda. 'I think he likes you,' said Carol.

'He's really tame,' said Belinda wonderingly. 'What do you suppose we should do with him?'

But just then a dull throbbing marked the regular exercise of half a dozen military helicopters of the type which boast a particularly satisfied sort of throb and the llama, startled, swivelled and galloped away towards the church, where it quickly disappeared from view.

'Oh dear,' said Belinda, 'what do we do? We can't leave him out all night. He might get cold.'

'I don't think so,' said Carol, 'they're not tropical animals, you know, and I think he's been around for a few days. We can't catch him anyway. I think we'd better just let the police know.'

'We can't turn him in,' said Belinda, 'surely?'

'Well he's obviously somebody's,' said Carol, 'and they're probably missing him.'

Roger the policeman had not got to be a policeman, he liked to say, without knowing a wind-up when he heard one. Actually, this wasn't true. Roger the policeman had, in fact, never been able to spot a wind-up, not even when it was a herd of stray moose tied to a lorry near Thetford to distract him from the real varmints, the ones smuggling Marks and

Spencer's chocolates into Belgium, in the next lorry along. Once again, today, Roger fell into the profound misjudgement hole, a large, gaping and suction-enhanced hole which had dogged him, well, doggedly, really, for virtually the whole of his police career. No, actually for the whole of his police career. Even his one success, the apprehension of a poacher who had been caught red-handed at a private lake with three sticks of dynamite and a very large net had only come to pass because he completely misjudged an Ordnance Survey map when trying to find a short cut between Toppesfield and Braintree and ended up in the water surrounded by a large number of suspiciously dead trout. And even then he had only arrested the poacher for cruel laughter.

So when yet another phone caller with a silly posh voice rang him claiming to have seen a llama in Parvum Magna Roger refused to be riled. He refused to be wound up. He would not let it get to him. He was not going to be even slightly, teensily, minutely cross. The fact that his Biro snapped in two as he wrote in the log book did not mean he was cross. He wrote, 'Another nuisance call, claiming sightings of large wild animal in village of Parvum Magna. Action: None', and left it at that.

Carol had asked Mrs Clayton in the post office to let everyone know there would be a brief meeting in the church that evening, as the hall was currently full of sawdust and workmen. Mrs Clayton affected dubiousness – 'I'm not sure, Mrs Pendragon, we close at twelve . . .' – but the power of post offices to spread news is legendary, and there was probably no-one in the Western world Mrs Clayton could not have reached by quarter-past ten if she had wanted to.

Carol had arranged to meet Giles in a pub in Bumpstaple first, as she wanted to see him without the possibility of Neil interrupting and glaring, and she had no idea when Neil was coming back. Neil wouldn't understand why she liked Giles, of course, and she wanted to be able to ask Giles's advice. Actually, she felt very much at ease with Giles, which was unusual for her, as she was rarely relaxed with anyone she hadn't known for a decade or had sex with. Only Neil scored on both counts and recently she hadn't felt very much at ease with him at all. He was obsessed with the money; she just couldn't get excited about it. So what if Uncle Percy didn't mean the village to have it? Serve him right. After all, he was a nasty old beggar. He wouldn't have wanted me to have it either, thought Carol. He told me he'd never forgive me for bringing shame on his house, and he never did. Only left me the farm because he knew I hated it. Thought I hated it, rather.

Giles was already settled in a corner of the lounge bar with a pint of real ale and a local history leaflet when she arrived. Carol reflected for a split second on the fact that Neil would never have taken a seat out of the central area, would have preferred to chat to anyone till she arrived with that cheerful bonhomie of his that was so expansive, so attractive and, in truth, so false. She kicked herself mentally. What is it with you, Carol, is it knock Neil day just because he doesn't think you should give the treasure away and won't see his GP?

'Hi,' she said to Giles, 'how are you?'

Giles, standing, was pleased to see her. Who isn't pleased at the chance of a chat with a beautiful woman? Absently, he admired the way the hair grew into a V at the nape of her neck. It was such a good place for kissing, just there.

'Hi. I'm great. Would you like a drink?'

'Yes, please, Campari,' said Carol, then thought how disgusting it was when she tasted it. But we always drink this in London, she thought. But then she hadn't been in London for . . . well, it was only a couple of weeks, but it felt like longer. She was being absorbed back into Parvum Magna without choosing. She'd better think whether she really wanted to be, before it was too late.

'So,' said Giles when they were settled, making good eye contact and surprising her with the greenness of his eyes. 'You'll be wanting to know what I know.' As she nodded he began to explain about the treasure.

By the time he had finished Carol was impressed. 'Will any museum want to buy it?'

'Well, certainly lots would love to,' said Giles, 'but the price would be beyond most of them. As a fail-safe the British Museum would almost certainly pay up, but it would take a huge bite out of their budget, and there are several major works about to leave the country which they want to buy. Anyway, I think they'd almost certainly feel a local museum was more appropriate. St Alupent's museum has a huge endowment – we could certainly afford it, and we want it. We're also local, which is perfect.'

'Gosh,' said Carol, not noticing the Serendipityism creeping in. Giles noticed, and found it rather endearing. 'I've got to execute the will, you know.'

'I know. Poor you – a sort of judgement of Solomon. Goodness me – I have to say that in my experience the only thing that causes more rows than sex is money.'

'Hugh says you think it's a can of worms,' said Carol, smiling.

'A remarkable young man,' said Giles. 'All my genes, of course.'

Carol was curious. 'Tell me about yourself,' she said. 'Do you have a girlfriend?' Then was appalled at her question and the obvious link. 'Oh I'm sorry, I . . .'

'That's all right,' said Giles, 'and no. I hadn't found the right woman till •very recently.' *Shut up, you fool*, he thought. 'And there's not much to tell. I went to Cambridge from school, spent three years at Oxford doing research then came back to a fellowship here.'

'Brothers? Sisters?' Carol discovered that she was interested.

Giles smiled. 'Two brothers, four sisters, giant impoverished family with ancient father, now a retired bishop, living by the sea in Sussex. I read poetry in strange languages, play rugby and particularly enjoy listening to jazz. I don't watch TV and I don't like sherry, and my ideal holiday would be a week in Tuscany with a side of Parma ham and a beautiful woman.'

'Sounds perfect,' said Carol, and blushed. 'Tuscany, I mean. And your family, of course.'

Giles smiled. 'They are, quite. You'd like them. Of course one of my sisters is Hugh's mother, Sarah, and another one lives in Bumpstaple.' *What am I saying? She's not my date.* He pulled himself up sharply. 'Anyway, what are you going to do?'

God, how stupid of me, thought Carol. Now he thinks I'm some awful predatory woman, and the sad thing is his opinion quite matters. I like him. 'I don't know,' she said aloud, 'although I'm planning on spending as much of it as I can on renovating the village hall. It's going to go way over budget – half a million, if I can manage it. The less I have to share out, the better.'

'I'm afraid that barely covers the value of Boudicca's crown,' said Giles, 'you've a bit to go at yet.'

Carol sighed. 'I could be torn apart by lions, couldn't I? However I share it out will be wrong, and they'll all be coveting oxen and asses and maidservants for ever after. It'll all be my fault, of course. This could be worse than the poll tax.'

'Not that bad,' said Giles, who had been a protesting student at the time, facing the police horses in Trafalgar Square, 'but I see your point.'

Carol swirled the Campari in her glass, thinking of Serendipity and Clive, of the rich Bollivants and the poor but obnoxious Clayton boys. 'Perhaps I should just throw it all back,' she said, 'into the mud. Before it does any more damage.'

Giles winced. 'Oh no. That would be awful. Especially not the crown.' He would have liked to see Carol in the crown. And nothing else. Stop it, man!

'What would you do?' Carol met his eyes over his Theakston's Old Peculiar and he felt a little peculiar himself.

'Well,' he said, 'since you ask . . .'

They made the meeting on time, with a detour via Serendipity to explain the planned announcement. Carol didn't want Serendipity to be disappointed if she was already planning her trip to Everest.

But Serendipity, as much to her own surprise as anyone else's, wasn't disappointed. 'I couldn't leave the children to climb Everest,' she said. 'I think I probably knew that all along.' She did look a little wistful, though. The thing was, she said to Clive afterwards, both Carol and Felix had had faith in her. They had really believed she could climb Everest if she wanted to, and that was what mattered.

On the way to the church Carol saw lights on at Greatbottom Farm. Neil was back. But he wouldn't know about the meeting, she should be fine.

She was wrong. Neil had every intention of attending the meeting, which dear Alice had rung to tell him about – an arrangement he had effected when he had first seen Carol showing this strange, unstable streak – but he didn't want Carol to know. He believed in playing his cards close to his chest, and it did not strike him as odd that he was suddenly seeing his own wife as an adversary in all this. Neil saw everyone as an adversary. That, he felt, was the secret of his success.

So the meeting began promptly, and quickly became as civilized and courteous as school dinner time. The turnout was predictably high, and the topic was predictably money, and who got what. Everyone who was there had something to say (and as meetings go, the Annual Convention of People who Like to Shout Very Loudly and who Never Agree with Anything – usually held on an island in the North Atlantic a very long way from anywhere else – is probably a calmer and more productive affair. At least there everyone can be sure that if they make a great deal of noise they will go home satisfied.) But the promise of sudden wealth is like the threat of bad weather on the beach – it sends everyone scurrying around and bumping into one another a lot, and most of them get very cross.

Giles Perry opened the proceedings by telling them about the inquest. 'We have had the chance to look in a little detail at the hoard,' he said. 'I've prepared a full inventory of the treasure as your receipt. Let me read it out . . . it's very interesting as it's a mixture of Icenian gold and Roman gold, suggesting that it dates from the time the two sides fought after the Romans marched south from Lincoln.'

'Get on with it,' muttered Jean Clayton's elder son, Terry, who had not done history at school and didn't much care whose gold it had been as long as some of it was now his.

Giles shrugged. Carol smiled at him encouragingly, and it struck him again what lovely dimples she had. Odd that, on first acquaintance, she had displayed all the classic signs of being not his type (most women who were Giles's type were long on blondeness and short on intellect, an unfortunate combination of preferences for a Cambridge fellow). Still. Married. To a real pillock, true, but married. 'Well, for those of you that are interested, we found over five hundred gold coins dating from around AD 60, the biggest find of this sort I can recall. Most of them are Icenian, dating from the reign of Prasutagus, and his wife Boudicca, but about a hundred are Roman aurei from Nero's reign. There are also some Roman ingots and simple items of gold jewellery, several gold dress fasteners, and a buckle. Finding all of these together is particularly interesting to historians as it suggests that the treasure may have been lost or hidden at some time when the Romans and Iceni met, possibly even at the time of their famous confrontation with the Roman Ninth Legion under Petulius Cerialis, from the battlefield itself. Now the Icknield Way passes very close to Parvum Magna . . .'

'Excuse me,' said Sidney Antrobus, and Giles, who had been in danger of galloping off towards Verulamium himself in his enthusiasm, forgetting that it was now called St Albans and suffered from a lot of traffic lights and a paucity of Britannic slaves, hauled in his mental reins, and looking a little bemused, as a man does when his mind is racing towards the spectacle of a naked but splendidly crowned Carol Pendragon about to be flogged by a legionnaire.

'Er . . . yes?'

'I think what these good folk could really do with knowing,' said Sid, voicing the same thought that anyone who has ever watched an *Antiques Roadshow* presenter building up to telling a little old lady that the chamber pot she kept her lavatory brush in is worth more than the entire contents of a Long Melford antique shop, as Alice Bollivant put her nose towards Pluto and tried to look as though she thought the question too common for words, 'is what's it all going to be worth?'

Giles was not a man to avoid biting the bullet when the bullet was shoved between his teeth, but he had more to say first. 'The Icenian coins are of extraordinary quality – there must be some strange preserving qualities in that mud – and the ingots and other small jewellery items are fairly unusual. It's the crown that crowns the collection, of course, and it's hard to put a value on that as it's unique, particularly if it might actually be attributable to Boadicea herself. I think you can probably expect something of the order of two thousand each for the coins, but with the jewellery, especially the crown, I think you could be looking at around two million pounds.'

Neil, listening at the door, gasped. Two million pounds! Not even the chairmen of privatized utilities got that much from Santa these days, not even when they had managed to convince the masses of how cheap everything was while hoisting up their prices like the Union Jack on VE Day. Carol couldn't give away two million pounds. He would find out some way of stopping this bloody bequest, whether Carol wanted him to or not. She might make a useful City wife in these enlightened days when a high-flyer's woman was at least expected to run her own business, but he had clearly misjudged her backbone. He didn't much like the Carol he was discovering now: she was not his sort at all.

As Neil crept away through the silent village, not noticing the softly chomping llama which regarded him boredly from behind the church hedge, the inside of the church erupted into the kind of arguments which most people think only take place on soap operas.

'I don't see what you're doing here anyway, Cosmo Featherstone . . .'

'I've lived in this village for thirty-five years . . .'

'I've lived here all my life . . .'

'You're only twenty-five . . .'

'You're under age, you don't count . . .'

'Just because you've got six children, don't think you're on for a bigger share of it . . .'

'I don't see why I should lose out because I only rent – I'm in the Young Wives' Club . . .'

'You're not a proper villager . . .'

'You've always been a snob . . .'

'I don't see why you should both get shares when you're married . . .'

'Well, you'd only spend yours on women and drink . . .'

'Sounds a blooming good idea to me . . .'

'You've got enough money, anyway, look at you with your floodlit tennis court . . .'

'I think it should be means tested . . .'

The noise rose and rose, from a hum to a murmur to a cacophony to a din . . .

'Means tested? Everything's bloody means tested. You have to be means tested to stuff a bloody chicken these days . . .'

'Sidney Antrobus, will you shut up moaning about that? Someone else might need that job . . .'

'I needed that job. All my friends did that job. What on earth are we here for anyway . . .?'

'He's right. You've only just moved in. I've lived in this village for—'

'*Will you all shut up!*'

There was sudden, complete and absolute silence. Into it Carol Pendragon, trembling slightly, dropped her voice carefully, each syllable carefully produced and thrown like a magician lobbing pearls of extraordinary whiteness into a pond of extraordinary calm.

'There is only one person who can decide how this money is distributed, and that is me. As my uncle's executor the decision as to how the money is divided is mine. My lawyer has confirmed that. And as you know, with all of your agreement, I have begun to renovate and extend the village hall in accordance with the old plans which everyone who was here agreed to years ago: a renovation which everyone agreed more recently was a good idea. Well, I have now decided the rest of the money will also be spent on something for the village for everyone to enjoy. Every penny. No individual handouts at all. You see, it's quite impossible to find a fair way of sharing this sort of money between a group of individuals which it is impossible to define. I have had letters from many of you asking for money' – there was much condemnatory murmuring of a denying sort from the listeners – '. . . I have had letters from others of you telling me how it should be shared out' (more murmurs). 'I have had letters from people in Bumpstaple who once lived here, and letters from people in Broomhill who intend to live here . . .' – downright cross noises from Alice, who sometimes behaved as though Broomhill was a pit into which the ungodly had been put and stirred – 'So I'm doing things in a way that I think is fair. And you will have to *put up with it*. Because what on earth is the point of leaving something to the village if the village falls apart squabbling as a result? So you've got two weeks to submit ideas, plans, suggestions, proposals, what have you . . . then I'll – then *we'll* look at them, and we'll decide what to do. Thank you for coming!'

There was a brief silence before it all erupted again. It was enough of a silence for Carol to grab her bag, grab Giles by one surprised arm, and flee the church. Serendipity too was taken aback by the sheer aplomb of the delivery, even though she had been expecting it, but as the door shut behind Carol she burst into spontaneous applause. Lady Sybil Ormondroyd, who had already said that she didn't want any money but liked to hear a nice row, joined in enthusiastically, hoping that someone would black someone's eye next (life used to be more fun when there was wrestling on TV every night). Alice, not wishing to appear anything other than community spirited (but sod it, she could have had decent floodlighting *and* an outdoor pool) joined in politely, then Hector, Clive and the Antrobuses, and gradually almost everyone else.

But beneath the applause they were still muttering . . .

'She can't do that, can she?'

'Stuck-up cow, who does she think she is?'

'I wanted a new garden shed . . .'

'Looks like you won't be purchasing your floodlight, my dear . . .'

'The White Russians were arrogant, too, and look what happened to them . . .'

'Oh, shut up, Brian, you're not at the Communists' Club now, you know . . .'

Alice rose above it. After all, you couldn't expect much better when the group included Cosmo whom no-one took seriously (those robes) and the Clayton family, a group as public spirited as the Viking King Hagmar, once known across East Anglia as Hagmar the Not Very Public Spirited At All.

*   *   *

Penelope Forbes had not been at the meeting which she had felt, with surprising prescience, would be beneath her dignity. In the absence of Miranda, who hadn't yet grown tired of being muddy but cool in a hole on the would-be Broomhill bypass, she had offered to babysit for her daughter. It gave her a chance to work on a poem about Lily, watched admiringly by Hugh who had not, he said, ever seen real poetry being written before, and by Belinda, who was giving him plenty of opportunity to see her in a good light by sitting underneath the lamp.

Penelope was very pleased with the poem. It was one of the best she had ever written. It seemed, though, to be all about lizards, which wasn't what she had intended. Still, she read it to Serendipity when she returned, weary but cheerful, from the meeting. Serendipity was not, she had to admit, wildly impressed.

'Iguanas don't have monthly cycles, Mother.'

'Of course they do,' said Penelope crossly, 'we are all sisters under the skin. This poem was inspired by Ignatius.'

Hugh was revolted. 'I'd *know* if Ignatius had periods,' he said. Ignatius squatted on the back of the sofa and glared palely in several directions at once.

'Don't worry, Hugh,' said Serendipity cheerlessly, 'my mother thinks everything has monthly cycles, even the space station Mir. She doesn't mean periods as such.'

Hugh was relieved. 'Well, that's good, then. That's one less thing for you to worry about. If you ever have an iguana, of course,' and he was gone with that cheery wave which was so reminiscent of the Teletubbies.

'I like that boy,' said Penelope, 'he's full of ideas.'

'He's full of something,' said Serendipity, who despite the fact that Hugh and his iguana had gone was sure she could still see Ignatius's eyes staring at her from the space where he had been, like the Cheshire Cat in *Alice in Wonderland*, 'that's for sure.'

'So tell me,' said Penelope, 'what's happening to the treasure?'

'Well, there's to be an inquest,' said Serendipity, 'at which it will be declared treasure trove and of national interest, and St Alupent's Museum will buy it at the agreed value.

But no-one's getting a penny of the money – Carol has community plans for it.'

'Nothing for my lobster charity?'

'Nothing.'

'She ought to think about sending everyone on a course for channelling their psychic energies,' said Penelope, resigned; 'the results could be startling.'

'You can say that again,' said Clive. 'I shudder to think what sort of dead Indian might be attracted to Alice's shoulder.'

Penelope glared. 'Handsome Dog is a spirit guide,' she said loftily, 'not a parrot. He doesn't sit on my shoulder, he floats above it, in my aura.'

'But what about the crown?' Belinda wanted this clarified: 'shouldn't the Queen get it? After all, if she's descended from Boadicea then she would have got it in her will.' She was mentally plotting a wonderful novel. A novel set in Middle Earth, peopled by children and peacocks and Boadicea's crown and, well, elves and goblins and hobbits . . .

'Sorry, darling, but the Queen's not descended from Boadicea,' said Penelope, 'she's descended from William the Conqueror and some Germans.'

'Oh. Well, what happened to Boadicea's descendants?'

'The Romans got their revenge in the end and wiped them all out,' said Clive, 'apart from your grandmother, of course. I can just see her commanding a tribe of wild woad-wearing women.'

'Thank you, Clive,' said Penelope warmly, 'that's one of the nicest compliments I've ever received.'

'It's gross,' said Felix. 'Hugh says Iceni women didn't wear deodorant.'

'Poor pampered boy,' effused Penelope, standing. 'You young people are out of touch with bodily must.'

'Felix isn't,' said Belinda, 'he touches his own socks.'

'Well, I'm off,' said Penelope. 'I'm going down to spend a night with Miranda at the protest.'

'Oh. Give her my love,' said Serendipity a little wistfully, as Lily came tearing down the stairs in her nightie. 'I'd come with you if I could.' How nice just to be able to do your own thing, she thought. Carol has never been tied like this.

Penelope gave her daughter a kind look. 'You've enough to do,' she said.

Lily stood on tiptoe, gripping and ungripping her hands strangely. She looked for all the world like a fairy statue which has come to life desperate to take wing, only to find that someone has cemented its feet to the plinth. Serendipity stroked her hair, watching her mother through the front window. If we were rich, she thought, I could have a nanny, and then I'd be free . . .

'You can go if you like,' offered Clive, seeing her expression. 'I'll look after the kids,' but she shook her head.

'No. I don't want to leave Lily.' I've got to stop envying other people, she thought; envy is worse than pineapple juice for getting into things and making them all black and smelly. Yet the truth is I don't want to go when I'm offered the chance. And if I can't even leave Lily to go to Broomhill for the night, Everest was always right out. I sort of said that to Carol earlier, and didn't realize I really meant it. But I did.

Chapter Nine

Neil had an appointment to fulfil the following morning, and one or two other things to do – which was how Serendipity came to see him. She might have missed him, as he wasn't in the Range Rover. The sports car was much more Neil anyway, she thought: a man who acts like a complete penis is bound to drive a car that looks like one.

She was glowering tensely out of the window of the dentist's waiting room at the time. This was a good spot for glowering, protected as it was from the road outside by those vertically slatted fabric blinds whose prime purpose is to attract dust and annoy the cleaning lady. There was a little bobbly plastic cord which was apparently intended to adjust the blind but whose real function was to drive slowly mad those poor souls who attempted to use it to adjust the quantity of light entering the room. Only the blind designers ever knew how the bobbly plastic cord worked, but as they are probably all long-term inmates in buildings with white walls and lots of five-lever mortice locks, they are unable to enlighten the rest of us.

Glaring out at the passing traffic was a popular diversion, as otherwise you had to stare at the walls which were horribly adorned with posters about teeth. (Since this was the place where you waited for your dental check-up, any distraction from teeth was welcome.) Pregnant women, in particular are much troubled by teeth. Actually it's not the teeth, so much – the teeth are usually fine – it's the dentist. Show a dentist a pregnant woman and he develops an evangelical urge to make sure her teeth are perfect for ever – just when she thought it would be quite nice if he wasn't very good at his job really and failed to notice a filling or two until later. And then there's the talking, of course, when your mouth is fuller than at almost any other time during a sexually active life; the constant questioning with the expectation of intelligible answers. So the waiting room is like the holding room for those TV shows where you think they'll send you for a fortnight in Barbados, but when you take the blindfold off you've got a week clearing ditches on a reclaimed industrial site just outside Basildon, while Chris Evans interviews you constantly but cheerily from behind a camera and beneath an umbrella: it is a room full of the willing hoping for the best but expecting the worst. Going beyond it, to the dental chair itself, is rather like an expedition to monitor the mating behaviour of the two-bottomed tortoise fish of the inner Patagonian rainforest – anything can happen. The one can lead to a clean bill of health or ten violent fillings and a serious sanding with the kind of whirringly unpleasant object that only diamond cutters and people on the production line for satellite parts could possibly admire. The other can lead to scientific and spiritual enlightenment or trench foot and a distressingly personal encounter with leeches. In either case, the best one can hope for after the event is not to be in greater pain than before it.

Outside the window the usual queue – around ten cars and a van carrying electrical goods – waited at Broomhill's mini-roundabout while an articulated lorry the size of Liechtenstein attempted to negotiate the kind of turning manoeuvre that requires a full right-hand lock in a Morris Minor.

Serendipity made a quick mental wager with herself: '. . . and if I win I won't need a filling . . . fifty per cent or more indulging in unacceptable personal habits . . .' then counted. Six of the stationary drivers were picking their noses, two were smoking, the man in the electrical appliance van seemed to have lost a winning lottery ticket in his right ear, and the man in the Porsche . . .

She had won the bet anyway, but that hardly mattered now. That was Neil's car. She was sure of it, because that was Neil in it. But whoever was in the front with him was not, judging by the smile on Neil's face, asleep in his lap, and it wasn't Carol – at least not unless Carol had dyed herself blond and developed a penchant for frizzy perms.

How do you tell your best friend that you've just seen her

husband receiving a blow job on a double mini-roundabout? The easy answer, thought Serendipity, is that you don't, but then I thought that before, when he propositioned me at the dinner party. This time I'll *have* to tell her. But when? How?

Neil Pendragon, who was not a man troubled by conscience with any sort of monotonous regularity (in fact, in the conscience stakes, he was so far behind the rest of the field that if the field had been the flat course at Newmarket he would have been in Stow-on-the-Wold) dropped his casual acquaintance off near the roundabout before making his way to the offices of Fosdyke, Mortle and Penge, solicitors to the now-deceased Percival Greatbottom. He did not see Hilda Antrobus as he passed the Jobcentre on his way – indeed, he would not have recognized Hilda if he had seen her. She was wearing dark glasses and a big floppy hat.

Hilda had found the woman in the Jobcentre most helpful. 'Yes, Mrs Antrobus,' she had assured her, 'we can ask applicants to fill out a form, and then we'll forward the forms to you. We won't give out your name, I can assure you of that. A little light housework, you say – you mean dusting, tidying, that sort of thing?'

'And a bit of cleaning,' Hilda had said, embarrassed, thinking, if someone wants to earn the money, it's market forces, that's what it is: 'just in the kitchen.'

On the way out she saw Frank Brown from Brigstock Road, going in, the man who always complained to the Council about everything and who organized the neighbourhood watch. She hurried on. Wouldn't want to get caught in conversation – she was in a hurry, and besides, what would she find to say? Asking if he'd noticed how the stock market had bumped along in the last few days would hardly be appropriate, and asking if he'd won the lottery yet, their old joke, would probably go down like a lead balloon. It struck Hilda suddenly that it could be a bit lonely, being this rich, that there was something a bit disorientating about it – but she pushed the thought away and turned determinedly back into the Jobcentre. 'And bathrooms,' she told the startled woman in there: 'she'll have to clean bathrooms.'

*　　*　　*

'To be honest,' said Mr Fosdyke, looking awkwardly at Neil, 'I shouldn't be discussing this with you.'

'Oh good Lord, John,' said Neil, as smooth as satin, 'I wouldn't want you to betray any professional confidence. I was speaking purely hypothetically – though I am concerned for my wife, you understand. I do worry that if her uncle had known that he was bequeathing something of such great value to the village, he would not have done so, but my dear Carol is such an . . . unworldly woman. But I feel that an accidental bequest of this nature could probably be challenged. Particularly as she was herself the finder of the treasure. Don't you think so? After all, we are talking two million pounds. So I'm sure a substantial legal . . . fighting fund could be made available.'

Mr Fosdyke fought down an urge to smooth the five hairs on his head. His wife was always telling him not to fiddle. He felt a little wrongfooted by the directness of Neil's approach. Actually he felt so wrongfooted that he had fallen right over his metaphorical feet. He was a country solicitor. He was not used to smooth bribery. Coarse bribery, adultery, lust, slander, the wilful desecration of someone else's sugar beet or the poisoning of their delphiniums . . . all these things he encountered regularly in his working life – but smooth and oily, well, you don't get that in East Anglia. (That's probably why it is such a good part of the world for delphiniums.) He floundered, flounderishly. 'Ahem, well, yes, Mr Pendragon . . .'

'Oh, please do call me Neil. Incidentally, my firm – you've perhaps heard of us – Pendragon, Pendragon and Fitz-Gilbert? – are looking for local legal representatives to take on some of our extensive business in Suffolk . . . but yes: Neil. Do go on.'

'Well, er – yes, speaking hypothetically, I'm sure a bequest could be challenged on the basis that it had become subject to events unforeseen at the time of death. However, I do think that your wife would have to be the one to challenge it. And as to the law of treasure trove, it is rather a difficult one, you see, as the treasure was found on the surface, and on village property, and as Mrs Pendragon simply helped retrieve it, I don't think she has a particular claim. She would have more chance if she were to challenge the will, I think, not the distribution of the treasure under treasure laws.'

Neil smiled a conqueror's smile. It was only on the inside of course, but it appeared that he had now got what he wanted twice in a row, and at very low cost. Twenty pounds and a short ride in a Porsche the first time, a mere hint the second. 'I want my wife to contest the will – I feel it would be in her best interests – and I think such advice would be better coming from you. If you were to urge her to fight this – on the basis, say, that you feel her uncle was not of sound mind when he made the bequest – then I think she might give the matter some serious thought. And of course, in the meantime, here's my card. I'll get someone in the firm's London office to contact you very shortly.'

That would do. These country solicitors were as simple to land as a coarse fish, easily blinded by a taste of the big time – and it wasn't as if he was trying to cheat Carol . . . but a lot of money was involved. She couldn't just give it away. He was her husband. At least half of it was his.

But Neil had misjudged Mr Fosdyke. He should have realized that the mental processes of a man capable of coming face to face with that hair in the shaving mirror every morning, and yet continuing with his day, were likely to be far beyond his grasp. For Fosdyke, chewing his lip in mild consternation, was no trout. Just because he was having a bad hair day – just because every day was a bad hair day – that didn't mean he didn't know when he was being offered bait with a hook in it. He didn't need to see a pair of waders and a man with a reel. And this man in front of him had a harpoon gun.

Mr Fosdyke had always prided himself on his decisiveness. We all have some indecisive element to our personalities, except possibly *Blue Peter* presenters, but all of the indecisiveness contained within John Fosdyke was channelled into his hair (which he could not decide to cut, even though he knew it made him look more ridiculous than a baboon's bottom). This left absolutely none for the rest of him. He therefore stood, decisively (as one might expect).

'Mr Pendragon,' he said, not trying to disguise his opinion

of Neil's methods, 'I will not try to disguise my opinion of your methods. Fosdyke, Mortle and Penge is a firm of long standing. We take our ethics to the highest degree, and we do not discuss our clients' business with anyone. I'm very sorry, but I am certainly not prepared to try to influence my client when I have no reason to doubt her uncle's sanity.'

Neil stood, swift, smooth as baby lotion, unruffled by sudden defeat. 'Very well, Mr Fosdyke, I'm sorry to have troubled you.' Anyone who tried it on as often as Neil did, in all areas of his life, was accustomed to a verbal smack in the face and was skilled at taking it gracefully. There was always another route to try, that was his motto. He could not, however, resist a final dig at Mr Hair Transplant here. 'I trust Mr Mortle and Mr Penge will not mourn too dearly the loss of my firm's business.'

'I doubt it,' said Mr Fosdyke. 'They've been dead for some time.'

Neil was not unduly concerned. He had decided to make a big effort with Carol – apologize for the row, romance her a bit, remind her of everything she saw in him (and there was so much, he thought, with what he felt was a modest lack of superlative). Perhaps he'd even encourage her to have some medical tests done. He did want a son after all, a son who would wear smart clothes and never be grubby nor, (particularly nor) snotty. A son who would have a succession of attractive blonde nannies from nice nanny places like Finland. A son who would go off to boarding school with a proud stride at seven, for there is nothing like serious private education for serious networking – think of all the big City players he would meet at sports day just because their snotty son played rugby with Neil Junior . . . He just didn't want to admit that there might be something wrong with himself in order to obtain a son: he certainly wasn't going to provide anything in a pot. But he could, at a pinch, accept that there might be something wrong with Carol. Wasn't it always the woman? So if he paid up and got her sorted out (Neil believed it could always be sorted out if you paid) she'd be grateful, and a grateful woman is always persuadable.

Mind you, a sensible man hedges his bets. He didn't quite trust Carol – lately she had seemed not to be the sparkling, ruthless woman he had married, but more a marshmallow of a person. You never knew what people might do when they went soft in the middle – she needed an eye keeping on her. So bearing that in mind, thought Neil, he had another call to make in Broomhill. Performing a swift U-turn in the road, sending an elderly woman in a Metro scurrying into a ditch (silly old bag, shouldn't be on the road at her age), he purred through Broomhill to the office of one Jeremy Brash, ex-army, ex-CID, ex-film extra, ex-decent human being, where he found a man who looked more like Philip Marlowe than anyone he had ever met. And that was very appropriate, really.

Hugh and Felix did not believe Belinda at first. The trouble was, believing her not only involved accepting that a llama could really be at large in Parvum Magna, it also meant letting go of the one piece of hard evidence that they had both entered the world of cannabis-induced fantasy by partaking in a joint llama-hallucinatory experience. If Belinda had seen the llama, then they had seen the llama, and if they had seen the llama, then . . .

'And it wasn't cannabis at all,' said Belinda, watching their faces with the smugness of one who has been unwittingly left out of something which later proved not to be worth being indulged in anyway. 'You were in the wrong field.'

'It was cannabis,' said Felix hotly, 'it made us all strange.'

'Well, if it had made you all normal I might be a bit more impressed,' said Belinda, 'but I wanted to talk to you about the llama.' She looked at Hugh. 'I'm worried about it. It shouldn't just be on the loose. I think we should try to find it.'

'Maybe we should tell the police,' said Felix, but Hugh was dubious.

'I don't know. The police might take it off to some dreadful sort of llama farm with no room for it to stretch its legs, where it would probably end up being eaten. I think we should trap it ourselves.'

Belinda was convinced. Hugh sensed it – he had become very good at that kind of thing and had realized it might be a useful skill in later life. He glowed a little, and added, 'I know a bit about trapping animals – my aunt keeps a pig. What we need to do first is to build a hide in your garden . . .'

Belinda and Felix, who had never possessed a pet more exotic than three peacocks who thought they were radish hounds, and a dog who thought he was a bath mat, were dubious. 'Why would we want to hide? We're supposed to be finding the llama, not the other way round,' said Felix, with impeccable logic.

But Hugh was certain of his argument. 'That's the way it is with wild animals,' he said: 'you have to disguise yourself as a part of the landscape, then they come to you. Then you watch them, and when you know all about them – then you can catch them.'

Felix and Belinda were impressed by such science of purpose, and so they began to plan their construction.

Serendipity, however, was not impressed when she saw what had appeared in her garden.

'It's for watching birds and wild animals,' said Hugh, rightly guessing that introducing a llama into the equation at this point might not be the wisest thing he had ever done.

'It looks,' said Serendipity, eyeing the heap of branches and string with some distaste, 'like the sort of thing Pocahontas might have thrown together in a panic if Powhatan had abandoned her on the coast near Cromer.'

Hugh, whose teenagerish tendencies were becoming ever more marked, produced a book to prove her wrong. *Survival Guide*, claimed the book on the front: *how to Survive Alone in the Wilderness*. 'So you see,' he added charmingly, 'you don't even have to bring us sandwiches. We can live off the land in this.'

'If you want to live on bits of snail and grass seed you're welcome,' said Belinda, who would only go so far for love, 'but I'm going to make a ham sandwich if we've got to spend the night in there.'

'The night? I don't remember agreeing to a night,' said Serendipity in some alarm, but Hugh was full of reassurance.

'It's OK, Mrs Rowan, I was kicked out of the nest at an early age. You learn survival at boarding school – you'd be surprised what they expect us to live off.'

Serendipity was not convinced. 'Spending the night in a home-made wigwam is hardly comparable to a night in the dorm at St Alupent's.'

'God, of course not,' said Hugh, glad she understood, 'but I wouldn't expect Felix and Belinda to stay at St Alupent's. In any case, we'll have my iguana to stand guard. They make excellent guard dogs, actually.'

'Really?' said Serendipity, in her driest voice. It was, as voices go, slightly drier than a dried sea slug, and rather more disbelieving. If a dried sea slug had been present, Serendipity's disbelief would have made its own profound lack of interest look like a fascinated attendance upon Hugh's every word.

'Ignatius is brilliant,' said Felix, jumping in with enthusiasm. 'Just think – a totally silent guard dog. He'd wake you up without barking.'

'I won't ask how,' said Serendipity, 'but I've a horrible feeling you'll tell me anyway.' Hugh made frantic don't-push-it faces at Felix, but Felix had not yet learned to employ tact or caution.

'He'd crawl up your pillow and lick your ear,' he said cheerfully.

Serendipity raised an eyebrow. 'Really?' she said, noncommittally. 'What's that ratty smell I can smell around here?'

'I don't know what you—'

'You are not,' said Serendipity, 'having an iguana, and you are not sleeping in that – and anyway, we have a meeting to go to tonight. I thought you might be interested. Look – this came through the door.'

Upstairs, Lily Rowan was unusually quiet. She was in her bedroom, looking through her treasure. Lily had a lot of treasure in her room, although adults rarely see things as children do, and few people saw things as Lily did, so it was unlikely that most people would have thought much of Lily's treasure. There were several Mavises, there was a scuba mask off an Action Man, there were some rather smooth stones and a ponytail bobble that glittered. And there were four shiny gold coins, dating back to the Iron Age. Lily smiled and pushed them into the bottom of her hiding place.

'Come and see your village's future,' said the note which Alice had given Hector to put through everyone's door. She had found an architect friend on one of her committees to draw some impressions, and wanted to get in quickly with it, before anyone else came up with any dreadful common or tasteless ideas for spending the village money. So the plans were on display in the church (the hall now lacked a roof), with Alice presiding over them like Lady Bountiful, and a glass of chilled white wine for those who came. (Hector had bought the wine from the cash and carry, telling Alice he'd been to a wine merchant. The label sounded French – probably came off the back of one of those lorries that endlessly got lost in Broomhill trying to get back off the half-a-bypass. No matter. She'd never know.)

Serendipity, arriving at the hall at the same time as Carol and Neil, gave Neil a hard look. I'm going to tell Carol about you, she thought, but I can't tell her here. Can I? God. I don't know if I can tell her at all . . .

'Hello, Neil,' she said, in Electrolux tones.

'Hello,' said Neil, giving her his I know-you-fancy-me look. 'Haven't seen you for a while.'

'No,' she said shortly, thinking, you are so slimy, actually, that frogs would have trouble relating to you. Yet Carol adores you. This reminds me of those friendship quizzes they had in teenage magazines when we were little (not like now, when the magazines are full of sexual position of the month and teenage road tests on condoms): how do you tell your best friend that her bloke is being unfaithful, and do you tell her at all? I seem to remember, she thought, the answer was always that you *should* tell her, yet I'm not sure I've got the nerve. If she doesn't believe me, she'll hate me, and I couldn't bear for her to hate me again so soon.

Neil, oblivious, patted her shoulder, moved over to talk to

Alice and accepted wine. He wasn't sure about this evening, what stand he should take. He certainly didn't want to encourage Carol towards giving the money away, but at the same time he needed to stay on top of the situation and keep in touch with where things were at (Neil even thought in management-speak). 'So which firm does your architect friend work for, Alice . . .?'

Carol, watching Serendipity curiously, edged her away. 'You don't like Neil, do you?'

'I . . .'

'Do come and see, everyone,' called Alice, and Serendipity put it on hold.

The plans for the village leisure centre were spread across several pews and the altar. It looked immense. Serendipity examined the artist's sketch of the swimming pool. Vast and plant-lined, it reminded her of the pool complexes at those forest park holiday centres so popular with middle-class families exhausted by their children. The last time they had been to one – to visit Alice and Hector for a day in their executive villa (same as a normal villa, but with a Jacuzzi, champagne, and, oddly, a free copy of *Cosmopolitan*), they had found the place interestingly surreal, a sort of forest idyll peopled with huge numbers of Canada geese so over-stuffed with holidaymakers' left-over muesli that if they had all landed in the lake at once they might have set up a tidal wave sufficient to sweep all the happy executives in a giant surge to Thetford. There was a long chute, like a giant Fallopian tube, out of which villagers could shoot, spermishly, into frothing waters filled with excited children (spermishly again, really) and a miniature pool in which small children could paddle and piddle. There was a gym, a tennis court (floodlit to an extraordinary degree) and a bar. There was even, clearly marked, a coffee room for tennis coaches. Serendipity looked at Clive. 'Do you honestly think this is right for the village?'

He shrugged. 'Not many villages have a set-up like this. God, this wine is disgusting.'

'Not many villages have a strip club either, but it doesn't mean they want one – it's another of those things that rather stops them from being villages, you see.'

Clive grinned, 'I rather like the Fallopian Flumes. The one in Broomhill is very popular.'

'Well,' said Serendipity ominously, 'then.'

'Isn't it brilliant?' demanded Felix rhetorically, coming up behind them. 'Just think, I could spend all day in the pool. You'd never have to worry about me going to raves and snogging girls with cold sores again.'

'Don't be revolting, Felix,' said Belinda. 'Mum, this is a monstrosity. We can't have this here.'

'I agree,' said Hugh, who was of the age when you think your opinions must fascinate the world. 'Think of all the natural habitats this could destroy – my aunt says there are orange-bellied newts in Parvum Magna.'

Neil, eyeing Hugh as one eyes something the cat has put on the garden path (which usually turns out to be the bit of a mouse that cats never eat), sidled over. 'I don't think,' he said, with just the right level of dry patronization, 'that a couple of reptiles should stand in the way of something of such benefit to the community.' He thought Alice's idea rather good. And once Carol understood that all the treasure was rightfully hers then he – and she, of course – would own the whole complex. They could make a fortune.

Hugh said indignantly, 'If you were a lizard you might see things differently.' He had not seen Neil before, but was quite prepared to go for the full dislike-thoroughly-at-first-glance option. Crocodile shoes. That said it all.

'Well fortunately,' said Neil, fixing Hugh with the sort of look that could impale directors and city financiers, 'the opinions of children have little bearing on the ultimate decision.'

'Semper bufo etis,' said Hugh cheerfully – he found Latin a useful language for calling people names. Neil, who had of course been to the sort of school where Latin was taught, but who had never been listening when it was, turned his back.

'I think he probably is a lizard,' said Serendipity to Hugh, after Neil had patronized off to eavesdrop elsewhere, 'although perhaps I'm being unfair to lizards.'

'You are,' said Hugh who should, after all, know. 'Lizards aren't slimy. I called him a toad, but actually he's more of a tomato frog. They have sticky lips. And I think this is daft. A decent village hall with a snooker table would be much more sensible.'

'I agree,' said Serendipity. 'I'm just not sure how to tell Alice. She's so proud of the whole idea.'

'Just watch me,' said Clive, 'I know how to handle women.'

'By the tickly bits, you said,' said Felix, and Serendipity glared at him, warningly.

Clive looked at Hugh, 'Sticky lips?'

'Don't worry,' said Hugh kindly, 'you don't need to understand.'

Alice bustled up, notebook in hand. 'Well, Serendipity, Clive, what do you think? I was very impressed with the tennis club, of course, and the outdoor salt pool. And isn't this lovely Chablis? From a little wine merchant Hector found in Cambridge, you know. Not a label I've seen before, and quite expensive . . .'

'I'm on orange juice.' Serendipity took a breath: 'To be frank, Alice . . .'

'Oh, can I be Ernest?' Clive beamed, then withered in seconds beneath Alice's frosty look, the one she could switch on and blaze at you like Buzz Lightyear's laser.

Alice raised a cultivated brow (recently shaped and plucked by Carole from Great Barking, who had just started doing home beauty sessions for her wealthier, more treasure-related clients), 'Yes, do be frank, Serendipity.'

'OK, Alice, who's going to use it? There are under two hundred people in this village. If you restrict it to the village it will be mainly empty most of the time. There'll just be the odd exciting day when we'll have the blood-chilling prospect of watching you frothing down the rapids entangled in Brian Baggins's hairy limbs. On the other hand, if we open it to the public we won't be able to get in ourselves in the holidays, and if we do get into the pool in the summer we'll be overwhelmed by unfettered ten-year-old boys endowed with Superman swimming trunks and a liberal sprinkling of athlete's foot.'

Alice was so stunned by the vision that her Chablis began to shake like the puddles in *Jurassic Park* just before the bit everyone knew was going to happen, happened. 'Serendipity,' she managed on a weak gasp, 'oh dear.'

'Think about it, Alice,' said Serendipity. 'Do you really want to turn Parvum Magna into Broomhill's answer to Center Parcs for the sake of a couple of floodlit tennis courts and the chance to drink gin and tonic with a tennis coach called Zack?'

'How did you . . .?'

'They're always,' said Serendipity, 'called Zack.'

Sidney Antrobus, peering at the modest pitch and putt course, also had his doubts. 'Looks like a hooray sort of place to me,' he said. 'Waste of money. What we need is a decent place for playing darts and a coach for outings.'

Hilda sniffed. 'Shut up betraying your ignorance, Sidney Antrobus,' she hissed in his ear.

Sidney glowered. 'Nearly thirty years of married life I've been Chicken Sid,' he told her. 'I'll not be Sidney Antrobus now, not if I never stuff a chicken again.'

'It does seem a bit extraordinary,' Carol was saying to Neil. 'It's like the sort of thing you get in the Home Counties where they're too terrified of having their Rolexes pinched to simply enjoy the fresh air without a fence.'

Neil shrugged. It could take a while to contest the will. If this went ahead he – and Carol, of course – could eventually make a fortune, once it was all theirs. They could turn it into the Queen's Club and Ragdale Hall rolled into one. It could be worth millions in time . . . He was brightening visibly, like a baboon's bottom at moments of particular pleasure. Alice Bollivant was clearly an intelligent woman. She might be a good reserve line of attack . . . She would understand that treasure was only treasure when it was divided a very few ways. Any further and it is merely small change. Alice had influence – if recruited as an ally she might be able to help keep the number of ways small. But of course he had Carol to work on this evening, and the champagne was chilling at the farm . . .

Serendipity watched him turning on the charm with Carol. I'm going to tell her about him, she vowed, but I'll have to wait till I can get her alone. I can't do it here in front of everyone – she'd never forgive me – although from the

221

looks of him if I wait till later they'll already be thrashing around in bed.

The other villagers who had turned up to view Alice's plans had varying opinions. Muriel, who ran the Dragon Arms, was dubious. What might this do to the pub's trade? She whispered her worries to her husband Dirk, but Dirk was not concerned. 'Silly old bag. It'll make us a mint. We won't need to work, we'll be rich.'

Muriel retreated to a corner and frowned. Not work? So they would do what, precisely, she demanded? Watch satellite TV and pick their noses all day if I know Dirk Mullins. It was a shame there was quite so much money really, she thought, a little bit less and they could have kept their own shares of it without things changing too much – have a nice meal, a trip to Clacton, a new bedroom carpet . . . But this much? This much was just plain trouble.

Carol, watching and listening, sighed heavily. Just because she had shouted at everyone and told them they wouldn't be getting any money, that didn't seem to have got her off the hook. They were still arguing, and she could tell, from the surreptitious dark looks aimed in her direction, that it was still all her fault.

'Don't worry,' said Hugh at her elbow: 'where two or three are gathered, there will always be an argument. That's what my RE teacher says.'

'He's very wise.' She smiled ruefully. 'The trouble is, I seem to have started this one.'

Hugh shrugged. 'Our headmaster says if you can't please all of the people any of the time, then why not please all of the people none of the time? It's his excuse for detention and school semolina.'

'Well,' said Carol, thinking that Hugh's school sounded to be a fount of wisdom and sanity, 'so far that seems to be exactly what I've done.'

Alice felt uneasy afterwards. It had all seemed so clear – that money was a good thing, that more of it was always better. A grand scheme for the village was much to be preferred over something modest . . . But after this evening this whole treasure thing seemed to have something oiky about it, a whiff of commonness, of sausage sandwiches and scratch cards and caravanning in Skegness with men called Derek and dogs called Killer. Incredibly, she was beginning to have just the sneakiest wish that the treasure had never been found, because actually, fame itself was oiky, wasn't it? She sighed and lay back.

'You know, a little foreplay might be nice, just occasionally.'

'Really, Hector. I am a busy woman. I have a lot on my mind.' She would ring Carol in the morning, put her revised point of view forward. After all, she must keep her influence on how the treasure was spent.

Hector sighed. That was the trouble with Alice – she was always thinking of the next thing, and this meant that the only time she was thinking about sex was when she was doing something else entirely. The thought of her deeply focused on his willy whilst conducting one of her endless committee meetings cheered him, but it was poor compensation for her failing to think about his willy at all when she was actually within firing range of it, so to speak.

Alice, trying now to direct at least a little attention to the business in hand, suppressed a yawn. The way she saw it, the trouble with sex was that it was always the same. What was the point in spending hours working up to it when in the end it was always essentially the same. It went in, it plunged around, it came out again. That was the bottom line. What more could you do, really? Alice's trouble was her complete lack of a sexual fantasy life. It wasn't that she couldn't fantasize about anything. It was just that it had never occurred to her to try. Hector, seeing the glazed look in her eyes, sighed inwardly and focused his ears on the owls outside.

Neil spent a frustrating night trying to win his wife over with caviare, sex and champagne. His concessions were just not enough: she was being totally unreasonable. He had said she could go and have tests done. He had even offered to pay. He just was not prepared to accompany her to see a doctor, or put something in a pot for a doctor to explore. It was all far too demeaning – and unnecessary. How could anything be wrong with a man who could perform as often and as effectively as he did? He particularly didn't need some country doctor poking him about. He had never understood why people became doctors anyway – all that time spent with people's bottoms and hardly a penny to show for it. It made Clive a completely different species to himself. A much stupider species.

Still, he tried everything to get Carol into responsive mode, but even the old snuggle-up-behind-her-and-poke-her-in-the-back routine brought no response at all. It finally resulted in a detumescence of spectacular inadequacy, and by the following morning they were not speaking at all. When Neil got up and dressed Carol was still faking sleep. Only when he said 'I'm off, darling – Brussels – I'll see you in two days', did he get a grudging farewell.

As Neil drove out of the gates of Greatbottom Farm, Hector Bollivant passed the end of his drive, motoring off towards errands in Broomhill. Ah, thought Neil, knowledge is opportunity. Why not take the chance to soften Alice Bollivant – you never knew when she might come in useful. She was his sort of woman. It wasn't that he fancied her physically, exactly, he told himself, but he did wonder what she'd be like in bed, which made her worth a visit anyway.

'I thought your ideas quite splendid last night,' he said to Alice over her kitchen table: 'you obviously have a sound business mind.'

Alice, making Earl Grey in her best teapot, the one she planned to use if the Queen, passing through Parvum Magna *en route* to Sandringham, ever suffered a blow-out and called at the first house with tennis court (and floodlight) she could see in order to await the RAC, was flattered. She might have gone off the idea of her sports complex a little, but she liked Neil. He was rich. He was successful. He had eyebrows like Roger Moore's. But mainly, although she had not admitted it to herself, she liked that predatory twinkle in his eye. She was rather glad that Hector had popped over to the garden centre for a bag of compost and a lawn aerating tool.

Alice had no plans to be unfaithful to Hector. The Queen-*en-route* fantasy was her only fantasy, but she did enjoy feeling Neil's carnal interest. It made her feel attractive. It made her feel desirable. It had, since she first met Neil and recognized the gleam in his eye, enabled Hector to make love to her in the conservatory on one occasion, and she had even hinted that she might be willing to consider the tennis court as a possible future venue, were it first to acquire another floodlight. Hector was mulling over the proposal. He was, it's true, prepared to go to some lengths to introduce a little more adventure on the marital front but, on the other hand, sex on the tennis court was just sex on the tennis court. Different venue, same sex. Rather like when *Songs of Praise* goes to the harbourside in Stornoway, in a sense. Now were she to offer to wear a ballet tutu, perhaps, or a pearl choker with crown and sash – *then* he would be willing to erect, in addition to the obvious, a dozen floodlights, right outside the back door.

'Thank you, Neil. Though I do think,' said Alice now, pouring tea for Neil and guessing that he was far too sophisticated (or pretentious) to want milk in it, 'that perhaps our plans were a little too downmarket. Something more exclusive is called for.' If *Serendipity* had subtly managed to attach a naff label to the whole idea, she thought, when her children go to state schools and she keeps peacocks for affected regality, then it must be really naff.

Neil smoothed himself and adopted an earnest face which suited him as well as French suited Biggles (who once, baling out over northern Europe, told a rescuing Belgian farmer 'Sorry, I have spat in your field of kidneys', due to a confusion of verbs and things). 'Well, I am sure your good taste will prevail. Understatement has such class,' he said smarmily.

Alice nodded seriously, much flattered, and Hector jumped up a little in her estimation. Perhaps their one floodlight wasn't such a bad thing. After all, didn't Oscar Wilde have a similar idea – to have one floodlight might suggest genteel upper classness; to have two might be considered vulgar. Well at least I haven't lost my touch, thought Neil, as he said his goodbyes and noted the willing look in Alice's eyes. I'll put Alice on hold.

*   *   *

225

After he had left, Alice rang Carol. They might not be best friends, but you had to keep in with people – it was a constant battle – and it wouldn't do for Carol to think she still supported those common plans which Hector's architect had come up with.

Carol sighed when she heard Alice's voice.

'Oh, Carol, dear, could I have a quick word?' Alice took silence as agreement. She had switched on her extremely tactful voice now, a voice that was in fact so extraordinarily tactful that it fell right off the edge of the tactful world and became completely tactless. 'I thought that the plans last night were just a little much, and I want you to know that I shall be backing a major rethink.'

Carol sighed again. Her morning was not going well so far. 'Alice, the way I'm feeling I might just drop all the bloody treasure back in the hole it came out of,' she said now. 'I'm just fed up with all the angst.'

'Oh, but . . .' Alice sniffed as the dialling tone cut in. They could stick their treasure, she thought, she wasn't going to be insulted over it, not for all the floodlights in England. At least she had an admirer in Neil. She wandered over to the mirror to check the progress of her new anti-ageing cream. She was only doing one eye with it at the moment, as a trial run, and it seemed to her, now, that her right eye had a twinkle, a lift, a sprightliness not seen on the left. Definitely time to order a larger tub. She didn't need Hector's hidden credit card to order – she knew the number by heart.

Because it was summer holidays Penelope Forbes was sitting by the ford, ostensibly composing poetry but actually waiting to harass any small summer-holiday boys who might come to dangle pigs' trotters in the river in the hope of catching her lobsters, and wondering whether, despite what she had said, Carol might still like to set up some sort of a lobster trust with some of the treasure money. 'Oh no,' she liked to shriek as another crustacean was hauled dripping from the water clinging grimly to a trotter in an act of unwitting self-sacrifice rendered all the more poignant by the fact that the murder weapon was, in her view, a piece of one who had been murdered earlier, 'I can hear it screaming. Drop it at once!' Although the boys did not generally believe her, the only thing boys fear more than relegation to reserve goalie in the fifth team is a mad female poet trying to tell them that lobsters can think.

Hugh, Felix and Belinda wandered down to the river to see her. It was a blistering day. The greenhouse effect was in full blaze, boiling up East Anglia's water and turning it into snow over Guatemala, while water company officials sat in offices chewing their fists and wondering about their bonuses. Hugh and Felix were peeved at Serendipity for insisting on plastering them with Factor 30 before allowing them out of the house, although Belinda welcomed it as she hoped to remain pale and interesting and not to be contaminated by freckles. They were OK on Hugh, but he had red hair. A natural blonde needs her pallor. Hugh had plastered Ignatius with the same gloopy stuff, and Ignatius was not, as a result, speaking to any of them.

Now they came to sit beside Penelope watching the lobsters.

'I don't think they like nesting under rocks,' said Belinda, 'it must be frightfully uncomfortable.'

Felix sneered mildly. 'I suppose you'd give them a little pink house with a white door and a tiny brass bed. You could call it Dun-nipping.'

Belinda glowered. 'What makes you so sure they wouldn't like that? Hugh, where do lobsters live?' she asked.

'Crevices,' said Hugh, who was not about to give ground to Belinda. That was no way to start a relationship . . .

'Lily loves them,' said Belinda; 'she got really excited over one the other day.'

Hugh's face lit up, giving him the golden, luminous quality of a harvest moon. 'Does she?' he said. 'My dad never let me have one as a pet. He said he drew the line at getting sentimental about work, and my mother went on about them being the only thing that got him going and if we had one in the kitchen she didn't know where it might end.'

Belinda saw an opening. 'Lily always gets what she wants,' she said.

*   *   *

'We brought him to show Lily,' they told Serendipity, 'then we'll put him back.'

'Why is it called Leonardo?' asked Serendipity, thinking, I'm going to regret asking that because I've given them an opening. I have failed to be implacable, and when your implacability cracks in front of a fourteen-year-old boy with a lobster in a bucket you may as well pack in all resistance and agree to the parrot and the Vietnamese potbellied pig.

'Well,' said Hugh, not disappointing her, 'you know Leonardo da Vinci drew that man with eight arms? Well, look –' he held Leonardo up for inspection, and Leonardo waved his frondy things at Serendipity in what was, she agreed reluctantly, a Da-Vinci-ish fashion. I don't know which of those bits are legs, she thought resignedly, and which are something else, but I don't want to.

'He's waving hello,' said Felix.

Serendipity treated them all to a baleful look. 'Mum,' said Belinda crossly, 'you could say hello back.'

It's easier to give in, thought Serendipity, greeting Leonardo like an old friend. They always win in the end.

Lily was ecstatic when she saw the lobster in the kitchen. It was an ecstasy so extraordinarily huge and all-encompassing, so totally rapt and Lilyish, that Serendipity felt overwhelmed with guilt that Lily had not had a lobster before. Still, she thought, at least it's not an iguana. At least it doesn't sit on people and stare.

'See,' said Belinda wheedlingly, 'how she loves animals. Gran says—'

'I can imagine what Gran says,' said Serendipity. 'And we are not having an iguana. I'd actually rather keep a lobster in my kitchen.'

Neil did not ring from Brussels; not that Carol cared, of course. He might as well have been in Timbuktu. It felt as though they were miles apart in more ways than merely being miles apart. She was alone at the farm trying to convince herself that a lazy bath and a facial would make her feel better, when Giles Perry called around.

'Hi there.' He peered in through the kitchen window at her, and Carol felt oddly self-conscious because she was wearing her dressing gown, even though it covered rather more of her than a mountaineer's thermal undies. Still, it is the intimacy of the garment, rather than what it does and does not reveal, that makes the difference.

'Oh, hi. What are you doing here?'

'Just passing,' said Giles, who had been just passing in the way that aeroplanes flying from Abu Dhabi to Murmansk just pass Llandudno, 'and I thought I'd take an interested peep at the mud spring and say hello.'

'Come in,' said Carol, 'have a coffee. I'll just dress.'

Giles gave her a shy but admiring look. 'Don't dress on my account,' he said, and blushed.

Carol was astonished to find herself completely confused. 'I – er – won't be a minute,' she said, with slightly less panache than an agitated bumble bee, and shot upstairs to spend an inordinately long time deciding what to put casually on.

'How's it going with the treasure?' called Giles up the stairs.

Carol appeared again, flustered, not wanting to admit that her heart was racing oddly because of the way Giles was looking at her. 'Awful, actually. I'm beginning to wish we'd never found it. Some people are unpleasant about it and that makes me feel terrible. Some of them are terribly noble and tell me their life's ambition, which I might have fulfilled for them, doesn't matter at all. But the end result is the same – I still feel terrible. Even Neil . . .' She stopped. *What am I doing, telling Giles about Neil?*

Giles let it pass. 'D'you fancy a coffee? You can tell me all of your problems. There, now you don't get an offer like that every day.'

'I do actually,' said Carol, then giggled, surprising herself. 'Do fancy a coffee, that is, not do get an offer. But I don't have problems, not really. It's just that Neil feels I shouldn't be giving up the treasure at all. He thinks I should challenge the will and get the mud spring back, and that if I spend any of the money on the village hall then there's no way of getting it back.' She looked into Giles's sympathetic face. She didn't want to talk about Neil with him. I'm imagining this, she thought, I must be. He's not my type. He's nothing like

229

Neil. Neil's my type. 'The money is upsetting everything.'

'Money does that,' said Giles cheerily, trying not to let Carol's sexy giggle get to him. 'One of the advantages of never having had any is that you can see it objectively, from a distance, as it were.' He watched her filling the coffee cups, tried to stop wondering what it would be like to kiss her. 'You and your husband seem an unlikely couple,' he said.

Carol let that pass, it was too dangerous in her present mood, and instead said, 'What would you do, right now, if you had to spend a pile of money on something everyone would want, if everyone already hated you for not dividing it up, but if you did divide it up they'd hate you even more, and if the only thing you could think of to spend it on was a village hall project that wouldn't even use a quarter of it, not even with more floodlights than Wimbledon?' She sat at the kitchen table and pushed a mug over to him.

'Well,' said Giles, carefully, sitting down opposite her, 'that depends on whether you're asking me with my historian's hat on, or with my friendly listener's hat on. Which would you like me to be?'

'Try both hats,' said Carol, noticing again what nice eyes he had. Neil's eyes were rather muddy brown. Giles's were warm and hazel, with little gold flecks – if you got closer there were other colours there too . . .

Giles smiled. 'The historian would say it doesn't matter what you do in the long run, so why worry? It will pass. And the friend . . .' He looked at her. Her eyes were just stunning. Those lashes . . .

'Yes?' Carol found she was holding her breath. She should look away really. She took a deep breath and watched herself load sugar, which she didn't take in coffee, ever, into her cup.

'The friend,' said Giles, following, 'would say chuck it all back where it came from.'

'If only I dared,' said Carol, 'I think I jolly well would.' I hope you're my friend, she thought, I really do.

'You have to tell her,' said Clive, when Serendipity explained the predicament.

'I know,' she sighed, 'it's just awful, being the bearer of bad news. I'm surprised at Neil.'

'I thought you didn't like him?'

'I don't – actually, he's *such* a slime, I'd have thought he fancied himself far too much to have any spare capacity. Anyway, what is it they say, curse not the messenger, or something?'

'Tell me about it,' said Clive, 'I'm a doctor, remember. I'm always the messenger. What's this?'

'Beetroot soup,' said Serendipity, a little too proudly, 'I saved you some. We ate earlier.'

Clive ate a little and grimaced. 'Where's it from?'

'Hungary,' said Serendipity, 'at least the recipe is. Don't you like it?'

'I think I now know why central European history followed the course it did,' said Clive. 'Do I have to eat with that lobster watching me? It's adding insult to injury.'

Serendipity sighed. 'Lily loves it, and it's better than the alternative. Do you suppose she loves him?'

Clive pulled a French pouf face. 'Perhaps,' he said Gérard Depardieu-ishly, 'but after me, everything else would always be second best.'

The telephone rang, narrowly saving Clive from having beetroot soup poured on his head. 'Don't answer it . . . you can now.'

'Hello, Mother,' said Clive into the phone, 'no, she hasn't had it yet. No, I'm afraid she can't come to the phone. She's in the bath. Yes, a lot of baths – it helps her backache. Yes, well, it can be a sign of labour, you're right, but I think it's just backache . . .'

Serendipity rolled her eyes and went to make Clive an omelette.

'Why didn't you want me to answer the phone?' he asked.

'It might have been Miranda,' said Serendipity, 'we have a code. Two tings, then a pause, then three rings means she wants to be picked up.'

'Ah,' said Clive, 'ingenious. An unbreakable code. So what would three rings, a pause and a ting mean?'

'Why? Has that happened?'

'It means she's being set upon by three children's TV

presenters with a wet haddock,' said Felix airily, coming in
search of bread. 'Can Hugh stay over if we promise not to
sleep in the hide?'

'Just let me know when he's checking out,' said
Serendipity, in resigned tones, and Felix retreated to plot.

Chapter Ten

Brian Baggins was very worried about the treasure, and he didn't like the feeling that these smug middle-class people were having all the say in what it got spent on. Why shouldn't he have his own share, anyhow? This daft idea with the pool and the palm trees was something to do with those Rowans. They should bugger off back to London, those Rowans. Then he remembered that the Rowans were Parvum Magnates, born and bred. Still, they were middle class, and they were just too smug. It was all very well Mrs Pendragon deciding how to spend it, she was a good woman, that one. Nice legs – but in his opinion that Serendipity had too much influence, just because her children had found it. Brian had never really liked Belinda Rowan, not since her essay entitled 'Country pursuits – the annual peasant shoot in Parvum Magna' had been published, with spelling errors, by an amused editor of the *Broomhill Gazette* under the headline, THE PEASANTS ARE PROBABLY REVOLTING. This had offended Brian's proletarian sensibilities to a high degree. Mind you, he didn't actually like Serendipity much either. Pretentious, she was, going on about the way the treasure was spent as if it was hers. So when he was in the post office he had a good moan.

There had been a lot of moaning in there that morning. Everyone in the village had an opinion on how the treasure should be spent, and most of them had decided to be unhappy with Carol's ideas so far, as they did not involve immediate cash in hand. Not since the last round of party political conferences had so many people tried to appear to be engaged in constructive debate when their points of view were about as negotiable as bank charges.

'I think,' said Jean Clayton, who had spent far too many of her evenings *seeing* that floodlight of the Bollivants, (light pollution, it was, if she leaned right out of her upstairs window she could just catch a glimpse of it,) 'I think that some people in this village are trying to take over. Patronizing, that's what it is.'

Mrs Featherstone, still up from Glastonbury (and thus far unchanged apart from a cardigan based on the Book of Kells and a birthstone jewel glued into her navel – Glastonbury can have that effect on the suggestible) agreed. 'A sports complex is no use to me,' she said. 'I would prefer simply to have my share.'

'You've moved out,' said Brian, who had never liked Mrs Featherstone much either. 'You shouldn't get a share, and I can't see Cosmo going down the flumes in those bloody robes.'

'I'm still on the electoral roll,' said Mrs Featherstone indignantly, 'and so is Cosmo.'

'As what? Guinevere?' Mr Baggins did not like Cosmo. It was amazing, in fact, how many people he was discovering profound dislike for since this treasure had appeared. It was hard work feeling like this about everyone.

'If Cosmo were here with me,' said Mrs Featherstone haughtily, 'he could explain to you about his earlier incarnations.'

'I bet he could,' said Brian nastily, 'and does each of them want a share as well, then? Where is he, anyway? Sneaking about talking to trees?'

'He had to go back to Glastonbury,' said Mrs Featherstone. 'It was very important for his aura now that the moon is entering Virgo.'

'Goodness,' said Jean Clayton, unsure of such language. 'I don't think . . .'

'Well, I don't know which is worse,' said Penelope Forbes, coming in at the tail end of the conversation, 'you all fighting over this blasted treasure or Carol Pendragon's plan to turn the whole village into a resort for happy campers so you all move away anyway.'

'Well, you've no need to worry,' said Brian.

'What do you mean by that, Brian?'

'Well, you're well in whatever happens,' said Brian. 'Your daughter's acting as if it's all hers already.'

'Actually,' said Penelope, 'I don't want a penny of it, and

Belinda and Felix could have staked a finder's claim for half of it, but didn't. I will admit that initially I hoped that the League of Vegetarian Women Poets might stand to gain a little, and I was hoping to start a lobster protection group, but now it seems to me that there is no advantage at all in any of this. If I had my way it would go right back where it came from.'

Jean Clayton was dismissive: 'You've never been short of money, so that's easy for you to say. My son Terry lost a fortune on the horses last season. He just can't afford to live on his benefits, what with the price of cigarettes and the subscription to cable. And you can't do without cable, everyone has it now. After all, what on earth would his kids do all day without the Disney Channel? I do what I can, but he's always short.'

Penelope shrugged. 'It depends what you mean by short. I've never envied anyone anything, Jean, and I'm not about to start. And isn't wealth defined as spending a penny less than you earn? A bag of sugar, please, I'm making a cake for Lily.'

After she had gone Brian, who had never liked her either, he now felt, gave a scornful 'ha'. 'She's got a screw loose, that one,' he told the other two. 'Do you know she swims in the river in the altogether, and plays whooping noises on her radio while she does it? Every full moon. I see her.'

'She's sounding more sensible by the minute to me,' said Mrs Featherstone.

But when Brian got home to Brenda he was very concerned. 'They're talking about throwing it back,' he said, 'they're all barmy.'

'Well, we can put a stop to that,' said Brenda, who had just been turned down for the cleaning job with Hilda Antrobus and was feeling a real sense of proletarian injustice (so much for the bloody people's bloody lottery).

'How do you mean?'

'Ring the papers,' said Brenda, who read only the tabloids and therefore had a somewhat simplified and excessively optimistic view of the power of the press. 'Then it'll all be out in the open and everything will have to be sorted out fairly.'

Brian enjoyed ˉringing the newspaper. He did it from the public phone box near the church, as he wanted to be an anonymous tipster, although when they asked his name he quite forgot and gave it anyway. It was nice to feel important, though. No-one had ever treated Brian as though he was important before. The girl on the desk at the *Broomhill Gazette* promised to pass the information about Boadicea's crown on to one of their journalists, and he put the phone down with a smug smile, preparing to stride home and be regaled with tea, a modern hero. At the *Gazette* office the girl put Brian's message on the pile for crank calls and carried on doing her nails. Pretty quickly it was obscured by a call from a woman who had seen a llama drinking at a pub.

But danger can lurk in the most banal of situations, on the most usual of days, and as he turned to push open the door of the phone booth, Brian froze. There was a creature outside and it was looking in at him.

The llama, who was called Eric, was blessed with rather a supercilious face, particularly when eating dahlias, and he was eating dahlias now. He had found them in those nice tubs outside the pub, and had wandered off, munching. He was, in truth, feeling a little peculiar, having finished off some brown frothy stuff he had found in a few abandoned glasses on a wooden table, and he was having trouble focusing on Brian. He pushed his face against the glass and tried to raise his eyebrows and blow bubbles.

Brian eyed Eric nervously. A llama, he thought, proud of his extensive knowledge (he had seen the TV programme with that nice Michael Palin in Patagonia), but an insane llama, clearly. It was frothing at the mouth. What was it doing here? What did it want? Why was it wearing a collar saying 'Eric'? He searched frantically in his mind for all he knew about llamas, but in fact there wasn't very much in there, and it did not give him the information he required – were llamas flesh eaters, and, if so, how could he tell if this one was hungry? Holding Eric's gaze with his own he felt for the telephone again with trembling hands, dialled 999 and got put through to Broomhill police station, where Roger was desk sergeant for the day.

'A llama, sir. And where might you be phoning from?'

'I'm in a phone box,' said Brian, keeping his wary gaze on Eric, 'and I have to tell you, officer, this is a particularly suspicious-looking llama.'

'Suspicious-looking, you say,' said Roger, imbuing his voice with just a subtle hint of irony. Subtlety was not Roger's strong point, and his voice was about as ironic as a big piece of iron. 'In what way does he look suspicious? Does he seem to be trying to hot-wire your car?'

'Don't be so bloody ridiculous,' said Brian furiously, 'whoever heard of a car being hot-wired by a llama?'

'Well, you wouldn't would you, sir,' said Roger happily, enjoying his revenge more and more by the minute. All the scam calls, all the Morris Minor incidents, those blasted moose in Thetford . . . 'Llama don't dob, you see. You never hear of a llama supergrass.'

'Don't dob? What the hell is dob? For God's sake. He's staring at me,' said Brian, becoming ever so slightly frantic now that he sensed he was not being taken seriously. 'He has wild staring eyes and a lurch to the left.' Eric, sensing excitement, rolled his eyes a little, and pressed his lips harder against the glass.

'And would he be called Nobby, by any chance, or perhaps Sid?'

'I don't know what he's bloody well called,' shouted Brian in a panic, 'you've got to save me. I can't get away.'

'Ahem,' said Roger's sergeant at his shoulder, 'and would this be a distressed member of the public on the telephone?'

'It's another of those hoax calls,' said Roger smugly, 'they keep ringing, sir. They keep saying they've seen a llama.'

'And would this llama by any chance match the description of the llama on this memo on your desk, the one answering to the name of Eric that has escaped from the pets corner at Linton Zoo?' He waved a piece of paper at Roger: 'This memo that is sitting in your out tray – implying that it has, at some point, journeyed there from your in tray, via the gap between your *ears*!'

Roger gulped.

At the telephone booth Eric thought Brian looked fun. He

liked the way his eyes rolled. Eric smiled a llama smile, and belched a llama belch.

'Oh my God!' shouted Brian. 'I think he's going to eat me . . .'

Although the hide had been a great deal of fun to build it was, in the end, absolutely not necessary for catching the llama. In fact the llama drama began, as far as Belinda could see, with the police constable named Roger. The one with the grim mouth and rather wildly staring eyes. Roger was stressed and angry. Multiple past encounters with moose, Morris Minors, circuses and other assorted tomfoolery had rendered him thus – angry, in particular, with anything that seemed even the teeniest weeniest bit odd. Morris Minors were odd. They made a funny noise and had wooden bits where other cars have the decency to have chrome. Morris Minor drivers were odd. They were appallingly cheerful, frustratingly law-abiding and infuriatingly nice. Moose were odd. They pulled the bumpers off panda cars. (Panda. There you are again, he had told his sergeant. Odd.) Worst of all, they looked at you in that suspicious, mooseish way. Where were the people called Nobby and Sid with the black masks, the striped shirts, and the bags marked 'swag' that had been in the police training video?

It did not enhance the quality of Roger's day when he was told to proceed out of Great Barking in a northerly direction along the Parvum Magna road in pursuit of a llama called Eric.

'Why Eric?' he demanded of his sergeant furiously. 'Why can't it have a llama sort of name?' A llama called Eric definitely fell into the category of odd, and Roger knew that he would end up coming off worst. Experience had taught him this, and he was already beginning to wonder if he was suited to the surreal quality of life in the East Anglian force.

'What name would you suggest?' asked the sergeant icily. He had had some trouble with Roger, who was being circulated between police forces like impossible patients are between doctors, having six months with each. He carried with him a reputation for attracting trouble, particularly the kind of trouble that makes the funny page in the local press.

Once the sergeant had found out that he was being allocated Roger, the news about the llama really had come as no surprise. 'Howard, perhaps, or Sebastian?'

'Something stupid,' glowered Roger unaccountably, 'like Big Ears or Rover,' and with that he stormed out to his waiting panda and kicked it soundly on the wheel hub.

Lady Angela Ormondroyd, grande dame of Parvum Magna, paid her taxes. Well technically she didn't, her husband George paid them, but she was rich and so that was the same thing. Moreover, she was pregnant, and pregnancy made her grouchy – more grouchy, that is, than she usually was, so she gave Roger's sergeant a substantial piece of her mind when she found Eric eating her begonias.

'There is a llama in my garden, officer,' she informed him imperiously, 'and the forces of law and order are doing nothing. Nothing! I am a pregnant woman – who knows what kind of strange diseases these beasts carry. They come from Peru, you know.'

'I know,' said the sergeant, riled at the implication that he was a mere pen-pusher who observed, read and knew nothing. He watched David Attenborough every time he was on TV. 'I know where they come from. What worries me is where this one's going. But fear not, madam, the intrepid forces of the law are on their way.' Bloody aristocracy, he thought, for he had a lot in common with Brian Baggins beneath his uniformed exterior . . . but better mobilize a few more units. Wasn't her husband on the Police Complaints Committee?

Hugh and Felix were cycling without their hands on the bars down the Parvum Magna road, having sneaked away from Belinda while she was finishing her Lily chores. The Lily chores had taken up rather more time than usual due to Lily's unfortunate acquisition of a pot of green finger paint, which she had liberally applied to all Serendipity's red dahlias. Serendipity had only red dahlias – the peacocks, apparently, found yellow and orange delicious, mauve and crimson palatable, but red completely disgusting.

'I bet you've never unicycled,' said Felix, pulling up.

'Have you?' Hugh stopped beside him.

'No,' said Felix. 'Where's Ignatius?'

'He doesn't like cycling,' said Hugh, 'although he's brilliant on horseback.'

'What, on his own?' Felix wondered if Ignatius wore a hat, and how he held the reins.

'No stupid. He's an iguana. How could he ride a horse? Anyway, I left him at your house.'

Felix was surprised. 'On his own?'

'Belinda,' said Hugh a little uneasily, 'said she'd look after him.'

'Is she going to be your second girlfriend?' Felix longed to have just one, although you couldn't be envious of someone who went out with your own sister. Yuk.

'She might.' Hugh was coming round to the idea. The break-up with Lucy, who had made the fatal mistake of coveting his cockroach, had faded into distant memory. (She was, in any case, now passionate about a vet's son in the year above him, and he really didn't care, although he had surprised a suspiciously wistful look on Ignatius's face from time to time.) In the distance they could hear the wail of a siren.

'It's probably the drugs,' said Felix, impressed. 'They've probably come for the cannabis.'

Hugh looked dubious. The siren came closer. 'Why would they want the cannabis?'

'Well, they probably saw it on *News East* and worked out where it was.'

Hugh frowned. 'It wouldn't have been on *News East* if it was secret, surely.'

'I don't know,' said Felix, 'there could have been a leak.'

Hugh was intrigued. 'If that's so, everyone will be after it. There could be gangs of Colombian drug dealers infiltrating Parvum Magna even as we speak. Maybe Mr Baggins is a plant.'

'How could he be a plant?'

'Oh, don't be daft,' said Hugh. 'Still, he could be the leek, I suppose.'

Felix was not quite used to Hugh yet. 'If that's where they're going, we could go and see.'

Hugh thought they should, for the sake of press freedom.

'What pet would you like next?' asked Felix, as they rode.

Hugh pulled up by the cannabis field with a flourish to consider this. 'A tarantula,' he said eventually, 'a giant red-kneed one.'

Felix was impressed. 'Miranda would love that. She's even afraid of bats.'

'Huh.'

'Yeah.' Both boys made that particular noise which demonstrates so well the incredible scorn and derision due to teenage girls who fear bats.

The siren was now clearly on their road, approaching from Bumpstaple.

'I wonder what . . .' began Felix, and then there was a clatter of hooves, and something large and white cantered past them and headed towards Parvum Magna.

'It's a push-me-pull-you,' said Felix, 'like in *Dr Dolittle*!'

'No it's not,' said Hugh in some excitement, 'it's our llama.'

The llama moved up to a gallop, then they saw it leap over a hedge and head towards St Alupent's church. A moment later a police panda car came tearing around the bend behind them and screeched to a halt.

'Tango Victor X-Ray calling base we need backup, repeat, we need backup,' Roger was shouting into his radio. His partner, a WPC called Cordelia, wound the window down.

'Have you two boys seen a llama going this way?'

'I . . .' began Felix, but Hugh shouldered him aside, determined that his acting experience would not have been for nothing, even if it did mean he got mobbed whenever he stood outside Tammy Girl eating a burger and chips.

'What colour llama?' If Hugh had been any cooler he would have frozen. Unfortunately, TV production companies do like to encourage children to overact, on the basis that this must surely make them more endearing to viewers. But Hugh overacting at ten as Just William on TV was quite different to Hugh at fourteen on a bike, in a country lane where a deadly llama was known to be at large. The one was endearing, the other suspicious. Roger who, despite his many faults was as suspicious a man as any Chief Constable could ever hope to find on the force, got out of the car and subjected Hugh to a gimlet look.

'If you withhold information from a police officer in pursuit of his duties,' he said darkly, 'you could be arrested for obstructing the police in their inquiries.'

Hugh ignored Roger, and gave the WPC a melting look. 'If I see a llama,' he said, 'of any colour, I'll be sure to tell you.'

Cordelia melted appropriately, 'a white llama would be of particular interest,' she told him, 'answering to the name of Eric.'

'I'll look out for him,' said Hugh, beaming.

Roger narrowed his eyes. There was something vaguely familiar about this boy. On the other hand, all boys of this age had that same look. In Roger's view the Baroness of Vulgaria had had the right idea in *Chitty Chitty Bang Bang*. A Childcatcher with a big nose and a horse-drawn cage, that's what was needed here. 'You just do that,' he said, using level two of implied menace as detailed in the 'Handbook for Beat Officers' he carried everywhere, – 'son.' He got back into the car with extreme dignity, spoiling the effect by knocking off his hat on the way in. (He was a tall man who had never quite come to terms with his height.)

Cordelia said nothing, but in the distance they could hear several more sirens. She looked at him.

'What?' he demanded. 'What?'

'I didn't say anything,' she said. 'Which way?'

'Forwards,' said Roger tightly, and they pulled away.

Hugh waited till they were round the bend and out of sight. 'Quick,' he said, 'head Eric off at the pass,' and he and Felix hauled their bicycles over the ditch at the side of the road and proceeded to use them for what mountain bikes are best at, scrambling over the Greatbottom meadows towards the mud spring.

Belinda was thoroughly annoyed to discover that Hugh and Felix had gone on a cycle ride without her. The frustration of being nearly his girlfriend, but not quite girlfriend enough for her to display him to her friends, was becoming too much. She put on one of Miranda's best floaty dresses (safe in the knowledge that Miranda now preferred to spend her time in right-on green trousers and the sort of lace-up metal-toed ankle boots that got riot police a bad name), adjusted her new bra (size AAA cup, but it was a bra in principle, and that was what counted, despite the face the fitting woman had pulled at her mother), arranged Ignatius on her shoulder as elegantly as she could (Vivienne Westwood would almost certainly have been interested), and arranged herself gracefully beside the mud spring, where she had a reasonable vantage point over the road. Thus she was well placed to view the unfolding llama drama. She heard the sirens first, and at that point she moved away from the spring to take up a better position up in the oak tree. From there she could see all the three roads that met at the centre of Parvum Magna.

She saw the llama first, as it leapt impressively over a hedge and legged it with surprising grace in her direction. Then she saw police cars. There were two on the Bumpstaple road, one on the Barking Road and three coming out from Broomhill. All had sirens wailing. In the distance, too, she could see Hugh and Felix cycling like mad things over the field.

Belinda was a bright girl: she had a Tolkien-inspired sense of self-sacrifice and bravery, with just a hint of the Mills and Boon. If she could stop the llama, which Hugh was so obviously pursuing, then it stood to reason that he would be filled with admiration. He would ask her out at last – possibly on the spot. Maybe even on one knee. She was already seeing several alternative romantic scenarios in her head, and sorting them into order of preference, as she scrambled down from the tree and rushed out to meet the llama. She had no real idea how you stopped a llama, but as long as Hugh saw her try, that was what counted, and she and the llama *were* old friends.

She was thus poorly placed to witness the unhappy spectacle of six police cars with sirens so loud that they could not hear one another, all braking a little too late, but she heard the crashing noise, and she even heard someone shouting 'Roger! Not you again!'

The llama liked the look of Belinda, and he stopped. She was not shrieking and wailing, she wasn't running after him, and she definitely wasn't a vicuña. (He did not like vicuña.)

243

Perhaps she would have some radishes. Those begonias had given him indigestion.

Hugh and Felix, hurtling up behind, were impressed, although they did not show it – Felix because it is not cool to be impressed by a sister, and Hugh because he knew from earlier experience what happened when you were visibly impressed by girls. Before you knew it, they had stolen the loyalty of your iguana. He mustered a coolly unimpressed expression.

Belinda was rather taken by the llama – almost as taken as she was by Hugh, as it happened. As they approached she put a protective arm over its neck.

'What's going on?' she demanded.

'Police,' said Felix, enjoying a conspiracy with a noble cause. 'We've got to hide him.'

'Hide him? Where on earth can we hide a llama? He's not a Spitfire pilot the Germans have just shot down, you know, he won't hide in a barn under a heap of straw or pretend to be a local farm worker who never speaks.' Belinda glared at Hugh. She looked, he thought, rather splendid in defiance.

'They're not going to notice much for a while,' he said, indicating the direction of the junction where the loud and not terribly measured tones of police officers arguing wildly about who was going to explain this to the sergeant could be heard carrying musically on the summer air.

'I suppose we could put him in our garden,' said Felix, 'they'll never see him over the hedge.'

'What will your mother say?' asked Hugh, whose own mother had already told him she would embarrass him unspeakably if he brought so much as one more unsolicited animal home. Since he thought his mother was unspeakably embarrassing already (fancy kissing him at prize day) such threats had to be taken seriously.

'She's pregnant,' said Belinda; 'it makes her funny. We'll tell her he's sad and homeless and she'll love him. She cries when they advertise nappies.'

'She cries when they advertise engine oil,' said Felix.

Hugh was dubious. 'When my aunt was pregnant,' he said, 'she got all funny. I offered her the most perfectly sensible advice about giving birth in a field. That's what they do in African villages, and then they carry on gathering the crop in too. But she just wouldn't listen. I couldn't even get her to squat down in the house.'

'It might not come with us,' said Felix, 'we can hardly carry it.'

'I bet it would come if we called it by name,' said Belinda.

'What do you mean?'

'I think you'll find,' said Belinda, 'he's named Eric.'

'How on earth do you know that?'

'It says so on his collar,' said Belinda, with coquettish accuracy, and Hugh was impressed.

'Oh,' said Felix, 'he must be somebody's, then.'

'Course he is,' said Hugh, 'you don't get spontaneous llama in Suffolk, you know. Or did you think they lived in burrows on the riverbank?'

Felix glared.

'Come on, Eric,' said Belinda, and as Eric followed them meekly down towards Peacocks' Barn, Hugh was even more impressed, and Belinda glowed.

'Mother,' said Serendipity into the telephone, using her crossest voice, which was unfortunately not very different from her usual voice, except that it squeaked more, 'what the hell is this in my garden?'

'Let me guess,' said Penelope happily. 'Is it green? Does it grow in the ground? You'll have to give me another clue.'

'Of course it isn't bloody green. It's a llama.'

'Why is there a llama in your garden, darling?'

'Mother,' said Serendipity through gritted teeth, 'that's what I'm asking you.'

'Really, Serendipity, just because there's a llama in your garden doesn't mean you have to blame me.'

'Don't use your hurt tones with me, Mother.' Serendipity was exasperated. 'I've got some of your genes, remember? Felix told me you thought animal therapy would help Lily, so I put two and two together. Anyway, you are the only person I know who would put a llama in my garden. You release lobsters into the wild and liberate council round-abouts.'

Penelope sniffed. 'You can think what you like, but it

wasn't me. I wish it had been, it's an excellent idea. What are you going to call it?'

'Call it? I'm not going to call it anything. It's not my bloody llama.'

'You shouldn't swear, darling, Lily might hear.'

'Lily won't hear,' said Serendipity, 'because Lily is in the garden communing with the llama.'

'Goodness, darling, don't they spit when they get cross?'

'Now there's an idea,' said Serendipity. Putting the phone down she rushed out to make certain that Lily was not about to be spat on, but Lily and the llama appeared to be in a state of considerable mutual admiration.

'Sheep, Mummy,' said Lily when she saw her. 'Big sheep.'

The llama chomped loudly and ominously. There was something reassuringly familiar about the sound. 'You're my ghostly cow,' Serendipity told it, suddenly feeling oddly cheered by this. 'At least this means I didn't imagine you.'

Hilda Antrobus had heard none of the fuss. Not even the repeated arrival of breakdown trucks followed by their departure towing the dented remains of police panda cars disturbed her. (Perhaps, Hugh had remarked to Roger when he had gone for a look at the mess, they ought to be called llama cars, thus confirming Roger's view that having red hair and freckles ought to be a criminal offence.) Hilda was not disturbed because she was interviewing prospective cleaners, and she was not impressed by what she had seen so far. The familiarity of the women! Hilda, indeed. She had never called any of her employers by their Christian name. That woman from the village had even turned up in rollers. And as for that man. Whoever heard of a male Mrs Mop? 'Haven't you heard of equal opportunities, dear?' asked Chicken Sid genially, looking up from the *Sun* crossword as she grumbled about the poverty of applications from decent cleaners.

Hilda glowered. 'I only want a woman for a few hours. And you can put that paper down, Sidney Antrobus, it's all about bosoms. We read the quality press now.'

Sid glared at the artfully arranged copies of *Hello* on the coffee table. 'I think you're getting above yourself, Hilda. You always said that the day you couldn't clean your own skirting boards would be the day you were carried off in a box.'

Hilda put her nose in the air. 'We have a responsibility to help those less fortunate than ourselves,' she said haughtily.

Sidney was dubious. 'Strikes me,' he said, 'we're turning into the sort of people we always used to look down on,' and he had skulked off into the garden before Hilda could think of a suitable reply. She watched him as he pottered off down to the garden shed, ran a thoughtful finger along the wooden skirting, and sighed. It was confusing, all this money. She was one of them now. They both were. Sidney would just have to see it. Resolutely she found the Yellow Pages and looked up 'Domestic Services'. She'd better find someone quickly – if this lot in the village came into money, as they seemed to think they should, then they might snap up all the available staff and there would be no-one left for her. Typical, really, that the minute she and Sidney came by some easy money, everyone around them came by some too. Unjust, that's what it was.

'Llama,' said Hugh, 'make wonderful pets.'

'We are absolutely not keeping it,' said Serendipity, as firmly as she felt, which was in fact as firm as a very firm thing indeed. 'There is no *room* for a llama in our lives. It's too big and it's too hairy and it's too greedy and it chomps. And I've got a sore throat. Since you arrived here, Hugh, fond though we all are of you and your uncle, we have developed a lobster and an iguana. I'm blowed if I'm going to add a llama to that list. Not even in the garden. And in any case, as I understand it, it's a hot llama.'

Eric the llama looked wounded. It was his usual look, as he was not actually a very expressive llama. If there had been a Royal Shakespeare Company for llamas Eric could not even have landed the part of chief tree in Dunsinane forest, not even if he had stood motionless for a week with an oak branch glued to his head.

'Look,' said Belinda, seizing the moment with pathos, 'he looks really sad.'

'I don't care if he's in the grip of psychotic depression,'

247

said Serendipity, 'he's not staying in my – ow! Lily! Lily, get off me. Felix, I hope you didn't put her up to biting me, I thought she'd stopped all that.'

Felix had the grace to look guilty. 'No, of course not, but she's sad. You know she loves animals.' Lily had gone slightly further than in rehearsal, but then, that was Lily for you, always going to extremes.

Serendipity folded her arms and looked levelly into their artless faces. 'If this is all about me buying an iguana,' she said, 'then let me just say that not since 1869 when Eastern and Oriental Railways built their first track out of wood, only to have it entirely consumed by ants before a single train could run, has so much effort been so pointlessly expended. Just because Lily is in love with a llama, it does not follow that I will buy her a reptile. We are not reptile people. We are small and undoglike dog people. We might even, at a pinch, a very very tight pinch, be temporary llama sort of people – but I draw the line at iguanas.'

Did I just give in to the llama, she thought? Hugh, Felix and Belinda were being grateful. She must have done.

Clive was not impressed when he got home, after a more-than-usually fraught surgery during which two parents threatened to sue him for suggesting that their children didn't have head lice, and another two threatened to sue him for suggesting that they did. An Englishman's home, though, is meant to have that medieval, fortressy feel to it in times of adversity. It is not meant to have strange zoo animals skulking amongst its dahlias.

'Hello,' he said to Eric, icily, 'do I know you?'

Eric, wisely, said nothing, although Hugh thought he tutted a bit. 'And you lot can stop sidling about,' added Clive. 'One thing doctors learn to excel at when they're still medical students is sidling. We sidle onto ward rounds, we sidle off them again, we sidle out of lectures and into tutorials. Sidling is one of the hidden arts of the medical brotherhood. You can't catch me out by sidling – it would take you years to be as good at it as me.'

Belinda rolled her eyes. 'He often gets stressed when he's on call,' she told Hugh.

'I know,' said Hugh sympathetically, 'my dad's the same when he gets home and finds a lot of carrier bags in the hall.'

'Stressed? I am not stressed. Why would I be stressed?' Clive strode past them to the house, muttering, 'I am not even going to ask . . .'

'Hello,' said Serendipity. 'Bad day?'

Clive enveloped his wife and her mother in a dark glance which also covered Leonardo as he sat between them on the table. 'Why do you ask?'

Serendipity raised her eyebrows as high as they would go and looked at Clive from beneath them. 'Well, put it this way, I wouldn't carry any garden implements around while you've got that face on, or someone might mistake you for the Grim Reaper and nail you to a cathedral door.'

'Ha ha. Very funny. OK. Yes. I have had a bad day. It was a bad day even before I found a zoo in my back garden.'

'It's not a zoo, Clive, dear,' said Penelope, smiling at Belinda, Hugh and Felix as they sidled sheepishly into the kitchen, 'it's a llama. Only a temporary one.'

'Oh is that all? I ask, you understand, to make sure there are no other furry surprises awaiting my arrival elsewhere in the house. A parrot, perhaps, or a sea lion, or a giant man-eating wood louse?'

'Now, Clive, don't exaggerate. Although I must say, a parrot sounds an excellent— Darling, don't kick me, I am your mother.'

Clive took a deep breath. 'He's not staying. He's trouble.'

'He's no trouble at all,' said Belinda indignantly, 'you just don't like animals.'

'Yes I do . . .'

'No you don't, you said goldfish would be too noisy.'

'Much good it did me,' said Clive, 'I'm being crowded out of my own home by a dog that barks all morning, an iguana that glares all evening, and now a llama that snores all night.'

'Well, if you throw him out he'll go to the pound,' said Belinda, distraught, 'and he'll probably be fed on dog food and get BSE. And he's probably from some dreadful llama farm where they're fattening him up with terrible drugs so they can make him into steaks for the barbecue.'

'Da! dadadadadadadad!' Lily hurtled through the kitchen and flung herself adoringly at Clive's legs. He steadied himself against a wall and picked her up. 'Hi Lily,' he said affectionately, rubbing her hair.

'Dadadadad . . . Llama,' said Lily, with huge pride, and hugged him blissfully. Penelope grinned.

'All right,' said Clive. 'He can stay for a few days. Just till you find out where he's from. Then we'll discuss it again.'

'You won't regret it,' said Belinda, hugging him. 'He'll be really pleased.'

'He doesn't look pleased,' said Clive, looking out of the window at Eric, who wandered over and peered in, 'he looks snooty.'

'He's genetically snooty,' said Hugh, 'he can't help it. He comes from the Andes, you know, so he expects to be above everyone else. Look, I think he wants to come in.'

'If you give that llama an inch,' said Clive, 'he'll have our bedroom and we'll be in the shed. I can tell.'

The following morning, when Hugh had gone off for the day for a summer granny-frightening, and Belinda was mourning the fact that she still was not his official girlfriend, the llama was still in the garden, and Serendipity still had a sore throat. Now, though, she also had the full complement of other viral features to match. She contemplated the llama though her kitchen window. 'It's very sweet,' she said to Lily, 'but you do know it can't stay here for long.'

'Lily sheep,' said Lily.

'I've decided I think it's interesting,' said Clive, shovelling in muesli with Alpine enthusiasm, 'a useful addition to our extended family.'

'Oh, be serious,' said Serendipity crossly. 'You don't have to be so relentlessly funny.'

'Oh, I do,' said Clive, 'I'm a doctor,' and he was gone before you could say Paul Daniels.

'Clive! You forgot . . .' called Serendipity, but it was too late.

'Good morning, how are you?' Carol was taking the morning air, trying to nerve herself for her imminent appointment at the surgery. Blood test results, to see if she was in basic working order. You can't expect Neil to understand, she told herself fiercely, when he doesn't have absolutely all the facts. He doesn't know I was ever pregnant.

Serendipity wasn't pleased to see her. She sneezed miserably, her guilt at what she was meant to be telling Carol right now this minute adding to the pressure in her sinuses. 'I feel as though my head is full of wood shavings and forty thousand champagne corks have been forced up my nose,' she said, 'and I've acquired a llama I never asked for. Don't let me give it to you.'

'I wouldn't,' said Carol, 'I don't want a llama.'

'I meant the cold,' said Serendipity grimly. Ever since Carol came back, she thought now, things have been very difficult around here. She felt unfairly irritated with Carol. 'It's a Suffolk cold – I expect I got it out of the river with the lobster. Or perhaps I got it from Eric. Londoners probably have no immunity.' I should be talking to Carol about Neil, she thought, but I feel too ill. I have to wait until I can take a breath without planning it first.

Carol was slightly annoyed by that 'Londoners' – not because she considered herself a Suffolker, not really. No, it was because Londoner made her sound like someone who bought jellied eel sandwiches off a barrow at lunchtime and then swept chimneys till tea. When asked, she always said that she lived in Highgate Village. Never London. Still, Serendipity was so provincial, she probably wouldn't understand. I'm not going to ask who Eric is, she thought. Aloud, she said, 'Has Lily got it too?'

'Lily never gets anything,' said Serendipity, 'she's got the constitution of an ox. Anyhow, what are you up to?'

'I needed an excuse to get out of the house,' said Carol. 'Every day the post is a nightmare. This morning I've been sent plans for a skating rink which would involve flattening the church and the village hall, plans for a ten-pin bowling alley that also take out the post office, and plans for a polo ground that don't leave much of the village standing at all, apart from Sir George Ormondroyd's tied cottages at the far end.'

'God. Who suggested that?'

'Sir George Ormondroyd,' said Carol.

'My mother wants you to set up a village charity for lobsters,' said Serendipity, 'to help her continue her pointless hobby of saving lobsters from the Hebrides so that they can get caught in Sudbury.'

'Well, at least that does have the advantage of benefiting absolutely no-one,' said Carol. 'Perhaps you and Clive could start a llama sanctuary too.'

But Serendipity was not in an easily-amused-by-llama mood. The llama had turned out to have a penchant for red dahlias, which meant she had no dahlias at all now. And Lily loved the llama with the kind of passion she had hitherto reserved for dolls called Mavis. A future which featured an iguana was, Serendipity felt, looming large. She sneezed again.

'Do you need anything? I mean, have you got to go anywhere?'

'Just to the surgery,' said Serendipity thinking, I'm surprised she let that pass. 'Londoner' sounds like the chimney sweep out of *Mary Poppins* – not like Carol, who gives her address as Highgate Village. Ironic really, after all that talk about the stifling nature of villages which preceded her departure so many years ago. 'I'll probably go in a minute. There's no point staying to guard my dahlias now – there are none left.'

'They'll grow again,' said Carol comfortingly, but Serendipity looked sympathetically superior.

'I can tell you've been in London. You've forgotten the importance of dahlias in places like Parvum Magna.'

Carol was annoyed again. Why should Serendipity claim unique insight into country living? Hadn't she grown up here too?

'We have gardens in Highgate too, you know,' she said, a little haughtily, but Serendipity just smiled. She always did that when I was annoyed with her, thought Carol crossly, acted as though she'd been on a Relate course on deflecting negative emotion before she was six. She took a grip on herself. This was childish.

'I'm surprised you need to go out, though. I thought your doctor came to you.' Not that he really is yours, because he was mine first. Stop it, Carol, stop getting annoyed with her. She's your friend. Neil is the cause of your bad mood.

'Clive's not my doctor,' said Serendipity, thinking, don't take it out on Carol, just because you feel guilty that you can't face telling her, 'I couldn't handle that. Imagine having a breast check done by your own husband. Or a smear. Ugh.' She wondered why Carol had registered at the surgery, but could not ask as she shouldn't really know. It was awkward being a doctor's wife sometimes – things you might know about people anyway had to be kept secret in case you only knew them because you were married to the man who had to know.

Carol grinned suddenly. 'Surely he could just do it as part of the normal run of things,' she said, 'you know, while he was in the area.'

'Oh, don't. Anyhow, I was going to drop something off, that's all. Clive forgot it, and it has to be in by ten when the samples go off to the lab.'

'Oh. D'you want me to take it? I'm going in there anyway. I've – er – got to get a repeat prescription.'

'Well, OK, if you don't mind. It's Clive's sperm sample.' Serendipity looked embarrassed.

'Why does – no, I'm sorry. I don't mean to pry.' We may be friends again, thought Carol, but I don't think we're at the talking-about-sperm stage yet. But why on earth should Clive need his sperm checked? Didn't five children convince him he must have billions? Was this one of those well man things, perhaps, like the well woman clinic which she had always thought was a gratuitous excuse for frightening her with talk about hormones?

'That's OK. It's because of his vasectomy,' said Serendipity, assuming knowledge Carol didn't have. 'It just needs dropping off at the desk.'

The bag of what were surely potential fertilizing sperms sat beside Carol on the leather bucket seat of the Mercedes all the way to Broomhill. She could sense it, muttering and rumbling with the sheer overwhelming might of active DNA it so obviously contained. It was teeming with hungry genes. What's more, she told herself, if this was Clive's pre-vasectomy sample then the op must be imminent, so even if she seduced him soon he might be firing blanks by then. Not that she had even thought of seducing him, of course. How could she when he had no visible abdominal muscles, and, in any case, he was the kind of man who wouldn't notice a mating signal unless it interrupted the Paul Daniels magic show by being openly made by the feathered, much sawn-in-half but ever-beautiful Debbie McGee. She'd be just as likely to seduce . . . well, Giles Perry, to pluck one extraordinarily unlikely name out of a hat. Just as likely. She sighed and pulled up in the car park.

The unspeakable had probably occurred to her the moment she saw the bag, but some things are impossible to admit, especially to yourself (Mars Bars, usually, and the inexplicable satisfaction of belching in private). It was still, though, with a sense of unreality that she found herself paying for a plastic syringe in Boots. And even that wasn't straightforward, as she had no cash and therefore had to buy an assortment of other things, both to justify using her credit card and to push the syringe into the realms of afterthought, rather than defining it as the main purchase. Bath oil for Serendipity, a CD for Miranda – not that I'm assuaging any sort of guilt, of course . . . Serendipity clearly doesn't need any more of Clive's little tadpoles swimming up her Fallopian tubes, whereas mine . . . mine are so desperate for the sight of a tadpole with mischief in its heart that they'd consider having sex with a frog. And he was my boyfriend first, and although we didn't sleep together, back then, I would have done if it hadn't been for Cosmo and everything going wrong. Because if it hadn't been for Cosmo I'd be Serendipity and she'd be me and she wouldn't be nearly so smug . . .

Sometimes a bit of resentment, however artificially induced, is enough, and the impossible unspeakable deed becomes just do-able enough to get done. Half the sample would have to go to the surgery, thought Carol in her car, or they'd wonder, but she had to be quick, and if she had to be quick then there wasn't time to think about what she was doing. Lots of babies are conceived in cars. This was no time for moral dilemmas. Sperm don't last, and in any case there was a real risk that if she allowed the ethical part of her cortex to make contact with the bit that wanted a baby she might change her mind.

As Carol wrestled with her conscience and threw it out of the ring, a draught blew in through the doors at the *Broomhill Gazette*, and sent the pile of crank calls flying across the office, where Ned Perkins, Broomhill's roving reporter, began to pick it up. One sheet caught his eye and he stopped to read it . . .

That was why, barely an hour later, when Serendipity returned from her morning walk with Lily, she found a small but insistent posse of journalists exploring the buried treasure story which had reached them courtesy of Brian Baggins's anonymous tip-off. Please God, she thought, don't let them see the llama. I don't feel up to explaining that one today.

The *Broomhill Gazette* didn't get many really juicy stories. Broomhill's only lottery winner so far had been quite appallingly nice, and had resolutely refused to become estranged from his wife or cut off his children without a bean – and their local novelist's toy boy, though twenty years younger than her, was even so sixty-five, and only *Blind Date* could have made entertainment out of that. So the discovery of Boadicea's crown on their patch represented real saleable news, and they had come to interview everyone, apparently on the grounds that drivel attributable to the residents of a village where treasure has been found is inherently far more interesting to the general public than drivel attributable to anyone else. Unfortunately the village had proved relatively quiet this morning, and so far they had only been able to interview one another.

Three of them rushed after Serendipity as she tried to stop Lily from saying 'sheep come too' in that give-away fashion. She closed her garden gate firmly behind the two of them.

'Mrs Rowan! Can we have a word?' they called winsomely.

'Certainly not,' said Serendipity, wondering if Lily's eating something would put them off. Probably not.

Ned Perkin from the 'Broomhill Gazette' was persistent. She had, he was pleased to see, a very large bosom, so the tabloid journalist in him was happy. There was, as it happened, no other sort of journalist in Ned.

'How old is your mummy?' he asked Lily cheerily.

Lily did not let her mother down. 'Lily go wee wee,' she said dramatically, feeling obviously for her knicker elastic.

Ned looked a little nervous. 'She won't, will she?' he asked Serendipity.

'Oh, almost certainly,' said Serendipity happily. 'She does it to ward off strangers.'

Ned thought he might as well grasp the bull by the horns. 'Was it you who found the treasure?' he asked. 'I understand it includes Boadicea's crown. Have you tried it on? Do you believe in reincarnation? Have you heard the story that Boadicea is asleep somewhere beneath the village waiting to return miraculously in our hour of need? What do you think of the rumour that Boadicea was a lesbian?'

'I don't know about you,' said Serendipity, 'but my hour of need is right now, and if Boadicea can miraculously bring a lavatory she can satisfy it. Otherwise I need the bathroom.'

The man from the *Sun* was dubious. He knew about pregnant women. They could be peculiar. 'We could talk through the bathroom door,' he offered, 'we've done that before.'

'You could get stuffed,' said Serendipity pleasantly, 'just as easily. I expect you've done that before too.' I'm just not in the mood for this, she thought.

'We'll just wait here, then,' said Ned, frowning stubbornly.

'If you do,' said Serendipity, 'I'll set my dog on you.' She wondered whether, if she did so, they would realize he was a dog, or just mistake him for some sort of salivating bath mat.

'Perhaps,' said the intrepid man from the *Sun*, elbowing Ned aside tabloidishly, 'I could arrange an interview later.' He winked. 'It'd make you famous. There might be something in it for you.'

Serendipity thought that would be something she almost certainly would not want, especially as she was sure that whatever she said in her interview would bear no discernible resemblance to anything that was subsequently printed, and they would certainly get her age wrong, too.

'No,' she said, adding, with a flash of inspiration, 'and you'd better watch out. The peacocks are coming.'

'Oh?' Ned was unsure of his ground.

'Well, they can be very nasty with strangers. Big claws, you see. And anyway, it's Alice Bollivant you need to talk to. She's the one who wanted to wear the crown.'

Well, she'll enjoy the attention, thought Serendipity defensively as she watched them depart like bloodhounds for the Bollivants' house.

'Very wise,' said Felix, appearing with the borrowed iguana when they had gone.

Serendipity sighed. 'Do you know, Felix, with that creature on your shoulder you almost look as though you have two heads. It's really quite unnerving.'

'I could turn him backwards,' said Felix brightly, 'if it would help.'

'I have to say,' said Serendipity, 'I don't think looking at an iguana's bottom when I speak to you has any particular merit either.'

'Thank you for helping hide our llama, by the way,' said Felix, feeling rather fond of his mother all of a sudden. It would be awful if she went off to Everest without him. 'Hugh thinks you've got a magical touch with camelids – and with iguanas, too.'

I never saw myself as a camelid and iguana sort of woman, thought Serendipity, after he had disappeared upstairs to store Ignatius before school, but then I always saw myself waving a Union Jack on the top of a mountain or orbiting the earth in a big silver suit, and I was wrong about that too. The thought no longer depressed her, though. Actually, she thought, even if I had the money, I don't think I'd want to go. Nearly having it has made me realize that Everest isn't my personal Everest any more. Maybe I don't need one.

Chapter Eleven

Alice was on the one o'clock *News East* spot, looking like an extra from *Dynasty* and affecting to be casually pruning her roses, although roses in villages are never casually pruned – nothing about village flowers is ever casual. There are far too many envious eyes giving your flowerbeds marks out of ten, and judging you slyly by the quality of the arrangements you bring into church when it is your month. (January was Serendipity's month. That way no-one could sneer when her flowers came from the Scillies via Sainsbury's.) 'Some local children,' Alice was saying, making them sound like shoe-less street urchins, 'found the crown. It is not here now – it is currently being examined in Cambridge.'

'That's really going to stir everyone up,' said Clive, home for a sandwich as Alice extolled the incredible nature of the village find, the beast-swallowing reputation of the mud spring, and the unfortunately titillating story of what upset Queen Boudicca in the first place. 'The next thing you know Hollywood will be making "Boadicea, the Legend" and Alice will be auditioning for the starring role.'

'Hector would love that,' said Serendipity, unloading the laundry basket onto the table and fantasizing mildly about Alice, wearing a bronze bikini top and a pair of bearskin knickers, ravaging Hector within an inch of his life in a spiked chariot parked on the would-be Broomhill bypass. 'Oh, my God, Clive, that's Miranda!'

The news had moved to the Broomhill bypass itself, where a small and motley band of protesting types, ac-companied by one with clean blond hair, were standing, arms linked, for the cameras. 'Look – that's the one Miranda thought was handsome. God, he's hairy!'

The protest, reported the programme with some delight, was continuing. The sheriff had arrived, and had asked the protesters to leave. They had refused. A dutiful camera shot then followed of the sheriff (who, to Belinda's disappointment, did not wear a tin-plate star and a Stetson) saying politely, 'Would you mind leaving now?' And the hairy type who had caught Miranda's eye saying, 'No, sorry, mate.'

'That was all staged,' said Serendipity, tearful now, 'to look civilized. Do you think they'll go in with tear gas?'

'Of course not,' said Clive. 'It's all very polite and courteous, you know, everyone knows what's expected of them. It'll be weeks before they move them out, but it will all be very jolly when they do.'

'How can you know that? There might be dozens of riot police with truncheons and CS gas just off camera.'

'Dozens? This is Suffolk.'

'OK, a couple, then.'

'It's not like that, honestly. The police and the protesters are the best of friends. They play rummy every evening. Anyhow, didn't you see Miranda's hair? It's not like that to win the admiration of the tunnel-dweller. Trust me – I've been down there every day.'

'Have you? Oh Clive, you are nice.'

'You make me sound like a biscuit. But it's terribly civilized. Lots of, "do you mind if we drag you out of your tunnel now?" and "oh, all right, if you must". So don't worry.'

'Easily said,' said Serendipity, guilty that she had not been there, but secretly a little unnerved at the prospect. A thought occurred to her. 'Did you see Carol in surgery?'

'She saw John Potter,' said Clive, and Serendipity heaved an inner sigh of relief. So Carol's smear was not her husband's province. There had been just that little fear, that echo of ancient jealousy. Carol had been oddly unforgiving again this morning. Mind you, she thought, I deserve it. I haven't told her what I have to tell her about Neil. And I owe her one, anyway, for having Clive. If only I felt more up to things, she thought – but even though she was now loaded with Lemsip she felt every bit as fluey, just more lemony.

'Did you drop off my sample?' Clive's voice broke into her thoughts. 'I left it.'

'Carol dropped it off,' said Serendipity. 'She was going in anyway, and I feel rough.'

'Carol dropped off my sample? Oh Ren.'

'What? Why does that matter?'

'That's just gross,' said Clive.

Serendipity stared. 'I'll never,' she said, 'understand the mentality of doctors.'

Hilda Antrobus had watched Alice on the news too, watched her accent carefully. It could be useful, a nice clipped accent like that. She tried a few experimental vowels.

Hilda had finally given up on the Jobcentre and was pursuing the 'qualified' option. It was now clear to her that the sort of person capable of the standards she required would probably be working as a housekeeper to the gentry. Not that she was becoming a snob, of course – but it would be ridiculous if she, a lottery winner, had to tolerate a house less sparkling than those inhabited by all those relatively impoverished but snobby women for whom she had once cleaned.

The agency, pleasingly titled Butlers, Footmen, Housemaids Inc., sent a very smarmy chap round to take her details. He wore a three-piece tweed suit and drove an old Jaguar. Yes, he had class, and Hilda wanted some of it. Not snooty sort of class, of course. Not aristocracy-snobbery class – for she and Sidney weren't like that, they were working class and proud of it . . . No, Hilda meant good taste. That's what she meant. So when a couple of applications dropped through the gold-plated letterbox (well, the other had been a bit draughty, so they'd needed a new one, and it had been a bargain) she settled down to read them with a warm glow.

Outside Sid watched mournfully as their trusty old caravan was driven away by a couple who seemed to him to have taken the old Hilda and Sid along with it. It wasn't in keeping, Hilda had said, with the house – and in any case, with their money, they would be able to stay at the Swan at Southwold. They would never again have to queue for the campsite showers.

'But I liked queuing,' said Sid, 'I met a lot of interesting people queuing. And I don't want to stay at the Swan. Our sort of people don't stay there.'

'For goodness sake, Sidney,' said Hilda, 'we're a different sort now. We're wealthy, we can afford to live it up a little, eat well and drink fine wines . . .'

'I don't like fine wines,' said Sid sulkily, 'I like lager and lime. So why you've joined that bloody wine club I can't imagine. You'll be ordering caviare next.'

Hilda said nothing. It was already in the fridge.

'Hi, Ren, it's Carol. I wondered – are you doing anything?'

'Er – just sneezing a lot. Why?'

'I just fancied a chat,' said Carol, thinking, oh God, I am just so venal, how on earth am I going to tell her what I've done? I can't believe I did it. What vile impulse, what unbelievably wicked urge drove me to . . . I must be mad. I know they looked at me strangely at the surgery when I handed in such a small sample. Surely they couldn't have guessed already – what if they've told Clive their suspicions? Doctors' receptionists have all sorts of funny senses denied the rest of us. They can probably spot a recently inseminated woman as easily as the rest of us would spot a lime green rhinoceros with the Queen of Belgium on its back.

'Well, come and have a coffee,' said Serendipity, thinking, Oh God, I'll have to tell her now. I can't kid myself the right opportunity hasn't arisen any more. But what if she doesn't believe me?

Carol seemed rather uneasy, Serendipity thought, unwrapping biscuits that neither of them ought to be eating but both of them felt they needed – but then maybe that's me transferring my feelings because of what I've got to say. 'Where's Neil?' she asked awkwardly. As an opening gambit it was, she thought, about as subtle as Hitler's march on Poland.

'Oh, Neil's in Brussels for two days,' said Carol, 'although to be honest, if he was in orbit around Mars I wouldn't be much interested.'

'Oh dear. Have you had a row?'

Carol sighed, finding the confidences more soothing than telling her best friend what she had done with her husband's sperm sample. Considerably more soothing. 'I think it's worse than that,' she said, 'I don't think we like one another any more. The awful thing is, I'm not at all sure we ever did. I think we were both trophies – it's not his fault, really, I was just as bad. Trophy wife and trophy husband. We'd be all right if all we had to do was sit on a shelf and be admired.' It was the sort of bitter self-criticism that the Chinese political system would love to extract from its dissidents.

'Surely you just feel this way because you've had a row,' said Serendipity, thinking, stop defending him, woman. You need to portray him as a cross between Henry VIII and Ivan the Terrible here.

But Carol sighed. 'It goes far deeper than one row,' she said. 'It goes so deep it goes right to the very bottom of me. The Greatbottom bottom, rather than the Pendragon one, that is.' She managed a weak smile. 'I seem to have discovered myself again, coming back here, as though all these years there's been a veneer on top that wasn't really me. And it was only the veneer that Neil liked. And only the veneer liked him.'

'It sounds serious,' said Serendipity.

'Fairly fundamental,' agreed Carol, thinking, this conversation is going to lead very quickly to that sperm. It's like being in a canoe on the Amazon, when suddenly you realize you're coming to a giant waterfall, and you can't row backwards because you just threw away your oars. You get sucked in, and although you know what's coming miles away, there's nothing you can do but go with the flow.

But she was wrong. Serendipity, wielding an oar of her own, rowed manfully away from the waterfall of sperm without even knowing it was there. She took a deep breath, the sort of breath you need when you have to tell someone something terrible, because you know if you stop in the middle to take another one you might never be able to finish. 'Carol, I have to tell you something,' she said, 'and I don't know how to say it, so I'll just say it, and please don't hate me – but I saw Neil with another woman, doing the kinds of things that you don't do with just a friend.'

Carol stared. It wasn't that Neil being with another woman was such a shock, it was just that she had been so geared towards her own confession that this unexpected pincer attack had left her completely winded. 'What?' she whispered: it was about all she could manage.

'I'm sorry,' said Serendipity, distraught. Please don't let me go into labour right now, she thought, I need to concentrate, and for that I need a non-contracting uterus. 'I know this is terrible – but I couldn't not tell you. It was Neil I saw. He was with a blonde woman in his car in Broomhill. She had her head in his lap and she wasn't asleep.'

Carol was pale, two red patches on her cheeks. She could feel a fine tremor in both of her hands. Was it shock, or was it rage? She wasn't sure. 'Blonde, did you say?'

Serendipity nodded miserably. 'And there's something else I should have told you before. He made a pass at me at dinner.'

There was a brief, drawn silence, then, 'It was a blonde last time,' said Carol, her voice as tight as an E string. She felt icy, but unsurprised, 'and also my friend Louisa.'

Serendipity was horrified. 'You mean he's had affairs before?'

'Oh no,' said Carol, 'it wasn't an affair.'

'Do you mean . . . ?'

'Louisa turned him down,' said Carol, 'so he didn't have an affair with her. She tried to tell me, but I didn't believe her. I lost myself a friend over the whole thing.'

'And the blonde?'

'Oh, she was never a friend,' said Carol, 'more of a working acquaintance.'

'Oh no. Not his secretary?'

'Oh, for heaven's sake, Serendipity,' said Carol, exasperated, 'don't you know what a working girl is?'

Serendipity sensed a trap, guessed the nature of its jaws. 'You mean Neil *paid* her?'

'Well, put it this way,' said Carol, with bland stoicism, 'they called her Mrs Whippy and she didn't sell ice-cream.'

'Oh Carol. Did you . . . does he know you know?'

'Oh yes,' said Carol, 'but he promised it would never happen again, and I somehow put it aside. Our lives in London were . . . well, not like here. We didn't have time for one another, not really, not the way you do. We were very proud of each other, but somehow it was always distant, rushing around, never really talking. Not like you and Clive do. I suppose I thought it was partly my fault, and that since it was just sex, it didn't really matter . . .'

'I expect he said that,' said Serendipity. 'Don't they always?'

'How would you know?' asked Carol, in a flash of bitterness. 'You were never dumped.'

'That's not true,' said Serendipity. 'Cosmo dumped me for you.'

Carol sniffed miserably. 'So he did,' she said, 'so he did.' And that's it, she thought. My marriage just came to the end of the road, because the road fell off the edge of acceptable existence, and I feel . . . strangely unsurprised.

'What are you going to do?'

Carol sighed. 'I think I should stew a while, like good tea. By the time he gets back from Brussels I'll know what to do. I should be nice and strong by then.'

'Carol?'

'What?'

'Well, you don't seem very . . .'

'No, I don't, do I? The thing is, the Parvum Magna version of me was already pretty much at odds with Neil.' I don't know who I am, actually, she thought, but I know who I'm imagining being comforted by. I wonder what Giles is doing right now . . . Mind you, I might be pregnant by Clive. Oh God. Perhaps I'm worse than Neil anyway.

Later, Carol sat at the kitchen table, adjusting her mental spectacles in an attempt to alter her perspective on what Neil was, had done. Unfortunately, the only angle from which he did not look like an enormous vile betrayer was a very distant angle. An angle so distant that even a gargantuan potato cod could have been mistaken for Miss Stow on the Wold. Ten years of marriage, and all that went with it, she thought, down the drain. But what did come with it, exactly, other than a shared sense of our mutual superiority and an original Hockney? Was there ever any real emotion? If I don't know now, now that Neil has just slung it all away, I guess I never will.

I bet Serendipity's marriage isn't this sterile. If only I had married someone like Clive, she thought. But were there, are there, any other men like Clive? Were there ever?

'Sorry for making you jump,' said Hugh, appearing in the doorway and making her jump. 'Mrs Rowan says are you OK and do you need the brandy, or just the sherry?'

Carol suppressed a smile. 'No, tell her things aren't that bad.'

'Good,' said Hugh. 'Has Neil gone?'

'Permanently,' said Carol. 'Unfortunately I've just discovered that I don't like him.'

Hugh nodded wisely. 'I never liked him either,' he said sagely.

'Why?' asked Carol, curious despite her sense of stunned unwantedness.

'He reminded me of my last girlfriend. In the end she was more interested in my cockroach than me.'

'That's exactly what he's like,' said Carol, 'exactly.' Who'd have imagined, she thought, that a fourteen-year-old boy would understand how I feel – but cockroaches, treasure, what's the diference?

'In that case,' said Hugh, shrugging the shrug of the emotionally unwounded, 'he's not worth worrying about.'

'You're so right,' said Carol. 'It's rather odd when you first realize it, that's all.'

'If I were you,' said Hugh, with that peculiar astuteness of which teenagers are occasionally capable, 'I'd ring Uncle Giles. I'm sure he'd understand. Mum told me he's always being walked all over by the wrong sort of women.'

Carol suppressed an unexpected smile, thinking, poor Giles, endlessly ground under stilettos and walked all over. Makes him sound like a pavement. 'I should think the last thing he wants is to be landed with cheering up someone else's reject,' she said wistfully.

'Oh no,' said Hugh, with the sensitive tact of a mating Galapagos turtle (a particularly tactless breed when the hormones are flowing). 'Aunt Tessa says when you're his age there's not so much choice. He told her he wished he'd met someone like you, but the best ones were all taken by thirty. She said that was like Quality Street, and he said if it was, you were the hazelnut in caramel.'

'Oh,' said Carol, much flattered, 'that's my favourite.'

'There you are, then,' said Hugh. 'What was Neil's favourite?'

'He didn't like them,' said Carol, 'which just goes to show.' Perhaps that ought to be part of marriage guidance from now on, she thought, if you don't like the same Quality Street you're doomed. 'But you might be wrong – he might have been talking about someone else.'

'Oh no,' said Hugh, 'I'm always right. My headmaster says that's the most annoying thing about me.'

The idea of ringing Giles echoed in Carol's head as she watched Alice again on the half-past-six local news. Then it grew until there was no more room in her head for anything else. Both Alice and Miranda had been trimmed this time to make way for an article about St Alupent's College and its museum, and that brought Giles right into the forefront of her consciousness. The thought of the way his eyes smiled at her warmed her already. And to think she had once thought him lanky, thought that handsome nose inelegant. It just went to show, really, what a poor judge of men she had been . . .

And when he was there she found that she really was seeing him with different eyes altogether, the sort of eyes the last dodo might have had if he had wandered round a corner in the misty Mauritian rainforest to discover that he was actually the last-but-one dodo, and the other one was a girl with a pert little bunch of tail feathers and a come-and-get-me beak. How could I not have noticed, she wondered, that I fancied him this much? But perhaps I did notice, and was just very good at ignoring it.

Giles was delighted to hear from Carol; even more so to be asked to dinner. He was a little surprised, on arrival, to find that the starter was Carol and she hadn't got round to cooking a main course. Even he, though, despite coming from a learned college where the fellows found sex about as easy to obtain as a Nobel prize when not doing very much, was not keen on one-night stands, and Carol was a married woman.

'I'm very flattered,' he told Carol, 'but you're married.'

'Not for much longer,' said Carol, moving closer. 'He prefers blondes.'

'Ah,' said Giles thoughtfully, 'you're on the rebound.'

Carol, slipping off the something slinky she had slipped on earlier, and not even waiting for the oysters, nodded, 'I am so much on the rebound that if you don't catch me I'll probably hurtle in a wild and ungainly fashion all the way to Newmarket.'

'Oh, I wouldn't do that,' said Giles, very close to her lips, 'they're very fast in Newmarket.' He examined his conscience. Married women were in the vetoed area, together with students, philosophers and women with moustaches. Rebounding women seemed to be OK. Especially this one – her scent was going to his head. Anything a dodo could do, he could definitely . . .

Carol sighed softly, feathering his lips with her breath: 'Do I have to spell it out? Giles, please come to bed with me. I badly need to feel . . . desired, and if possible by someone who likes hazelnut in caramel. And I want you. I've actually wanted you for ages. I just kept it deeply buried in the mud.'

There was really only one thing to do. Giles invoked the ex-MP's motto, the one they allegedly use when someone offers them alleged envelopes full of alleged cash. The one that generally leads to their becoming ex-MPs; that if he didn't do it, someone else would, and they'd be bound to make a hash of it. Giles left his conscience on the table and accepted Carol's offer with alacrity.

Alice rang Carol almost before Carol had finished enjoying herself – but as she had been enjoying herself for quite some time that perhaps didn't matter *so* much.

'Carol? Alice Bollivant here. Listen, *News East* are *very* interested in the treasure. They would like to come and film us presenting it to Professor Perry. I wondered if you knew where to get hold of him.'

Carol, superhumanly not laughing, said that she knew exactly where to get hold of him, and demonstrated it, although not to Alice. 'I'll ring him later,' she promised, 'I happen to know he won't be in till then.'

'You're wrong,' said Giles sexily, when Alice had gone, 'I

shall be in very soon,' and then showed, to Carol's continued amazement, what she had been missing for all these years by sleeping with a man who was far too deeply in love with his own body to be properly in love with hers.

Neither of them, lost in the experience, noticed the small, lascivious man in a grey boiler suit and a cap bearing the logo of a burglar alarm company. He had been in the village for a few hours, but he was the sort of man who could make himself invisible. This is an unusual skill, the key to which he told his trainees, is to look as though you have a role to play. Then no-one notices you. It was, though, a tribute to his extreme skills as a private detective that no-one noticed him even when he was perched on a ladder outside their bedroom window taking multiple photographs of them with a single-use camera from Boots. Mind you, they were very busy.

People had always envied Carol and Neil their marriage. Their envy had been a palpable thing, it had glowed with the serious intensity of the moon. It had been, if Carol was truly honest with herself, one of life's thrills, knowing yourself to be the object of that luminous peer envy. And of all of her friends, Louisa's envy had been the best, the one that was the most sexually zingy if conjured up at the right moment. For Louisa had tried to tell her that Neil had made a pass, a very clumsy, very crude pass, backstage at a dinner party. And the then-Carol had known that such an extraordinary claim had to be manufactured out of envy, had to have a structure as nebulous and hollow as a bar of Aero, for Louisa was plain, and Louisa was plump. Louisa was, amongst Carol's circle, known as NSFC – Not Suitable For Chanel. But Louisa was also rich enough to have the Chanel made to measure if she wished, and so her envy, her sexual envy in particular, had been an enjoyable thing to have. Carol had often used the thought of Louisa imagining her with Neil to put sexual fire into her performance, a fire that had sometimes been oddly lacking otherwise.

Louisa was no longer a friend, of course. Carol had not believed Louisa then – but she believed Serendipity now,

268

and so, for good measure, she rang Louisa's answering machine and apologized to it. Answering machines, despite the fact that many people hate talking to them, are wonderful tools for apologies: their very inability to answer back enables the apologizing one to launch into an enthusiastic monologue and get everything said that needs to be said, without any risk of the machine suddenly saying, 'Go and stick your apology in your bottom.'

This done, Carol waited for Neil to return. Giles, given the bald facts, had offered to be there for moral support, but she refused. 'I have to do this by myself,' she said, 'it's important not to show Neil signs of weakness.' (Showing Giles signs of weakness, on the other hand, was something she had discovered she very much enjoyed. How could she ever have thought that spare athletic frame skinny? And what could be more sexy than the Depardieu nose?)

But in the end she went round to Serendipity's for moral support when Neil's flight appeared on Ceefax, and the first person she ran into there was Hugh. And if Hugh wasn't good moral support she didn't know what was.

'I need you,' she told him. 'Come and see Neil with me.'

'It's a pleasure,' said Hugh fervently. There might be a chance here, he thought, unaware that he had missed the boat by an entire Atlantic crossing, for his Uncle Giles.

So when Neil breezed in from Brussels he found Carol and Hugh sitting at the kitchen table playing cards as if they hadn't a care in the world. They ignored him and Neil, who was unaccustomed to being ignored, noticed this. 'Have I done something wrong here?' he asked eventually, in the irritated tones of one who cannot conceive that there is anything he could possibly do that would be wrong, being half sexual dreamboat and half saint.

'You made a pass at Serendipity,' said Carol, 'for a start. You won, Hugh.'

Neil was confused. 'I *what*? Surely you don't believe I'd be attracted to a pregnant woman?' He came towards her with the same indulgent expression he had worn when she had told him of Louisa's claims. She glared.

'You can take that look off your face, Neil – or should I say, Vile Betrayer?'

'I think you should,' said Hugh brightly from behind her. 'My turn to cut the pack.'

'What the hell is he doing here?' asked Neil.

'Keeping me company,' said Carol, 'since you won't be.'

'Since I won't be . . . what exactly do you mean?' Rejection and Neil were not familiar friends. As a concept he found it sank in slightly less easily than elephants do into igneous rock. 'Where are you going?'

'Ever onwards and upwards,' said Carol cheerfully, 'without you. Your turn to deal, Hugh.'

'That's very good,' said Hugh. 'It would make a brilliant school motto. Without the last bit, of course. Much better than our school motto. "Fear not the dragons". I mean, I ask you, what have dragons got to do with anything?'

'I quite agree,' said Carol, who had come to feel that fourteen-year-old boys are like mud springs in terms of hidden depths and useful outpourings.

Neil looked from one to the other with the dawning incredulity often shown on adverts for sanitary wear by women talking about thinness and absorption. 'Do you mean to tell me that Serendipity has sold you some ridiculous story fed by her own jealousy and you believe her?'

'Serendipity is the least jealous person I know,' said Carol, 'and you are without a doubt the most slimy. Please go, Neil. You're interrupting our rummy. You'll hear from my solicitor – whom, I gather, you attempted to coerce.'

If it weren't for the treasure, Neil thought, I'd walk away. 'You can't manage without me,' he said: 'it's not worth splitting up over a minor indiscretion. Darling, don't go all sanctimonious on me – we're two of a kind, you and I.'

'Rummy,' said Hugh, 'or whist?'

'D'you know, Neil,' said Carol with cutting absence of subtlety, 'if you didn't love yourself so much that would be a real insult. And I'll be as sanctimonious as I like in my own house. I'd prefer, though, that you took your perfidious person somewhere else.'

'That's nonsense,' said Neil, who quite enjoyed hard-to-get games. 'You know you're desperate for me.'

'Actually,' said Carol, with wounding clarity, 'you are as desirable as plankton.'

'Whales might not think so,' said Hugh, and Neil frowned.

'I don't think he follows you,' said Carol.

'Don't worry,' said Hugh, in the mournful tones of the much misunderstood, 'I'm used to it.'

Neil glared a glare then sighed a sigh. 'You'll come round, darling,' he told Carol loftily, 'I know you too well. You'll be begging forgiveness this time next week.' I'm a businessman, he thought, I can cut my losses if need be. 'In any case, half of what you have is mine,' he said. 'I shall want my share of the treasure, of course. A million, plus the town house and I'll give up my claim to this farm.'

'Neil,' said Carol, 'I'll see you in court. Your bags are in the hall.'

Neil's eyes narrowed. 'You'll regret this,' he said levelly, 'I promise you you'll be sorry.'

'I thought diamonds were trumps,' said Hugh. 'You're not concentrating.'

'I've got more on you than you think,' said Neil, unmasking at last and revealing his very nasty side, hitherto cunningly concealed behind his particularly nasty side, 'I've got photographs.'

Carol raised her eyebrows. 'So?'

'Well, put it this way, I think I'll win on the infidelity grounds.'

'I should think it's equally likely that a hundred drug-crazed Canadian Mounties will come around that corner singing "Waltzing Matilda". Do you know, you are so full of hot air, Neil, that I'm surprised you stay anchored to the ground. Perhaps it's because you're heavy with treachery.'

'Oh you think so? Well, you'll smile on the other side of your face when you see the prints,' said Neil. 'Does the name Giles Perry mean anything to you?'

Carol felt her cheeks tighten. 'Why?' she asked carefully.

'I'm a businessman,' said Neil. 'I like to keep an eye on my assets. There is a very good private detective in Broomhill, particularly good on marital infidelity, and his focal range is excellent. I'll let you have a couple of prints' – he dropped a brown envelope on the table – 'but I thought I'd hang onto the negatives' – he patted his breast pocket – 'if you get my drift.' He left before she could get in a reply.

'Wow,' said Hugh after he had gone, closing the door behind him with deliberate menace, 'so slimy he's a species all of his own.'

Carol agreed. 'He's actually on a par with that animated cold sore that lives on the lips of Norwegian lobsters.'

Hugh was impressed by her knowledge, but wounded by its application. 'That,' he said, with dignified hurt, 'was a new phylum – the most significant biological find for centuries. My dad has a photo of it by his bed.'

'Oh Hugh,' said Carol, wondering what secret elixir kept Hugh's mother's sanity, and if she could have some, 'you are a breath of fresh air.' She eyed the envelope, thinking, I don't want to even think about this.

'Just think,' said Hugh, seizing his chance, 'if you had children with my Uncle Giles, they might be just like me.'

'Now that,' said Carol, feeling her emotional bruises a little soothed, 'is an almost overpowering thought.'

Hugh had gone to see Leonardo when Mrs Baggins bosomed in looking like a character from a bad sitcom, the sort where the cleaning lady is fat and warty and never takes her curlers out.

'Morning, Mrs P. Hubby gone off again, has he? My Brian always says absence makes the heart grow fonder.'

I bet he does, thought Carol, secretly hoping for a meteorite to crash randomly through the atmosphere and create a giant pit into which Mrs Baggins would fall, rollers intact, still gossiping.

There were, alas, no meteorites in Parvum Magna that day (they were all over Cape Canaveral taunting the men from NASA, who had watched far too many B disaster movies entitled *Meteorite!* and *Asteroid!* to take them lightly.) However, Hugh was back, and he was almost as good as a meteorite.

'Serendipity says we're all going to the seaside and you can come too,' he said, sounding like a reworked Sixties pop song.

'Er,' said Carol, who still found Hugh's brand of rapid speech rather daunting.

'Felix, Belinda and Lily are going,' said Hugh, 'and me.

She says we're going to escape oppression.' He grinned.

'Ah,' said Carol, 'oppression.' Mrs Baggins, she knew, was living proof that 100 is merely the average IQ of the population, some being much lower to balance out the Jimmy Saviles. She would not spot the reference to the all-pervading atmosphere of treasure-greed and treachery. And Lily was going . . .

'Whereabouts?' she asked cautiously.

'I don't know,' said Hugh. 'My mum always goes to Southwold. Oh, and bring your jelly shoes.'

'I don't have any jelly shoes,' said Carol, a touch mournfully. What has my life become, she thought, that I have no jelly shoes?

'Never mind.' Hugh was impatient. 'We're going right now, so you can get some when we're there, wherever it is.'

'Not in Southwold,' said Carol, 'surely?'

'You go on, dear,' said Mrs Baggins encouragingly, apparently under the impression that Carol needed her permission before leaving. She privately thought that Carol was just becoming an East Anglian again, after all these years in a foreign place. London was foreign. It churned out people who drank coffee with a head on it and expected to buy their knickers at railway stations. The true art of corsetry, thought Mrs Baggins, lies in those little shops in which huge-bosomed women with hands like ice personally pour you into fiendishly constructed whalebone devices which are not so far removed in size and shape from the original whale. 'It will do you good. Give me chance to get on with the tidying.'

And prying, thought Carol, and you'll work out that Neil's gone. Even you, though, could never reconstruct those photos out of the pulped shreds in the bin. 'Why didn't Serendipity ring me?' she asked Hugh.

'She said you'd find an excuse not to come,' said Hugh, 'but she says she can't cope with our combined intellect without you.'

Carol smiled suddenly. Oppressive was the right word. She felt Neil sitting on her subconscious like a huge fat unpleasant thing with suckers, and it would be good to throw him off and breathe the sea air again. 'She's not wrong,' she told Hugh. 'Give me two minutes and I'll be with you.'

Hugh, who had both a mother and, almost now, a girl-friend (if he could only be sure it wouldn't all turn out badly again – heartache is one thing, but to risk losing a pet, now that is another), felt he knew all about women and minutes. He settled down to wait with a couple of biscuits and a wildlife magazine.

I'm not desolate, thought Carol upstairs, rooting for her deck shoes (for posing on company yachts – they had never got so much as a water mark on them). I'm angry and I'm hurt and I'm wounded, but I'm not desolate. It's a good job there never was a baby, because he really can't have been the right man. Not if this is all I feel. Mind you, there might still be a baby . . . Oh God, what about the sperm?

She could think of nothing else after that, and they were driving up Newmarket High Street to the accompaniment of a spirited (and surprisingly musical) rendering of 'Mummies on the bus are learned and wise' when it occurred to her that Southwold was the other way.

'Oh, I thought we'd go to Hunstanton,' said Serendipity, with the happy insouciance of one who clearly does not know that something truly awful once happened to her best friend at Hunstanton, and that the friend has never really got over it. It was the one thing which could, and did, put the sperm out of Carol's mind.

Carol sighed. She seemed to be having a summer of con-fronting her demons. Cosmo, Clive, Serendipity, all people she had thought never to see again – yet she was still intact, still sane . . . Neil, who she would prefer never to see again, shedding a skin and revealing a less pleasant one beneath – and yet she was still able to sing children's songs . . . Giles, whom she had planned to use briefly for sex, in revenge, turning out to be quite surprisingly good at it . . . Next to all that, a day trip to Hunstanton seemed a minor problem.

It took just over an hour, in which time Lily had counted a hundred and forty-two red cars, forty-six female drivers, four cars with dogs in the front and eleven Morris Minors, only two of which were Travellers (she had an extraordinary memory for numbers, and an ability to store all sorts of ongoing things at once). Felix, Hugh and Belinda had sung every verse of 'Mummies on the Bus' from 'learned and wise' to 'much better drivers', and Dog had eaten a whole packet of extra-strong mints, together with the paper, and begun to pass horrible wind in the back.

The day was turquoise, with scuddy white fluff-clouds, and the sort of warm breeze that calls to mind hula girls and whispering oleanders on hibiscus-strewn, palm-fronded shores. It was a day for parting from your husband, particularly if you had finally realized that he had the charm of a lugworm and was as necessary to your happiness as a lard sandwich.

The drive was easy. A short cut around Ely admiring the cathedral gazing majestically across the marshes which Hereward defended. Downham Market, King's Lynn, follow the signs for Cromer. ('I was conceived at Cromer,' said Belinda proudly, and Serendipity knew that Belinda believed this referred to her parents coming up with the idea of having her, rather than the actual execution of their plan.) Eventually, Hunstanton, and the cry of seagulls telling stories of the sea.

It didn't look the same on the way in. There were new houses, a lavender farm with a posh sign and a children's playground, a petrol station, then signs for the south beach ('I'm sure there was only one beach last time,' said Carol) and they pulled into the car park where a nice man saw Lily's orange disabled car badge and waved them through, free and cheerful. And then they were within sight of the big dipper and the sea.

Carol had waited for Hunstanton to hit her, with a huge punch of memory, but none came. She felt like laughing aloud. It's just a place, hooted a voice in her head. Just a seaside town with a funfair and a beach, with thousands of lives running through it every day like sand through fingers. Just because I was once one of the grains, she thought, I shouldn't expect Hunstanton to remember me. What did I expect? A tourist information sign pointing the way to the doubtless defunct bus shelter where Carol Greatbottom well and truly lost her virginity to Cosmo Featherstone in a flurry of reluctance, embarrassment and pain? Perhaps it's time I stopped weeping at remembered tragedies.

Back in Parvum Magna Neil, trying hard to convince himself that either the break-up of his marriage was not imminent or, if it was, that he didn't care, glared at the mud spring and blamed it, this mysterious quagmire of infinite capacity and resource. That bloody sign was a bit arrogant, too. *Envy none, and all shall envy thee*? What rot. Envy drives the world round. Without envy it would probably stop turning and we'd all fall off. Neil wrenched the sign from the tree to which it was nailed and flung it meanly into the mud, where it sank silently and inevitably, a piece of lost history in payment for a crown.

Lily saw the dragon first, and she was off, shrieking and laughing. 'Catch up with her!' shouted Serendipity, lumbering from the car like an American beefburger-eating champion after a particularly tough match, and Felix, Belinda and Hugh tore off in hot pursuit. They looked like characters from an Enid Blyton book, silhouetted in carefree exuberance.

'It's so different,' said Carol, eating a pot of prawns with a wooden cocktail stick some time later. Lily, having had a pancake with chocolate sauce and pineapple chunks and three rides on the big dipper dragon, had been sick in the ghost train, and they had retreated to the beach to look for crabs. At least the pancake man had taken it well when Lily had ecstatically and innocently informed him he was a great tosser. Down on the beach the children sparkled and played, and she sighed. 'It must be nice to feel that free,' she said wistfully.

Serendipity followed her gaze. 'Life moves, though, doesn't it? Responsibility is the price of control. We were like them once, and one day they'll be like us – it's a natural progression.'

'That's very clever,' said Carol.

'Isn't it? I often think God ought to get a Nobel prize for people.'

'No, I meant you're clever. It isn't quite the same as I remember it, though. There was a funfair before, but I remember it as bigger – darker.'

'That's a funny choice of adjective,' said Serendipity, frowning. 'Darker? It was a roasting hot, sunny day when we all came here.' She watched Felix and Hugh swinging Lily between them as they ran down the wave-ridged sands. The sea, almost half a mile out, sparkled in the sunshine, tranquil as a bathtub without Lily in it. Between the promenade steps and the sea was an unexplored continent of warm shallow pools populated by shrimps and crabs and tiny unsuspecting fish who had no idea what a Lily was.

Carol sighed. 'It wasn't a very nice day for me,' she said, a wisp of dark hair playing against her cheek.

'Nor me.' Serendipity looked at her with that frank blue look. 'You disappeared off with Cosmo. At the time, I was quite put out.'

Carol looked out to sea, watching quicksilver dancing on the waves. 'I know. It wasn't my best move ever.'

'He was a bit of a creep, though, wasn't he?' Serendipity smiled.

Carol laughed bitterly. 'You've no idea, have you?' she said, in a voice dragged by old agonies.

Serendipity was startled. 'What do you mean?' Half her mind was watching Lily crouching, looking at something. The sun was bright and she squinted. Were Belinda and Hugh holding hands?

Carol looked too, saw the dancing, laughing children, and felt the sharp shaft of pain so familiar to the unwittingly childless. But suddenly, here, it was easy to say the thing that had stuck in her throat so many other times, that had never wanted to be said.

'Cosmo raped me,' she said baldly. Then, embarrassed by the drama of the word, added, 'Well, he pressured me. To be fair it wasn't quite rape, not in the accepted sense, but it was in a bus shelter. Behind a bus shelter.'

Serendipity seemed frozen, her face a mask. 'We looked for you for ages,' she said in a tight, little voice. 'Really ages . . . Then you just turned up, but by then Clive thought you had ditched him for Cosmo, and I thought the same, and . . .'

'You were right,' said Carol, 'I had. Cosmo made it clear he was interested in me, and I wanted him to be. I always felt second best to you.'

Serendipity shook her head, surprised, 'You weren't. I only went out with him because you had Clive, and Cosmo only went out with me to get to you.'

Carol started to laugh, then began to cry. 'How bloody ironic. I only went off with him because I was jealous that he fancied you.'

'But you had Clive.' Serendipity was mystified, both by the story and by the tears – it hardly mattered now.

'Clive only ever went on about you. It was you he wanted all the time. He only dated me first because I asked him out and he didn't know how to say no.'

'Ma!' screamed Lily an inch from her right eardrum, and she jumped. Lily had caught a crab. Well, to be precise, the crab had caught Lily – it was hanging onto the flesh of her thumb with the tenacity of a double glazing salesman. Lily, who often seemed immune to pain, was delighted. 'Spider, a, Spider!'

By the time Lily and the crab had been separated, Felix, Belinda and Hugh had returned demanding entertainment, and Carol's tears were gone if not forgotten. Serendipity got the feeling that a huge monster lay shallowly buried, like those fossilized dinosaurs they occasionally find in the sands of the Gobi desert, and she planned a little dig later.

The dig didn't materialize until much later in the day, after they had been for lunch and to the Sea Life centre, a magical marine adventure where Lily had been mesmerized by a pair of jellyfish which glooped and lollopped about their tank with the ethereal and endless choreography of a screensaver, and Hugh had fallen in love with four catfish, grey igneous-skinned creatures with teeth like needles and faces so ugly that they were quite exquisite. The fact that they were squeezed against the glass, and had squashed an anemone there showed, he said, that they were desperate to get out. Belinda, determined to prove herself his soul mate in every respect, agreed. They were, she said, interesting, and obviously quite affectionate.

'You're joking,' said Serendipity. 'If you want to fancy something in here as a pet, why don't you pick on those sweet little plankton?'

'How on earth can plankton be sweet?' Felix asked in some scorn, carelessly throwing away the chance, Hugh pointed out later, of cultivating a litre of microscopic sea creatures which might, like a surreal lucky dip, turn out to contain catfish, jellyfish, or even an octopus.

Lily was finally persuaded to leave Sea Life by the purchase of a plastic shark named Mavis. After a ride on the horse carousel, she opted for the big dipper dragon again. It took Serendipity, Carol and the man who collected the money quite some effort to drag her off it after her eighth go. 'D'you know, one of these days I'm going to go into labour trying to drag Lily from somewhere,' said Serendipity, rubbing her back. 'Clive's mother keeps ringing up convinced I've given birth without telling her.'

'Don't do it here,' said Carol in alarm. 'I don't think I'm up to delivering babies.'

'I am,' said Hugh helpfully. 'I've been at a birth,' and Serendipity shuddered.

'I've heard about you, Hugh, from your Aunt Tessa,' she told him. 'She said the vicar was sitting on you in the hall when she gave birth. Suffice to say I'd rather my own labour attendants were three extras from *Star Trek*. The ones with the funny-shaped heads.'

Hugh was wounded but phlegmatic. Geniuses, he said, are rarely understood. After that, exhausted, they went back to the beach. The sun was sinking gently towards the sea, coating the watery sand with molten silver. Carol and Serendipity walked along the flats, as the children raced from pool to pool shrieking and laughing (or, in Lily's case, shrieking and shrieking).

A baby sat in the ethereal silver, gurgling at the ridges of sand. Carol's gaze alighted, twisted then ripped. My baby . . . and she was shocked at the tearing pain still there beneath the old unhealed wound. She gasped, and Serendipity saw her face. 'Carol, are you all right? You look as if you've seen a ghost.'

'I have,' said Carol, in a whisper of the past, 'in a way.'

She could not take her eyes off the baby, a little girl of about twelve months, chubby, fair, laughing . . .

Serendipity was suddenly alarmed. Had she missed something out when mentally plotting the course of Carol's life over the last eighteen years? Had there been a child, lost? She fumbled for words. 'Is it the baby?' she asked.

Carol took a deep breath, as is always necessary when you prepare to say something which has never been said, despite needing to be for such a long time . . .

'Fairy,' said Lily with bell-like clarity, and they jumped. Lily squatted, peered at something in the warm water.

'Oh look,' said Serendipity, charmed, 'starfish.'

There were two of them, surely mother and child, for it suits us always to see things that way. They were drifting starfishily in a pool, and curling their legs when Lily touched them. Lily, convinced of their fairyhood, perhaps, did not seem to want to pick them out and eat them.

'C'mon, Lily,' shouted Belinda from the next pool, 'big dead crab,' and Lily rushed over, the starfish forgotten already, presumably entranced by the prospect of pulling the crab's legs off.

'So what's really the matter?' asked Serendipity, watching where the edges of clouds which overlay the sun shone with an impossible, mercurial fire.

'I was pregnant,' said Carol. 'I thought you might have known. I thought a lot of people did.' At the edge of the sea, silhouetted against the brightness, a lone horse trod gingerly in the surf, its rider relaxed, enviable.

'Oh, Carol.' In her mind Serendipity felt that time had just wrinkled up like an unstarched sheet so that she could step back a split second into her ghost self, the sixteen-year-old Serendipity who haunted Hunstanton beach. Half her mind watched the rider and horse, seeming to draw a mutual breath of anticipation of the open beach ahead. The other half fought with the realization that Carol's life had been engulfed in a drama she had never even guessed at. And yet a drama that was so familiar . . .

Carol, finding unexpected relief in telling it as it really was rather than as she had always told herself it was, said, 'Cosmo didn't rape me, I'm not being fair, thinking of it that way even now, using that word. He made me feel cheap. That's the truth. Then when I realized I was pregnant, at the end of that summer, there was a terrible row at home. Uncle Percy threw us out.'

The horse and rider took off through the surf, galloping with joyous release as though all their problems had been left behind on the breakwater where the dogfish grumbled.

'So that's why you left so suddenly?'

Carol smiled ruefully. 'He was a foul old man, you know. No morals himself, but fire and brimstone where I was involved. Called me the whore of Babylon, actually.'

'Did you . . . have your baby?'

Carol swallowed. 'No, Mum wanted me to have an abortion, and I said no because I was full of daft ideas of myself as some sort of glorious mother figure. I think Mum would have stood by me – well, teetered next to me on her stilettos, but she never got the chance. I had a miscarriage. It was quite early. I hadn't even been for my scan. I really regret that, that I never had the scan, that I never saw . . .' She kept her eyes wide open, fixed on the far horizon tightly and hard, took a breath, 'They were awfully nice in the hospital. No-one said it was for the best, not once. They all said I'd have lots of babies one day, when I planned them.' Her voice thickened suddenly, revealingly. 'But they lied. I've been planning them for ages and I haven't had any at all.' Oh God, said the voice in her mind, what have I done? Those weren't my sperm. I'm going to have to tell her now – this conversation has gone too far.

Serendipity put a hand on her arm. 'Do you know why you lost him – or her?'

Carol shook her head, noticing gratefully that Serendipity did not use 'it'. Perhaps mothers understand the importance of that 'he or she'. *Sperm, sperm, sperm,* said a voice inside, rattled but noisy. 'No – just one of those things. I felt marked by it for years – a woman who failed, who had a miscarriage. Then, when I married, I decided to forget it. I didn't tell Neil – I thought, it's not what life throws at us but how we respond to it that defines us, so I'm not going to be Carol Greatbottom who had a miscarriage any more, I'm going to be Carol Pendragon who succeeds, who has a baby. But I haven't had a baby, and I'm starting to think maybe I can't.'

'Have you seen anyone – you know, medically.'

'Neil wouldn't hear of it, and I suppose I let him convince me. I did finally see someone recently, but I could only take things so far without Neil. He could never concede there might be anything wrong with him, you see. Neil had to be perfect.'

Serendipity thought of Neil with distaste. 'Would you want to patch things up with him, if he asked – if he begged?'

Carol shook her head. 'Not if he hung from the minute hand of Big Ben for forty-eight hours wearing nothing but a G-string and an apologetic expression. Things are way past that point. You see, since coming back here I've redis-covered myself, my real self, and I like her much better than the other one. The trouble is, she likes Neil even less than he likes her. He even threatened me, in front of Hugh. He hired a private detective to take photos of me with Giles Perry.'

'You and *Giles*? . . .You didn't . . . ?'

'Oh we did. I'm not in the slightest bit ashamed of that. He must have taken a whole film, though. God knows how he managed it.'

'What will he do with the photos?'

'His ruthless worst,' said Carol, 'and I admit I'm not par-ticularly looking forward to seeing my bare behind stuck up on flyers all over the City of London, even if I have finally made peace with my own cellulite. But I'm certainly not going to cave in to Neil over it.'

'Who'd have thought the treasure would trigger all this?' said Serendipity sadly.

'Oh, it wasn't the treasure, although it was coming home that made me see that Neil and I haven't wanted the same things for a long time now. Our not having a child has become more and more important to me. Neil's life is merely dominated by the need to disperse his seed as widely as possible.' Oh God, I've said it. I've said the taboo word.

'Funny,' said Serendipity, before she could stop herself, 'my life has been dominated by sperm too. You and I are like reflections of one another, aren't we?'

Now I have to tell her, thought Carol, feeling the

upwelling of confessions racing towards a climax, towards the subject of Clive's diverted seminal sample and where, precisely, it had been diverted to. She could no more give it a wide berth than boarding schoolboys can vats of baked beans. She wondered if Serendipity would storm off and leave her behind in Hunstanton. But she couldn't allow that: Serendipity might go into labour on the way home. 'I . . .'

'I suppose,' said Serendipity awkwardly, blithely unaware of Carol's inner churnings, 'that when you took that sample of Clive's down you must have felt I was adding insult to injury.'

'No, I . . .'

'At least our sperm problems are over now. Mind you – we haven't had the result yet. But it's bound to show no more little spermies.'

Carol looked at her, frowned. 'No more?'

'Well, of course. It was Clive's post-vasectomy sample – didn't I say? You have to wait three months or thirty-five – er – clearances. That only took him a week and a half.'

'So he's . . .'

'Almost certainly slightly less fertile than the North face of Everest,' said Serendipity wistfully, 'and nothing grows there.'

Carol thought she was going to be sick.

'Poor Carol was quite ill coming home,' said Serendipity to Clive later that night. 'It must have been the prawns.'

Clive, deep in a magic book, did not respond.

'Clive?'

'Mmm,' he said, 'is she?'

Perhaps, Serendipity thought, I should saw myself in half or stick feathers in my head and disappear. 'Clive?'

'Mmm?'

'Clive put that bloody book down or I'll make soup out of it. Listen to me. I want you to think.'

'Now, be reasonable,' said Clive, 'I'm a GP.'

'I'm serious. Do you remember the time we all went to Hunstanton?'

'You mean last bank holiday after Lily got us thrown out of the tea shop in Southwold?'

'No, I mean eighteen years ago. You and I and Carol and Cosmo – in Cosmo's car?'

'Of course I remember. We made Miranda that day, you and I.'

'I know we did. But Clive, did Cosmo say anything to you? I mean, anything boastful?'

'Why?'

'Just tell me – did he?'

Clive sighed. 'Well, he did brag a bit.'

'God,' said Serendipity furiously, 'what a bastard.'

'Well, it was a nice car. I'd have bragged.'

'You mean he bragged about the *car*?'

'Yes, of course. What did you think I meant?' He was already reabsorbed in the technicalities of how to extract whole eggs from the ears of impressed onlookers, and was not interested.

So at least he didn't brag, thought Serendipity. He didn't brag, and I – neither Clive nor I – ever knew. Carol conceived her baby, left the village, lost her baby – and yet no-one said a word. It's as if we were all taking part in the same play but on different stages. And now she has nothing to show for it but the wound. And I have Miranda. And to think I envied Carol . . .

'Where have you been all day?' demanded Neil down the telephone.

'Catching crabs,' said Carol cheerfully.

'You filthy bitch,' said Neil, 'I might have known you'd—'

'On Hunstanton beach, Neil,' said Carol, with all the dignity she could muster. 'In East Anglia crabs are little crunchy things with legs that run sideways through the sand trying to avoid seagulls. It's only in Neilsville that they're little teensy things with legs that run through your groin trying to avoid louse shampoo.'

Neil let that pass. 'Have you thought about my offer? The photos for a fair division of assets?'

'Your offer,' said Carol, 'had about as much impact on my life as Bill Clinton's cat, which wasn't a lot.'

'I could ruin your business,' said Neil. 'One word from me, and the City—'

'Feel free,' said Carol, 'although it might interest you that I've sold my business to Fiona.'

'You sold your business to your office manager?'

'Why not? She wants it. I don't any more. I'm staying here, Neil. This is where I belong.'

'Perhaps you should look properly at the pictures,' said Neil smoothly, 'they're taken from a fascinating angle.'

'I won't bother,' said Carol, 'I can quite imagine what sort of photograph a man with the charm of a plate of salmonella would find fascinating.' She hung up.

Chapter Twelve

Talk amongst women in Broomhill that 'did' was that Hilda Antrobus was the world's worst employer. She was mean, was Hilda, yet she expected to be able to criticize you over the shine on her knobs and the dust on her kitchen shelves – always peering over your shoulder like Mr Sheen fallen off his rocket. Brenda Baggins had warned everyone about Hilda, and she had been right.

Hilda, meanwhile, was inspecting the handiwork of the latest appointee to be offered a trial. It wasn't good enough. Oh, it was good – there was barely a grain of dust on the skirting boards, and a lot of people wouldn't have thought to check the inside of the cutlery drainer. Hilda had high standards, though, and just because Hermione Beadle had cleaned for Sir George and Lady Angela Ormondroyd, that did not in itself make her good enough for Hilda Antrobus.

'Do you know, Sidney,' she told her husband, who was in the process of systematically pulling the feathers out of their newest sofa, made to order by a firm he felt should be called Very Expensive Sofas Inc., 'you just can't find people to do a job properly. I could do it better myself.'

'That's what you always used to do, dear,' said Sid mildly.

Hilda sniffed. 'That was then, this is now. Money brings responsibilities, and status, Sidney.'

Sidney glared. 'I'm off for a walk,' he said.

He didn't have far to go. 'I'll do it for nothing,' he told the foreman at Broomhill Poultry, 'if you promise not to tell Hilda. I just want some company and – well – I know they're not much to look at, but I miss the chickens.'

The foreman had worked in poultry processing for thirty years, man and boy. He knew all about the love that can develop between man and plucked chicken. He agreed.

Hilda was delighted to hear that Sid had a new hobby.

'A bird-watching club? That sounds marvellous.' 'Marvellous' was a good word – she had heard it on morning TV. 'Smashing' never got used, though, nor 'grand'. 'Tell them about those owls you've found that hoot back.'

'I'll do that,' said Sidney, thinking, another six hours and I'll have something to stuff again.

As Sidney plotted and paced, Carol girded herself mentally until she felt like, well, a girder. She had something to tell Serendipity. She had to tell her what she had done, even though it didn't matter any more, at least not as much, because there's nothing else you can do with a horrible secret. You have to get rid of it, because otherwise it sits on your chest like a giant Thelwell pony, impossible to shift and impossible to ignore.

Lily Rowan spotted her from indoors. She had taken a huge liking to Carol, and when Lily liked someone, she made certain they knew it. Lily raced out to greet her before anyone else and rushed forward to offer her love, her whole self, and every breath in her body.

'Ma!' she shrieked, with her usual gift for the superlative, and flung herself upon Carol with the sort of exuberance you might expect in a man released from Center Parcs after an entire week with the grandchildren.

'Hello, Lily.' Carol stroked the golden hair. At first she hadn't known quite how to respond, but it was easier now that she had realized it didn't matter, because however she responded, Lily would still adore her. As she adored Lily. And if when she told Serendipity, Serendipity hated her and she lost Lily too, that would be unbearable. Lily beamed then danced away, practising the ballet steps she had recently learned at school. The ballet teacher hadn't been sure about taking Lily on, but Lily had got her way by joining in anyway (and then proving better than everyone else at almost everything the ballet teacher suggested). At Lily's level in ballet, exuberance was a fine thing.

Carol found Serendipity sitting at the kitchen table weeping over something that had clearly come in the post. From his tank on the kitchen unit, Leonardo watched, puzzled and frondy. From the kitchen table, Ignatius observed the proceedings coolly and implacably.

'Oh dear,' said Carol, remembering fleetingly that in London she had not had the sort of friends whose grief she could comfortably walk in on – she would have sneaked back out telling herself that she did not want to embarrass them, whilst knowing that she did not want to embarrass herself. 'Bad news? Or are you just overwhelmed by wildlife?' Well, she couldn't give her friend bad news when she was already upset. Mind you, that never stopped Banquo – but then, look what happened to Macbeth.

Serendipity shook her head. 'No, not at all. It's Lily's school report. She's doing brilliantly.'

'Well, that's good, isn't it?'

'Of course it is.' Lily pushed herself against her mother like a cat offering comfort, and tried to steal the report. 'Don't be a toad, Lily. Let go. No, of course it is. It's just that one of the other mothers at the assessment centre has been on the phone to me. Her little girl's report is just the opposite – they don't think she'll ever speak.' Lily beamed, and seized Ignatius, who sat happily upon her shoulder and gloated at Serendipity.

'No,' said Serendipity to Ignatius.

'Why are you talking to the creature?' Carol frowned.

'He wants me to get him a wife,' said Serendipity, well aware of Hugh, Felix and Belinda plotting an earshot away on the stairs, 'and I'm not going to.'

'So you feel bad for your friend.'

'And guilty,' said Serendipity, 'for leaving Tara behind.'

'Lily was never that bad though, surely?'

'Lily and Tara were just the same two years ago. They've just gone in different directions. Forwards and backwards.'

'Perhaps they never had the same thing. You can't feel guilty because someone else is worse off than you.'

'Can't you?' Serendipity looked at Lily. 'No, of course you can't. But it's far easier to envy than to be envied.'

Is it? wondered Carol, I've found envying Serendipity a rather painful process myself, whereas I rather enjoyed being half of the golden couple who were the envy of Highgate.

'It's probably genetic anyway,' said Serendipity, not noticing Carol's expression.

'What is?'

'Lily. You know, the way she is.'

'You mean Lily's . . . her autism . . . is inherited? But I thought no-one knew what caused it.' It had actually never, ever occurred to Carol to think about it. Illness, you thought of that as inherited, but not – well – oddness.

Serendipity was unaware of the churning of Carol's emotions. 'Probably – at least partly – but no-one really knows. It does seem to have a tendency to run in some families, put it that way.'

How Carol retained her composure she would never know. There is a God, said a voice in her head, and he's passed judgement on me. Now I'll always wonder if I'd have had a Lily with Clive, if only that sample had been a real sample with real sperms in it – I would have *loved* a Lily . . . But I should never have imagined I could steal fatherhood from Clive. How could I ever have thought it was as simple as a quick syringing in a car park? If I'd had Clive's baby it might have looked like Lily – it might have been like Lily – they would have *known* . . . 'Your family, or Clive's?' she said softly.

'I've no idea. No way of knowing. We stopped worrying about it long ago.'

'And you still decided to have another baby?'

Serendipity shrugged. 'We live our lives and take what that brings.'

I can't do this, thought Carol, I just can't tell her. I haven't thought properly how to tell her. What if she never wants to see me again? So, taking Lily with her, she went up to the village hall to have a look at the renovations. It was looking really rather grand – in fact, if the Sultan of Brunei had had a village hall, it wouldn't have been much grander than this. Maybe a bit more gold, but no grander. Now there's a thought, thought Carol. Perhaps I should have gone for solid gold light fittings . . . Still, it was certainly fit for *News East*.

Serendipity was still weeping when Clive got home for lunch, as she had opened the rest of the mail. If the postman, who was a sensitive soul, had known what bad tidings he carried, he would probably have taken the day off and gone to the Sea Life centre in Hunstanton to watch the jellyfish instead, but he did not know, and was by now delivering huge piles of unsolicited home shopping mail to the inhabitants of Bumpstaple. Bumpstaple, although residents did not know it, had been targeted as a village whose residents were particularly likely to order by mail, and as a result was on the prime target list of everything from companies which sold gadgets no-one should be without to companies which sold gadgets no-one would want. The parent companies were, of course, the same.

'When you said you'd like to have the kitchen units distressed,' said Clive, with inappropriate facetiousness, 'I thought you were referring to a paint finish. I didn't realize that you planned to render them suicidal with grief.'

Serendipity tried to sniff through a nose swollen by crying, but failed and gasped for breath. Clive sighed, went over and put an arm around her shoulders. 'Come on, what's the matter?'

Serendipity hiccuped and waved a pink form at him wordlessly.

'What is it?' Mystified, he peered at the figures on the form, then saw his own name. 'Ah, my sample result at last. At least we sent enough this time. The staff will never let me forget not producing enough the first time. Still, we're all clear now. We can have wild uninhibited sex. That's good news, isn't it?'

'We're really infertile,' sobbed Serendipity into half a hundredweight of kitchen towel (she never bought proper tissues, which seemed so extravagant for use on mere noses, but compensated admirably for such frugality by using Sainsbury's economy kitchen towel three sheets at a time whenever she sneezed). 'We'll never have any more babies.' She put a hand on her stomach. 'Phoebe is the very last. The last Rowan baby,'

Clive sat down. 'But you knew that. I've had a vasectomy to achieve that very end.'

'I know,' said Serendipity woefully, 'I even told Carol I knew – but I didn't really really *know* – I mean I knew you probably were, but I think I still thought you might not be. It might not have worked, don't you see? But now it's here in black and white . . .'

'Black and pink,' said Clive, in the interests of accuracy.

'Black and pink. It's confirmed. No sperm. Not a single sperm. Not even one.'

Clive sighed, sat at the table and took her hands. 'I thought that was the idea. We wanted to spend some time with the ones we've got – and there are already times when I feel overwhelmed by mascara, even though Belinda and Lily haven't got any yet.'

'Lily has,' sniffed Serendipity: 'she stole mine and used it to draw teletubbies on the bathroom wall.'

'And,' said Clive firmly, 'we have a Lily. She makes three or four on her own. We were sure that we had the full complement of children. Weren't we?'

'Yes, we were. We are. I don't want to be pregnant again anyway. I just wasn't ready to be told I'm infertile. It's called distressed ambivalence.'

'You're not infertile,' pointed out Clive reasonably, 'I am.'

'Well, that's fairly academic since I'm not sleeping with anyone else,' said Serendipity, wiping her eyes at last, 'but doesn't it make you sad?'

'In a way, but not to be distraught over. Men don't cry when they're ambivalent.'

'New men do,' said Serendipity, 'and they wash up.'

'What about slightly used men?'

'They at least sniff a bit.'

He sighed. 'Come on, Ren, contraception has never been our strong point.'

'It might have been if you'd remembered to put it on.' She ignored her own twinges of guilt – she had known full well he hadn't been wearing a condom, but it was far too late to admit it now. Besides, she was the one with the varicose vein . . . 'But that's not the point. I liked knowing I still had it in me.'

Clive started to laugh rudely, then saw her expression and stopped. 'This is precisely why we had sperm stored,' he said: 'so if you changed your mind we still could.'

'Except I'd have to be inseminated by a plastic syringe. It's not very romantic, is it?'

'Oh, I don't know. I could do it for you wearing a black tie with "True Love" playing in the background.'

Serendipity giggled weakly. 'I suppose you could.'

'Look,' he said, 'why don't we go out for a meal tonight? Last chance before Phoebe?'

'We can't,' said Serendipity, 'it's the Broomhill opera tonight.'

Carol, scanning her answering machine for any messages she wanted to hear found Giles on it and rang him.

'Carol? Hello.' It amazed her how her heart flipped when she heard his voice.

'Hello Giles, how are you?'

'Longing to see you,' said Giles, who didn't believe in subtlety or playing hard to get when it came to women. They were confusing enough as it was.

'Come over,' said Carol. 'Perhaps you could help me deal with my gargantuan guilt.'

'Your what? You've not got Hugh with you, have you?'

'It's a long story,' said Carol. 'Can you come? We've got trial by opera tonight.'

'I'm sorry,' said Giles, 'I've a lecture and a tutorial. I wanted to tell you that the College Council have agreed to pay two million pounds for the treasure. It's well above the likely valuation, so I'm sure it will stand. The crown alone is worth about a quarter of that. I thought you might like to tell your village.'

'Actually,' said Carol, 'I think I'd prefer it to being tattooed all over with pictures of Alice and put on display in Broomhill library, but only slightly. Thank you for sharing that with me.'

'Any time,' said Giles cheerfully. He had a poor sense of irony. When two Russian cosmonauts, leaving their room for the short walk to their rocket, prior to blast-off for Mir, got their sitting room door jammed and had to be rescued with the aid of two Philips screwdrivers and a Sacha Distel record, Giles had not found that ironic either. 'I should be over tomorrow.'

Carol sighed as she put the phone down. I haven't managed to spend even a quarter of two million pounds on the the village hall, she thought, and no-one else has come up with a single practical idea (although Brian Baggins had suggested, rather incongruously, a giant observatory and bird hide). What on earth can I do with the rest? If I'm not quick it will keep gathering interest, and then there'll be even more of it. Resignedly, she played the other messages. The first was the Broomhill football club, ringing to see if she would like to discuss plans for a small stadium. Nothing too excessive, but obviously it would have to be all seats, regulations being what they were . . . The second was someone from *News East* wanting to arrange to see her and discuss the new village hall. Last was Mr Fosdyke, sounding wounded.

'Fosdyke here. I – er – thought you should know that I have been approached by several parties from your village questioning your right to distribute the proceeds of the treasure from your late uncle's spring. I have informed the parties I cannot possibly act for them, and that in any case I do not believe they have grounds to challenge you as executor. Um. I'm afraid they were then – erm – rather rude about my hair. Do feel free to give me a call if you want to discuss things. Goodbye.'

Things, Carol thought, are going from bad to worse. Perhaps this is the revenge of the mud spring god, because of what I did in the car park behind Boots.

That evening the curtain rose at last on the Broomhill Amateur Operatic Society's open air production of *La Bohème*, produced at Greatbottom Farm, in the field that immediately adjoined the mud spring. It was an entirely local production, from the cast to the set manager, but there was a large audience; this included Eric, although he was not obvious as he was on the other side of a hedge from everyone else. Even Gromit, Flange and Peebles, who had almost finished their work on the village hall, stopped for the night to listen – it was the least they could do, they said, when Carol insisted on paying them so much more than the going rate. (They had, though, left behind the man doing the maple worktops as after a lifetime of sawing and sanding he was completely tone deaf and only went to brass band concerts, because they at least made his head vibrate when he got really close to the tubas).

It began well, the Broomhill Symphony Orchestra supporting the cast admirably, and even managing to drown them out when the trills got too much. Alice, well cleavaged in the lead soprano role (it wasn't tarty, this was art), seemed rather more capable of passion than usual (Hector watched with lustful eyes) and Dirk Mullins, though not entirely convincing as a man who thought Alice the love of his life, tried hard. So if some people thought they might have been more convincing as starving artists if they hadn't carried more weight between them than the government of Tonga, they did not say so, and since most of the audience had been coerced into their seats and had absolutely no idea that the opera was about anything other than two fat people singing on a stage, they were not particularly critical. It was actually very difficult for anyone who lived in Parvum Magna not to attend. Alice, who sold more tickets than any-one else, did not tolerate excuses. Besides, the noise of the production was far less tolerable if you didn't go than if you did. Only Brian Baggins, proletarian to a fault, declared to Alice's face that it was all far too elitist for the likes of him, and Alice was too flattered by this to wish to challenge it.

Unfortunately, given Eric's interest, the production was doomed from the start. Llamas do not like opera. They like pan pipes and drums, and the sound of rapids rushing through breathtaking gorges impassable to man and beast. They like the cry of the high mountain eagles, the tinkle of herdsmen's bells and the humming of Andean child shepherds bringing them in for a night on the straw. They like raindrops on coca leaves, and Elton John. (It is one of the world's great tragedies that most llama never get to hear Elton John and so are deprived of the opportunity to enter the state of cosmic bliss which is so familiar to London-Zoo-based llamas, who insist on 'Goodbye, Yellow Brick Road' before they'll do anything or go anywhere.) Opera, though, they can do without: anyone who has ever counted the number of llama at Glyndebourne on a summer night can vouch for that.

Felix, Belinda and Hugh sat together at the back. Hugh had not brought Ignatius, fearing that Ignatius might not appreciate the trills. 'Lady iguanas make the same noise,' he told Belinda, 'when they're receptive. I don't know what he might do if he heard Mrs Bollivant.'

'He'll be fine at your house with Lily and Gran,' said Belinda, who had brushed her blond hair out and was contriving to have the breeze waft it at Hugh. She had doused it liberally with Miranda's favourite perfume, and was hoping to appeal to his subconscious. 'It'll make her love him more.'

Hugh smiled approvingly. Although his senses had been on danger alert ever since he met Belinda, he was beginning to relax. She was not showing the classic signs of iguana envy, and had already shown an uncanny ability to tame wild llama. Well, almost wild. She would be quite a good person to share a life of hunting for tomato frogs in the Madagascan jungle.

Serendipity was quite enjoying it. Clive wasn't on call for once, and he wasn't practising magic tricks, he was sitting next to her, which made the evening quite unusual to begin with. Phoebe, gestating enthusiastically, seemed to be enjoying the music too, shifting around excitedly whenever Alice hurled herself into a crescendo. Carol looked a little pensive, she thought. She leaned towards her. 'Are you OK?'

'Oh, I'm just tired,' whispered Carol back.

'You look stressed. Is it Neil, making trouble?'

It was nice having a friend who really knew you, thought Carol, who had wiped several grovelling messages from Neil from her answering machine (if I had one of those lie detector phones, she thought, he'd have blown it up). 'To be honest it's the stress of being on display. I can feel everyone looking at me, saying, "that's the woman, look, the one who gets to spend all the money, Lady Bountiful of Greatbottom Farm."'

'Oh, I'm sure they're not,' whispered Serendipity, certain that they were.

Carol sighed. 'I sometimes wish things had been different.'

'You mean you think you shouldn't have come back?' On stage Alice noticed them whispering and sang from the depths of her bosom, which was a very long way.

'Oh no,' whispered Carol, 'this is home. I mean it would have been easier without the treasure.'

'You might not have found out about Neil without the treasure,' said Serendipity, thinking, if my husband was a rat I'd like to know about it. But then I know Clive would never be a rat, so that's easy for me to say.

But Carol shrugged. 'It would have happened eventually,' she said. It was impossible to imagine things lasting with Neil, now that she wouldn't touch him with a barge pole so long that if a bargee had tried to use it to push off with it he would have vaulted out of his barge and all the way to Ely. But I might not have met Giles without the treasure, she thought. Funny thing, fate.

The final act was playing dramatically and tragically, but it was about to become a little more dramatic and tragic than the performers intended.

Eric was now in a state of llama-hype. The opera had worked him to a frenzy, and he had realized that Alice was the originator of the trills that particularly offended his inner ear.

Belinda saw Eric first, and clutched Hugh to warn him. Hugh, entirely misinterpreting the clutch, jumped three feet in the air and started to think of an excuse . . . However, it was already too late, for there is nothing more determined than an excited llama.

Alice was meant to be in the process of fading away, although as a serious egotist she was completely unable to sing pianissimo, and her Mimi sounded extraordinarily robust and lusty as she coughed her last. Afterwards it was said of her that the only true high note she ever sang was when she closed her eyes for Rodolfo's final embrace, only to be slobbered upon as Eric delivered his most sumptuous kiss in an effort to shut her up.

'Now there's something you don't see every day,' said Clive, with a smile on his face like Captain Birdseye. He didn't like opera anyway. He was, he told Hugh, starting to see the merit in llamas.

'Just think,' said Belinda, considering her potential love-life, even when poised to rush to Eric, 'how useful a family iguana could be.'

After that the opera ended in some disarray. Belinda, Felix and Hugh managed to seize Eric and whisk him from the scene before anyone wondered where he had gone, but they were a subdued trio as they hurried him through the mêlée, hastened by the sound of distant sirens. Eric's gaff, Hugh said, was surely blown. It was only a matter of time before someone came to get him for some dreadful llama farm where they were hormoned via their radishes and shaved of an entire jumper every single day – or worse, divided into component bits for display on the exotic counter at Sainsbury's. Still, it's surprising what you can get away with on the llama front. By the time Roger the police-man arrived, this time armed with a special issue large game stun gun he had commandeered from the vet, and people had stopped running around screaming like extras in *Meteorite 3*, no-one knew what direction the llama had appeared from, where the llama had gone, nor, even, in some cases, that he was a llama (Terry Clayton swore he was a giraffe).

Serendipity watched with slight sadness, both for Alice, and for Eric (who had, after all, kissed Alice), but particularly when she remembered how completely Eric had become Lily's llama, and how certain it was now that he was only a very temporary addition to their family. 'I wonder,' she said to Clive, 'how long we've got.'

They arrived home to find Miranda, flush with the excitement of her expulsion from the protest site by the special police anti road protester squad (a squad consisting entirely of officers from outside the county who had no sense of smell. This wasn't only because they spent an awful lot of time drinking minestrone soup out of thermoses, but also because a tunnel can be a bit niffy when six road protesters have failed to wash in it for a week). Miranda had breezed in as casually as though she had not just been carried, still protesting, from a tunnel by three burly, handsome but anosmic policemen, all of whom had wanted her telephone number before they would put her down, but only one of whom she had given it to. Her long blond hair looked suspiciously clean and brushed, even though the rest of her was affecting the unkempt, unwashed and un-thought-about style. Miranda was not a girl to let her hair look a mess. Her combat fatigues looked good when they were filthy, she reasoned, her jumper was meant to look as though it had done three rounds with a welterweight, but her hair was her best asset and should be nurtured.

Serendipity was horrified. 'I thought they weren't moving in on you till tomorrow,' she said, 'and I was at the opera. What a pathetic mother that makes me.'

'Don't be silly – I didn't tell you,' said Miranda. 'It would have rather spoiled the look of the thing if a whole lot of middle-class parents had come tearing down to lay into the police and then gone into labour all over the place. Anyway, it was all quite civilized, really.'

'You mean you don't trust us to be civilized?'

'Certainly not,' said Miranda. 'Yours was the rebel generation.'

But it had, she told her mother, taught her a lot. In particular, she said, after Hugh, Felix and Belinda had gone off somewhere to worry about Eric, it had taught her that sleeping in holes in the ground showed a person in their true light, and Luke was not for her. He had been pressuring her, she said, for sex. 'Mum,' she asked, 'did Dad pressure you for sex when you were sixteen? I mean, how did it *happen* that you got pregnant with me? I mean, how come you let it?'

Serendipity sighed. 'It happened . . .' What on earth am I to say? that I've got regrets, when Miranda was the result? Or that I haven't, and it's great to get pregnant before A levels? 'It happened on impulse,' she said impulsively. 'We weren't equipped with the means to avoid it. Well, we were, but we dropped it. We got carried away. It's easy to do, believe me.'

'And then you got me,' said Miranda thoughtfully, then, cheerily: 'so at least that was a bit of good luck.'

And just then Carol called in for coffee and finally met Miranda, and after weeks of assumptions about Serendipity's life history, added two and two successfully for the first time in a while.

Of course she knew about Miranda – she knew there was a Miranda, anyway. She knew Miranda was seventeen, and that was fine. Seventeen was a nice age, an age of discovery, an age with little responsibility but much anticipation. She had never been seventeen herself in Parvum Magna; seventeen had been London and the new start, new school, new and posher friends, forgetting there ever was a place where cows fell into bogs and old men gossiped next to the graves of their ancestors, a place where you belonged to the land in a way that no-one in cities belongs to anywhere any more, and where Harvest Festival has a particular resonance in a church filled with giant onions and even huger beetroot.

Carol was not particularly surprised to find her tall, as Clive was tall, but when you meet your best friend's teenaged offspring for the first time you are obliged by convention to say something inane, so she said, 'Gosh, you are tall. I don't remember Serendipity being this tall at seventeen.'

'It would be surprising if you did,' said Serendipity drily, 'as I'm still not that tall now. But Miranda is eighteen next week.'

'That's right,' agreed Miranda. 'I'm nearly ripe.'

'Frankly, darling,' said Serendipity, 'you're over-ripe. Why don't you go and avail yourself of some running water?'

It had taken a while to sink into Carol, but finally it did. Serendipity had an *eighteen*-year-old daughter – but she and Clive had been married . . . not quite eighteen years. Eighteen years ago I left this village – well, eighteen and a bit – but the bit was not enough, not nearly enough, for Serendipity to have got pregnant and had a daughter of nearly eighteen in. And if Serendipity didn't get pregnant after I left Parvum Magna, she must have been pregnant before I left. She must have been pregnant when I was pregnant. She must have . . .

'What's the matter?' asked Serendipity, 'you look as though you've seen a ghost.'

Carol stared at her. 'I . . .' Half of her wanted to get up and go. Serendipity had betrayed her, she must have slept with Clive when he still wasn't hers to sleep with. She must have done. Mustn't she? Carol searched her mind for timings, dates . . . She looked at Miranda, who looked like a girl from a shampoo advert who had fallen on mucky times. 'How can you be nearly eighteen?' she asked.

'It all dates back eighteen years,' said Miranda brightly, mistaking all this for a compliment on Serendipity's youthful looks or her own youthful looks, or a comment on the incredible swiftness with which time had managed to pass. 'Or more, actually. I was conceived nine months before that, you know, in the back of a car in Hunstanton.'

Carol looked at Serendipity. A picture of the beach at Hunstanton, silver-lit and magical, flashed into her mind's eye. She felt her face tingling. This is finally it, she thought, I'm finally turning pale, like the heroine of one of those dreadful Loveday and Blott novels. 'Is this true?'

Miranda looked from one to another, not sure why the atmosphere had suddenly thickened, but aware it was not the sort of atmosphere you would want to use for the usual things like breathing. 'Er . . . I'm off to wash my hair,' she attempted breezily, although it didn't quite come out that way. It didn't much matter, no-one heard, and she slipped off to shower herself into the sort of girl that a policeman might fancy.

Serendipity nodded and swallowed. 'Oh,' she said, then, 'oh I see. Of course. You want to know exactly when . . . well, Miranda's right. I got pregnant the day we went to Hunstanton.'

'*That* day?'

'Yes.'

'So while Cosmo was . . . you were . . .' This is ridiculous, thought Carol, I'm behaving as if I were still sixteen. This is *years* ago.

'Yes,' said Serendipity, defiantly, 'you'd gone off with Cosmo and we couldn't find you – and we put two and two together and . . .'

'And I suppose you thought you might as well nick my boyfriend if I'd got yours. That is just so low.'

'Well, *hadn't* you? Hadn't you stolen him? I know you regretted it afterwards, but you didn't think about me when you sneaked off with him.'

'You didn't want him – you wanted Clive.'

'You didn't know that, though. You *stole* him.'

'Well, you stole Clive . . .' Oh God, thought Carol, and look what I did with his *sperm.* I'm no angel.

They had been glaring at one another for several seconds, like gunfighters at the OK Corral, but they deflated suddenly and simultaneously. 'I can't believe we're arguing about this now,' said Serendipity incredulously. 'It was years ago. We're acting as if we're Belinda's age.'

'I think it was a row that needed finishing,' said Carol, wondering if she could bring herself to confess, knowing she couldn't and was putting it off again to a more auspicious, warmer, sunnier, less fraught, more friendly . . . *later* moment. 'I ran off before we could shout at one another, originally.'

'You're right,' said Serendipity, 'but is it over now?'

'I think so,' said Carol, compressing the sperm back into their tiny corner of her mind, where they wriggled uncomfortably, making her brain itch. 'Tell me what happened.'

'I got pregnant,' said Serendipity, 'as Miranda just told you so charmingly. I didn't realize it at once, of course, not until nearly four months had gone by. I wanted to talk to you, but you were so distant, and then you left. I told Mother in the end.'

'How was it?'

'Not bad, really,' said Serendipity. 'Clive's mother was far the worst. She tried to get me into a whalebone corset for the wedding, but it was no use as everyone knew by then. She said it proved I was a hussy. I was nearly seven months pregnant when we married.'

Carol sighed. 'I wish I'd been here.'

'No you don't,' said Serendipity, 'you'd have hated me. It was a nice wedding, though. I wore a wheatsheaf on my head and came disguised as the Goddess of Fertility.'

'Are you serious?'

'Absolutely. That's what I looked like. Mother dressed me, and I think she was on something at the time. Clive wore a top hat . . .' she looked wistful. 'He was very handsome.'

'Neil wore tails,' said Carol darkly, 'and a waistcoat from Savile Row, and I went as a giant meringue because mother was at the height of her Zsa Zsa phase. We had two hundred guests and I hardly knew any of them, and Neil and I rowed for weeks because I wouldn't say "obey."'

'I didn't say it,' said Serendipity.

'Oh,' said Carol. 'I – oh.'

'What?'

'Just period pain,' said Carol. 'I think I'll pop home for a good night's sleep.' And she insisted, despite Serendipity's worried fussing, on going alone.

But she went to the mud spring instead, because it all suddenly seemed too much, and there she began to cry, slow, silent painful tears, squeezing from her eyes like blood from a stone. Sitting on the old tree stump she felt them creating paths through her make-up like the little streams you get on the beach, and wondered, more in habit than in concern, what sort of a mess this was making of her mascara.

'I never met a man worth that sort of fuss,' said the dry voice of Penelope Forbes at her shoulder.

Carol swallowed, embarrassment muting the free expression of self-indulgent grief. 'I'm not crying over him,' she managed between hiccups, 'I'm facing a moral dilemma.'

'Oh, is that all?' said Penelope, sitting next to Carol and producing something from her pocket. She proffered it: 'Creme egg?'

Carol stared, then began to giggle through the tears. 'I haven't wanted one of those in years,' she said, taking it, 'but I seem to be doing a lot of things I haven't done for years.'

'That's what happens when you come home,' said Penelope: 'all your old habits pop up from where you left them and jump right back on board.'

Carol smiled and bit the top off the egg. It was just as she remembered creme eggs to be. 'I'm probably really crying because I'm not pregnant,' she said, matter-of-factly.

'Well, that makes a change – eighteen years ago it was Serendipity there crying because she was,' said Penelope, also matter-of-factly. 'Mind you, if you were it would be by that egotistical creature who had the nerve to make a pass at me.'

'He didn't!'

'He did,' said Penelope. 'I was having an innocent late-night bathe when he happened upon me and offered to join me.'

'What did you say?'

'Well, he had stripped by then – I think he thought that would sway me. I remarked on how much like a pig's trotter his equipment might seem, subterraneanly – from a lobster's point of view – and it seemed to put him off. I presume he would have been the father.'

'Not definitely,' admitted Carol. 'Oh God, I've been so awful.' She began to cry again.

Penelope finished her creme egg. 'Well, you certainly sound as if you've been a bit of a hussy.'

'Oh, I've been much worse than that.' Carol looked at her through tear-filled eyes: 'I've done something so awful that no hussy would even consider it, not even the Chief Hussy of the Real Old Hussy Society. I can't even bear to say it to myself.'

'I'm sure it can't be that bad,' said Penelope comfortably, 'but would you like to give me a clue?'

Carol wanted to tell her, but still shook her head. 'I stole something,' she said. The mud spring sat, unmoved and gloopy, before them. Perhaps I should throw myself in, she thought, because when I finally do confess to Serendipity and Clive they'll throw me in for sure.

'Oh yes?'

Carol nodded. 'Something that belonged to Clive and Serendipity. They didn't need it, and I thought I did. But it wasn't any use because he'd already had a vasectomy, and I'd done this foul thing by the time I realized' – she began to cry even more loudly – 'with a plastic syringe in the car park behind Boots.'

'Dear me,' said Penelope, 'this does sound interesting. I must say, though, if what you're after is a quick fertilizing then I'd highly recommend Macclesfield. Would you like another creme egg?'

Carol sniffed, trying to compose herself. 'I think I might be sick if I ate another one. You've guessed, haven't you? You know I used Clive's sperm sample on myself.'

'As you say, a rather pointless exercise,' said Penelope prosaically.

'Awful, though,' said Carol. 'How on earth am I going to tell them?'

'Take my advice,' said Penelope, 'and don't. Tell the mud spring instead. It's a good repository for nasty secrets. They just sink away into the depths of time.'

'They'll come back up eventually,' said Carol mournfully. 'Secrets are like buried treasure – there's always someone digging around for them, so they turn up again in the end.'

'Don't bank on it,' said Penelope encouragingly. 'There are a lot of them in there, believe me, and I haven't seen a single one come back up yet, so I wouldn't worry. We all have terrible secrets – it's the price of growing up.'

'What are yours?'

'Oh, the mud spring has most of mine,' said Penelope, 'so I don't worry. But I did use an electrician rather as you used Clive's sample. The poor man had only come to fix my wiring. It was five and fifteen amp in those days, you see. He came to rid me of my round-pin plugs. At least you did the work yourself, you and your syringe . . .'

'Lost it? How in heaven's name can you lose a llama?'

'Well, by the time we got there it had just disappeared into the crowd, sir.'

'Disappeared into the crowd? What sort of a crowd are we talking about?'

'Villagers, sir,' said Roger, able to see where the conversation was going; not able to stop it.

'And were any of these villagers,' said the sergeant, glowing slightly, 'unusually hairy or camel like? Did any of them have four legs and sport particularly supercilious expressions? I ask, you understand, because I would like to be sure I have a clear picture of the situation before I *bawl you out of my office*!'

Roger attempted a little humour to defuse the situation. 'No sir, they were typical East Anglians, although the lead soprano did say that the tenor and the llama were virtually indistinguishable with her eyes closed.' He smiled hopefully. The delivery had been good, the expression satisfactory. Shame about the audience really. He would have got a less critical reception at the Comedy Store – or even possibly from the Russian-speaking crew of a cod trawler while they were asleep. Night duty it was, then. He sighed.

The following morning Serendipity was seized by a mammoth urge to build nests, and was mowing the lawn for a second time to try to get that nice crisscross effect they have at Fulham football ground when a tell-tale but unsurprising pop told her that all was not as it had been. Carol, arriving in post-Penelope mood (full of chocolate, slightly fragile and humming uncanny tunes which sounded a bit like Oasis but a bit not) found her squatting next to the mower, humming a similar tune.

'Hi, are you making grass grow?' she asked cheerfully. Her secret was consigned to the mud, and she only carried the one problem now, the one of spending the rest of two million pounds, and that seemed a small one by comparison to the other, and not worth getting too het up about.

'Not exactly. It's a little more primitive than that,' said Serendipity, vaguely wondering if Carol would cotton on, or if she was too distant from childbirth to pick up the vibes.

'You're in labour?' Carol, cottoning on rapidly, burst into tears again. I seem to be doing this a lot, she thought.

Serendipity gazed at her with a semi-detached sympathy. 'I think I'm the one who's supposed to do that,' she said thoughtfully after a while, 'but I'm afraid I'm going to have to spend a little time squatting inelegantly now and imagining I'm a water lily. Please will you ring Clive?'

Carol nodded mutely, tears still running down her face, and went to phone. Clive, said the receptionist, was on an urgent visit to a patient. They'd get him home as soon as they could. Meanwhile, was there anything they could do?

Carol had no idea. She was, she discovered, totally ignorant of what you did when your best friend went into labour. Miranda appeared, then went off, disconcertingly, to make raspberry tea. Serendipity seemed calm enough. After all, she told Carol cheerfully, she was pretty sure that Phoebe had been conceived on a lawnmower, so it was all quite appropriate. Even so, Carol felt herself trembling.

'What's happening now?'

'I'm trying to concentrate on the opening petals of a flower,' said Serendipity, with a pained expression, 'but all I can see in my mind's eye is these giant metal teeth. I think it might help if you talked to me.'

'I could ask you something,' said Carol, 'if you don't mind?'

'Oooph,' said Serendipity, 'please do.'

'OK. Tell me about your scan. Was it really magical?'

Serendipity heard the wistful note. 'It is – although you have to make your own magic. They don't worry much about ambience – actually, from the time I was allotted you'd have thought I was gestating a gallstone.'

'So don't they go away,' asked Miranda, appearing with herb tea, 'and leave you, you know, to quietly commune with the screen?'

'Certainly not,' said Serendipity, 'although I think I spend most of pregnancy communing silently anyway – especially when she moves.'

'That must feel weird,' said Miranda, sympathetically.

'It's lovely – but I've felt it so often now that when I'm not pregnant I occasionally get the same feeling, and I pat it with a smug glow and say a silent hello even though it's only a rumble in the plumbing – hang on – ooooooooph. God, I remember this now. Those bloody metal teeth.'

'I wouldn't have thought you could forget it,' said Carol, fascinated.

'Oh you do,' said Serendipity, 'you remember that it hurts, but you don't remember what that feels like. The same as with life. It's God, being crafty, making sure you have another one. Where was I? Oh, yes, when I had my scan with Lily, they showed me her bile duct.'

'What on earth for?'

'Because it was there,' said Serendipity, 'and because it was a nice one, apparently. Miranda, will you look after Lily. I think I can hear Clive.'

'I'll look after them if you like,' said Carol, who felt that she easily equalled Lily in the mutual adoration stakes.

'Oh no,' said Serendipity, 'I need you to stay with me. You should have been here the first time.'

It's only in books that the heroine gives birth in two minutes because either she's had a silent and painless labour, she's been held hostage by Uzbek terrorists on a stationary 737 at Stansted, or she's been snowed in at home with phone lines down (and of all these possibilities, the last is by far the least likely). The reality, as Carol discovered, was slightly more long-winded. As Clive loaded them into the car and Penelope fussed about trying to get her to take the right tapes ('Tapes, Mother? I don't want to listen to tapes. I plan to make far too much noise to appreciate whalesong') Serendipity insisted, 'Carol, will you come with us?'

And there wasn't time to think about it, so Carol went.

It was, in the end, the most extraordinary thing that had ever happened to her. It was untidy and uncontrolled, it was undignified and noisy, it was characterized by bad jokes from Clive and completely unfunny jokes from Serendipity, who was high on something she was getting through a mask and seemed to think she was an extra in *Baywatch*, and it was completely lacking in the sort of reverence that Carol had always imagined would attend childbirth. The most unbelievable thing of all, she thought, watching Clive cut his daughter's umbilical cord, is that so many people do it – and then they do it again. Bloody hell, my mother did this (I wonder if she took her shoes off?) And when it was all over, there was one more person in the world than there had been before, and her name was Phoebe. And Carol thought: at least if I never do have a baby of my own, I know now what it's like, I was here. It's not a secret from me any more.

But I will have a baby, she thought, feeling hope spring in that eternal way it has, and it will be without using a plastic syringe, too. It was amazing, she thought, that Serendipity had realized how *good* it would be for her, Carol, to have been there. Most people would have thought it would be the worst thing for her to have to watch someone else give birth, but Serendipity had known it would be the best thing, the biggest gift. And that, thought Carol, is what best friends are for.

Sidney Antrobus, just off shift and a happier man by far, now that he had something proper to do with his hands again, saw the Rowans and Carol Pendragon getting out of a car. Serendipity Rowan was clearly arriving home with yet another baby. Why, only yesterday she had still been pregnant. It just went to show, Sidney felt, that women were very like chickens really, they just popped another one out between mealtimes and got on with it. His Hilda had always just got on with it too, until now. In fact, at moments of particular passion he had been known to call her his little bantam – but best not to think of that. Now this money had turned her into an imitation snooty bag.

The mud spring sat alone, abandoned beneath shining skies, thinking of ages past and interesting species it had known, things with wings and things with claws. Nothing with udders, though. It looked pensive, thought Sidney Antrobus, as he approached it, reflective, as though it had a lot of secrets hidden down there in its bowels. Well, he had another secret for it. Glancing surreptitiously round he wrapped his wage slip round a stone, flung it into the very middle, and watched it slip away. Broomhill Poultry liked to do things properly. They might be prepared to pay him the grand rate of absolutely nothing per hour (just a tiny bit less than the recommended minimum wage, then) but they insisted on giving him a slip. And Sidney did not want Hilda seeing those slips – she'd make his life misery. It was bad enough her employing dragons to polish the inside of his underwear drawer.

Chapter Thirteen

It took Alice a few days to get over the trauma, but even she commented that a kiss from a llama was not so very different from a kiss from Dirk Mullins, in the end. Clive said it was no less than he had expected all along, but as doctors are trained to say 'I told you so' at every available opportunity, no-one took a great deal of notice. Meanwhile, Lily remained cheerful, and Eric remained greedy, whilst Serendipity wrapped herself in Phoebe and wept copiously whenever anyone said anything soppy, even 'pass me the tomato sauce'. Carol felt better than she had for a long time. With Giles teaching her, at appropriate moments of course, to talk dirty in ancient Icelandic (whoever said that Cambridge professors have no relevance to modern life?) and with Phoebe, via her mother, having booked her in already as godmother, the spending of the rest of the treasure money seemed but a minor worry. Since Hugh had volunteered to start sifting through her mail and replying as necessary, she didn't even have to put up with the flak any more . . .

Dear Mrs Pendragon, I have never lived in Parvum Magna but I have always wanted to . . . Yours sincerely, Bertha Bates

Dear Bertha, You wouldn't like it here, really. We are turning the village into an open safari park experiment, so that lions and other creatures will be roaming freely at night . . . Yours sincerely, Hugh Appleton, Private Sec. to Mrs Pendragon

Dear Mrs Pendragon, I lived in Parvum Magna for twenty years, and was a good friend to your dear Uncle Albert, who would have remembered me in his will . . . Yours sincerely, Edna Tibbett

Dear Elsie, Sorry, his memory was obviously even worse than yours. Hugh Appleton, Sec. to Mrs Pendragon

Dear Mrs Pendragon, I am six feet two inches tall and very handsome, and I saw your picture in the paper . . .

Dear Tall One, My ex-husband is very rich and particularly likes tall men. Please refer your question to Neil Pendragon, 8 Tunstall Road, London N6 . . . Yours sincerely, Hugh Appleton, etc.

Hugh hadn't had this much fun since the English teacher had had a momentary lapse of Hugh-consciousness, and set an essay on 'The Ethics of Keeping Pets' in the summer exam (he was still marking it).

Miranda cooed so much over her new sister that Serendipity began to fear she had wakened latent broody feelings that might otherwise have slept on for a decade, like King Arthur in his alleged bedroom beneath the mud spring. But she need not have feared. Road protest seemed to have opened up Miranda's horizons. Now, cradling Phoebe in the sitting room while Clive finished seeing all the head lice he'd missed earlier in the day (Broomhill was a middle-class town, so genuine nits were considered a medical emergency), Serendipity heard her daughter in the hall. She was obviously meant to hear: perhaps the presence of her mother was a form of moral support. I don't know that I'm much good, though, thought Serendipity, confrontations make me weep. Mind you, there's always Leonardo. He'd be OK in a fight. She waved at Leonardo who, eerily, waved back.

'I don't see why you're so against the idea of sex,' Luke was saying, and Serendipity shivered. Would teenage pregnancy be an ever-recurring spectre in her life? Why are we all blessed with so much hindsight and so little foresight, she wondered.

'I'm not,' said Miranda's voice loudly, with a cheerful lack of tact, 'I'm just against it with you.'

'You don't mean that,' came Luke's voice. Oops, thought Serendipity, too cocky. You've had it now. 'After all we've

310

been through together at the road protest.'

'I didn't see you throwing missiles at the police when they carried me out,' said Miranda pointedly.

Luke sighed audibly. 'What would have been the point? You were loving it. Come here,' he added in what were obviously intended to be come-to-bed tones, 'you know you can't say no to me.' Serendipity winced. Why are men so bad at that tone? she wondered.

'Touch me and I'll vomit,' said Miranda, offering, it had to be said, minimal encouragement. Serendipity decided it was time for the rescue. She opened the door.

'Hi, you two,' she managed with the false airy breeziness of TV presenters who have just heard from the microphone in their ear that their knickers have been showing for twenty minutes and that viewers are phoning to complain, 'you're back. Would you both like a coffee? I was just making some.'

She was not immensely surprised when Luke refused the coffee.

'Are you OK?' she asked Miranda, after he had gone.

Miranda swallowed hard. 'Absolutely OK,' she said, with the convincing ring of Mystic Meg. 'Really.'

'Oh dear, I'm sorry. Had you just gone off him, or is there something else you'd like to talk to me about?'

Miranda sighed. 'No. He was just getting too serious.'

'No, you hadn't gone off him?'

'No, I hadn't. Well – maybe a little. But he was talking about our future, and I don't want to end up . . .' her voice trailed away.

'Like me? It's all right. I haven't spent the last seventeen years bringing you up in the hope that you'd be married by now, you know. I don't want you to end up like me either.'

Miranda looked at her mother as if she was seeing her for the first time. 'You're not unhappy, are you, Mum? I mean, I always assumed you were happy. You're not sorry you had us?'

'Oh, of course I'm not!' cried Serendipity, dismayed. 'I didn't mean it like that at all. I just want you to have a chance to make up your own mind what you want before life takes over.'

'Oh.' Miranda looked doubtful. 'Well, to be honest,

311

actually I quite fancied one of the policemen, and Luke showed the emotional depth of a pot noodle most of the time. It worries me a bit, that you can go off someone so much, when you were on them so much only a few weeks earlier. It's like a change of focus.'

'So you've got new glasses, so to speak?'

Miranda sighed. 'I suppose so, but it worries me – I mean, how do I know I won't keep wanting to change them? I mean, look at Carol – she'd had her glasses on for years.'

'You don't know,' said Serendipity. 'I sometimes think it's more luck than judgement.'

'Greg says that luck is just something invented by people who haven't got religion, to convince them they don't face the odds alone,' said Miranda. 'We had lots of talks around the campfire.'

'Oh, and who's Greg?' Serendipity thought it all sounded rather jolly, but was not sure she was quite ready for a boyfriend who did not believe in washing.

'My policeman,' said Miranda, 'he's gorgeous.' She frowned. 'For now.'

'Stop worrying,' said Serendipity: 'one day you'll feel ready to take a chance, and you will. I just took mine early.'

'You don't regret marrying Dad?'

Clive, coming in through the kitchen door, heard her say, 'Never for a second of my life,' and smiled.

'So you'll keep me for now, then?' He kissed the top of her head, and beamed soppily at Phoebe.

Serendipity grinned. 'Just for now.'

He was followed in by Hugh, Belinda and Felix, who had just popped home to satisfy an acute cornflakes craving.

'Spoon,' said Clive pointedly, watching them shovel cereal in a manner reminiscent of feeding time in the Serengeti just after an entire herd of particularly juicy wildebeest have spontaneously died of old age.

'Hmm?' said Felix without curiosity.

Clive glared at him. 'I've spent the last four million years evolving to the point at which I could use a spoon,' he said; 'what have you been doing?'

'Carving,' said Belinda, immune to sarcasm, 'and it's thirsty work. We're off back to the mud spring. Hugh and I are making a new sign – someone took the other one away. And then we're going to make a new sign for the builders, too.'

Serendipity grinned. 'You mean Gromit, Flange and Peebles, the erect trio? I'm not surprised they never got any work.'

'Why?' asked Belinda.

'People,' said Serendipity obscurely, 'probably weren't too sure about them.'

'That's what Hugh said,' said Belinda, 'which is why they're paying us to make them a new sign when we've finished this one.'

'Girls can't carve,' said Felix sullenly. It was becoming clear to him that Hugh and Belinda were forming an attachment of which he could not be a part. He went with them anyway. You never knew, he reasoned, what they might spell wrong without him.

I wonder what it will say, thought Serendipity, cradling Phoebe as they left the house. My generation would have carved something gormless on the tree, she thought, but somehow our children seem a lot wiser than we were.

Hilda Antrobus was very worried. Sidney was up to something. He was out all the time, recently. She might have everything anyone could ever want – a proper cleaner, a house to die for, underwear from Marks and Spencer – but she wasn't happy. For a traitorous voice had begun to whisper in her head, what if Sidney has another woman? What if, after twenty-nine years of wedded bliss, the planned cake with the big thirty iced on top was about to slip irrevocably from their grasp? Her Sid might not be that much to look at – he was a difficult man to hug unless you had arms like Guy the gorilla, and threading the cord through his pyjama bottoms took all morning – but he was a man of means now, and money attracts the sort of nubile young blondes with bosoms like traffic cones who are capable of breaking the land-speed record when they hear the chink of brass . . .

That silly cow Hermione Beadle was no help at all. 'Well, madam,' she had said, when Hilda had opined that Sidney was hardly ever at home, 'at least he isn't treading mud into the carpets.' Hermione had never married, and she read Esme Smuts novels in her spare time. That said it all, really.

Hilda missed Sid, and she missed his mud. She missed the look on his face when she used to bring him a cuppa at the end of a hard afternoon on the chicken shift. She missed the laughs they used to have at the bingo (for how can you go to bingo when you're rich? The others would hate it if you won, and there's no point going there to lose). She missed him calling her his little bantam. She resolved to have things out. She was a resolute woman when the chips were down.

'I don't feel comfortable in my own house,' said Sid, when she tackled him on his way out in the morning. 'It doesn't feel like my house, especially now you've employed a dragon to hoover the hall.'

'You just have to get used to her,' said Hilda, 'she's got a nice smile.'

'If I could crack a route through that permafrost she wears as a facial expression I might find out,' said Sid, 'but I doubt it. Hilda, I miss the way things were. I don't want a dragon in my house. I want—'

'Sidney, I think you'd better just tell me,' said Hilda, bracing herself for the worst: 'where have you been spending all your time? You go out alone for hours.'

Sidney Antrobus was an honest man. He had never lied to his Hilda, not direct, like, and he wasn't about to start now. There might be some in the factory who kept mum about the size of the annual Christmas stuffing bonus in their wage packet, or who pretended there was never any cider drunk on the annual works trip to Great Yarmouth, but Sid had never been one of them. 'Hilda,' he told her, looking her firmly in the eye, 'I have been plucking and stuffing chickens, and I'm proud of it.'

Neil was not a happy man. Sitting in the Highgate house, contemplating the expensive hi-fi, the wide-screen TV and the silver-framed photographs of himself dotted about, he was experiencing a peculiar, ants-in-the-pants feeling which he did not recognize as loneliness. Despite the throughput, over the last two weeks, of a string of attractive blondes of every body type, despite spending several evenings at an insalubrious establishment named the Bristol Club which boasted no discernible link with anywhere in the county of Avon, he just was not content. The idea that he might be missing Carol did not occur to him for a moment, although he did ring her up and tell her that if she didn't come down to London to talk he would make sure she wouldn't see a penny of her half of the house. His astonishment when Carol had said, 'Fine, keep the house, I've got a house, I don't need two' had been palpable. In Neil's world you hung onto your assets. She didn't even seem worried by the photos he had of her with that prawn-like creature she had the fling with (he patted his breast pocket where the negatives still lodged). She had become quite peculiar. Not his sort of woman at all – but, try as he might, Neil could not quite convince himself that he had no use for Carol.

It was then that it came to him in a blinding flash. Of course! Carol was mentally unbalanced. She was ill. That explained it all. It explained her apparently going off him, her strange but forgivable lapse with that streak of dishwater from the Cambridge college, her insistence that money was not important to her, her crazy scheme to give away the Parvum Magna treasure, treasure that she had found herself, on land that was rightfully hers . . . Perhaps those villagers had put her on something, thought Neil. Clive Rowan was her doctor, wasn't he? Obviously he had drugged her in order to manipulate her mind. That was it, it all fitted. He was a magician as well, was he not? Neil had heard about magicians. He knew all about the things they could do. Disappearance, levitation, hypnosis . . . he had spent years trying to perfect hypnosis himself, in fact, driven by the fantasy of what women might be prepared to do for him while they were under. Imagine the possible misuse of those powers by a GP! Neil had himself convinced. He must get back to Parvum Magna today. He must save the money – no, he must save Carol. He *must* save Carol. And the money, of course.

He rang first, but she wasn't in, so he simply seized his package of photos, jumped into his new Lotus, feeling like a knight in shining armour, and drove hell for leather up the

M11, thoroughly upsetting fifty-one members of the Morris Minor Owners Club who were proceeding at just under the legal limit towards Diss, which is a Mecca for Morris Minors.

Hector Bollivant was also indulging in a little fantasy. Alice had been, he felt, quite superb in her operatic role. Another emerald had been called for. (Alice was rather keen on emeralds, something she had in common with Penelope. Penelope believed that they represented female power, the strength of women in labour. Alice believed they were expensive.) And Alice, flush with her musical triumph, had been quite taken with his suggestion that the costume jewellery she had worn had made her look ravishing, like the sort of woman who should be lying bejewelled upon silk sheets in a house with two outdoor floodlights. Of course, opera purists would have said that the penurious students of *La Bohème* would not have worn jewels, when they couldn't afford food – but Alice had told the wardrobe woman it was artistic licence, and perhaps they had been once-wealthy students fallen upon hard times at a time when no-one would buy second-hand jewels, not even for the price of a bowl of soup.

Having got thus far, Hector had reached the point of trying to insert into Alice's mind the idea that wearing a crown would enhance her features to an incredible degree. He had an ace of temptation up his sleeve in the form of the floodlight. All he needed was the crown – perhaps Alice could arrange to borrow it? He would work on it.

Carol was not expecting Neil, although she was expecting Pamela Piggott, roving reporter from *News East*. Pamela was doing the story on the Broomhill treasure, and had come to arrange for the cameras to cover the official opening of the restored village hall. Carol had decided to have this the following day, to get it over with before the Featherstones had the chance to find out about it or Alice Bollivant turned it into a huge affair and crowned herself queen.

Pamela arrived ten minutes early, as the best journalists always do, for you never know what you might catch people doing if you're early. She was dressed in her extracting confidences outfit – chainstore, unthreatening, absolutely not her at all, but the production company paid for it so that was all right.

'What would be really good . . .' Pamela told Carol as she sipped tea in her kitchen, unaware that Giles Perry was drinking the rest of the pot in the pink bedroom, recently redecorated but still pink, having been hurriedly abandoned there only five minutes earlier. Carol offered ginger biscuits, which reporters never eat as they might stick their jaws together and thus hinder the necessary two hundred questions per hour of rapier-like penetration. She was unaware that Neil and his latest Lotus had reached the A11 junction on the motorway and were heading rapidly into Suffolk. 'No thanks – what would be really good would be if we could get the treasure here, and show you presenting it to someone from St Alupent's. I'm sure our viewers would be interested in the crown.'

'I don't know,' said Carol dubiously. 'It's all in St Alupent's museum. I'm sure it's much safer there.'

But Pamela was not an intrepid reporter for nothing. She had been reporting on these peculiar villages around Broomhill for some years, and she knew the score. They said no, you persuaded, they were polite, you begged, they said yes. She tried it on Carol. It was local history, she said . . . people would be fascinated . . . it was the BBC's duty to educate . . . Boadicea was a local queen . . . she fought Romans who were probably their very own ancestors . . . it was an upbeat, feel-good story, it would encourage other villages to do the same ('What, flog their tribal queens?' asked Carol, with flippancy which fell, stone-like, into the pit of Pamela Piggott's family-programme awareness.)

Eventually it worked: Pamela had worn Carol down as subtly as industrial sanding machines wear down very soft things.

'I'll speak to the professor who's in charge of the collection,' Carol promised, 'and see if we can arrange to have it away . . . have it here, that is, for you to film tomorrow.'

Pamela caught the slip – her slip-catching skills had been honed well by her time working for the tabloid press, before she made it to the heady heights of front-of-camera. Only one more step to take – to her own, daily, agony show. She was already stocking up on suitable suits (all agony aunts wear suits. Somehow jumpers and jeans are unsuitable for agony – which may be why clinical psychologists and bereavement counsellors, who always wear leggings, find their work so difficult). Pamela knew more about psychology than Freud, and firmly believed that nothing pops out accidentally and without cause. 'A friend of yours, is he, this professor?' she asked archly, and Carol blushed.

'Er – yes,' she said.

Pamela beamed. 'Well I'm sure he'll arrange it for you,' she oozed at Carol. 'We'll come over with the crew early tomorrow morning, when the light is fresh, to set up and film the treasure and the village hall, then we'll film the presentation itself at a more civilized hour – say, nine? If we start early enough it should be ready to go out at lunchtime.'

'I'm not sure that we could arrange to get the treasure over here that early in the morning,' said Carol, frowning. There was a loud knock at the door, and she stood up.

Pamela was airy. This should be a bit of a scoop, and the woman was easily managed. She got the feeling this Professor Perry was easily managing her. 'Well, just get the treasure over here tonight,' she said. 'Nothing will happen to it overnight in Parvum Magna – this isn't New York, you know. Anyway, the Broomhill police will send someone to stand guard over it till morning – they could do with a bit of decent publicity at the moment, and I know the sergeant.'

'Oh, I don't . . .' began Carol, opening the door, and there was – 'Neil! What are you doing here?'

'Came to see how you were, darling. I've been worried about you,' breezed Neil, aglow with dribbling charm.

Behind her Carol could sense all of Pamela's mental antennae shooting out at once, like the prongs on a mine. Dangerous.

'This is my ex-husband,' she told her firmly, as Neil listened with narrowed ears, 'and I'm afraid I need to speak to him alone. I'll arrange everything, as you said. Goodbye.'

'What about our early start?'

'Everything will be absolutely fine,' said Carol, who right

then would have agreed to dance naked round the village hall coated in cake mix and pursued by a dozen hungry llamas if it would have got rid of Pamela. The last thing she needed was to read about her private life in the press.

As Pamela left, disappointed, Neil was settling himself into his favourite chair. Well, they were all revolting flowery chairs, but it was his least unfavourite, he thought. Carol watched with some satisfaction (never having told him that it was the one Uncle Percy had died in, with Cruella riding high) as he explained her dangerous mental state.

Carol heard him out, although only because she didn't want to storm out of the room and leave him there in case he wandered around and found the post-coital Giles upstairs. As he told her how ill she was, how poisoned by villagers, hypnotized and drugged, she became increasingly incredulous.

'Do you realize what you're accusing Clive of, Neil? My God, if he'd done what you say he'd be guilty of – I don't know – extreme misconduct or something. He's my friend, and this sounds like one of your more perverse fantasies. I'm not mad, I'm perfectly sane. I've come home, that's all, and realized that there are things, lots and lots of things, that are more important than money and business success.'

Neil was genuinely mystified. 'What things?'

Carol, watching his puzzled expression, felt momentarily sorry for him. 'Love, Neil. Children, friendship, loyalty.'

Neil's face twisted into a mask of scorn. 'And I suppose you think you'll get pregnant here by that radish you've been screwing and live happily ever after with the seven dwarfs and all the pretty little woodland creatures.'

Carol's sympathy faded. 'Don't be silly, Neil.'

'Silly? At least I'm not deluded. Let me tell you, dear, I've made more women pregnant than you'll ever know. If someone round here is as dry as Namibia it's you.'

'Well, maybe I am, Neil, and maybe it's you – and maybe I'll never have a baby, but I can live in hope, and I can live happily.'

'No you can't. Frigid women don't get pregnant, and I've screwed more responsive . . . screws!'

319

Carol was white. With her dark hair flying round her face and a patch of pink on each cheek she looked like one of those china dolls that antique programme presenters get most excited over when they're particularly ugly. But Carol did not look ugly, Neil noticed, she looked rather striking. He started to get out of his chair to come towards her . . .

Carol exploded like a microwaved mango, only more messily. 'Get out!' she shouted at him. 'Get out of my house, you . . . you smarmy, git-faced, faithless, cheating *bastard*! Get out of that bloody chair that Uncle Percy popped his socks in, and get out of my space. Take your bastard face and your bastard body and your bastard bastard washboard bastard abdomen and . . . and . . . *fuck off*!'

'Jolly well said,' said Giles Perry from the doorway as Neil slammed out of the house. 'Now, where were we?'

Carol burst into tears.

Neil, or Nefarious Neil, as he might more accurately have been known by this time, had had enough of this vilification. Why was he being seen as the villain of the piece? He had been genuinely concerned about his wife all along. It's true, he told himself, and may God make me unattractive to women if I tell a lie. But now, storming out of the farm in search of something to kick, he felt there were only two choices: further pleading, or revenge. And revenge was starting to look rather attractive. But what revenge?

As Neil stewed, Giles and Carol, holding hands, went to inspect the completed, refurbished and extended village hall and tennis court, whilst Messrs Gromit, Flange and Peebles stood proudly by.

Their renovation of the old hall and erection of its new extension had been swift and efficient – as indeed erections so often are. Besides, Gromit, Flange and Peebles had been promised such a high rate that they had been desperate to finish and get off to the Bahamas for a holiday.

'It's wonderful,' Giles told Carol, 'although I think you were probably wise to do without the floodlights in the end. You haven't managed to spend it all, though. As I said, the crown alone will cover the cost of this.'

'I know,' Carol sighed. 'I've been trying to avoid

having another meeting. It always brings the Featherstones back from Glastonbury like the ghosts of Christmas past, and the sort of ideas pouring in by post were enough to send me screaming. Hugh answers them for me now.'

'I bet those letters are interesting,' said Giles, smiling.

Carol smiled back. 'I don't look – but I still get cornered in the village all the time. Brian Baggins now thinks I should build a mausoleum with wax effigies of dead communists in it. He thinks it would be a tourist attraction.'

Giles grinned. 'Stop worrying. Things always work out, you know. Anyway, this is brilliant, you should be proud.'

'I am,' said Carol, 'really.'

'I suppose you'll be going back to London soon.' *Don't scare her off, Giles, good women don't come along very often.* 'Your business must need you.'

'No it won't,' said Carol; 'they haven't needed me in the slightest. I've sold up to my manager. I'm staying.'

'Really?' Giles tried not to jump up and clap his hands, but didn't quite manage it. 'That's great. So – er – what are your plans?'

Carol grinned back. 'I haven't gone through all this just to let someone else have all the fun of playing bingo here, you know. And my next plan is to spend a great deal of time in bed with you. As for Parvum Magna, I'm here to stay.'

Giles smiled. 'So where shall we put the treasure? We can bring it over from St Alupent's this evening.'

'I don't know,' said Carol, 'but we'd better decide. It's six o'clock already.'

'Carol, Professor Perry, how nice to see you.' That was Alice, appearing in the doorway. 'Carol, dear, I wondered if perhaps you would let me have the new keys for safe keeping. I am, after all, Parish Council secretary, and Hector is chairman, you know.'

'Of course,' said Carol, trying not to beam broadly – but how nice to be handing the whole thing over. 'Here, Alice, but you'll have to wait around for the treasure, I'm afraid. They're not here yet, and we were just going for a drink.'

Alice did not seem to mind. Indeed she thought it a wonderful opportunity. They left her inspecting the snooker table and went to see Serendipity and Phoebe.

As darkness fell, Roger the policeman was not impressed with this latest task. As a rural community constable he had hoped to cycle around elegantly on a shiny bike receiving rhubarb from little old ladies. Unfortunately, his personal fitness level was such that the microscopic gradients between Broomhill and Parvum Magna left him exhausted and gasping, so he had now been issued with a 50cc moped. It made a noise like a hundred schoolboys farting and granted him the street cred normally reserved, he felt, for old Greek men on donkeys. Now, to add insult to injury, he and the scooter were to spend a night in Parvum Magna's village hall guarding this bloody stupid treasure from God knows who. That bloody llama, probably. It had clearly been up to no good the last time he saw it.

Being close to the church all night worried Roger. He watched enough re-runs of *Scooby-Doo* when he wasn't studying criminology (which he wasn't studying most of the time) to know that ghostly beings lurk at every turn in a law enforcer's life. (Roger had rather missed the point in *Scooby-Doo*, which was generally that the ghosts are never real, but are nefarious wrongdoers posing in completely unconvincing ghost costumes. He was perhaps the only man alive more gormless than Shaggy.)

The sound of something chomping only served to heighten his nerves. It was a regular chomp, a menacing chomp, the sort of chomp that you might hear from a creature who had been chewing on the same piece of something chompable for years and years . . . a creature which no longer tasted that which it chomped, but which chomped for mere effect, out of a devilish desire to strike fear and trepidation into the hearts of those who upheld the law in all its glory. It was the chomp, he felt, with incandescent palpitations, of a zombie. There was no doubt, surely, that what he was hearing was none other than Tulip, the ghostly cow of Parvum Magna, haunting the churchyard down the years in search of the man who, through his deficient fencing skills, had despatched her to her gruesome grave. Tulip was searching for the remains of Percival Greatbottom . . .

Roger could stand it no longer. Even in his state of

adrenalin-charged cow-phobia he realized that a call to base for back-up would interrupt the evening coffee break and snooker down at the station. A plea for support would draw laughter and derision, and make him yet again the unwilling target of police snooker-room wit, so he took the only course possible. One can only live with fear for so long, and Roger might be afraid but he was also brave. He would confront the cow.

Serendipity had finally given in to the sleep-in-the-hide pressure, and had made a humungous pile of ham sandwiches and set up a two-way baby monitor, which Felix had immediately switched off so that he, Hugh and Belinda could tell one another all the rude jokes they knew, thus continuing the endless exchange of vulgarity between different school populations that so influences the intellects of young people today. Intermittently they checked the churchyard, where Eric had gone for a late-night feast (grass is often particularly lush in churchyards, though it is probably best not to spend too long wondering why).

'There was a young lady of Australia,' began Felix, 'who went to a dance as a dahlia, but the petals revealed what they should have concealed, and the dance, as a dance, was a failure.' He giggled hilariously at his own humour, while Belinda glowered.

'That's really sexist. Gran says that sexist men emasculate themselves.'

'That's rubbish,' said Felix. 'Why should being sexist make you clean?'

'Sssh,' said Hugh, 'someone's coming. Look.'

'Wha—?' began Felix, but Hugh put a hand over his mouth and they all watched through the tangle of hedge which made up the outer wall of their hide as Roger's torch beam appeared cautiously on the other side of it.

'He'll see Eric,' hissed Felix into Hugh's ear.

'No he won't – Eric's gone around the other side of the church . . .'

Allowing Eric out for an evening constitutional was part of Hugh's plot to tame him, so convincing Serendipity that he did not need to be betrayed to the Broomhill police. You gave him what he wanted, he became docile, then you trained him. That was the plan, though so far it had not gone well – Eric seemed to be in the grip of a relentless determination to eat, so profound and all-consuming that there was absolutely no room for standing on his hind legs or performing dressage. He was still eating now.

'I knew something was going on,' said Hugh in a forced whisper as they crouched together in the darkness and peered through the hedge. 'Just watch.'

Belinda regarded Hugh with admiration. 'You're very brave,' she told him.

Hugh was modest. 'Not really. Being brave is tackling your worst fear,' he said, 'and I'm not afraid of Roger. If I was as brave as a Piaroa Indian, then I'd be brave.'

'Why?'

'They eat freshly roasted tarantula thorax,' said Hugh, 'and hang the fangs round their necks.'

'Wow,' said Belinda, 'we must ask Gran what Handsome Dog eats.'

'Oh, stop making cows' eyes at him,' said Felix, annoyed at the gooseberry feelings washing over him.

Hugh assumed a superior expression to hide his secret pleasure. 'Just hush,' he said, 'and watch. That policeman is still creeping about, and we may need to rescue Eric again.'

Inside the hall Boadicea's treasure was set out ready for the presentation and TV cameras next morning. It was valuable, but it had a police guard, it had an alarm, no-one outside the village knew about it, so it seemed safe enough. In any case, Roger did not plan to leave it for long. Once round the village hall he would go, to face the fear head-on. He would challenge Tulip, that's what he would do. Humming, oddly, the 'Marseillaise', Roger strode forth. No matter that ghostly cows have staring eyes and huge swinging udders. No matter that the average cow passes enough wind each week to inflate the Virgin Atlantic Challenger. No matter that Tulip was a *ghost* . . .

Neil had been to Broomhill but had to return for his bags as they were Louis Vuitton. He saw the lights in the church hall as he drove back into the village, trying to decide what final, wounding thing he might say to Carol. Then he would return to Highgate and the life he knew. Carol could keep her twee little existence in crocheted teacosy land. He was out of here. She was unforgivable . . .

When he saw the lights his mind worked quickly, the synapses firing international bankerishly to reach a conclusion, to find some advantage, as there always is for someone, in the unexplained and uncanny. He was certain that something was going on . . . something in the churchyard – that was, without a doubt, a policeman over there.

Neil began to put the available twos together. Carol's mystery visitor earlier, who had the aura of the press about her. That Perry fellow hanging around like the smell of surreptitiously entertained ladies. The renovated village hall . . . it all made sense suddenly. The bloody treasure was here in the village hall, with no-one guarding it but that daft praddock in uniform who couldn't spot a burglar if he ran down the High Street carrying twenty thousand in used notes and a sack of ten pees with a screaming cashier shouting 'Stop, thief!' still attached to the other side. He'd bet he was right. And if the treasure was in the village hall, he knew who would have the key.

Of course he wouldn't steal it. Neil would not be stupid enough to commit that sort of crime. No, if Neil wanted to commit a crime it would be the kind of crime to baffle the Serious Fraud Squad for years. It would involve millions, and he'd have a doctor's note saying he had early-onset Alzheimer's disease prepared well in advance of needing any sort of legal advice.

But revenge. Cold revenge, Chinese style. Now that was an idea. And what would be the best revenge of all? How to hurt Carol and her new yokel friends? Take away something they valued. The treasure. The wealth. Neil was on vengeful ground that he understood.

So, as Roger crept valiantly clockwise around the village hall (for he was well aware that if he went anticlockwise he might be eaten by goblins or disappear into a passing wrinkle in time), and as the llama also went clockwise (for he was, he realized, in the northern hemisphere now), Neil put his cunning plan into action and pulled his car up outside Alice's house.

Alice was feeling neglected. Very neglected. It was bad enough that Hector was out late at his gardening club but, worse still, she had ventured into Argos today to take shelter from a shower, and had seen her emerald ring there. *Her* emerald ring, the one of which she had been so proud, the emerald so deep green and so flawless that she had thought it must for once have been the most expensive one Hector could find, was not a true emerald ring at all. It was a manufactured emerald. Man, rather than God, had fashioned it. It didn't matter, now, that she had loved the perfection of the stone and the simplicity of its setting. It didn't matter that she knew in her heart of hearts that whatever she owned there would always be someone with a bigger, better or more valuable one at Butterton School sports day. All that mattered was the knowledge that Hector had deceived her. He had not used all of his annual bonus to buy her ring. He had used only a small proportion of it. A very small proportion. The rest had obviously gone on this secret vice of his, this collection which she had found in the potting shed together with the Argos catalogue. It is always a shock when you discover that the man you thought you knew is an avid collector of Rupert the Bear memorabilia.

So because of all this, Alice was open to Neil's suggestion, a suggestion that the vain and greedy corner of her personality had, perhaps, always hoped that he would make. And it did not take her long, at the height of their encounter, to see the merit in his suggestion that Boadicea was actually a sexual icon, and that the wearing of her crown during the act itself would add a great deal to their enjoyment. Hector had suggested something similar, actually, but she had just thought he was being silly.

Neil was rather thrown to discover that Alice had the crown in her bedroom already, as the plan had involved her giving him the keys to go off and fetch it. This meant that he did have to completely seduce her rather than just make a start – but that was all right, it wouldn't take long and it wouldn't take much effort. Sex was, to Neil, primarily for demonstrating his own prowess rather than enjoying someone else's, and he could do that with almost anyone.

Alice told him she had decided to look after the crown for added security (it was really so that she could spend the evening trying it with a variety of different outfits), but as the keys to the village hall were in the drawer of her dressing table with it, Neil's task was no harder than he had anticipated. Once he had exhausted her – leaving himself barely breathless, of course – and she was asleep (smiling like a well-fed dormouse) he was off, keys in hand. After a little thought, he left the crown behind. She had looped her arm through it in her sleep, and he did not want to wake her. Besides, it did look rather good on her. It might give Hector a thrill.

Roger and Eric, meanwhile, had successfully avoided one another in the churchyard, and Eric was heading back towards the garden of Peacocks' Barn (it wasn't quite Patagonia, but it was home). Neil, creeping up the church path, saw the sheen of white on Eric's coat, and frowned. There was something decidedly peculiar about this village. He would be glad to leave it. He patted his breast pocket reassuringly. The photos were there, surely still his passport to a decent settlement from Carol.

It was Hugh, Felix and Belinda, then, who saw the movement in the shadows as Neil slipped into the village hall as stealthily and nefariously as a true villain might.

Alice had not been much impressed with Neil's performance. The trouble was that his ego had been the biggest thing in the bed by far and had taken up most of his attention. Beside him Hector, whom she had always assumed to be Mr Average, now seemed something of a cross between Cyrano de Bergerac and Casanova. True, Neil had had a few interesting ideas – particularly the crown – but now she found herself wondering exactly what Neil had intended by his seduction. She was no fool. It had been quite plain all along that Neil had wanted something – something, that is, distinct from that which he had already obtained.

Thoughtfully she opened the drawer where the keys to the village hall were kept, awaiting the grand opening tomorrow. They were gone. Alice frowned and dressed quickly . . .

'I told you our hide would come in useful,' hissed Felix, 'look. I bet he's going to steal the treasure.'

'We should call the police,' said Belinda, turning back towards the house. Hugh grabbed her arm.

'Think about what you just said. The policeman's name is . . . ?'

'Roger,' said Belinda. 'I see what you mean.'

'C'mon,' said Felix, 'we can look in through the window if we stand on Belinda.'

'Dream on,' said his sister.

Roger, oblivious to the grand larceny being attempted right under his nose, was pacing the perimeter of the churchyard looking for cowprints with his special torch. It was special because if you switched the switch the other way it was a siren. Roger was very proud of it. Eric, concealed behind a yew tree, watched Roger with interest but not enthusiasm.

'Hurry up,' said Felix, grumbling, 'you weigh a ton.'

'It's Neil – Carol's old Neil, I mean,' said Belinda, classifying Neil in that one casual phrase with brands of tampon Carol no longer favoured and brands of expensive washing powder that had failed to get the stains out. 'He's putting the treasure in a big bag. Actually, I think it's a pillowcase – he's just scooping it in.'

'Get down, then,' said Hugh, 'and we'll pow-wow.'

'I think he might hear us if we sing,' said Belinda dubiously.

'Pow-wow means discuss, idiot,' said Felix, and Belinda glared. At the edge of the churchyard Roger had almost completed his circuit when he found a . . . Could it be . . . ? Was it? It could be – there were certainly no live cows available for this sort of thing in the village. The lads at forensics ought to be able to tell him. He felt in his pockets for an evidence bag. He knew he would have one – he usually carried several, for he had always longed to have something to send to the lads at forensics. That's what they did on *Morse.*

Neil, heading towards his Lotus with laboured steps, saw Roger bent examining the unexaminable, and paused. He would not be able to get past Roger – so which way should he go? His eye alighted on the lych gate which led to the field where the mud spring sat. The gate was open.

The sack was very heavy. It was taking all of Neil's gym-honed strength to move it without lots of clinking and jangling. He certainly did not have attention to spare for noticing Felix, Hugh and Belinda. However, as they crept after him, whispering amongst themselves in debate of the best way for two fourteen-year-olds and a twelve-year-old to apprehend an angry villain, someone else noticed them. Alice watched in brief fascination, then hurried to the hall to check on the treasure.

Neil could feel his anger fading. After spending the last two weeks trying to find ways of separating Carol from her money, and discovering that even the interesting photographs he had of her with Giles Perry were unlikely to achieve any more than embarrassment, he had at last found a face-saving course of action.

Neil hated Parvum Magna. It had turned Carol against him. It had turned her into a person he did not like. A country person. A weepy person. The sort of person who covenanted money to charity and stood by people when they were in trouble. Neil had no use for that type of person, they were weak and achieved little, and he blamed this bloody place for it. This place and its people. Neil's opinion of it had sunk to an all-time low when he had discovered Penelope Forbes swimming naked in the ford to the sound of whale song. They were all weirdoes. That's what they were, and Neil would hit them where it hurt, where everyone was most vulnerable – in their pockets.

It was a shame that he had had to leave the crown with Alice, but this would do. He would throw all these bloody coins and other junk back into the spring they came out of, and there was sod all anyone would be able to do about it.

Alice stared at the empty treasure display in disbelief. It was all gone. Every penny. After all the discussion, the arguments, the wrangling, the ill-feeling, the rivalry, the resentment . . . and then she began to laugh. She was still laughing when Roger found her and, unable to get any sense out of her, took her round to Serendipity, still wearing the crown. There seemed, as Alice said, little point worrying about leaving the village hall door unattended now, when the treasure had already bolted.

Serendipity was up anyway – babies do that and Phoebe was no exception. Serendipity took exception, though, to their story.

'I don't believe it,' she said to Roger, while Alice giggled into a mug of strong tea: 'you let someone take the treasure from right under your nose?'

Roger looked miserable. 'My sergeant will murder me,' he said. 'Nothing ever goes right for me. I suppose you think I'm useless too.'

'Well put it this way,' said Serendipity: 'on a usefulness scale of one to a hundred, you would score nothing, and an armadillo with its shoelaces tied together would score one. Would you like some tea?'

Penelope, fresh from her midnight bathe in the River Stour – a useful way of communicating with her lobsters and recharging her psychic energies – crept up the field towards the mud spring. Penelope was not a medium for nothing. Her psychic powers were strong tonight, and Handsome Dog had directed her to the mud spring. Something was going to happen, Penelope had no doubt about it, and she was needed there.

Penelope's powers as a medium had been somewhat neglected in recent years. She had at one time had a slot in the local paper offering words of comfort and wisdom to those in need, but unfortunately all most people ever seemed in need of was an accurate National Lottery prediction, and at that she was no better than Mystic Meg. The newspaper had finally dropped her when she had uncannily directed one of their newshounds to a major scoop, and this had turned out to be the news that their own editor was enjoying an uninhibited but covert lunchtime liaison in a caravan on the Cambridge Road with a woman called Lucy

Loveshackles. Penelope had attributed her Sight on this occasion to her intense dislike for the gentleman concerned, but he was unimpressed and replaced her with an agony aunt called Rose Bush, who dispensed no-nonsense advice on the subjects of morals, corsetry and sex. Now, however, Penelope's powers were serving her well, and she reached the mud spring just a few moments before Neil.

Neil, breathing heavily, was not angry now, he was triumphant. He had spent several days considering his revenge-against-Carol schemes before coming up with this, the most effective. Once his London solicitor had convinced him that he had no chance of wresting half of the money from Carol, and that her insanity as demonstrated by her inexplicable infidelity with a man who looked like a lugworm did not in itself constitute a reason to challenge Uncle Percy's will, this seemed the best plan.

So Penelope watched silently as Neil dumped his bulky (and obviously villainous) sack beside the spring and began to throw gold coins back into it muttering, 'and that one's for that idiot Hector . . . and that one's for Seren-bloody-dipity . . .' before deciding that this was far too slow, and picking up the whole sack again with the intent to throw it, and with an almost religious determination.

It was clear, thought Penelope, what he was doing, and doubtless her duty as a citizen of the village (can one be a citizen of a village?) was to wrestle him to the ground and save the treasure. But something held Penelope back, and she liked to think it was her karma, her deep inner knowledge that treasure was not the answer to very much, her conviction that this particular treasure might actually be better off in the mud, rather than causing all the trouble and strife which it seemed to have managed on land. So she watched, thoughtfully, as Hugh, Belinda and Felix came careering up like John Wayne and one of his trusty posses, to save the day. At her shoulder, Handsome Dog nodded approvingly.

It was neither Penelope nor the children that startled Neil: it was the creature. Not having been at the opera, he was not forewarned as to the kind of exotic wild creatures that inhabited this corner of Suffolk at the moment. As far as Neil was concerned, you don't see llama in Suffolk, particularly not nocturnal llama. It was a bloody inappropriate creature. And it belched loudly and unselfconsciously at his right shoulder just as he was flinging the entire sack of treasure into the mud, consigning it to the oblivion whence it came.

Unfortunately, the effort involved in flinging a large quantity of gold into a large quantity of mud is fairly substantial, even to a man who regards himself as the Hercules of Highgate, and it had unbalanced Neil. Swinging round to see more clearly the white hairy thing in his peripheral vision, he took two rapid unbalanced steps backwards and cannoned into Penelope, then staggered forwards from her into a bush. He might have been safe but, as Hugh said afterwards, he couldn't see the mud for the trees, or rather the tree, which had just enough give in it to bounce him effectively into the mud spring. The mud, displaying, as Hugh also observed, a level of bad taste surprising even in one accustomed to eating cows of poor yield, seized Neil's left ankle, and yanked sharply. Neil grasped frantically anything that might save him, and fell backwards into the quagmire clutching billions of air molecules. Penelope, obeying the laws of momentum, bounced cheerfully away from the spring and the wildly flailing Neil, landing firmly on the grass beside Eric, winded but otherwise unharmed. There, as Neil began to squeak in rage, she began to laugh uproariously.

'Well,' said Hugh, with a jolly equanimity oddly appropriate amidst such chaos, 'at least you could say that Neil has managed to strike a happy medium.'

Neil, knee deep and sinking, called Hugh something almost as rude as saying 'son of a turtle egg' in Chinese, but not quite as clever. It was difficult to be terrifically clever in the circumstances – the mud spring, apart from its other peculiar properties in the geological department, was what the very top geologists call bloody smelly, and it rather upset his concentration. 'So get a bloody move on and pull me out,' he added, 'or I'll sue you.'

Hugh beamed. 'I think you might be too heavy,' he said cheerfully.

'Too fucking what? I'll fucking too heavy you. Just pull me out of this bloody mess or I swear you'll live to regret it.' Neil was starting to panic.

Hugh though, was in control. Belinda and Felix watched his not-intimidatedness with admiration, Penelope with delight, as he explained that Neil might – just – be light enough to pull out were he to relieve himself of the added weight of the negatives in his breast pocket. And Neil, feeling the indescribably gloopy sensation of being sucked ever downwards by a hungry pond, handed them over with only a 'now get me out of here', adding hastily, for face-saving sake, 'you evil little bastard'.

Hugh suggested towing him out with Eric. Eric, however, was not interested in verbal cleverness, was not impressed at being called a bloody inappropriate creature, and trotted away haughtily in search of somewhere more like Patagonia – or, failing that, that nice garden with the dahlias. It didn't matter really, because, as Neil said, loudly and shrilly, that bloody animal had already hurled him into the mud, he didn't need any more help from it when he was trying to get out, thank you.

In the end it took Felix, Hugh, Penelope and Belinda all of their strength to haul him out. It wasn't easy – the mud hung on tight, and by the time they got a grip on him he was already in it up to his thighs – but as Hugh said afterwards, it was worth the effort not to have him hanging round in the village for centuries, glowering and muttering. Neil was immune to Hugh's advice – 'Lie down in it, and pretend you're swimming' – but he struggled so wildly as they pulled that very little of him was not caked in mud when he eventually emerged, with the kind of noise that moose make when they pass wind after eating cheese and pickle sandwiches.

Gasping, they all collapsed in a heap like a triumphant tug-of-war team. The mud spring, as disappointed as a geological oddity can be, glooped once, rumblingly, then was silent. The Parvum Magna treasure was nowhere to be seen. It had gone back to the sedimentary depths from which it had, so recently, been temptingly flung – but then that had been the whole aim of Neil's exercise. There was not a coin or buckle to be seen – nothing, in fact, save possibly a faint aura of smug satisfaction hanging over the mud itself.

Neil had succeeded, and he was trying to feel victorious, despite the smell. The treasure was as lost as if he had thrown it off the edge of the world (which, as most southerners are aware, is only just beyond Teddington service station on the M1, after which the entire motorway drops out of rural Bedfordshire into nothingness, depositing travelling salesmen and articulated lorries in a huge happy heap in another dimension, one full of people who want to buy things and giant roundabouts which are easier to negotiate than Murmansk airfield). Parvum Magna could sink back into the unattractive quagmire of rural impoverishment from which it had so nearly been raised. And how they would weep! He had, he now told himself, thrown himself into the mud instinctively after being startled by Eric. His reactions were honed, that's what they were: a man of his level of fitness could take evasive action in a fraction of a second. A man like him needed to be able to respond rapidly and efficiently to threat. Not for anything would he admit that in that first moment, when he had sensed the presence of something white behind him, he had believed, for a tiny but significant blink of Time's eye, that the ghost of the unfortunate Tulip had appeared to haunt him and extract a ghastly revenge.

'God,' he said now, standing on the bank, brown and shaking like an enraged Easter Egg, 'just look at me. I'm wet, I'm muddy, and I smell like a latrine! I can't possibly get into my car like this, I've only just taken the polythene covers off.' He glared at Hugh. That hair. Those freckles. There'd been one of him at school. 'I might have known you would be in on this. I expect you to help.'

Chapter Fourteen

News East might have been extremely disappointed if there had been no treasure to see, so it was rather lucky that Alice had taken the crown home for safe keeping, and the wandering llama in the background did make good TV. True, he ate the furry cover off the sound man's mike (and they are incredibly expensive as they are manufactured secretly in Stornoway from the coats of defunct Emu puppets, by a team of ex-NASA scientists who opted out of the rat race after being overwhelmed by just one too many meteorite disaster movies). All in all, though, the presentation went rather well, even if it did take three hours to film what would ultimately comprise less than three minutes of TV. ('Gawd,' said Brian Baggins, watching, 'imagine how long that Linda Leatherstrumpet must have had to spend starkers, then – she's on screen all night.')

Alice, wearing a suede suit purchased specially for the occasion, and a hairstyle which particularly suited a crown, just in case she should be asked to try it on for the viewers, enjoyed every minute. 'On behalf of the village of Parvum Magna,' she trilled over and over to the cameras, 'I would like to present this historical crown to St Alupent's museum. You know, I could sing too, if you like – I am an opera singer.' Surprisingly Eric, as hero of the hour, enjoyed every minute too. The fact that the cameraman had a CD of Elton John in his Walkman encouraged him to walk backwards and forwards endlessly, ruminating and humming a song of the High Andes. It was all about growing apricots, and he just couldn't get the tune out of his head. Carol, standing rather closer to Giles Perry than was absolutely necessary for the presentation, thought the whole thing had ended perfectly. St Alupent's College would have the crown, and in return they would pay the bill from Gromit, Flange and Peebles – and that, as they say, would be that. Apart from the sex with Giles, of course, but she would be having that later.

Belinda, Hugh and Felix were not immune to the feel-good factor which seemed to have settled on the village like a giant, smiling fruit bat (indeed, one of the government's special feel-good seeker teams had got wind of what was going on and had already notified Downing Street of a feel-good story opportunity.)

'What really went wrong with your first girlfriend?' asked Belinda, taking the opportunity to chat with Hugh while they were waiting to be interviewed about their part in the find.

Hugh sighed sorrowfully. 'She started off quite normal,' he said, 'but she got more and more interested in my pets. In the end she only wanted me for my breeding cockroach, Miss Trust.'

'That would never happen with me,' said Belinda re-assuringly, 'I've got Leonardo.'

Hugh finally stopped wriggling on the hook which, in truth, he had known he was attached to for weeks. He gave in to the inevitable, and took hold of her hand. 'That's OK, then,' he said.

Behind him Felix scowled furiously in recognition of the fact that there was absolutely nothing he could do. He'd seen films. All there was left for them to do now was kiss. It was definitely time for him to go and play with Lily.

Hilda Antrobus missed all the excitement of *News East*, as she was in bed with pains in her stomach. Sid was quite worried about her. His Hilda was such a stoic – she never got ill. So he called in sick for the first time in forty years, then telephoned Clive Rowan.

Clive examined Hilda's large girth thoroughly, then stood back and applied his bedside manner, gleaned, as all the best doctors glean it, from watching *Dr Finlay* and the nice docs on those American casualty soaps. When he was a medical student his whole group had been subject to a bedside manner controlled trial, in which half the students were forced to watch children's TV every day for twelve months, and the other half watched programmes about nice doctors, heroic doctors, the sort of doctors that inspire adverts for aftershave and four-wheel-drive cars. Clive, in the latter group, felt he had come out of it fairly well, and had a good line in serious faces and heroic diagnoses ('I'm afraid I think we're dealing with the common cold here – but don't worry, I can prescribe you something . . .') unlike his colleague John Potter who, after a year of manic presenters, magic shows and the Muppets, constantly wore bright orange trousers, and tried to entertain his more distraught patients by making the practice receptionists disappear. Mind you, he could do a grand impersonation of Kermit the Frog, and he was quite useful at the staff Christmas dinner when they wanted the sprouts to disappear.

'What have you been eating, recently?' Clive asked.

'Er,' said Hilda.

'Rubbish,' said Sid, 'that's what she eats.'

Clive looked at Hilda and raised a brow. 'What did you eat for breakfast?'

'Oysters,' said Hilda a little sheepishly.

'And yesterday?'

'Caviare,' said Hilda, becoming as sheepish as a sheep. 'Beluga. And *foie gras* and truffles. I wanted to try them – but the truffles repeated on me something rotten.'

'Anything else?'

'Champagne,' said Hilda, now more sheepish than New Zealand, 'and a glass or two of port. 1955 Taylors.'

Clive put his stethoscope away. 'Then I would advise a low-caviare diet,' he told her firmly but heroically, 'and forget the truffles.'

Hilda avoided Sid's eye for quite a long time after Clive had gone but at last this became impossible.

'OK, Sid, so it was silly. I've got above myself, I can see it now.'

'Bloody silly,' said Sid, 'and so far above yourself I didn't recognize you. At least I'm Sid again, now. Does this mean we can go back to how we were?'

Hilda sighed and nodded meekly Their old life. The struggle. But at least they would be themselves. At least she would get her anniversary cake. At least she would have her Sid. 'OK, Chicken Sid, the dragon goes. Her skirting boards weren't anything like mine anyway. The caviare goes. To be honest it tasted like cold cockles. What about the house, Sid? And do we have to give *all* the money away?'

'Give it away? Certainly not. I may be working class,' said Sid, 'but that doesn't mean I'm stupid.'

The first item on *News East* that night was about the crown of Boudicca of the Iceni, the renovated Parvum Magna village hall, and the fact that the crown of Boudicca had paid for it. Even the Prime Minister had mentioned the project during question time (there is nothing prime ministers like more than a heart-warming story to tell to fill some of those dangerous minutes. He had been determined to get it in, even if this meant using it to answer a question about the proposed closure of a condom factory in County Durham). Sadly there was no mention of three valiant children and a llama – but then, Serendipity pointed out, a two-minute news item had to be simple and to the point; if they told the whole story it would have to be on TV all night.

First they showed Alice, in a glowing pink suit of alarming luminosity, proudly handing the crown to Giles Perry, with a beaming Carol at her side, and then Lady Angela Ormondroyd, the hugely pregnant wheel-in aristocrat from Great Barking whom Alice had wheeled in to officially open the village hall and rename it the Moot House declaring, 'I now declare this Moot House open. Oooh.' Then she was carried away, huffing and puffing. Poor Lady Angela. Her first child had begun her entry into the world when her waters broke at dinner with an earl. Now her twins had done the same thing on national TV.

It had been Belinda's suggestion to rename the village hall the Moot House, a moot being amongst other things a meeting of the tree people in *Lord of the Rings*. Since whether or not it was renovated at all had been a moot point, the village, with a surprising show of the sort of shared humour not often seen outside the live audiences for *One Foot in the Grave*, had agreed.

'There we are!' shouted Felix unnecessarily, seeing himself on screen at last. 'Look. Belinda, you look like a lovesick baboon. Wow – don't we look all different?'

'You look clean,' said Belinda, 'that's what's different, and you combed your hair. Hugh looks just the same.'

Hugh shrugged nonchalantly. 'You tend to get used to TV,' he said, with panache. He knew he was hooked up again, but he had given it careful thought before the hormones had won – an official girlfriend is at least some sort of protection from the crowds of other wannabes out there.

Belinda felt smug. It would be quite clear to all of her friends now that she was one of the in-crowd, one of the boyfriended class. Already Sarah Porter, with the pierced ears and the belly button ring, had rung her to ask how you grew your hair that long, and that was even before *News East* had gone out. Sarah had seen the trailer at lunchtime, and was now having hair extensions for her birthday. Plaits, it seemed, were about to be 'in' at Broomhill High. 'Oh look, I didn't realize Eric had come into shot,' she said, as Lily hooted and pointed.

'I'm afraid,' said Serendipity, putting a bit of a dampener on the proceedings, 'that by courting TV stardom Eric may have finally blown his cover. No-one is going to believe he's one of our peacocks after this.'

'We could still brazen it out,' said Clive, cheered at the prospect of one less zoo animal glaring at him over breakfast. Perhaps Leonardo could be next – there's nothing worse than the soulful stare of a lonely lobster when you're finishing Lily's fish fingers. 'I suppose there's an outside chance we could tell them he's Sir George Ormondroyd. Some of the aristocracy are very inbred.'

'Hush,' said Belinda, 'listen.'

'The village of Parvum Magna has been recommended for a Community Award for their project to rebuild their village hall with a difference,' trilled the presenter. 'The crown of Boadicea, Queen of the Iceni, recently found in a secret location near here, provided the funding for this excellent project, which has facilities for catering, for sport, for after-school clubs and for village meetings of many kinds. There is even an outdoor tennis court under construction, and floodlighting is being actively considered.' A quick shot of the would-be court showed Gromit, Flange and Peebles leaning winsomely on their spades, next to their new sign which (in spite of Hugh's pleading with them to cut three

339

words out) read, *Gromit, Flange and Peebles,* LTD. PERFECTION IN ERECTION, FOR ALL YOUR BUILDING NEEDS. 'The Prime Minister, speaking in the Commons today, called the village a blueprint for villages all over the country who should consider similar moves.'

The scene moved to the Commons, where bits of screwed-up paper were flying everywhere and a large row of fuschia-clad lady MPs, artfully seated behind the Prime Minister by a right-on PR man, were breastfeeding in synchrony. 'People in communities of many sorts could learn from this project,' beamed the Prime Minister, with an eye on the next election, another on those members of the party who might mount a leadership challenge (bastards), and another on the shadow Culture Minister (all prime ministers need at least three eyes). 'This shows how much a community can achieve if they all work together in a spirit of co-operation. I hope this Moot House will provide facilities for the village of Parvum Magna well into the next century.'

The cameras left the scene before Opposition shouts of 'Answer the question' could peal across the land like dissenting bells, and returned to Parvum Magna for a brief panoramic shot of grinning villagers outside the Moot House. In the background someone could be seen peering through its windows with a rather wild expression.

'My God,' said Carol, 'that's Neil. What on earth was he still doing in there?'

'After Eric pushed him into the mud spring,' said Felix, 'he insisted we let him in there, then Alice locked him in the back room to keep him away from the cameras.'

'Why did he *want* to be in there? He'd already stolen the treasure.'

'Because of his legs,' said Belinda. 'They were a bit cold.'

'Cold? I don't see . . . why was he hiding?'

'Well, he couldn't really come out,' said Hugh, 'not with *News East* there – it would have been a bit embarrassing for him when he had no trousers.'

'Why on earth did he have no trousers?' This is exhausting, thought Carol.

'It's a long story,' said Felix, emerging from the kitchen,

'and very complicated. But Eric didn't like the look of him, so he pushed him in to the mud spring, and basically when we pulled him out his trousers were mucky, so he made us take them off to wash them.'

Carol giggled. 'Neil hates dirt. So what happened to his trousers?'

'He said it was our fault and we had to wash them for him,' said Hugh, 'while he waited in the Moot House. Unfortunately we rinsed them in the river and they got carried away.'

'The current's not that strong,' said Carol suspiciously. 'Do you mean you threw them in?'

'Of course not,' said Hugh indignantly. 'We're not the sort of people who would deliberately throw away someone's trousers. No, they really got carried away – by Mrs Forbes.'

'My mother,' said Serendipity absently. 'Now why am I not surprised? But whyever did my mother want Neil's trousers?'

'Nesting,' said Hugh, 'for lobsters.' He looked as though butter wouldn't melt in his mouth, not even if he chewed it. 'It was after I told her that the lobsters probably wouldn't go off downstream to Sudbury if they had some decent bedding here. She said Prince of Wales check would be perfect, so she took them away to cut them up.'

'Gosh, Neil must have been furious,' said Carol, torn between amusement and delight. 'Where is he now?'

'He's gone back to London,' said Felix. 'We found him a chorister's robe in the vestry after the TV people had gone.'

As he spoke *News East* broke into the second item, the arrest of Neil Pendragon whilst breaking into his own house, for the theft and subsequent vandalistic disposal of the Parvum Magna treasure. The Metropolitan Police had gone to collect him. (Roger had offered to go with them, but they had, unaccountably, refused.) Neil was clearly seen to be shoeless, trouserless, and dressed in a cassock.

'God, Neil will be wild,' said Carol, impressed.

'Oh absolutely,' said Hugh. 'It can't have been very easy getting home with four flat tyres, either. Oh, and he gave me some negatives for safe keeping before we pulled him out'

– he beamed at Carol – 'but I accidentally went too near the mud spring and they just got sucked in.'

'You,' said Carol, delighted, 'are all stars.' Hugh looked modest – this was something he already knew – but Felix and Belinda basked in the glory and wondered what to ask for before it wore off. Just think, thought Carol, if Giles and I – well – we might have a Hugh . . .

'What will happen to Neil?' asked Serendipity, eyes round.

Carol smiled. 'Oh, I thought the humiliation would be enough. I don't want to press charges – but no-one will tell him that for a day or two.'

Unfortunately they came for Eric later that day. He was led away by a very nice man from Linton Zoo who had, he said, been hunting for him for ages. Hugh, Felix and Belinda were somewhat abashed, especially when they saw the enthusiasm with which Eric greeted his keeper. After all, it is one thing to wilfully conceal a llama when you believe you are saving him from incarceration in some unspeakable llama farm, but quite another to hide him when he is from Linton Zoo and all the little kiddies are weeping because he is not there.

'I'm sorry,' Belinda told the keeper. 'We thought he was a battery llama.'

'Oh no,' said the Linton man cheerily, for it is a village of much wit and ebullience, 'I'm sure he runs on gas.'

Once the cameras had gone, it was just a matter of accepting that this was a perfectly ordinary village again – with a rather smart village hall that was the envy of both Bumpstaple and Great Barking, a village with a bit of a history, perhaps – (but then, haven't they all?) It was not a village of rage and retribution. In fact Neil would have been surprised – astonished, actually – to discover that the village bore him so little ill-feeling. The fact was, though, that everyone had noticed that the all-pervading atmosphere of ill-will which had dogged the place recently had dispersed as swiftly and sweetly as a queue of men outside an underwear sale once the leopardskin thongs are sold out. Brian

Baggins summed it up when he said, 'all we needed was a new village hall, and we've got that, so why complain?' But Neil was not about to venture back into Suffolk to discover this: he was sure his face must feature on 'Wanted' posters from Broomhill to the coast. Rural Suffolk, he felt, was full of the rural mafia – peculiar people who wore muddy wellies and thought sugar beet was interesting – and it wasn't for him. Carol was welcome to it.

Serendipity had barely given the treasure a thought – but then, she was floating on a cotton wool sea of motherhood, in which baby Phoebe, who was beautiful beyond any sort of reasonableness, was declared adorable at least three times a day by all who saw her, especially Carol and Giles, and Everest had receded to a very distant place. To the Himalayas, in fact. She missed Leonardo, who had turned out to be the ideal pet (waved hello a lot, never argued, did not fart and lived on sausages) before Penelope had insisted he be returned to his family in the river.

She had had to give in to the iguana – Lily had been distraught at Eric's departure. The number of trips they had needed to make to Linton Zoo had eventually become rather difficult. It is a lovely zoo, but one can only spend so many hours contemplating the cassowaries and anyway, as Miranda said, the place had to close sometimes.

And so it was that Serendipity found herself in Chelmsford with Hugh who was an old hand at this sort of thing, and Miranda, who felt she should come along in case Serendipity was seized by too many other zoological urges while she was out.

'Just think,' Serendipity told Phoebe cheerfully as they pulled into a parking space, 'your first trip out, and it's to a pet shop. What will become of us?'

'What was my first trip out?' asked Miranda curiously.

'To see your grandmother,' said Serendipity darkly. 'She spoke to her Indian to ask him for a name for you.'

'And he chose Miranda?'

'This is my mother we're talking about,' said Serendipity. 'She did not choose Miranda. You have only my common sense to thank that you weren't christened Hoar Frost.'

Miranda giggled. 'I don't know. It has a certain ring to it.'

'A loony ring. Have you heard from Luke?' asked Serendipity as they got out of the car.

Miranda sniffed. 'He's going out with Claire Kettle from Bumpstaple.'

'Yeuch,' said Hugh, 'that's my cousin. If you wanted revenge, you've got it. Here's the shop. Wow. Look at those. Look at their legs!'

Serendipity stared. 'It's a good job we left Lily at home,' she said. 'Let's go in.'

Lily was delighted with her new pet. Miranda felt they had got off lightly, having seen what they could have bought. The fact that she was happy with an iguana was, given Serendipity's generous state of mind, quite lucky for them all.

Felix was a little miffed when he saw it. 'I wanted an iguana first. Now Lily's got one and I never will have.'

Hugh though, was complacent. 'Ah, but birds of a feather flock together.'

'Now you're being obscure,' said Felix, 'it's not a bloody parrot.'

Hugh sighed, reflecting yet again on the misunderstood qualities of geniuses. 'Lily's got a lady iguana. What does that tell you?'

Felix was dubious. 'Ignatius wouldn't be seen dead with a mate called Mavis.'

'Don't be a killjoy,' said Belinda, 'and be grateful. An iguana in the hand is worth two in the bush.'

'Oh, ha ha,' said Felix, irritated.

Hugh smiled at Belinda. A girl who understood humour. He reflected that this time he'd clearly made a good choice.

There was one more opening ceremony yet to take place in Parvum Magna. It attracted a smaller audience than the last one, but as far as the life of the village was concerned, it was at least as important. All the people who counted were there, and Belinda, Hugh and Felix were rather relieved that the Bollivants were not.

'I now declare,' said Serendipity, for Phoebe – who was

not yet making speeches, but who, as the village's youngest resident, had been given the honour of performing the ceremony – 'this Mud Spring Sign . . . open.' She pulled the tea towel off.

'What do you think?' asked Belinda proudly, 'Hugh and Felix carved the letters, but it was my idea.'

They looked at the new sign on the tree by the mud spring. It read: ALL THAT GLISTERS IS NOT GOLD . . .

'That's very deep,' said Clive. 'What gave you that idea?'

Belinda sighed. Doctors, she thought, they're just so ignorant. 'Shakespeare,' she said aloud. '*The Merchant of Venice* . . . actually.'

'Couldn't he spell?' asked Clive.

Belinda rolled her eyes.

Afterwards, Serendipity contemplated the still flats of the mud spring, deep in thought, while Baby Phoebe slept in her papoose carrier.

'Hello. Are you throwing all your dark secrets in there?' asked Carol at her shoulder.

Serendipity smiled. 'You've been talking to Mother. Watch out, if you let her think she's making sense you'll wake up one morning to see she's bought you a wildebeest or turned your garden into an international centre for dead Red Indians. Anyway, all my dark secrets went in there long ago. Best place for them.'

They stood side by side, companionably, and the mud spring gave one of its intermittent gloops. 'Doesn't it make you wonder what will surface next?' asked Carol.

'You never know,' said Serendipity, 'it could be King Arthur next, or a mucky Lady of the Lake waving a sword and a cow. I don't suppose the treasure will be back for a few centuries, though.'

A short distance away Hector Bollivant had forgotten all about the unveiling. He had just been subject to a little unveiling of his own, and was now being transported to a level of ecstasy that had previously existed only in his wildest dreams (and wild dreams they had been). He was wearing his Rupert the Bear outfit, from the red jersey right

345

the way down to the nice, shiny shoes. Alice, who had flung him onto a bed of sheepskin in front of the roaring flames of the fire, was ravaging him within an inch of his life in the fiery scarlet glow, wearing a suede corset trimmed with fur, and a crown which Boudicca of the Iceni would have been proud to wear, had she had the opportunity.

She hadn't. It had last been worn by Mavis Entwhistle of Bumpstaple, the last person to hire it from Fantasy and Fun in Broomhill. Alice had not enjoyed herself this much for a long time, and had completely forgiven Hector for the emeralds. Emeralds are expensive, she now realized, but fantasies are free.

Roger had been on desk duty ever since the whole débâcle, but he didn't mind. It was far less stressful work – it was a jungle out there, after all.

'You know that sample you sent over to forensics?' said the sergeant interrupting his peaceful report copying.

'Oh yes?' Roger felt rather grand, like an extra on *Morse*.

'Well, do you mind telling me why you sent a heap of llama droppings to our forensic laboratory?'

Roger sighed. Llama, moose . . . his life was dogged by them. Perhaps God or the fates were trying to tell him something. Perhaps he wasn't destined to be a policeman. He had, after all, always wanted to join the circus when he was a boy . . . and he had this very week noticed an advertisement for a vicuña keeper at London Zoo. It might not pay very well, but the wool would knit up into lovely underpants.

They were all making an awful lot of fuss of the baby downstairs, as they were trying to go out shopping for shoes. The baby had to be wrapped in all sorts of things, then unwrapped, then wrapped again. Lily couldn't understand it, but she knew they were going out because she'd had to take her wellies off and put her knickers on. Lily liked going out, but she did not like fuss. Lily liked chocolate and presents and Christmas trees, and things with legs that tasted crunchy, and her creature, Mavis, but not fuss. For that matter, she didn't like being cheated either, and gold coins she couldn't unwrap now that she was ready for them, that didn't taste of chocolate – nor of anything, actually – were decidedly in the cheat sphere.

Creeping off to her bedroom and rooting under the edge of her bed where she kept most of her Mavises, Lily found the four gold coins that she had taken from the kitchen table, so long ago that she couldn't remember, although she knew it had been teatime and there had been peas which she had lined up in rows. They would do.

Lily liked the dog outside the shoe shop. She couldn't see why her mother was so desperate to get her away when there was such a nice dog here. There was a hole in the top of his head, which wasn't right. She pulled Serendipity's hand, then sat down and made herself very heavy and spread her limbs in as random an arrangement as possible. It made her impossible to lift.

'Come on, Lily,' said Serendipity, 'don't do this, not now.'

'Doggy hole,' said Lily, 'Lily put in doggy hole.'

Serendipity sighed and found a tenpence piece. 'Here, Lily, you put money in that hole.'

Lily was delighted. When you put the coin into the dog you could hear it rolling down into his insides. Then he tinged like a telephone. Obviously the dog wouldn't mind that these coins were not chocolate. She grinned and felt in her pocket, wanting him to ting again.

Epilogue

'There has been a surprising windfall for a charity in the region,' said the link man on *News East* a few days later. 'When the RSPCA opened their collection boxes from Broomhill last week, they were surprised to find four Iron Age gold coins in there. Pamela Piggott is in Broomhill talking about the unexpected windfall . . .'

Pamela Piggott now wore a BBC newsreader suit – all one colour, elegant, powerful – and proper newsreader hair – several colours (all blond) but still elegant and still powerful. She was interviewing an RSPCA man who, the caption said, was called Kevin.

'I know we have a reputation for not coming to empty the boxes very often, but we're sure someone must have been since these were last in circulation,' said Kevin, with a jolly smile and a lack of comic timing more often seen in policemen.

'And what have you been told they are worth?'

'Oh, several thousand pounds,' said Kevin even more cheerily. 'We're using them to launch our new River Life campaign.' Hugh pricked up his ears, which were as always finely tuned to anything involving animals (after all he had, according to his mother, inherited a lobster-loving gene from his father). Kevin went on: 'Suffolk has long been known for the numbers of crayfish breeding in the River Stour, and it seems now that there is also a large population of lobsters. We feel not only that it is time to stop the barbaric practice of eating these intelligent and harmless creatures, but also that we should be reintroducing some of our native river fish – pike, eel, grayling . . .'

Well now, thought Hugh, that gives me an idea. He wondered what his mother would think of a giant electric eel. Only one way to find out . . .

THE END

A Wing And A Prayer

Mary Selby

'A THOROUGHLY ENJOYABLE TONGUE-IN-CHEEK
LOOK AT VILLAGE LIFE . . . TERRIFIC FUN'
Daily Express

In the quiet village of Great Barking, strange doings are
afoot. Up at the Hall the squire, Sir George, seems to
have exhausted his wife Angela – leaving her quite
unable to contemplate the rigours of hosting the annual
village fête in the Hall grounds. Caroline, the doctor's
wife, has her time taken up with her three tiny children,
but feels that as a newcomer to the village she should
offer her own rather more modest garden as the venue
for this important local affair. But who is to open it?
Will Sir George's elderly mother, now somewhat
unpredictable, be asked, as tradition dictates? Or should
Sarah Struther, the voluptuous lady potter who prefers to
work unencumbered by clothing and who has just been
featured in a smart Sunday newspaper, be invited?

The village fête committee decides that a commission to
Sarah to fashion a special pot for the fête, to be entitled
The Organ (suggesting the need for funds to combat dry
rot in the organ loft) may be a better idea, little
suspecting that the title may be open to misconstruction.
And in the churchyard the tall privet bush has been
lovingly fashioned by old Jacob Bean into a shape so
curious that coachloads of sightseers start arriving to
view it . . .

0 552 99672 6

BLACK SWAN

That Awkward Age

Mary Selby

There is more to some vicars than meets the eye,
but when Robert Peabody, handsome, divorced and
forty-something, moved into the village of
Bumpstaple, few could have predicted just how
wildly different a vicar he would prove to be . . .
Mavis Entwhistle, creator of the world's most
terrible pastry, thought she had an inkling but then
she thought she had magical powers, too, so this
was not surprising. Certainly her surprisingly
lovely daughter Sally, exhausted by her mother's
efforts to marry her off, had no idea – although the
whole village decided Sally would make the
perfect vicar's wife.

Josh, Robert's son, found romance more easily
when he met Claire on the school bus. She was
fifteen, a truly awkward age to be, made worse by
spots and the dreadful embarrassment of her
mother Tessa's advancing pregnancy – and at her
age, too! And now cousin Hugh, the bug-collector
from Hell, was coming to stay until Christmas.
Robert planned a Carol Service, a triumphant
celebration of village life to bring his new parish
together, but it was Hugh who added the final extra
touch to the evening . . .

0 552 99671 8

BLACK SWAN

GARGOYLES AND PORT

Mary Selby

Intrigue, love and magic in a Cambridge summer

Serena Prime had been married to the bursar of St Alupent's College for long enough to know that she came very low down the list of his priorities. Anthony Prime's life revolved around the college, its finances, and the pretty young female undergraduates who occasionally had to ask him for help in eking out their grants. Serena had become fat and depressed, and found it hard to believe that, even if Anthony no longer found her attractive, there were other men who did – including Will Standish, a dishy research student and oarsman, and Crispin St Clair, the sex-obsessed organ scholar who fancied trying his hand at an older woman.

But now, St Alupent's was in crisis. In desperate need of an enormous amount of cash – immediately – it was casting around for help. Would the discovery of the bones of St Alupent – patron saint of dragon slayers – or the sale of its rare and precious port or even a generous donation from Gloria O'Flynn, Texan oil heiress, save the day? Or could young Hugh Appleton, insect fancier, cockroach collector and chorister at St Alupent's, come to rescue both the college and Serena's surprisingly complicated love life?

'A SALACIOUS, YET ENDEARINGLY FAMILIAR, TALE OF HIGH-TABLE LIFE'
The Times

0 552 99763 3

BLACK SWAN

A SELECTED LIST OF FINE WRITING AVAILABLE FROM BLACK SWAN

THE PRICES SHOWN BELOW WERE CORRECT AT THE TIME OF GOING TO PRESS. HOWEVER TRANSWORLD PUBLISHERS RESERVE THE RIGHT TO SHOW NEW RETAIL PRICES ON COVERS WHICH MAY DIFFER FROM THOSE PREVIOUSLY ADVERTISED IN THE TEXT OR ELSEWHERE.

99766 8	EVERY GOOD GIRL	*Judy Astley*	£6.99
99619 X	HUMAN CROQUET	*Kate Atkinson*	£6.99
99687 4	THE PURVEYOR OF ENCHANTMENT	*Marika Cobbold*	£6.99
99670 X	THE MISTRESS OF SPICES	*Chitra Banerjee Divakaruni*	£6.99
99730 7	FREEZING	*Penelope Evans*	£6.99
99622 X	THE GOLDEN YEAR	*Elizabeth Falconer*	£6.99
99656 4	THE TEN O'CLOCK HORSES	*Laurie Graham*	£5.99
99611 4	THE COURTYARD IN AUGUST	*Janette Griffiths*	£6.99
99774 9	THE CUCKOO'S PARTING CRY	*Anthea Halliwell*	£6.99
99754 5	CLOUD MUSIC	*Karen Hayes*	£6.99
99736 6	KISS AND KIN	*Angela Lambert*	£6.99
99771 4	MALLINGFORD	*Alison Love*	£6.99
99688 2	HOLY ASPIC	*Joan Marysmith*	£6.99
99649 1	WAITING TO EXHALE	*Terry McMillan*	£5.99
99696 3	THE VISITATION	*Sue Reidy*	£5.99
99747 1	M FOR MOTHER	*Marjorie Riddell*	£6.99
99608 4	LAURIE AND CLAIRE	*Kathleen Rowntree*	£6.99
99672 6	A WING AND A PRAYER	*Mary Selby*	£6.99
99671 8	THAT AWKWARD AGE	*Mary Selby*	£6.99
99663 6	GARGOYLES AND PORT	*Mary Selby*	£6.99
99753 6	AN ACCIDENTAL LIFE	*Titia Sutherland*	£6.99
99700 5	NEXT OF KIN	*Joanna Trollope*	£6.99
99646 7	A SCHOOL FOR LOVERS	*Jill Paton Walsh*	£6.99
99723 4	PART OF THE FURNITURE	*Mary Wesley*	£6.99
99761 7	THE GATEGRASHER	*Madeleine Wickham*	£6.99
99591 6	A MISLAID MAGIC	*Joyce Windsor*	£6.99

All Transworld titles are available by post from:

Book Services By Post, P.O. Box 29, Douglas, Isle of Man IM99 1BQ

Credit cards accepted. Please telephone 01624 675137,
fax 01624 670923 or Internet http://www.bookpost.co.uk.
or e-mail: bookshop@enterprise.net for details

Free postage and packing in the UK. Overseas customers: allow
£1 per book (paperbacks) and £3 per book (hardbacks).